Praise for
Lauraine Snelling and Her Books

"Reminding us that love can spring forth from ashes, that life can emerge from death, Lauraine Snelling writes a gripping and powerful novel that will inspire and uplift you."

—Lynne Hinton, author of *The Last Odd Day*

"Snelling writes about the foibles of human nature with keen insight and sweet honesty."

—National Church Library Association

"Snelling is good at creating suspenseful twists and turns."

—Bookbrowse.com

"Lauraine's writing is both humorous and convicting."

—Leslie Gould, author of *Beyond the Blue* and *Garden of Dreams*

"Snelling's captivating tale will immediately draw readers in. The grief process is accurately portrayed, and readers will be enthralled by the raw emotion of Jenna's and Nora's accounts."

—*Romantic Times Book Reviews* on *One Perfect Day*

"Two mothers. Two children. One tragedy. One miracle. Snelling, whose novels have sold more than two million copies, is sure to grab readers from the start of this holiday melodrama.... Fans of Christian women's fiction will enjoy this winning novel."

—*Publishers Weekly* on *One Perfect Day*

ALSO BY LAURAINE SNELLING

Breaking Free
One Perfect Day

Available from FaithWords wherever books are sold.

On Hummingbird Wings

A Novel

Lauraine Snelling

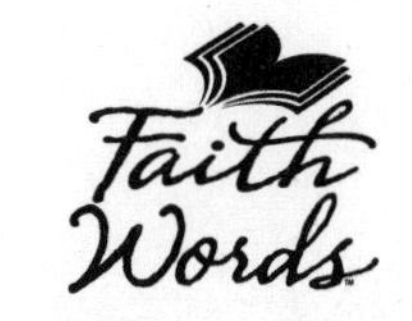

New York Boston Nashville

FaithWords
Hachette Book Group
237 Park Avenue
New York, NY 10017

www.faithwords.com

Printed in the United States of America

First Edition: April 2011
10 9 8 7 6 5 4 3 2 1

FaithWords is a division of Hachette Book Group, Inc.
The FaithWords name and logo are trademarks of Hachette Book Group, Inc.

Library of Congress Cataloging-in-Publication Data

Snelling, Lauraine.
On hummingbird wings / by Lauraine Snelling. — 1st ed.
p. cm.
ISBN 978-0-446-58211-7
I. Title.
PS3569.N39O5 2011
813'.54—dc22

2010031034

To all those who struggle to care for aging parents, may God grant you love and grace beyond your wildest dreams, and to you I dedicate *On Hummingbird Wings*.

On Hummingbird Wings

Chapter One

But Mother is *always* dying." Why had she ever let the call come through? "I'm putting you on speaker." Gillian Ormsby clicked the SPEAKER button without waiting for her sister's reply. At least this way she could continue to flip the screens on the computer. Glancing at the clock, she mentally allowed Allison two more minutes before returning to the report in front of her.

"No, this time it is really serious. I can't make her get out of bed."

Gillian rolled her eyes. Leave it to Miss Perfect Allison to hit the dramatics. "Look, you live twenty miles away and I live across the country. Surely you can find time in your busy schedule to sweet-talk Mother into doing what you want." *You always have.*

"You don't need to be sarcastic. Just because I'm not a high-powered executive with an office in New York City. It isn't like what I have to do isn't important, with two active teenagers and a busy husband."

"I didn't say that. But, Allie, there is no way I can leave right now. There are rumors of a possible buyout, and everyone is walking around whispering like someone died. Have you talked with her doctor? Surely if she is that bad, she should go to a nursing home to help get her back on her feet."

"That's part of the problem; she doesn't want to get back on her feet. She wants to die. She says life here has no meaning for her any longer and heaven will be a far better place."

"Mother said that?"

"And yes, I have talked with the doctor, but you know I don't understand a lot about medical things."

"Google it."

"Gillian, please. She needs *you.*"

"Mother has made it quite clear through the years that she much prefers your company to mine." *So suck it up, baby sister, and live with it.* She drummed her nails on the desk pad. "Look, I have to go. I'll call you back tonight." She checked her calendar. "No, make that tomorrow night, I have a commitment for tonight."

"What if she dies before then?"

Gillian closed her eyes and heaved a sigh. "Look, she's not going to die. She's threatened this for years. Every hangnail is mortal peril, you know that."

"You haven't seen her, in what—five years?"

Leave it to Allison to go for the stiletto. Although Gillian sent expensive gifts at the proper occasions, she'd not graced California with her presence in a long time. Surely, it hadn't been five years, had it? She counted back, using Christmas as the starting point. She'd spent the last one in Saint Croix, actually two of the last five; she needed warm weather by then. And while California was usually sunny in December, she'd wanted somewhere really warm and tropical to go along with it. One year she'd gone skiing, the first and last time in Vermont and the first and last time with Pierre. Since that debacle she'd sworn off both skiing and men.

That was three of the five. Where else had she gone? Oh, yes, one year she'd been home in bed—with the flu and her own rotten company.

"Gillian, are you listening to me?" The strident tone jerked her back to the moment.

"Of course I am." What had she missed?

"Well, then?"

"Well, what?"

"When are you coming?"

Gillian glanced heavenward as if hoping for deliverance. "Sorry, I have a call that I have to take. I'll get back to you." She hung up before her sister could respond. Clicking on her intercom, she instructed her assistant to hold any calls from Allison and collapsed against the back of her leather executive chair. Why now? She really didn't dare leave, not if she wanted to be sure of an office to come back to. Glancing around the room, she focused on a painting she'd found at a local art fair and hung opposite her desk to help relieve moments of stress. The painting depicted purple wisteria cascading over a white trellis that had one corner of its arch in need of repair. Much like she did right now. The four-paned cottage windows of the cozy house at the end of a brick walk beckoned her in. She drew in a deep breath, held it to the count of ten, and blew it all out on a gentle stream. Her shoulders relaxed immediately, as did the tension pulling from the back of her head, through her scalp, and to her eyebrows.

Someday she would own a cottage like that, maybe as a summer place; it didn't matter on which coast. What mattered was the garden and the sense of peace that seeped from the picture into her soul. Digging in the dirt did that for her. Gardening was the one thing she had in common with her mother.

Surely Mother isn't really dying.

Gillian flexed her fingers. Allie had been born exaggerating. No occasion was sufficient in and of itself; she always had to make it bigger and brighter, deeper and wider. Gillian stared at the computer screen where she'd been working on the proposal for a three o'clock meeting. The figures blurred, causing her to blink and blink again.

Her mother could not be dying. She was far too young and had always been robustly healthy. She claimed her gardening did that for her.

So what had happened to cause this, this manifestation of...of...of what? Granted even fingernail splits were traumatic to her mother, but she'd never taken to her bed before.

You don't have time to think on this now, she ordered herself. *Get that proposal done.* She pulled open her middle desk drawer and popped two squares of gum from the green box. Chewing vigorously, she focused on the computer screen. She knew the figures added up, but could she cut anywhere to reduce the bottom line?

The intercom clicked in. "Gillian, you have one hour."

She'd asked Shannon to remind her in case she lost track of time. "Thank you. I'm sending this to the printer. Would you make ten copies and put them in clear binders?"

"Of course... You didn't have lunch."

"I know. I'll eat a protein bar."

"I'll bring you a bottle of water."

"Thanks." Shannon was the kind of assistant all executives dreamed of, coveted by the rest of the R and D team at Fitch, Fitch, and Folsom, commonly known in the business world as Triple F, developer of systems for data transmitting. Retiring early from her successful twenty-year career there was one of Gillian's lifetime goals. Early, meaning in five to seven years. Her other dream had died a lingering death, killed by time.

When her assistant stepped through the door, Gillian knew immediately something was wrong. Shannon had obviously been shoving fingers through her normally sleek coif.

"What's up?" Gillian accepted the fresh-from-the-fridge bottle of water and pointed at the chair in front of her desk.

Shannon sat. "I just had a call from my mother. They took my father to the hospital via ambulance." She blinked back tears.

"And why are you still here?"

"Because you asked me to put the folders together."

"I see." This must be family intrusion day. "Then I suggest you hand the project over to Natalie and take yourself out the door as fast as possible."

"Thank you."

"And give your mother a hug from me, and know that we'll all be praying for your father."

Shannon nodded and stood at the same time. "You're the best."

"Get outta here." Gillian made shooing motions with her hand and raised the water bottle to her mouth. Forty-five minutes until the meeting.

Halfway through the protein bar, the phone rang again. Gillian hit the TALK button.

"Yes."

"Your sister is on the line."

Gillian stared at a water drop on her desk. "Put her through."

Reading the long pause and deep breath correctly, Natalie responded, "Guess I was supposed to hold your calls. Sorry, I didn't know."

"I know." Gillian clicked the OFF button and stared hard at the blinking light on line one. If only she could glare it away. With an even deeper exhale, she pressed the square button. "What now?"

"You don't have to be snappy."

"I told you I'd get back to you."

"I know, but since then I've talked with Mother, and she said she hopes to see you before she dies. After all, with even a minor stroke, who knows?"

Besides always being "on the brink of death," their mother was a maestro at laying on guilt. "So, why doesn't she call me and say that in person?" Gillian paused. "A stroke. You didn't mention that before."

"I know, but you know how private she is."

"Yes, I'm afraid I do. So here is my suggestion. You drive over there and physically see how she is. None of this phone-tag stuff. If I were you, before I went, I would put in a call to her primary care physician and make an appointment—for Mother, not for you. Look into this stroke thing."

"I intensely dislike sarcasm." She spoke in that hurt-little-girl voice of hers.

Oh, for Pete's sake, Allie, grow up. "Yes, well, I intensely dislike being cast in the unfeeling older sister role. Surely Jefferson could be put upon to haul his own children around for a change and not go hide out at the golf course." Gillian knew she was overstepping, but at the moment, she didn't give a rat's nose. "Now, I have a meeting that I have to not only be at, but lead, so I know you will handle this with your normal efficiency. Give Mother my love." She pushed the END button with a little more force than necessary. Heartburn was not her usual problem at this time of day, but right now, she needed help—in the form of a crunchable tablet. Or maybe half a bottle of the liquid stuff.

Surely her mother hadn't really had a stroke and not told her.

The packet in the middle drawer of Gillian's desk was empty, so she pulled out the pill container from her purse, but that, too, held nothing but air. She'd reminded herself on the way home last night that she needed to refill it from the large bottle she kept in the bathroom. So much for keeping on top of things. Stuffing the purse back into the lower drawer, she headed for Shannon's desk. Surely she had a supply. After all, nearly everyone in the building lived on antacids.

If this was an indication of the remainder of the day, she'd rather just head home now.

Hand to her chest, she pulled out the drawer where Shannon kept her personal things, and in the back of the divider she found a beat-up roll of antacids with two tablets left. Only two when right now the burning called for a handful. Crunching the two, she returned to her office, turned her chair so she could stare out the window, and sipped water to wash the last of the chalky bits down. *Relax.* The words didn't get past her clenched teeth. *Breathe deeply and exhale. Relax.* Her shoulders were tickling her earlobes, not a good sign.

Think of your favorite place, see yourself there, and inhale the clean air. All the instructions from the class she'd taken on relaxation less than a month ago raced each other around the storm-laced trees in her once peaceful place.

Mind control was needed. *Take every thought captive.* The verse usually worked. Not today. Her very un-captive thoughts chased after each other wielding meat cleavers. The headache that she'd stretched away a few minutes earlier returned with a vengeance along with a partner, each of them taking up residence behind an eye.

She closed her eyes and returned to the deep-breathing exercises.

A tap on the door made her turn her chair back around and respond. "Come in."

"Your folders are done." Natalie clasped the stack against her skinny chest, her eyes huge behind her thick glasses. Another forewarning of unforeseen circumstances.

"What now?"

"The printer server is down—tech support is working on it. I had to do these on the old one, so the typeface isn't quite as clear."

Gillian heaved another sigh. "Thanks for taking care of it."

"But it's not perfect, you know."

"I understand." What she really understood was that only those who looked too closely would notice the discrepancy. Natalie had hawk eyes when it came to fine print. "Don't worry about it, all right? Just set them on the corner of the desk and then hold all my calls. You'll be gone before I return."

"I could stay as long as you need me."

"Thank you. But once this meeting is done, I'm heading home immediately." *To get rid of this headache if nothing else*. When Natalie closed the door behind her, Gillian dug in her purse for whatever painkiller she still had in there. Obviously her entire purse and desk needed a restocking. She filled a glass of water in her private bathroom and prepared for her meeting. Hair, fine; add lipstick; check for mascara smudges. All in order.

She stared in the mirror. Surely her mother wasn't dying. Guilt dug like little needles under her skin. Of course Allison could take care of this latest fiasco.

One thing at a time. Get through this meeting and then think on Mother. If that were at all possible.

Chapter Two

Turned down. How could they be so shortsighted as not to see this plan was far better than the other one? Granted, the bottom line was lower on the other, but that team had not included several costs that would be necessary. As Senior V.P. of Marketing, Gillian had been so sure of her plan. She closed her eyes and mentally reviewed the meeting. Why did she have a feeling there had been a setup?

And the major question: what did this mean to the others on her team? If the rumors were indeed true... She blew out a breath and stared at the folder in front of her. Nothing further could be done today. Hauling her purse from the bottom drawer, she slung it over her shoulder, retrieved her raincoat from the closet, and headed out the door. As usual, she was the last in her department to leave, so she shut off the lights as she went, a carryover from her growing-up years when her parents always insisted that when one left the room, one turned out the lights.

Tonight the click of the switch felt symbolic. The meeting had thrown a switch inside of her. All that hard work for naught. Waiting for the elevator, she felt her cell phone vibrate in her purse. She flipped it open and said hello without checking to see who it was.

Big mistake.

"I'm at her house, Gillian, and I can't get her out of bed." Allie's voice came over the receiver. "Here. I'm sending you a picture I took with my cell."

Gillian considered hanging up or at least pretending she lost the transmission. Guilt alone prevented her from following through. What kind of an unfeeling daughter was she to even think of such a thing? One on serious overload, she argued back. The picture showed up on her screen. Even with the poor-quality reception, she could recognize her mother, eyes closed, mouth half open in sleep.

"Gillian, are you there?"

"I am." How she wished she weren't.

"Her pulse is slow, too. Should I call 9-1-1?"

"Is she comatose?"

"No, she refused to go to the doctor, refused to eat the hamburger I brought. I did manage to get her to drink some tea, but then she went back to sleep."

"So she would refuse the paramedics, too?" Gillian stepped out of the elevator and crossed the marble floor to the front exit. Tonight even the soaring beauty of the brass and glass lobby failed to lift her spirits.

"I suppose."

"Does she have food in the house, easy things to fix?"

"Of course. I do her shopping and make sure of that. This week she refused to go with me, even when I tried to bribe her with lunch at Lucia's."

Gillian didn't recognize the name, but much had probably changed in the twenty years since she left Martinez, California. Back then, oil refineries and cargo shipping had been pushing out the orchards and fishing around the small river town on its way to becoming a bedroom community for San Francisco. Her visit five years earlier made her even more grateful she'd left when she did.

She paused to put up her umbrella so she wouldn't get soaked on her walk to the subway. Had the weather been dry she would have walked home to her condo in Greenwich Village. The rain matched her mood.

"Look, Allie, there is nothing I can do from here. You will have to deal with this."

"Mother said you wouldn't come so not to waste my time. I guess she was right." The phone clicked off.

Gillian could hear her unspoken thrust. *And if she dies it is all your fault.* While the thought made no sense, she couldn't shut it out. With no place to sit on the subway, she hung on to a bar and tried to read the newspaper over a man's shoulder. The Dow fell yet again. An ad for cheap airfare caught her attention. Here it was Thursday; what if she flew out there tomorrow and caught a red-eye back to New York on Monday night? Would a few days make any difference—other than to her guilt level? She had plenty of vacation time, so that was not a problem.

The metallic voice announced her stop, and she followed the human herd out the door and up the steep stairs into more rain. Sunny California was looking better by the minute.

When she unlocked her door, the phone gave one last bleep and went to voice mail. The flashing light said there were more messages. She hung her coat on the hall tree to drip dry and tipped her umbrella into the stand to do the same. What would happen if she called her boss and said that due to a family emergency she would be out of town for the next few days, not working on Saturday as was her wont? Friday, either. Others took three- and four-day weekends every once in a while, but a two-day weekend was a treat for Gillian. Dedication to her career had always taken precedence.

Flipping through the messages, she shook her head. Allison had been busy. After the second one, she hit DELETE at the first sound of her sister's voice that was whinier by the message. The last message was different. Her boss's voice sounded tired, too.

"Give me a call when you get in, will you, Gillian? Thanks."

She checked the time of the call. She'd just missed it. Thirst drew her to the kitchen, where she pulled a bottle of Perrier from the refrigerator, popped the top, and poured it over ice cubes into a stemmed glass. Tonight she needed bubbles. Sipping her drink with her phone in hand, she sank down into her favorite leather recliner. With her feet propped up, she dialed Scot's number.

He answered on the second ring. "Thanks for returning my call. I just wanted to say how sorry I am that the board went with the other proposal."

"Thank you." *I guess. What else am I to say?*

"Between you and me, I think they made a big mistake."

She forced herself to take a sip and swallow before answering. "Obviously I do, too."

"Well, don't be discouraged, we'll work something out."

"Okay." And then her mouth took off without her permission. "I had several calls here from my sister in California. We are having a family emergency, and if I can get flights I think I'll fly out there tomorrow and come back Monday."

"I hope it is not too serious."

"I'll know more when I get there." *I can't believe I am saying this.*

"Well, go with my blessing and let me know how I can be of help."

"Thank you. I'll be in touch." They said their good-byes, but she kept hold of the phone. She really had done it. Not asked for time off, but stated it as fact.

He must be in a state of shock, for she certainly was.

Gillian caught the six a.m. flight to SFO Friday morning and called her sister from the airport as she caught the shuttle to the car rental. She ignored the e-mails on her phone; she'd have to check them later. None looked critical.

"Can you meet me at Mother's in an hour?" A slight shiver of vindictiveness caught her at the stutter on the other end.

"But why didn't you warn me? I'm on my way to a doctor's appointment with Sherrilyn and we can't miss that. It took me forever to get it. I'll get there as soon as I can."

Gillian could hear more muttering. It sounded like she'd thrown her sister into a real tizzy.

"Look, you wanted me to come, and I am here. Is the key still under the same rock?"

"Yes, at least I assume so."

"Good. I'll call you if it is, and you won't need to rearrange your schedule." She left out the adjective *precious* before schedule, but barely.

"I'll come as soon as I can."

"Fine." A four-letter word that housed a multitude of meanings. Gillian clicked her phone shut and prepared to exit the bus at the rental office.

Thanks to traffic on the Bay Bridge the trip took more than an hour, but when she had trouble recognizing her mother's street due to all the new houses in what used to be fields, she was even more grateful she no longer lived in the area. Recognizing the winery that had been there ever since she could remember helped. At least the homes on her mother's street had been kept up and the few vacant lots built on. She parked in the short driveway and stared at the front yard to her right. The jasmine that had always been the glory of her mother's yard lay brown and twisted, the leaves lifeless under the branches and stems.

Alarm sneaked in, followed by resentment. Couldn't her sister at least have turned on the sprinklers a few times? The small patch of lawn looked equally bereft, only the weeds poking through the dead grass. Her mom would probably get a citation from the city for neglect of the premises, if she hadn't already. Gillian opened her car door and, leaving her suitcase in the backseat, slung her bag over her shoulder and headed for the front door. The key lay under the same rock, but it failed to turn the lock in the door.

Gillian felt like banging her head against one of the curtain-obscured windowpanes in the door. Drapes drawn tight prevented any view into the house. She checked out the side of the house. The gate to the backyard was locked from the inside. By putting her eye to the crack between the gate and post she could barely make out a padlock. The six-foot cedar fence effectively cut off any access to the backyard.

Muttering a word that her mother would take exception to, Gillian headed back to the front door and pounded on it. "Mother, it's Gillian. Come open the door." She knew the effort was futile. Her mother's bedroom lay on the far end of the house, overlooking the backyard. "Please, God, let her be in the kitchen, or watching TV in the living room, or even getting up to go to the bathroom." As was the case lately, God did not seem to be listening.

What to do? She tried the key several more times, but nada. She called her mother's phone—no answer. Back in the car she punched in her sister's phone number only to have it go to voice mail. What now? Call 9-1-1 and get the fire department out here to let her in on the pretext that her mother needed medical help? She considered that. Unless Mother was comatose, she would refuse and they would not take her.

She dialed Allie again. No doubt she turned off her phone during the doctor's appointment. Were they still there? Nearly noon. Surely not. "Turn your phone back on, you..." No names sounded sufficient. Surely Allie would turn her phone on. Miss Perfect who kept track of everyone in the universe except their aging mother and her now furious sister.

Slamming her hand on the steering wheel did nothing but cause more pain. *Think, Gillian, think.* Were any of the neighbors long-term friends? Did her mother leave the key with anyone else? Probably not. She glared at an imprint the key had left on her palm. Why hadn't she called Allie from the airport in New York? Surely she could have worked something out to be here. She knew the reason—six thirty in New York was only three thirty in California. *But you could have called her last night.* Would the arguments in her head never cease?

Returning to the front door, she leaned on the doorbell. Not hearing a ring from inside, she heaved a sigh that sounded more like a groan. Was it broken? Disconnected? Why had Jefferson, Allie's perfect husband, not taken care of these things?

And now, on top of everything else, she needed to use the facilities. She should have stopped at the shopping center, but she'd known she'd be at her mother's house soon enough. Obviously not soon enough. She glanced around the yard and spied the brick edging along the sidewalk. It would be easier to put a new pane in the front door than to gamble on making it to a ladies' room at the shopping center. Checking the door for an emblem that said security and not finding one, she picked up the closest brick and lifted her arm.

"Stop!"

She heard the voice and the growl at the same time. She dropped the brick while spinning around. Her toes screamed from the force of the falling brick, and she yelped. The monster dog standing right at the edge of the single concrete step never made another sound. He didn't need to. One lip slightly raised and dark eyes that stared into her own slammed her back against the door. The screen door smacked her shins. Could she hide behind that?

"Sit, Thor."

Her gaze shifted to the middle-aged man striding up the walk. The scowl on his face about matched that of the monster. "Call off your dog!" Sure, that sounded like a line from a B-grade movie. She tried to swallow, but somehow her mouth had turned to dust.

"He seems to be doing his job just fine. Now, what are you doing here?" He glanced down at the brick, then back to her face.

"Trying to get into my mother's house, if it is any business of yours." At least total fear had momentarily dried up the other problem at the same time as her mouth.

He nodded, a slight glint touching his steely blue eyes. "You could have tried the key under the rock."

"I did. It didn't work!"

"And Allie?"

"Who are you?" *That you know all this.*

"My name is Adam Bentley and I live two doors up." He relaxed his shoulders, and the glint brightened. "You must be the long-lost daughter. Gillian, isn't it?"

The urge returned, more ferociously than before.

"Look, I have to get in the house." Big emphasis on *have*. "Allie is coming from a doctor's appointment, but who knows how soon. I can't rouse Mother and..." She shifted from one foot to the other, like a little kid.

He gave a slight nod. "I could boost you over the fence." He looked at her slacks and silk blouse, along with her trademark high heels. "Probably not."

"Look, I don't have any choice. I'm going to break the window and get it fixed this afternoon. Only, call off your dog because I don't dare move."

"Thor, come."

Gillian bent over, picked up the brick, and tapped the window. The glass fell inward. She started to reach through the eight inch pane, when his "watch it" made her jerk back.

"What?"

"The glass. You could cut yourself."

"I'm fine," she said through gritted teeth. *Please, body, hang in there*. She tapped a jagged tooth and, when the glass fell, reached through and felt for the handle. A rip in the arm of her silk shirt didn't stop her. Turning the handle, she pulled her hand out and opened the door. Sliding through, she crunched her way through the glass shards and hustled down the hall, fighting the buckle on her leather belt closure as she went.

When she'd finished her business, she heaved a sigh of relief, put herself back together, and washed her hands. She took a peek at her mother to make sure she was still breathing, then returned to the front door.

"Is your mother all right?" The guy had picked up the larger shards and stacked them by the wall. Thor sat on the sidewalk where he'd been told to sit.

"She's breathing, but all this noise didn't wake her. I'll

get a broom and dustpan." *Delayed reaction,* she thought as she started to shake. Her foot ached; she glanced down to see a scuff on the toe of her Ferragamo three-inch heels. Fury lit a flame. This was all his fault. Had he not appeared, she'd have broken the glass and entered in a nice, civilized manner. No broken toes, ruined shoes, heart palpitations or...

"Here, I'll take those." He reached for the broom and dustpan. "You're limping."

Up close the man looked like a giant—had to be at least six-five, broad-shouldered—a big man. She started to hang on to the cleaning utensils, but when her foot let out another shriek, she surrendered them. "Do you know my mother well?" She tried to remember his name. Adam something. *Mind your manners.* Her mother's voice of yore.

"No, not well, I've not lived here that long, but she and my mother were the best of friends."

She caught the *were*. Had there been a falling out? What happened?

"My mother died eighteen months ago."

"Oh, I'm so sorry." The light dawned, her mother had often spoken of her friend up the hill. Alice? Bentley, that was the last name. "Mother never told me." *Perhaps had you asked more often about her friends and activities, she would have told you.* If only she could order the voice in her head to take a vacation. Guilt was a strident hoyden, a demanding accuser.

"There." He held pan and broom. "Where can I dump this?"

"The trash is under the sink, in the kitchen." At least it used to be, but then her mother was never one for change. If something worked, she did not try to make it better. Gillian leaned against the half wall that bordered the living room. She started to lean over to take off her shoe, remembered the glass, and thought the better of it.

"You might want to take a vacuum to the carpet around the tiled area."

"I will."

"Did your mother know you were coming?"

Gillian shook her head. *No, she is sure I didn't care enough to come.* "My sister called me in a panic, and so I came."

"So you are Gillian from New York?"

"Yes. I don't know why the key doesn't work."

"Figures. They probably forgot to put a new one under the rock after they changed the locks."

"Changed the locks?" What had been going on in this neighborhood?

"We had a rash of burglaries last year, and the police suggested that those of us with older houses might want new locks with dead bolts."

Right now if she could get her fingers around Allie's neck she would have been seriously tempted to squeeze. Dead bolt. Thank God that wasn't in place; she'd never have gotten in in time. The thought flipped. *What good was a dead bolt if it wasn't used?*

"I see."

"Have you called your sister?"

"Yes." *What do you think I am, stupid?* Of course, had she called earlier…or come more often. She gritted her teeth. All she needed was another dose of guilt to make this a perfect day.

The dog whined outside from his place on the concrete walk. She flinched. Little dogs were fine, but this monster looked like he could be guarding a junkyard with ease. Broad of chest, salad plate–size paws, square muzzle with lots of shiny white teeth, one ear stood up, the other flopped forward.

"I'm coming, boy." Adam looked back to Gillian. "We'll stop back in when we get home in an hour or so to make sure you're all right. Maybe by then your sister will be here."

"I certainly hope so."

Gillian took a deep breath and let it out. Her cell phone was ringing in her purse she'd left outside the door.

He waited to see if it was Allie, and when she shook her head, he smiled and the two strode down the drive and turned to go down the hill. He stopped and called back. "You might want to get some ice on that foot."

"I will." She watched him leave. Bossy-man. She'd not even said thank you.

"What is it, Shannon?"

"Are you really in California?"

"Yes."

"But you never leave New York."

"True, but this time I did. Have you heard about the meeting? Oh, before you answer that, how is your father?"

"He's doing better, thank you for asking." She dropped her voice to a whisper. "Something strange is going on here, and I have no idea what it is. I keep hearing words like *takeover* and *reorganization*, but no one knows for sure."

Gillian heaved another sigh. "Well, keep me posted. I should be back in the office on Tuesday." *Barring any real catastrophes here, and if Allie doesn't arrive soon, she is going to be one of the casualties.*

Chapter Three

Since when had deep sighs become part of her modus operandi?

Gillian caught herself in another one. She peeled herself off the half wall and limped down the hallway. If she had brought her suitcase into the house, she would have changed shoes. Trying to ignore the pain, she entered her mother's bedroom. Not only were the drapes pulled but the blind was down, too. Strange since her mother had never closed the back drapes before. She loved seeing the first light of the day. The room smelled musty, empty like a house when no one was home. Where had the meticulous housekeeper gone? Good thing she could hear her mother breathing, since she could barely see her. Should she turn on the light? Would that be too much of a shock? She crossed the room to stand beside the double bed, the same bed she'd known as a child and had climbed into when the nightmares overwhelmed her. All those years ago, before her father had died. Even the lamp and shade on the nightstand were the same. Memories from her growing years whipped through her mind at warp speed.

With eyes more adjusted to the dimness and the light

from the doorway, she stared down at the frail woman in the bed. Gaunt was the only word she could think of. How long had her mother been like this? Was Mother really dying? From what she saw, it could happen at any minute.

"Mother." Gillian touched the thin hand lying on top of the blankets. "Mom." She gently stroked the fingers she remembered being strong enough to pull quack grass. Surely her mother wasn't comatose? Fear raced through her mind chased by larger ones.

A slow burn ignited. Why had Allie let their mother get to this state before attempting to do something? Gillian laid a hand on her mother's shoulder and shook a bit harder.

Her mother snorted and sniffed, her eyes slowly opening as if the weight was too much to lift. When she didn't focus immediately, Gillian took her hand. "Mother, it's Gillian. Can you hear me?"

Dorothy nodded and turned her head bit by bit. "You came?"

"Yes, Allie called me." *Called me twenty times or more.* The burn flickered higher.

Her mother looked straight forward again. "It's too late."

"What do you mean, too late?" She fought to keep the edge from her tone.

"I'm dying."

Gillian swallowed and blinked. "I brought you some See's Candies; you know the creams you like so well. I bought them here at the airport."

Another shake of the head.

You can't be dying, Mother, you are too young to die. But her argument didn't hold water as she stared down at the still form whose eyes were drifting closed again. Was Mother really so weak she couldn't even talk? Or sit up?

Or...or..."Can I get you something?" She forced herself to think. What did her mother like, other than the candies? "When did you eat last?"

She'd have missed the shrug had she not been staring so intently. "Okay, how about I heat up some soup and bring it in and feed you?" She took the non-answer as an affirmative. "I'll be right back."

Stopping at the door to the guest room, she removed her shoes and tried wiggling her toes. At least they worked, although the three smaller toes were already swollen. No wonder her shoes hurt so badly. As long as she stayed away from the front door and the glass, she should be all right.

Sunlight flooded through the south window and sliding glass door, warming the kitchen that included a dining area. The geraniums in front of the window side of the door looked about as shriveled as her mother. Did Allie ever water anything? Disgust warred with anger, and then the two teamed together. Obviously her visits were short, with a lack of assistance. Gillian's mind turned into list mode. Even though she would only be here for a couple of days, she could get some of this mess cleaned up.

With a bowl of chicken noodle soup heating in the microwave, she filled the under-the-sink pitcher with water and started watering the geraniums. When the water drained through the dry pots without pausing, she brought the plants to the sink. She put in the plug and after setting the temperature to lukewarm, set the three pots in the sink and gave them a good drenching. Upon closer inspection, the stalks still had a little bit of green to them. As did the violets on the north windowsill in the living room. She moved them to the other side of the deep two-sectioned sink to soak.

For crying out loud, how long does it take Allie to get

here? Surely she didn't take Sherrilyn out for lunch first. But knowing the time, of course she did. The girl couldn't go back to school without being fed.

The microwave beeped, so she dug a spoon out of the drawer and after dividing the soup into two bowls—from the same yellow set she remembered as a child—carried one bowl and spoon down the hall. She stopped at the table to retrieve a napkin from the yellow holder that had sat in the middle of the table ever since she could remember. Back in the bedroom that desperately needed airing, she set the bowl down and pulled the cord to open the drapes. While the horizontal blinds kept out the direct sun, at least she could see to feed her mother.

"Mother, I've brought you some soup."

No response.

She sat down on the edge of the bed and shook her mother's shoulder.

A grimace but at least a response.

"Open your eyes and I'll help you sit up."

Mother shook her head, slowly. "I can't."

"I understand that, so I am going to help you. I'll help pull you up and put the pillows behind you."

"No." Even two letters trailed off.

Leave her and let her be came from one side of Gillian's mind and *just do it* from the other. She gritted her teeth. She had been called to help and help she would. No matter if her mother wanted it or not. She would not be intimidated like her wimpy sister. Forcing a note of cheer into her voice, Gillian stood and leaned over the bed to pick up the other pillow.

"All right now, I'm going to put an arm around you to lift your head and add the pillow. Then we'll get you sitting up comfortably." In spite of her mother's shaking head, Gillian did exactly as she had explained. Although lifting someone who didn't want to move into a sitting position took more strength and determination than she had expected. But her mother was now halfway sitting against the pillows. At least she'd be able to swallow the soup without choking.

"There, how's that?" Gillian picked up the bowl and spoon. "Remember when you used to do this for us when we got sick?" She scooped out liquid and held the spoon to her mother's mouth. To her surprise, Mother did open her mouth and swallow the soup. "There, very good." *You sound like you're talking to a baby. This is your mother, remember?*

Without opening her eyes, Dorothy ate half the bowl before shaking her head and resisting the spoon against her mouth.

"Okay, we'll stop for now. Would you like coffee or tea?" She gently wiped her mother's mouth with the napkin. Waiting for an answer tugged at the end of her patience. "Mother, coffee or tea? Or if you have juice in the cupboard, I'll bring that. You have to get some liquids into you."

Faded blue eyes peered out of half-opened lids, but the face bore no appearances of a stroke. Not that Gillian knew a lot about strokes, but surely the damage would be visible if her mother were really dying from it. A bath was needed, her nose told her that much. The thought of giving her mother a sponge bath made her want to sigh again. And head for the rental car and the airport.

"Gillian?" Allie's voice came from the front door. "What happened here?"

"In the bedroom." Keep this light and easy. *Do not jump on her with both feet—both spiked heels feet—yet.* Her mind heard the warnings, but the rest of her fought going along with it. "Allie's here." Bright and breezy. Maybe she should have been on the stage instead of in the boardroom.

Her mother's jaw went slack as Gillian watched. In an instant, Dorothy Mae Ormsby was sound asleep again.

"What happened to the door?"

"What ever happened to 'hello, good to see you, thank you for coming'?"

"Don't get testy with me; I've had a hard morning." Allie set her leather hobo bag on the dresser by the doorway. "Now, what happened to the front door and why is there glass all over the floor?"

"There is not glass all over. It's already been swept up. Since the key did not work and I had to use the facilities and you were not here yet, I hit the glass with a brick and let myself in. Had you replaced the key when you replaced the lock on the door, none of this would have happened." Gillian stood, wishing for her heels so she could be taller and more imposing, and crossed her arms over her chest. She ignored Allie's sputtering and continued. "And if you had taken the time to come more often, perhaps things would not be in such bad shape." She didn't say, "including Mother," but she sure thought it loud.

"Now, I think we should adjourn to the kitchen. Mother has just finished half a bowl of soup and is resting." She marched forward and out the door. Again wishing for her shoes but wisely not trying to cram her wounded toes back into the fashionably pointy leather, she headed for the kitchen. Even if her mother did not want a cup of coffee, Gillian most certainly did.

"You got her to eat?"

"Yes, I fed her." Gillian opened the cupboard and found the can of coffee right where it had always sat, second shelf on the left. She shook the red plastic container. "How long has this been here?"

"How should I know?"

"You said you do all her shopping." Gillian located the coffeepot in the tall closet beside the stove. The same percolator even. "Couldn't you buy her a decent coffeemaker?"

"She didn't want one."

Gillian thought back. "I sent her one for Christmas two years ago."

"It's in the closet of the guest room. Along with most of the other things we've all given her. She's keeping them nice." Allie clipped her words.

Gillian turned around to recognize daggers flying at her. She heaved another one of those sighs she so deplored. "All right. That's enough. We're not getting anywhere sniping at each other." Talk about falling right back into old patterns. This was classic Gillian versus Allie. "I suggest that I pour us each a cup of coffee and we sit down at that table and discuss what we would like to accomplish here."

"I'll fix myself some iced tea. I hate that kind of coffee." Allie reached into the tall pantry cupboard and brought out a jar of peach-flavored instant tea mix.

"Mother drinks that?"

"At times, but mostly I keep this here for me. Her coffee is far too strong." As Allie went about making her iced tea, Gillian filled the white ceramic coffeepot with water to the eight cup line, poured the grounds in the basket, and with all the innards assembled, set the pot on the burner. Later she'd retrieve that new coffeemaker from the guest closet and set it up. Her stomach rumbled at the fragrance of the coffee. She should finish that soup.

"Have you eaten?" Gillian asked.

"Yes, Sherrilyn and I stopped for lunch." Allie glanced at her sister's face. "Well, I couldn't let her go back to school hungry. Her lunch period had already passed."

"I'm sure." Gillian set her bowl of soup in the microwave. While it heated she put the dish she'd served to her mother into the fridge. The lack of supplies caught her attention. "I thought you said there was plenty of food here."

"There is. Both canned and frozen. I didn't want things to go to waste. You know how Mother hates that." She sipped from her glass, her gaze flitting from her sister to the backyard and to the drink between her hands.

The microwave beeped, and Gillian retrieved the hot soup with potholders and set it on the table. The coffee was beginning to perk, sending the aroma to tease her nose. The coffeemaker would have finished brewing long before now. She sat down at the table.

"Why are you shaking your head?"

"The coffee thing. I try to make life easier for her, and she stuffs the gifts into the closet." Spooning her soup, she waited for her sister to say something.

"You could have let me know you were coming."

"Oh, Allie. By the time I hit the airport, it was three a.m. here. I spent the evening trying to get flights and packing. Let's just drop it and try to figure out what to do."

Allie rolled her eyes and heaved a sigh of her own. "All right. Just don't blame me for everything. Mother has a will of her own, in case you've forgotten."

So much for not sniping. "Look, I don't have a lot of time here, so let's make every minute count. First of all, do you know who I should call to fix the window?"

"The people I know would charge extra for driving clear up here, so look in the phone book."

"All right. Do you have her primary care doctor's phone number?"

"All her phone numbers are in the book by the telephone. And before you call, they will not give you information because you are not listed as immediate family."

"Great, so how do I get listed?" The soup she'd partially eaten only made her realize she wanted something more.

"They won't be open over the weekend anyway."

"So we have to deal with this today." Gillian glanced at her watch, glad she'd reset it on the plane. One thirty.

"What are we going to do?"

"Go over to the clinic and get me on that list."

"I think you have to have Mother's signature to do that."

"Good grief." Gillian tipped her head back and closed her eyes. This was enough to drive one to cocktails. Early cocktails.

"It's not my fault; it's the new privacy laws."

Gillian smiled around clenched teeth. "I didn't say it was your fault. We are two fairly intelligent women; surely we can come to some kind of agreement on how to get help for our mother."

"She doesn't want help."

Gillian placed her hands flat on the table, fingers spread. "So, according to you we just leave her here to die?"

"Yes... no." Big sigh. "I don't know." Allie's head wagged from side to side.

"Okay, here's what I see as the options. One: we leave her as is and she dies. Two: we talk to the doctor and get her opinion. Three: we call nine-one-one and have them take Mother to the hospital."

"His opinion." The words were mumbled into the iced tea glass held at her lips.

"What?" Gillian got up to pour herself a cup of coffee.

"His opinion. Mother's doctor is a man."

"Oh, for..." Man, woman, what did it matter? Stick to

the point. Gillian set her cup on the counter and crossed to the wall phone with the stand right below it. Funny, why did she feel so strongly that Mother had a woman doctor, and had so for years? "His name?"

"Isaacs. He's with the Martinez Medical Clinic by the hospital."

"When did you see Mother last?" Gillian picked up her mug of coffee and returned to the table.

"Yesterday."

"How long before that?"

"I talk to her every day." Her sister's petulant tone showed her defenses had sprung to attention.

"That's not what I asked you." Gillian kept her tone mild through fierce force of will. She stared out the glass door to the caricature of the former beauty of the backyard. Surely it hadn't been so hot here that the plants in the pots had died overnight. "Couldn't someone have turned the sprinklers on?"

"We had timers installed, but Mother turned them off. Said her water bill was too high."

So why didn't you pay it? Or ask me to? Things were not making sense. Gillian glanced at her watch again. "Okay, here's what we are going to do. I will get my bag out of the car, put some shoes on, and we will go over to the doctor's office and start the process so I can have access to Mother's medical information. We will see if Dr. Isaacs can fit us in for a quick conference. With you there, he can talk to me."

"But I have to pick up the kids at two thirty."

"Text them and tell them you will be a bit late. Waiting won't kill them. Tell them it's all my fault."

"This is not a boardroom with you in charge." Allie stood and took her glass to the sink, then pulled out her cell phone.

Gillian drained her mug, opened the dishwasher door, and pulled out the rack.

"No, you can't put those in there."

"Why not?"

"Mother doesn't like to use the dishwasher; it wastes too much power and water."

"I see. Does it work?"

"I guess so."

"Then I will use it and pay the power bill." *So, that's another thing we deal with—Mother's finances.* "Don't you usually take care of her financial things?"

Allie shook her head. "Oh, no. I offered and she about bit my head off. I'm not going there again."

"But has she been paying her bills?"

"I guess so. It's not…"

Gillian whirled around and shook her finger at her baby sister. "Do not say that again." She huffed a breath. "How long since she took to her bed?"

"Two weeks."

"And before that?"

Allie shrugged. She glanced down at her sister's bare feet. "You better put on shoes before you go to the car." She stared down. "Your toes are all swollen. What happened?"

"I dropped a brick."

Allie stared at her sister. "Give me your keys. I'll get your suitcase. And we'll take my car."

"But what about Mother?" Gillian wished she could take the words back. After all, her mother had been alone all this time, what difference would a couple of hours make?

Chapter Four

He'll never have time to see us."

Gillian swallowed the sigh this time. "Didn't Mother teach us a verse that said something about it never hurts to ask?"

Allie shook her head. "There were verses about asking, but that wasn't one of them."

"Well, what is it then?"

"I don't remember exactly, but that isn't it."

Gillian turned in her seat. "Do you still go to church?"

"Of course. Don't you?"

She knew that was another strike against her. "Not too often. Sunday is the only day I have off." She gazed out the window. Things sure had changed in the five years since she'd been back to Martinez. But she knew mentioning that would bring on more recriminations.

"Surely you don't have to work every Saturday."

"If I want to achieve my goals, long hours are part of the package."

"You and Jefferson." This was muttered under her breath.

"I thought he played a lot of golf."

"Well, he needs some form of relaxation from the pressure cooker where he works."

That sounded like a direct quote. What was wrong with relaxing at home? But she knew the excuse most men used. Golfing was also a good place to make contacts and conduct business in a more informal setting. She'd tried golfing but found the same criteria didn't always work for women. The men didn't want to golf with a woman, and there weren't too many women in her sphere of equals. Not that she'd thought much of a game where one hit a little white ball with a club and then hoped it fell into a hole in the grass.

"Can't relax with his family, eh?" She knew that was throwing down the gauntlet, but some demon inside slipped it into the conversation.

"You just don't know what life with two active teenagers is like. Jefferson is a good father and a great provider. You…" She sputtered as she turned into the clinic parking lot.

Gillian noticed her sister had not said what a great husband mister perfect Jefferson was. And yet, since his wife was driving a Lexus SUV he certainly was doing well, or was heavily in debt. The peril of going into debt was one thing that her mother had drilled into both girls, and it had stuck with Gillian. But then she didn't have to consult with a husband as to what to buy and when.

Don't go there, Gillian, the sweeter of the two internal voices whispered. "Is it always this crowded?"

"Yes, Martinez has grown a lot in the last years. Like everywhere else in the Bay Area." Allie expertly jockeyed the big vehicle into a parking place just vacated by a much smaller car.

Admiration for her sister's skill made her smile. One did not own an SUV or any other vehicle in NYC. Not if they had any common sense. New Yorkers rented cars as needed, which wasn't often.

"Not a lot of room to open the doors. Sorry."

She didn't sound too sorry. Gillian skinnied through the narrow space, her sister doing the same. Hopefully there'd be more space by the time they returned. She caught up with Allie who clicked the car lock with an over-the-shoulder aim of the key. *Cut the criticizing,* she ordered herself. *She lives this life, you don't.*

The sisters took the elevator to the third floor, obeying the no talking rule that seemed to dominate elevator users. As they opened the door to the office, she asked, "How long has Mother been this doctor's patient?"

"Forever."

"I see." *Come on, little sister, let's quit playing games here. Working together will accomplish a lot more.* They waited at the counter for the receptionist to hang up the phone.

"Hi, Jeanie, my sister is here from New York to help with Mother and we need to fill out the authorization forms for her to be informed about Mother's health."

The woman smiled at them both. "We can do that, but you'll need Dorothy to sign them."

"I was afraid of that. Mother isn't doing well right now. Is there any way we can get around that?"

"Nope, sorry. Do you need to make an appointment for her?"

Allie shook her head. "She won't come. I tried that."

The woman lost her smile. "Do we need to intervene?"

"I—I don't know what to do."

"You need to talk to Dr. Isaacs. Let me make you an appointment for next week."

Gillian waited for Allie to chime in, but when she didn't,

Gillian leaned forward. "That would be wonderful, but I need to be back in my office in New York on Tuesday bright and early. Is there any chance we could see him for a few minutes right now or . . . ?" She could feel Allie's glare.

Jeanie glanced down at her book. "He's really busy but . . ." She paused a moment. "Let me check." She picked up her phone, punched a button, and waited. "Hi, Sarah, is there any chance Dorothy Ormsby's daughters could talk with him for a couple of minutes?" She nodded. "Okay, I'll do that." She hung up and turned back to them. Leaning forward, she dropped her voice. "This never happens. Just shows how much concern he has for your mother. Follow me."

She showed them into the doctor's private office. "He'll be with you in a couple of minutes. He's squeezing you in between patients."

Allie stared at Gillian, all the while shaking her head. "You know what a miracle this is?"

"No, but I can guess." Gillian ignored the throbbing in her foot. She'd ice it when she got back to her mother's. Glancing around the office, she noted the family pictures on a bookshelf, including several of the doctor and a sailboat. Sailing was one of those things she'd never dreamed of, due to intense motion sickness the one time she'd tried.

She hated waiting for anyone; doctors were not exempt. *Relax*. She took a deep cleansing breath, paused, and let it all out. Sometimes obeying that inner voice was extremely wise. Allie's glare drilled into her. What was her problem? Gillian repeated her action and felt the tension leave her shoulders. At the same time, she hoped breathing would improve her armor against those unwanted and unearned dagger-glares.

"Have you never heard of breathing to relax?" Gillian spoke softly, refusing to let the barbs sink in.

"Yes." Even a yes sounded brittle when pushed through clenched teeth.

"You might try it."

Allie's foot began to swing, more like a twitch at first but escalating. She'd done the same as a little girl when she got restless. Deep breathing was far more effective.

The door opened and a deep voice preceded the white-coated man with silver hair any aging male would covet. "Sorry to keep you waiting. How are you, Allie?"

How often was her sister here that everyone knew her name? Surely her mother didn't need to come that often.

"Fine, Reuben, we're here about Mother."

Reuben? First names all around. Gillian made sure her face was smiling.

"I understand. Since I haven't seen her since that little TIA, I assumed she recovered well."

"This is my sister from New York, Gillian Ormsby."

He extended his hand. "Good to meet you. Your mother has often mentioned you."

Gillian hoped she caught the look of surprise that must have at least made it to her eyes. She shook his hand. "Thank you. You said she had a little TIA?"

"Yes, a very small stroke in other words."

"I see." Gillian understood about TIAs but was still having trouble associating that with her mother.

"Maybe more than one but nothing to be concerned about. Why?" His blue eyes looked right into her.

"She refuses to get out of bed. She says she is dying." Gillian kept the eye connection with the doctor. "Allie called me because she could not get Mother to cooperate."

He switched his attention to Allie. "How long has this been going on?"

"Two, three weeks. I wanted to call you, but Mother was adamant."

"Ah, I know what you mean about adamant. But where did this idea she was dying come from?"

"Mother has been dying all her life. Or at least she has said so." Gillian dropped into the conversation.

"I know she has a low threshold for pain, but dying?"

"She's also a drama queen." *And a narcissist of the first order.*

He half shook his head, and then rolled his lips together, as if keeping a smile inside. "Your mother can be a most charming woman."

"When she wants to."

"Gillian!"

Gillian almost waited for the pinch that used to come when she didn't do exactly as her mother wished. Often the wish wasn't verbally stated, but both girls had learned mind reading, or rather mother reading, at an early age.

"Is she taking her medication?" He looked to Allie.

"I—I think so. She's usually very careful about that."

"But she won't get out of bed. Is she eating? Drinking fluids?"

Allie shook her head. "Not to speak of."

"Unless something else has happened, she is in very good health. This makes no sense." He stared at the pictures on the shelf. "I could request an ambulance go get her and check her into the hospital for observation."

"They can't take her against her wishes." Allie stared down at her purse in her lap. "I asked a friend who is an EMT."

"And she's not comatose?"

"Sleeps all the time, but when you wake her, she is fairly alert."

"She did not answer the door when I rang, but once I was in the house, I shook her and she woke. She recognized me." Gillian leaned slightly forward. "I heated some soup and fed it to her. She ate about a cup before she refused any more."

"She can't stay by herself any longer, at least not like this. I recommend you look into an assisted living facility."

What are we to do, tie her up and haul her there? Gillian kept the thought to herself.

"I know she won't want to go. She made that clear to me one day when I suggested she think on it. But then she was fully cognizant and busy with her garden. She even brought me some tomatoes." He appeared to be thinking hard, his eyes half slitted. He was nodding slightly as he looked from one woman to the other. "She shouldn't be living alone especially if she refuses food and drink. Even if she's not sick now, she could will herself to that end, and we all know what a strong will she has."

"I can't leave my family at night, at least not for any length of time." Allie's voice climbed a notch.

"What about you?" He looked to Gillian.

"I have to be back in my office on Tuesday."

"I see. You can hire an attendant, but they are expensive and difficult to find. I don't think she needs a full-time nurse, but I can write orders for her to be monitored. I can also order that she gets physical therapy twice a week to get her strength back. But . . ." He started writing on a prescription pad, tearing one sheet off and then another. "I can also prescribe something to increase her appetite." He wrote out a third slip of paper and tore it off. "And tell her I expect to see her in here on Wednesday."

He looked to Gillian again. "If you could make different arrangements, even for two weeks, it could be very important." He extended his hand. "Good to meet you. Dorothy certainly has two lovely daughters." He shook Allie's hand, too. "Tell her I gave the orders."

"What about the papers we need to sign?" Allie asked.

"Pick them up and take them home. Have her sign them and send them back so you can both call for information when you need to."

"Thank you for working us in." Gillian stood and hooked her kid leather bag over her shoulder. After he left, she turned to look at Allie, who had yet to move.

"She won't come. She really wants to die. He didn't get it," Allie murmured.

"Yes, he thinks we have some kind of influence here. Well, maybe you do, but I know I don't. Come on, let's get the papers and get back to the house so I can see about fixing the window."

Once they were in the car and waiting at the stoplight to enter Alhambra Avenue, Gillian turned to Allie. "How do you know them all so well?"

"He used to be my doctor until we moved to San Ramon. For the last year or so, Mother has insisted that she can't drive down here."

"Not drive?"

"Oh, she drives but not to the clinic, not since they finished the hospital additions and Dr. Isaacs moved his office into this building."

"But that doesn't make any sense."

"Maybe not, but she made up her mind."

"I see." Gillian pondered a moment. "So she drives to church?"

A nod. Allie accelerated and turned south on the now four-lane street.

"To the grocery store?"

"She drove most places until about a month ago. After the stroke."

"Technically it was a stroke, but TIAs aren't usually debilitating. One of the men in the office had the same kind of thing."

"You tell Mother that. I tried."

"Did you go online and print out information for her to read?"

"No." Allie heaved a sigh. "They gave her a booklet about it."

"Did she read it?"

"How would I know? I'm not *her* mother." Allie checked her watch. "And now I am officially late."

"But you told them you would be."

"I know." Allie sped up to get through a light and onto Highway 4 going east.

"So, will you pick up the kids and then come back?"

"I can't. I have a commitment for this evening."

"And tomorrow?"

"I'll see what I can do. Sherrilyn has a soccer game at eight a.m., and Benson has tennis practice."

"What about Jefferson?"

"We haven't discussed the weekend much yet."

That seemed strange. Friday afternoon and they'd not discussed the weekend. Hmm. "What does your calendar say?"

"Look, I'll check and get back to you."

"I'd think since I came clear across the country, we might want to get together, the whole family for dinner or something. Perhaps Sunday evening?"

"If you had told me you were coming, I would have made arrangements. Now I will do what I can." Allie cut the corner a bit sharply onto Munson Street, earning a glare from the driver waiting to turn, and sped up the street. Pulling into the driveway as far as she could without clipping her sister's rental car, she stopped and clicked the door lock latch.

"Thanks for the ride." Gillian opened the door and stepped down. The vehicle was in motion almost before she slammed the door and backed out of the way. Her sister did not wave or smile. Watching her leave, Gillian blew out a long breath. Well, it was obvious they were going to have trouble working together on this. Doctor's orders or no. She shook her head and headed for the door. Good thing the window was open because she still had no key.

"Of all the stupid...!" She wasn't sure who she was referring to. At the moment, that didn't much matter. Hobbling to the door was enough for right now, then phone book for a glass repair shop and an ice pack for her toes, in that order. Oh, and check on Mother.

Chapter Five

Eight phone calls and three frozen toes later, Gillian still hadn't located a man to fix the window—today. The earliest possible opening was next Thursday.

"Thieves could steal the entire house by then," Gillian huffed, ignoring the fact there was no one to hear her. Besides, she would be back in New York. Feeling a bit like the little red hen in the children's story, she told herself, "So then, I will fix it myself."

She wished it was as easy to come up with a Plan B for Mother. She wasn't really sure if there had been a Plan A. Other than flying across the country to help when clearly, her mother didn't want her help. Allie wanted her to either take care of this situation or for the situation to just go away. What did Gillian want? She wanted her mother to get out of bed and be the mother she remembered, not that ghost in the bedroom. Impossible expectations.

She stared at the empty window frame. How difficult could this be? Measure the space, go to the nearest home fix-it store, buy the glass, come home, and put it in. She could ask at the store what other supplies she needed.

Your mother would know how, her inner voice prompted.

Maybe this would be enough to get her mother out of bed. She headed for the bedroom. As usual, waking Mother took some shoulder shaking.

"You're still here."

"Yes, I am." They'd been through this before. Perhaps there was something wrong with mother's mind. "Can you hear me?"

"I am not hard of hearing."

Good. A response at least. "I have a slight problem in that I can't find anyone to fix the broken window in the front door. Do you have the tools here that I will need?"

Dorothy's eyes opened. "A broken window?"

"Just one of the small panes." She thought of telling her mother the entire story but decided not to. "We can talk about that later."

"A broken window."

She should never have mentioned it, she knew it now. "Yes, Mother, a small one. I will fix it. Now, what can I get you to drink?"

Dorothy shook her head. "Nothing." Her voice sounded so weak that Gillian leaned closer to hear. "A broken window."

Patience! And she needed a full measure right now!

Dorothy shook her head, her eyes drifting shut again. She mumbled something that Gillian figured was the same as before. "Window" being the only word she heard clearly.

Back in the kitchen the telephone rang. Answer it—ignore it. "Hello?"

"Ah, is this Dorothy Ormsby's residence?" Surely that was a slight Italian accent. And male.

"Yes, this is her daughter Gillian. How may I help you?"

"Ah, Gillian. How delightful. I've heard about you."

I just bet. So what does one say to that? Yes? Thank you? "Oh." That seemed the safest.

"Yes, your mother is very proud of you." If he was as nice as his voice...

"I'm glad to hear that. What did you say your name is?"

"Oh, sorry, this is Enzio Delgado. I'd like to talk to Dorothy, if I may."

Oh, dear. Gillian thought a quick second. "I'll see if she's available." She laid the receiver on the stand and headed down the hall. "Mother, a man named Enzio Delgado would like to talk with you."

Without opening her eyes, her mother shook her head.

Gillian returned to the kitchen. "I'm sorry, but she's not able to come to the phone right now."

"Not able to or refuses?"

"How well do you know my mother?"

"We've been friends for a long time. We met at the senior center."

"I see. How about I have her call you back later? Does she have your number?"

"Yes. But, Gillian, I've been trying to reach her for days. She never answers the phone or the door. Is she all right?"

The truth or not? "I'm trying to determine that myself. We'll get back to you."

"Promise?"

After finding his phone number in the address book, she smiled to herself. He was nothing if not determined. "I promise. Bye." Wondering if Allie knew about this friendship, she grabbed her purse and headed out the door. The afternoon was already cooling off, not that it had been hot before. Typical October weather. The perfect season, she used to think. She slid her arms into the jacket she'd left in the car and shrugged the shoulders into place. Slubbed silk was perfect for fall and ecru, her favorite neutral color. Taking lipstick from her purse, she applied it using the mirror on the visor before checking her hair. As usual it swung perfectly in place, thanks to her master hairstylist.

Because she'd seen the home improvement store on her way in from the airport, she drove to it, parked, and followed the signs to the window and glass department. From the first question the clerk asked, she wished she knew more about windows.

Once she'd explained the situation, she handed him the measurements.

"Now, you're sure these are correct?"

"Yes." She did know how to read a tape measure.

"I always double check. Easy to make a mistake."

"Yes, it is correct. While you are cutting it, what other supplies do I need?"

"You need brads..."

At the look on her face, he sighed. "I'll get the things for you. Have you ever installed a pane of glass before?"

She shook her head. She'd always had a maintenance man in her building that took care of things like that. "I tried to get someone, but they were all busy."

"True, most glass guys don't like to make a trip to replace one small pane. I'll be right back."

Gillian waited...and waited...and waited. When he finally returned, she kept her smile firmly in place—with effort.

"Now, do you have a hammer?" At her nod, he continued. "And a caulking gun?" At her blank look, he held out a metal contraption that looked like a giant syringe. "You put the caulk tube in here and squeeze this handle to line the caulk around the window. That is after you put the points in to hold the glass in place. With a hammer. Gently." He appeared to be watching her for a reaction—any kind of reaction.

"I see. Thank you." Surely this couldn't be too difficult. She took her supplies to the counter, paid, and returned to her car. At least she was able to remember which one was hers and where she had parked it. She'd learned the importance of focusing on things like that with an earlier rental. The memory was not a good one.

When she returned to the house after a stop at the grocery store, a note on the door caught her attention.

"Gillian, I stopped by to see if you need any help. Call me if you do." It was signed with an A.

"Well, that was nice of him." Here she was talking to herself again. Was it becoming a habit, or a natural accompaniment to sighing? Glass crunched under her feet again as she entered. That had to be the next thing on the list. Vacuum up the glass. After checking on her mother—no change there—she hung her jacket in the closet. Maybe jeans and a cotton shirt would be more appropriate attire for replacing glass. Caulk on her slacks, two shades darker than her jacket, would probably destroy them. As she removed her blouse, she saw a rip in the left sleeve, the arm she'd put through the window to open the door. About an inch and a half long, it pronounced the shirt no longer usable. No dry cleaner could repair that.

Heaving a sigh after all, she hung her clothes in the closet and pulled on lightweight denim capri pants and a white long-sleeve blouse, rolling up the sleeves. Slip-on wedges for her feet and a promise to ice the toes again later, and she returned to the kitchen to put the groceries away. At home she would have music filling the rooms, a scented candle burning, and a bottle of white wine cooling in the fridge. She would not be gearing up to repair a broken window.

Maybe she could leave this until tomorrow and let Adam fix it. The thought rang with truth and good sense. "But how hard can putting that window back in be? After all, what good is locking a door when an intruder could open it as easily as you did?"

She thought of the silk shirt sleeve and her aching foot. Being able to tell her mother that she fixed the window had a certain cachet.

Of course, her mother probably had done something like this many times. She was the original do-it-yourselfer, most likely because she'd not had a husband to fix the small things around the house, nor the money to hire help. All those years she'd worked at the school to supplement the money she'd received from her late husband's life insurance policy and a small pension. And she was still home to take care of her two girls.

After vacuuming the hall and part of the living room to make sure she got all the slivers of glass, Gillian put the machine back in the hall closet. First thing: clean all the broken glass out of the space. She shouldn't have put the vacuum away. After removing the large pieces, she dampened a couple of paper towels and wiped any spare glass bits out of the window frame and off the vinyl flooring by the door. She considered getting something to eat before proceeding further.

"Don't be silly, just finish this and then make a good dinner. That salmon looked perfect." Back to talking to herself. "After all, how much time can this take?"

She carefully unwrapped the paper from around the glass and inserted it into the space. It didn't fit. Too long by a good quarter of an inch. She tried again, closed her eyes, tipped back her head, and deliberately loosened the jaw clamping her teeth together. Her options: Take it back and have the clerk re-cut it. Go back and order another pane and make sure she didn't talk with the same man. Search the tools for a glass cutter, whatever that looked like. Throw the whole thing in the trash, or against a wall, and let Adam take care of it in the morning.

Shutting the door with a little more force than necessary, she hauled the toolbox back to the garage, dragged out the vacuum, vacuumed and put it away—again. Maybe she should use the brick on this piece of glass, too. Or maybe she should just throw the brick.

Surely the empty pane would not be visible from the street with the stretched curtains pulled back in place. She sank into a chair at the oak table in the kitchen and contemplated the foot she'd raised up to rest on the adjacent chair. She knew elevating a foot was good for an injury. Her phone rang from deep within the bowels of her bag. What had happened to her? Her mind went out when she crossed the Rocky Mountains? Why wasn't the phone in its holster? It stopped ringing as she pulled it out. Checking the calls, she recognized the number. Allie. Call her back or wait to see if she left a message?

It rang again.

"Hello."

"How's Mother?"

"Sound asleep, what more can you expect?"

"You don't have to bite my head off."

"No, I don't, but consider yourself lucky you are not here or I might."

"Oh." Pause. "Did you get Mother to eat again?"

"No, she didn't like the coffee I brought her. And I've been a bit busy so I haven't started dinner yet."

"Doing what?"

"Trying to replace the window."

A silence extended.

"No one would come?"

"Not until Thursday, and their minimum charge was one hundred dollars."

"I see. Maybe I could ask..."

The doorbell rang. At least now she knew it worked. "Hang on. Let me see who's at the door."

"Just call me back."

Gillian tossed the phone into her bag and headed for the front door. She glanced through the lace curtain. Adam. Turning the lock, she opened the door. "Come on in."

"Couldn't get someone to fix it?"

"Nope."

"I can come back in the morning. You got a tape measure?"

"You don't need one." She picked up the paper-wrapped glass and handed it to him. "This is one quarter inch too tall." She pointed at the plastic bag sitting on the chair. "There's calking and pointy things in there."

He checked the bag. "I see you are well supplied."

"And if you say one word about this, I might be forced to lose my temper. Ask Allie, that is not a pretty picture."

He nodded, rolling his lips together. His mouth might not say anything, but the demon dancing in his eyes said more than enough.

"Someday this will be a funny story to tell at a gathering, but right now..."

He nodded. "It's not."

She unclenched her teeth again, she was going to end up with the TMJ at the rate she was going. "Can I get you something to drink?"

Adam shook his head. "What did the doctor say?"

"How did you know we went to the doctor?"

"Called Allie. I didn't have your phone number."

"She didn't fill you in?"

"Nope, just said you went and she had another call."

Leave it to Allie. "He said Mother had a TIA and shouldn't be having any trouble unless something else has happened. He wants to see her on Wednesday."

"But I thought..."

"I know. She said she was dying. But you see, Mother is always dying, at least according to her."

"But I've never heard her complain."

Gillian shook her head. Of course not. She only acted that way with her daughters. Unless... unless this time there really was something seriously wrong and even the doctor didn't know.

Later that evening after telling her mother good night, a wave of weariness nearly washed Gillian out to sea. She finished wiping down the counter and turned out the kitchen light. Nine o'clock seemed far too early to go to bed, unless one counted that her body was still on East Coast time. By the time she'd finished her nighttime routine, checked on her mother, and crawled in bed, another half hour had passed and her eyes refused to stay open.

Under her pillow she found a lavender sachet. Inhaling the fragrance, slight though it was, she smiled and settled in. Would she hear her mother if she needed anything? Both doors were open, so other than sleeping in the master bedroom, this was the best she could do.

Sometime later, she blinked at the clock beside the bed. Two a.m. She listened with every sense alert. Was someone at the door? The door that was now missing a windowpane? She crept from her bed, tiptoed down the hall, and peeped around the corner. No one there. The streetlight would have shown. A couple more steps and around another corner she could see through the glass doors to the backyard. No one there. She exhaled a breath she hadn't realized she'd been holding and went down the hall to peer into her mother's room. The streetlights gave enough illumination that she could faintly see the mound in the bed. She could hear breathing.

Heaving another breath, Gillian returned to her bed and collapsed into it. Maybe she'd look into an alarm system in the morning.

Four o'clock found her body wide awake, while her mind insisted she needed more sleep. But this was her normal waking time on the East Coast where it was now seven a.m. She laid there for a while before throwing back the covers, grabbing her wrapper off the chair by the bed, and making her way to the kitchen. At home her coffeemaker would have the pot all ready for her, the coffee brewed with freshly ground beans, its fragrance as vital as the hot liquid itself. She fumbled with the percolator and the can of ground coffee, trying not to make any noise that would disturb her mother. When the basket clattered into the sink, she gave up trying to be quiet. It would take the baying dogs from *The Hound of the Baskervilles* to disturb Mother.

While the coffee perked, she took a quick shower, dressed, checked on her mother, and returned to the kitchen. With doughnut quarters on a covered plate and a hefty mug of coffee in her hand, she trailed into the living room to look for the television remote. *Where would my mother keep that?* she wondered after searching every available space. The television clicked on when she turned the knob. Surely she'd bought a new TV since remotes came into being. She found the New York channel by turning the dial, rolled her eyes, and settled into the recliner she knew to be her mother's chair.

The morning news made her want to gag. Mayhem in

Afghanistan, bombings in Iraq, a junta in Central America, and the really good news: a serial murderer in Seattle had been taken into custody. *An alleged serial killer;* one must be careful of libel. While the commentators did their thing, she read the small print tracking across the bottom of the screen. "A hostile takeover at Fitch, Fitch, and Folsom and…" The rest of the message slid past her before she could read it all. What? Surely that hadn't been her company? Were there any other Fitches? Her stomach clenched, squeezing the coffee back up to burn her esophagus. She closed her eyes and leaned back against the doily that protected the plush fabric from oily hair. This was Saturday. Whom could she call? Eight o'clock, New York time. Was her boss in the office yet? Would he be going to the office? Would any of them have offices to go to? She headed to the bedroom for her computer. Would Scot be picking up messages today?

Chapter Six

You're up early for a Saturday."

Adam glanced up at his father with a smile. "Have to go fix that window at Dorothy's before I head to the marina. Found your glass cutter out in the shop." He snapped the paper to make it stand upright. "How was your night?"

"Okay."

But Adam could tell from his father's eyes that his dad had not slept well. Was it just the grief of losing his wife, or was there something else going on? No, not *just*. But it had been nearly two years. Shouldn't his father be recovering? Every article he'd read about grief said people responded in their own time, but usually by two years they were able to deal with life better. His father seemed to be getting older and weaker, not better.

"Coffee's ready and the orange juice is fresh squeezed." He'd been up early all right. Had he been dreaming of Gillian Ormsby or did he only think of her when he woke?

"Did you get to visit with Dorothy?" Bill set his coffee mug on the table and sat in his usual place where he could watch the action in the backyard. "You filled the bird feeders."

"Didn't dare go outside if I hadn't. Dive-bombed by

a hummingbird, scolded by the scrub jay, and the house finches put up such a chattering I thought they'd wake you." His hope to make his father smile paid off. For a man who used to wear a permanent smile, now he had to work at it.

"And the fishpond?"

"The hose is running into that now." Adam folded the paper and pushed it toward his father. "How about going out on the boat with me later?"

Bill studied the dark liquid in his cup. "I don't know. Maybe."

Adam knew "maybe" was just a polite way of declining. "Are you going into the office?"

His father shrugged. Bill owned two nurseries, one in Martinez and one in Pittsburg, up the river to the east. All those years he'd insisted that a man needed to spend the full weekend with his wife and family. But since losing Alice to cancer, he found more solace in his business.

Adam had come home ostensibly to help with the business, but the real reason was to cheer up his father and get him interested in living again. In the twelve months he'd been in Martinez, he'd not accomplished much of his goal.

"You want some eggs?"

"I guess. How about scrambled?"

"Bacon?"

"And a piece of toast."

They went through this every morning. Adam rose and turned on the stove. By the time he'd fixed breakfast, his father had wandered outside to check on his babies—starts of begonias from slips, irises from seeds he'd spent months hybridizing, and a flat of cyclamen he'd started just for fun.

Adam called out the door, "Come and eat, Dad." He waited until his father raised an arm in response and dished up the plates for the table. All the while Thor sat where he'd been told to, his gaze following Adam's every move. When both men sat down at the table, the dog sank to the floor, jaws on paws, only his eyes moving.

"Are you going to pot those cyclamen today?" Adam asked.

"I planned on it. Might have to mix more potting soil. I potted that little chrysanthemum you asked me to."

"The rust-colored one?"

"Actually there are several, take your pick."

"Why don't you come to Dorothy's with me? Maybe a visitor will help get her out of bed." He'd told his father the night before what Gillian had said about her mother.

"Your mother would have had her up. If there was someone who could talk a friend into living, it was Alice." He scooped the last of his eggs onto the corner of toast and ate it, before giving Thor the final bit of bacon.

Adam had given up telling his father that Thor had plenty of dog food, he didn't need people food. Only Adam was more important than Bill in Thor's eyes, but that was dubious when someone offered him bacon.

Bill gathered up the dishes for the dishwasher. The two had a bargain, one cooked, the other cleaned up. The two jobs were interchangeable.

Adam decided on the deep burgundy-colored mum, stuck a bow on a stick in the dirt, snapped the lead on Thor's collar, and headed down the hill. What a glorious morning, blue sky, trailing clouds, and birdsong, what more could he ask? Since it was Saturday, he and Thor could run around the field at the school, in spite of the soccer players. During school hours, he was afraid Thor would be too distracting for the students.

He stopped on the sidewalk in front of Dorothy's house. Still an empty window frame, but the sprinklers had been turned on. Maybe the jasmine would come back and the lawn would of course. But only if they could get Dorothy out of bed and on her feet. Since when had Gillian's fight become his? He wondered at that as he and Thor made their way to the front door and rang the bell.

"Coming."

He heard the voice from a distance. Perhaps Gillian was in the backyard. He waited a bit more and then he could see her outline against the light from the kitchen windows. "Good morning," he said as she opened the door. But one look at her face and he was sure she was not having a good morning.

"Come in." She stepped back and motioned.

"Thor, too?"

"Why not?" It was more a concession than an invitation.

So, do I ask or pretend I don't see anything wrong? He followed her to the kitchen and handed her the colorful pot. "My father sent this for your mother."

"How lovely." She set the pot in the middle of the table. "I'll take it to her when she wakes. Would you like some coffee?"

In spite of already having had his two cup quota for the morning, he nodded. Since Thor sat right beside him, he dropped his hand to the dog's head and scratched the black ears. "I know this probably isn't my place, but what's wrong? Your mother?"

Gillian shook her head. "I had a rather traumatic surprise this morning." He waited for her to continue.

"There was an announcement on television that my company is the victim of a hostile takeover. When I called my boss, he confirmed it. I have no job and until Wednesday to clean out my office." Her jaw clenched. "Just like that." She poured two mugs of coffee. "Cream or sugar?"

"Black."

When she set them on the table, her hands shook slightly. She took the chair at the other end of the table after a glance at Thor.

"He won't hurt you or anyone."

"Right." She raised her mug with both hands cupped around it and took a swallow.

While he saw her staring at the burgundy blossoms, he was sure she wasn't seeing them. "Miserable way to find out."

"He said he was waiting until he was sure the West Coast was awake before he phoned me, but I called him first."

Adam propped his elbows on the table. "Did he have the particulars for you?"

"He'll have them on Monday. I guess the other company wants the weekend to celebrate before dealing with realities." After a deep breath and exhale, she continued. "I've worked there all my career, from right out of college until now."

"That's pretty unusual in this day and age."

"I know. I hoped to retire in five to seven more years." After a dainty, ladylike snort, she continued. "Planned to actually, and everything was on track for that." Another huff. "Everyone knew something was happening, but this was one closely guarded secret."

Her voice sounded lost, not decisive like the day before. In fact if Adam were not staring right at her, he'd have had a hard time believing this was the same woman. What could he say? He drained his cup and set it back down. "Why don't I get that door fixed? Then I'm taking my boat out. Would you like to go for a sail?"

She raised her gaze to meet his, her head already beginning to shake. "Thank you, but no. I'm not much of a sailor.

I get terribly seasick." She looked over his shoulder. "And besides, there is Mother."

He should have known better. "All right. I see you got the sprinklers going."

"I have the flowerpots soaking as well. Hopefully some of the plants will come back."

"I would have set the sprinklers if I'd had a way to get into the backyard. Shame to watch all the plants die." He rose. "Where's the glass pane you bought?"

"It's too large."

"I know." He pulled the glass cutter from his pocket. "Do you have a steel ruler and a pair of pliers?"

"I guess. I'll get the toolbox."

She returned with the red box in hand. "What else do you need?"

"Nothing."

"I really appreciate this. I know Mother will, too."

Adam set about measuring the window frame, the glass, and then scribing the quarter inch off one end. Using the pliers, he broke the extra glass off on the line, the shards falling into the plastic trash can he'd pulled from under the sink. When he set the glass in place, he tapped the points in to hold it steady and then laid a thick bead of caulking around the glass. "The wood is going to need a touch-up."

"No problem. Mother always keeps little bottles of paint in the garage to cover up any dings or scratches that occur. She likes to keep her walls and moldings pristine."

"If not, the white is easy to match." He smoothed the caulk with a putty knife and put the supplies back into the plastic bag. "There. Done."

"Wish I knew something I could do for you in exchange. Thanks doesn't seem to be enough."

"Go sailing with me. I can bring anti-seasick meds."

A smile tried to light in her eyes but failed. "I need to get some other things done here before I leave for New York."

Why did even the mention of that make him feel sad? "I'll drop by tomorrow to see if you need anything."

She walked him to the door. "Thanks again."

Adam and Thor walked out to the sidewalk. Without looking, he knew she was watching. They headed down the street, his walk picking up to a jog. Shame she wouldn't go sailing. It might have made her feel better. Tough losing a job like that. From the little her mother and sister had ever said to him Adam knew Gillian was married to her job. When they reached Morello Avenue, they turned right and jogged the short blocks to the school where they turned in and picked up speed. As they both settled into their stride, Adam let go of everything but the pleasure of sun and breeze on his face and blood pumping through his veins. Glancing down he could see the same delight in his dog's face, pink tongue lolling, ears flapping. They ran to the trail along the dry creek, east to the edge of the school grounds, and back to the other side, picking up the driveway again where Adam slowed to a gradual walk. Both of them strolled with heaving sides.

"Good, huh, boy?" He reached down to thump Thor on the ribs. Stopping to watch the soccer players for a bit, Adam finally caught his breath, and his mind kicked back into thinking about the woman who had just walked into his life and was counting the days, or rather hours, until she would leave. What would she do with no job in New York City? Perhaps the new company would pick her up; sometimes takeovers did that.

But another thought made him smile. Maybe she would come back to Martinez to keep on helping her mother.

Chapter Seven

Why am I doing this?" she asked the walls as she returned to the kitchen after almost forcing her mother to eat a few bites and drink fluids of any kind.

Good question. Actually she knew it was because Allie guilted her into it. And she was frustrated at her proposal being turned down, so she bit. Not that it would make any difference now anyway. And because she was afraid her mother really might be dying this time, especially after Allie said the word *stroke*. People died from strokes. But not TIAs. How could Mother sleep all the time like this if there really were nothing biologically wrong? Now that was the major question.

Gillian slid open the glass door and stepped outside, closing the screen door behind her. At least the shrubs that bordered the six-foot wooden fence were still alive. And the weeds of course. Why could weeds survive when beloved plants died so quickly from lack of water? She bent over and sniffed a pink rose that bordered the patio on the west. The roses hadn't died at least, but they sure needed pruning, and a good feeding probably wouldn't hurt. When had her mother quit taking care of her yard?

Strange that Allie didn't have more concrete answers for her. She said she talked to Mother every day, but... Gillian thought a moment. There must be a telephone in the bedroom, too, or how could Allie have talked with her mother? She chewed on her lower lip while she tried to think the disparity through. When she let down her guard, the words *no job* leaped to the forefront of her thoughts, trampling out all others.

"Don't waste your time stewing on it when there is nothing you can do to change it." This was one of her life-based credos. Worry was a waste of time—and energy.

"So, make a list of the things you must do while here." She returned to the kitchen to fetch a paper and pencil and went back outside to sit at the round, glass-topped patio table. The umbrella was tightly bound with bungee cords, and the chairs, plus the table, held a thick coating of dust. Rather than giving up the idea of sitting in the sun, she turned on the hose wrapped in a perfect circle on the wall hanger and sprayed the table and chairs.

After wiping them down with a cloth from the kitchen, she sat down. Her mother lived to care for her flowers and plants, so what had caused such an abrupt cessation? Could the doctor's diagnosis really have caused her mother to quit like this?

Back to her list. Get her mother out of the bed and into the slipper chair where she usually sat to put her shoes on. Strip the bed, remake it with clean sheets. Shower or sponge bathe mother. Call Enzio if she could keep her mother sitting in the chair. Laundry.

A hummingbird zipped by her shoulder heading for the roses. Her mother used to love the flying jewels as she'd heard someone call them. How could Mother simply stop caring about all the things she loved? Including her daughters? The thought sneaked in, like a cat on a hunt.

As Gillian had always known, Allie was the favored child. She was born beautiful and stayed that way. She always minded, not a wayward thought in her little head. She lived to make her mother happy. And now her family. Not like Miss Independent gap-toothed, pudgy Gillian, whose hair never curled and who never cared for fluffy dresses—or wearing dresses at all during her younger days.

The one thing the three of them had always shared was the love of flowers and gardening. Allie had sat, chortling in her infant seat, between the rows of lettuce, carrots, and beans. The girls worked in the garden alongside their mother from the time they could bend over and identify the weeds.

Even today, wherever she traveled, Gillian strolled through public gardens and admired the beauty, but she only had three pots in her condo—one African violet and one with parsley, sage, and rosemary. Shiny-leaf sweet basil grew in the third container and was one of her favorite cooking ingredients. Her mother's herb garden looked like a collection of dried sticks among the yellow mustard and thistles going to seed.

How long had this hiding in the bed been going on? If the weather had been really hot the annuals would have died quickly, but the jasmine in the front yard should have deep enough roots to stay green. Glancing at her watch, she gathered her writing things and returned to the house. Time to lead the charge. One thing to do before rousing her mother—open all the windows and doors, including the garage, and let the breeze blow the stagnant air out of the house. With that accomplished, she headed for her mother's dark den.

On the way to get her mother out of bed she reopened the bedroom drapes and let the sunshine in through half-opened blinds.

"Mother." She accompanied her words with a moving hand on her thin shoulder.

"You're still here?"

"Yes, I am." She considered the interchange while she got her mother bathed and the bed changed, the latter being simple, the former cantankerous enough to send her running for her car or at least counting the hours until she could fly home. This trip would be a lot more pleasant if she heard one thank you.

When the kitchen phone rang, she answered, "Ormsby residence."

A man's chuckle greeted her. "A bit formal, aren't we?"

"Good morning, Mr. Delgado." Even the sound of his voice made her smile. If only her mother would talk with him, surely she would feel better. Her daughter surely did.

"Are you all right?"

Honesty was needed here. "I'm just tired." She listed the things she'd accomplished so far.

"Sounds like a full morning."

"Adam Bentley has been here and repaired the door, and I've watered all but the back garden..." *And my company was bought out so I have no job. No whining allowed. He doesn't want to know about your New York woes.*

His chuckle brought her smile back. "I tried calling a half hour or so ago, but there was no answer. I guess you were busy."

"I want to meet you." Her words shocked her into silence.

"Well, that's a nice thing for an old man to hear. When can we meet?"

Gillian heaved a sigh. "I don't know. I fly back home on Monday night."

"Oh, so soon?"

She could hear his regret over the phone.

"Do you think Dorothy would see me?"

"I doubt it, but if you want to come by and join me drinking iced tea out on the patio, I'd be delighted."

"I'll stop by the Italian bakery. Surprise you."

You dear, sweet man. "Fine, around two-ish?"

She couldn't stop smiling after they hung up and looked out the patio doors. What if she could get her mother out there on the chaise longue? How could she resist such a charming gentleman?

Allie hadn't called. The thought surprised her. She dialed her sister's cell.

No answer. She must still be at Sherrilyn's soccer game. Gillian picked up the tray with two coffees and a bud vase on top of a linen napkin and carried it into the bedroom.

Dorothy stared from the tray to her daughter and back to the tray. "The roses are still blooming?"

"Yes." Something to be thankful for, her mother had noticed the pink rose in the bud vase. "But things look really bad out there." When her mother didn't respond, Gillian decided to leap in with her questions. "When did you stop taking care of your yard and garden, and why?" The only response was a head shake. "Do you have pain anywhere? Mother, I need to know what happened to . . . " She stopped. "Where do you hurt?"

Dorothy only shook her head, slowly from side to side as if it were too heavy to hold up.

Gillian retreated behind her coffee. It looked like a change of tactics was in order. "Even the jasmine is dead. Or appears to be." She ransacked her brain trying to find a topic her mother might respond to. "You used to go watch the kids' games. Why did you stop?"

Nothing. Not even a head shake. "What if I left early?"

Her mother raised her head and glared at her. "You said you would stay until Monday night."

"I have a bargain for you. I will stay if you will answer some of my questions. Two at least."

Dorothy sipped from her cup and made a face.

"Do you want me to warm up the coffee?"

"No." She took a couple more swallows and made another face. "Yes."

Gillian left to refill the cup, mentally rejoicing over the response, and returned immediately. "I have news for you. A hummingbird nearly nicked my shoulder when I was sitting at the patio table."

No response. "If I were going to be here longer, I'd put up the feeders." How many years had it been since she'd watched the hummers dueling over the feeder? She wasn't even sure there were hummingbirds in New York City.

Something under the bed caught her eye. A telephone. So that's how Allie spoke with Mother. But the phone hadn't rung in here while she was bathing Mother. "Does your phone work?"

"The ringer is off."

"So, Allie said she talks with you every day. How can that be?"

Dorothy shrugged and clutched the sweater closer. "Sometimes I hear it."

Gillian let the subject drop. Criticizing Allie was never allowed. But pushing her sister for the truth was. The next time she saw her.

"I should open your window and air this room out, too." Gillian left the room smiling.

"No."

* * *

"Why can't you leave me alone?" her mother grumbled at the arrival of her daughter carrying in the lunch tray a while later. "I'm not hungry."

"Would you rather eat for me or go to a nursing home where they will force you to eat?" Playing a trump card was sometimes a gamble. When her mother took a bite of salmon, she knew it had been a good move. One she couldn't use too often, but then Monday was coming like a runaway train. *Who will do this when I leave?*

"We have a visitor coming this afternoon."

Dorothy laid her fork back down. "I will not see anyone." She paused. "But Allie."

"Shame. He seems so charming."

Dorothy shrugged and tried to lift the tray off her legs. When the dishes started to slide, Gillian grabbed the tray and set it on the floor. By the time she glanced back at the bed, her mother had lain back down, purple bruises under her eyes the only color in her pale face. Dorothy did indeed look exhausted. *Perhaps I am pushing her too fast? If only I knew what was the best thing to do.* Although common sense said to make her mother eat and move around, what if there was indeed something really wrong, that might be exacerbated by...? She heaved a sigh. Would Dr. Isaacs be on call or would he switch to a service since this was a weekend? She picked up the tray. Time to talk with her sister.

No answer on either Allie's cell or home phone. Gillian left pointed messages on each and hung up. Was Allie playing paybacks for Thursday? If so, it was pretty childish. Half an hour later, she called again and left more messages. If she knew where the soccer field and the tennis court were, she'd drive over there and have it out, in public if necessary. Did she have Jefferson's office number? He, like her, usually worked Saturdays. She checked her mother's address book to see if possibly she had it. Nada.

Did this family ever communicate with each other? *Allie, turn your phone on.*

Fuming was getting Gillian nowhere. With the towels in the dryer, she pulled out the vacuum cleaner and attacked the living room. Pretending it was Allie she was pushing around the furniture accomplished two things: a clean room and better feelings toward her sister. With the furniture dusted and waxed, she went to the closet where her mother saved all the gifts she'd been sent. A burning vanilla candle set on the coffee table not only looked nice but helped take away the musty odor as well as the musty feeling.

The doorbell rang.

"Oh, dear." Two o'clock by her watch, and the man was nothing if not prompt. She'd planned on changing clothes and...oh, well. She crossed to the door that was still open and unlatched the screen door. "Welcome." He looked much like she expected. Silver hair that any of the older movie stars dreamed of, dark twinkling eyes, and olive skin that looked like a permanent tan. The crinkles edging his eyes deepened with his smile. He was taller than she by only a couple of inches, and his trim body said he stayed active.

There was no way one could resist his smile, not that she wanted to. "Come in, come in." She extended her hand and he shook it, covering their clasp with his other hand.

"Your pictures do not begin to do you justice. How blessed your mother is with two such lovely daughters."

"Enzio, you are a charmer all right. Let's go outside." She ushered him through the house. "Do you like your tea plain or sweet?"

"Whatever you fix." He dropped his voice. "Your mother?"

"Is sound asleep, and this time she earned it. I'm afraid I might be pushing her too hard. I tried to get her to join us, but her no was pretty adamant."

"Don't you fret. We'll overcome all of her obstacles." He leaned his backside against the kitchen counter.

Gillian filled the glasses with ice and poured the tea she'd made earlier.

He lifted a white box tied with string. "We need plates for these. Hope you like napoleons."

"You didn't."

"Your mother used to love napoleons, too."

"How come Mother has never mentioned you?"

He shrugged. "That I don't know, but I plan to remedy her oversight."

Setting the small plates on the counter, Gillian turned around to see a look of dedication, his eyes slightly narrowed, jaw raised, as he stared back at her. "You mean that, don't you?"

"I do." He broke the string and laid the box open to reveal three of the sinfully delicious desserts. "I believe that positive thinking makes a difference."

Gillian transferred the delicacies to the plates, set out forks and napkins on the tray she was preparing, as he held out his hands.

"Let me."

I will let you, she thought as she nodded and smiled. "I think you will do my mother a world of good." Sliding open the screen door, she went out first and closed it behind him. A waft of subtle male shaving cream slipped past. One more tally mark in his favor. Too many men wore too heavy a cologne. Well, if she was thinking along those lines, many women did the same.

When they'd sat down and had their plates in front of

them, he held up his glass and she clinked hers to it, as he said, "To many happy years." Gillian nodded. Right now the year ahead was shading toward bleak, but she had no intentions of dimming his delight. She sipped her tea and set the glass down.

"So, tell me about yourself."

"Try that first." He indicated her plate.

"I hate to smash it, it's so pretty."

He nodded. "Pretty enough to eat."

She picked up her fork, cutting through the alternating crisp and creamy layers with difficulty and closed her eyes in delight as the confection's flavors burst upon her tongue. "Oh, my right arm. This is sublime."

"Ah, a woman who thinks like me." He followed her lead. "I would have one of these every day, if I could afford it." He grinned. "Calorie-wise, that is." His chuckle elicited an answering one from her.

"What do you like to do?"

"I play bocce ball—we have leagues here in Martinez—and I love to dance. My wife and I used to enter ballroom competitions. I enjoy cooking, and while the knees won't let me run any longer, I can walk mighty fast."

"So you're involved at the senior center?"

He nodded. "And my church. I drive people for their cancer treatments and I love birding and gardening. Your mother and I have much in common."

Except she was in there trying to die and he was grabbing life with both hands and loving it. Gillian heaved a sigh.

"Don't worry, she will come around."

"How long ago did your wife...?"

"Die? That is not a bad word, you know. She had cancer and she has gone home. I couldn't ask her to stay around and suffer. She said to me, 'How will I stand heaven until you get there?' And I told her that God knew the time and to keep her dancing shoes in shape because surely there is singing and dancing in heaven. She made me promise to keep on living and finding joy every day." His smile made Gillian wipe her eyes. And at first she'd thought this man could be a gigolo? How far from the truth could that be?

"Do you know the Bentleys?"

"Of course. My wife, Alice, and your mother were good friends."

"I forget how small a town Martinez really is."

"Not so small anymore. With all the new subdivisions, Martinez is a growing community."

"So, how many children do you have?"

"Two sons and two daughters. We have one daughter already waiting for us in heaven. She and my wife, I know they had a grand reunion."

"You really believe that?"

"I do, with all my heart." He stared right into her soul. "Do you not believe?"

"I—I'm not sure anymore." She scraped up the last bit of pastry filling with the tines of her fork. She could feel his gaze warming her head. When she looked up, she saw such love in his eyes that she caught her breath.

He reached across the table and laid his hand on top of hers. "Maybe that is one of the reasons you have come home."

After he left, Gillian remained seated at the table, watching the hummingbirds. If only she could get her mother out here to soak in the sun. She had forty-eight hours before she had to leave. The longer Mother stayed in bed, the harder it would be to get her healthy again.

Chapter Eight

Sailing was more fun with another person along.

Adam raised his face to the sun, catching the glint off a window high on the hill. Hand on the tiller, legs crossed at the ankles, he inhaled the bite of salt water on the wind that brought out even the most reluctant of sailors. Bright white or bold colors, sails dotted San Francisco Bay like huge kites tied to bits of wood skipping over the water's surface.

He should have worked harder to get his father to come with him. Concern for the man he loved most in this world dimmed the sun. Why was his dad not improving? Did he no longer have that will to live that got him through the first months after Mother had died? Was it depression? Just plain old tired? Or—was something seriously wrong physically? Bill Bentley was not that old. But then neither had his mother been.

To keep the sail from luffing, Adam tacked back but still on a northerly route so he could return to the moorage in Martinez. He'd hoped the wind would help clear his mind, but it only seemed to bring on more questions. Sometimes he felt his brain was really a series of boxes. He'd open the one labeled "Father," cogitate on that for a time, then close it and open another one. One big box was labeled "What do I do with the rest of my life?" Granted he would assume more of the responsibilities for the family's nurseries as needed, after all this was not only his inheritance but that of Jennifer and her two children. Maybe next time he took the boat out, he'd ask Jen along. His brother and his wife had loved to sail, but Jen sold their boat when Charles died. Said the memories were too difficult.

The business was improving again, thanks to his father, who had been a wise manager and had hired good people who had chosen to stay on with him. The slip had occurred after Alice had died; Bill had lost heart for the business for a time. Now it looked like it would grow again—if the economy held, that is. Adam tried to keep on top of prevailing shifts in the business climate, but he was hearing subtle murmurs of possible problems. Now was not the time to expand as his father had suggested. One of the many things Adam admired about his father was that Bill carried little to no debt, in both his personal and his company's finances. Surely an anachronism in this day and age.

Up ahead the Carquinez Bridge loomed closer, the entry to the delta where the Sacramento and the San Joaquin rivers flowed together before the straits that flowed into the San Francisco Bay.

Adam closed that box since no new ideas came to him and dallied with the one titled "Gillian," a new box and quite intriguing. Why bother thinking on her when she was planning on returning to New York City Monday night? He'd never had a company sold out from under him, but he'd sold one after his brother died. How would he feel in her place? He nodded and ducked as the boom swung in the opposite direction to tack again. As the boat heeled over, spray hit him, making him shiver. Glancing over his shoulder, he knew why. The fog was creeping over the western hills, making him glad he was nearly to his Martinez moorage. He'd been caught by fog on the bay before and had no desire to repeat the experience.

Gillian. He even liked the sound of her name. But what about her mother? Why would someone as vital as Dorothy Ormsby had always been go to bed to die like that? True, her best friend had died, but that couldn't be it. If the stroke she'd had was that severe, why was she not in rehab or a convalescent home? Was there some way he could help or would he only make matters worse?

Thor rose from where he'd been sleeping at Adam's feet and strolled forward, his life jacket hooked on a line to a metal cable so that if he ever went overboard, he'd be safe. He loved to sit where the breeze would blow his ears back and the spray could soak his fur.

Gillian. Go-getter would certainly fit. She stepped right in to help her mother the best way she knew how. But now she was leaving. Would she be back? That was the thousand-dollar question. Or ten-thousand. An oil tanker, guided by two puny appearing but powerful tugs, took up the middle of the waterway. Heading back out to sea, it was fully loaded, laying low in the water. Crossing the wake always made a sailor pay attention. Or lose the wind in the sails. The southbound Amtrak train wound along the southern shoreline, whistle blowing as it neared the station in Martinez. That was one of those major changes he'd noticed when he moved back here. The old station had been replaced with an attractive new building, but thankfully not at the expense of the waterfront park where he and Thor loved to run.

Taking tighter tacks now, Adam stood and kept his attention on the other boats heading into moorage. He lowered the mainsail, tied down the boom, and switched to engine power to make tying up far easier. He'd sailed in at times but not on a busy weekend like this one.

Thor barked as they neared the slip. Adam flipped out the bumper to keep from banging into the dock and tossed a line to George, who owned the neighboring boat and had just finished tying off his own sloop. He'd waited to help Adam tie up. Those that moored around him took their boats out often like he did, not like some of the boats that had been moored for months and years without being used.

"Thanks," Adam called.

"You're welcome. Have a good sail?"

"I did. Glad I got off the bay, the fog was coming in fast." He glanced up at the western hills. When the fog hit the tops of the hills, it poured down into Martinez like a huge, gray billowing river. He'd not seen fog do exactly that anywhere else, other than the hills that bordered the bay. "How about you?"

"We went up river, not as much sail traffic."

"But more powerboats."

"True." The man touched a finger to his forehead. "Have a good day." He strolled up the floating dock.

Adam tied down the rolled sails, put away his gear, and finally locked the entrance to the cabin. Stepping up onto the dock, he whistled for Thor, who was busy sniffing the dock, inhaling his own copy of the daily news. Maybe Gillian would like to go out to dinner with him?

The thought put a spring in his step and a smile in his mind. "Come on, Thor, pick up your feet." He could hear dog toenails eating up the dock as Thor surged past him to wait panting at the gate.

When they drove up the hill toward the house, Thor stood on the passenger's seat, his tail beating out his anticipation. Home meant dinner. So when the SUV stopped two doors down from home, both his ears and tail drooped. The look he shot over his shoulder at his owner said it all.

"I know you are hungry, but in case you've overlooked this minor point, you are always hungry. We'll go home in a few minutes. You wait; I'll be right back." Adam smiled as he opened the vehicle's door.

Thor sat on the seat, looking out the window, ignoring Adam's exit from the SUV. Even the door slamming didn't make him look over.

"Be that way." Adam crossed the street and strolled up the concrete walk. Since Gillian's car was parked in the driveway, he was pretty certain she was here. He rang the doorbell, checking out his window replacement. One corner of the caulking could do with the addition of a bit more.

He was about to ring again when Gillian opened the door, her smile widening when she saw who it was. "Sorry, I was out in the backyard. Come in."

"Looks like I need to add more caulking to that window. Don't care much for the new silicone caulks; the old stuff worked better."

"I wouldn't know, but I'm sure grateful it's fixed. Mother went on and on about a broken window until I could assure her that you had repaired it." She motioned toward the kitchen. "Want some iced tea?"

He watched her hook a lock of hair over her right ear. "What were you doing out back?"

"Trying to clean up some of the mess. I dead-headed the roses, so maybe they'll bloom some more." She smiled again. "Tea?"

He shrugged. "Why not? Thor's already put out with me because I stopped before going on home. I can't stay long."

She retrieved a pitcher from the refrigerator and two glasses from the cupboard.

Watching the easy way she moved pleased something inside him. "How's your mother doing?"

"Well, at least she's eating, not a lot, but probably enough for right now. I've had her up and out of bed a couple of times, which really pushes her buttons. But she has a bit more color in her face, so that's good."

"What does Allie say to all this?" He took the glass she held out to him.

Her eyebrows raised. "Now that is a bit of a sore subject." Leading the way outside, she took one of the chairs around the table.

"How so?"

"Can't get her to return my calls." She glanced up at him. "Sit down, be comfortable." The bite still tinged her words.

He sat and took a drink, noticing the wheelbarrow full of rose clippings. "Your mother grinds all the garden refuse and tosses it into the compost heap out back."

"Oh, great. Now, that I've never done. When I worked in the garden with her, she had a compost bin but no grinder."

"You worked in the garden?"

"We all did. Mother loved to garden and wanted us to join her. From some things Allie has said, I guess she's taught the grandchildren the same."

"What took you to New York City?"

"I wanted to get as far away from home as possible. Chose an East Coast college and worked my way through four years and later earned an MBA."

"I see." But he didn't really. Why would she want to leave this area? The climate seemed as close to perfect as any he'd found, with water for boating and mountains for skiing, what more could anyone want?

"Why the corporate life?"

"I always dreamed of being a successful woman in a man's world. You have to admit that the boardrooms are generally male dominated, although it has gotten better these last years." She sipped her drink. "What about you?"

"Started college, joined the navy, finished college, went to OCS, and before I realized it, I had twenty years in. Retired to go into business with my brother and sold that after he died. Now I'm here to help Dad."

"Interesting. Both of us here to help an aging parent. I sure didn't expect this."

"Neither did I." He gave a short nod.

"Did you take your boat out?"

"I did, and on the way home, I thought maybe you'd like to join me for dinner."

She paused. "I hate to leave Mother."

"I figured that, so my next suggestion is I go find us dinner and bring it back. For three if you like."

"I was going to make myself a salad and a can of soup for Mother."

"What kind of food? Chinese, sushi, Tai, Mexican, barbecue, seafood, pizza, you name it, I'll find it."

"Mother used to like Chinese, but I haven't had good Mexican food for a long time."

"I'll bring a variety." He stood and picked up his glass and carried it inside to the sink. "About an hour, hour and a half?"

Her smile made her seem far less intimidating than the frown she'd been wearing earlier that morning. But then the news that greeted her on the television would make anyone scowl.

"Thank you."

He whistled as he exited the house and returned to the

SUV, where Thor wagged his tail, disgust forgotten. That was one good thing about his black canine friend; he didn't hold a grudge. When Adam got home, he read a note on the kitchen table that said his dad had taken some of the plants he'd potted down to the Martinez store. So he went ahead and fed the dog, then sorted through the mail on the table while Thor ate. A note from Jennifer thanked him for the tickets to a local theater production. An invitation to a barbecue from the manager of the Pittsburg store for both he and his dad was tossed on the table. The power bill, circulars, two catalogs, and a plea for money rounded out the mail. All but the bill he ripped in half and tossed in the trash under the kitchen sink.

After a quick shower, he pulled on tan shorts and a navy Polo shirt, slid his feet into deck shoes, and snapped his watch back on his wrist. Staring into the mirror, he realized he needed a haircut, keeping his hair short kept the curl under control. A quick pass over his chin said the shave from the morning was sufficient. Could he actually call this a date? He shook his head. Jennifer kept trying to set him up with her friends, but until now, he'd not met anyone he wanted to date. And now that he'd found someone he might be interested in, she lived clear across the continent.

Thor followed him to the door and sat when Adam said no.

"Don't give me that. You were along with me all day." Adam ruffled his dog's ears. "Dad will be home soon. Take care of the place." He locked the door behind him and headed back for the truck.

An hour later he drove back up the hill to park in the same place. He gathered up the two large plastic bags filled with Styrofoam boxes of food, the smells setting his mouth to watering, and whistled his way across the street. When he thought about it, he realized he'd been whistling or humming much of the day.

"Come on in," Gillian called through the open door before he had time to push the doorbell. "I'm in the kitchen." She turned to smile at him and then drew back laughing, shock making her shake her head. "You must have enough food there for ten people."

"Probably, but I wanted a variety." He set the bags on the table. "Will Dorothy be joining us?"

A shadow passed over Gillian's face, but she smiled anyway. "I wish, but I'll be pleased if I can get her to eat some of it."

She'd changed clothes to a khaki skirt and a cream blouse with a red belt and red sandals. Her dangling red and white earrings drew Adam's attention to her face. Not that he needed any encouragement. Her perfume teased his nose, light but intriguing, just like the rest of her.

"What?" She drew back slightly, her hand going to check her earrings. "Am I missing something?"

"No, but just looking at you is a pleasure." He saw the flush start in her neck and work its way upward. "I mean..." He rolled his eyes. "Forgive me, maybe I shouldn't be let loose in female company. It's been so long, I've forgotten my manners."

Her smile returned. "I think this is all a compliment. Been a while since I've heard one, so we seem to be in the same boat."

Adam wished they had been. "I invited you, remember?"

"Trust me; you don't want me in a boat smaller than a cruise liner. You want to eat outside or in?"

"It's turning chilly now the sun's gone down. In might be best."

She fetched the plates from the cupboard and the silverware from the drawer and set the table.

"Don't bother with serving plates. I'll just open the boxes, but we'll probably need some serving utensils."

"Really casual."

"Is that all right with you?" She seemed a more formal person, but then he'd heard there was a world of difference between NYC and sunny California.

She glanced at him over her shoulder. "Fine. Iced tea?"

He nodded and removed the containers from the bags. "I hope you like this. Dad says the Cantina serves the best Mexican food around."

She brought two glasses to the table and set them at the plates. "I just realized I am starved."

"Good." He pulled back one chair and waited for her to sit down.

"Thank you." Gillian smiled up at him. "This is so much nicer than eating a salad alone."

Sitting down, he shook out his napkin. "You want to say grace, or shall I?" When she just shrugged, he bowed his head. "Thank you, Lord, for good food, new friends, and healing for Dorothy. May we be aware of all the ways you bless us. Amen." He looked up to find Gillian's gaze resting on him. If only he could read the mind behind those long eyelashes.

Chapter Nine

During the day Gillian had been able to keep the worry at bay, well mostly, but in that fragile land between awake and asleep, worry and his cohorts of fear and resentment attacked with full force. How much money would she lose in this takeover? How would she ever find another job she liked as well as this one? That paid as well? How could she leave her mother? She'd slip right back into dying mode. The questions pummeled her, retreated and attacked again.

She forced herself fully awake so she could deal with the fears with some kind of common sense. The problem was, awake or asleep she had no answers. She got up, peeked in her mother's room to hear regular breathing, and headed for the kitchen for a cup of chamomile tea, one of her mother's antidotes for sleeplessness. Something her mother used to say when Gillian was a little girl filtered through the battlefield of her mind.

"When you have nightmares, chase them away by praying. Put Jesus in your mind; nothing can stand against Him. His name is all powerful."

Cup in hand, she sat at the table and stared out at the moonlit backyard. Put Jesus in her mind. How could she have forgotten that? How many times in those childhood years had she crept into her mother's room, shivering in terror?

"Come, let's pray Jesus' name." The words, accompanied by a loving arm around her shoulders, had always brought her peace. The nightmares left and she could sleep. Was it the words, the loving arm, or was it as her mother always said, "Jesus' name is all powerful."

If it weren't so chilly out, she'd go outside and sit in the moonlight. Instead she shook her head. Just saying the name of Jesus was too simple. *Get a grip, girl,* she told herself. *You know you will solve all those things as they come up. You always have. You are known as a problem solver. That's what they pay you the big bucks for.* Oops, bad comment. They weren't going to be paying her any bucks, any longer. Surely there would be a severance package? Or since she'd been there so long would they force her to retire? Retirement? She was not ready to retire yet.

And so the battle fought to storm back in. She inhaled and let it out on a whoosh. God used to answer her prayers. That raised another question. Did He quit answering or did she quit praying? For years she'd kept a journal where she wrote down what she prayed about and then went back and logged in the answers. Had she taken that with her to New York or—or…? There were boxes in the garage labeled with her name, others with Allie's. She finished her tea and caught a yawn with her hand. Look for the boxes or go back to bed? Opting for bed, she mentally wrote herself a note to search in the morning. Right now, sleep sounded amazingly appealing.

Gillian woke to the ring of a telephone. Bounding out of bed, she trotted down the hall to the kitchen and snatched the receiver off the wall mount, hoping it was Allie.

"Hello?"

"I woke you, didn't I?" a male voice asked.

She finger-swept her hair back over the top of her head. "Ah, yes."

"I'm sorry. May I please speak with Mrs. Ormsby?"

"Who is this?"

"I am Nurse Ronald Smith. I have a memo here from Dr. Isaacs that I was to call Mrs. Ormsby on Sunday to remind her that she has an appointment with Dr. Isaacs on Wednesday morning at ten thirty and to see how she is doing."

"I see. This is her daughter Gillian Ormsby and I've been taking care of her the last couple of days."

"Good, that's what my notes indicate. May I talk with her?"

"She's still sleeping. Um, could you call back later? I would really like her to talk with you."

"Of course. When would be a good time?"

I wish I knew. Gillian stared at the clock on the stove. Eight fifteen? She had really slept in. "Would ten-ish be possible?" At his acquiescence she continued. "Since she has refused to talk with anyone since I arrived, I'm not sure how to make this happen, but I will try."

"Is she bedridden?"

"Yes, at this point."

"Is there a phone accessible?"

"Yes."

"Sometimes elderly people will talk with a medical person, you know how they respect doctors, and usually nurses, too. Let's hope this works for us." He paused. "I will review her chart more carefully before I call back. See if we can get some help for you."

Gillian heaved a sigh of relief. "Thank you. I have to

leave tomorrow night and I'm worried about what will happen here."

"When will you be back?"

"I don't know. I live in New York City..."

"But don't you have a sister who lives near here?" He mumbled a bit, obviously reading. "A Mrs. Miller?"

"Yes, but I've not talked with her yet this morning."

"I see."

No, he didn't. She didn't call back all day yesterday. Who knew what today would bring. "Hopefully I can talk with her before you call back. Thank you for calling." Gillian hung up the phone. Maybe this was the help she needed. But what were the chances she could get things in place by tomorrow night, especially if she couldn't get in contact with Allie?

First things first. Get dressed and get going.

As soon as she had set the coffee to perking, she made her bed and headed for the shower. *Try Allie first before she leaves for church.* Gillian dialed and waited, left a message again on the cell phone, then another one on the home phone. What, had they left on a vacation or something?

"You're still here." Dorothy stared at her daughter sometime later.

"I told you I would be. Coffee's ready." Gillian motioned to the steaming cup on the nightstand. "Let's get you sitting up."

Even though Dorothy shook her head, she semi-cooperated with the process. While she'd not said thank you, she did hold the mug herself and inhaled the steam. Gillian chose to mark that as progress.

"A male nurse called from your clinic, checking on you with a reminder of your appointment on Wednesday."

Her mother stared at the coffee mug and then finally glanced at Gillian. "I can't go."

"Why?"

She shook her head once and then kept on, barely moving it from side to side. Her mouth turned down even more, if that were possible.

Gillian waited for her to say more, but when she didn't, added, "Allie hasn't returned my calls."

A shrug.

"Mother, I have to leave tomorrow night and we need some kind of plan in place before that." When she didn't respond, Gillian continued. "Now what would you like for breakfast?"

No answer again. "Fine, then I will make oatmeal."

By the time she returned to the bedroom, her mother had rolled over and gone back to sleep. "You know this might be a lot more comfortable if you moved to the chair and I brought a TV tray in." She might as well be talking to a statue or the wall. Her mother didn't respond. Stubborn, bullheaded, willful, the adjectives rolled through her mind. Yesterday she'd been able to be patient. Things weren't looking so good for today.

Once Dorothy was sitting up again, Gillian willed her mother to look up and ask a question, complain, anything—but she didn't, only staring down at her hands clasped loosely in her lap.

"Mother, that nurse is going to call back at any time. You need to speak with him."

The shaking head was getting old.

"Between you and Allie . . ." Gillian caught herself shaking her own head. That along with her own sighing might make keeping her own sanity rather questionable. Why would she want to ever come back here?

Wanting and needing were two different things. She could hear the phone ringing in the kitchen. She knelt down and retrieved the old-fashioned desk phone from under the bed, answering it on her way back up. "Yes, thank you, she's right here." She sat the phone on the bed and handed her mother the receiver. "It's the nurse."

Dorothy lifted the receiver to her ear. "Yes."

Gillian wished the other phone was portable so she could listen in. But at least her mother was taking the call.

"No."

No what? Gillian headed for the kitchen, guilt halting her hand before she picked up the receiver. Should she listen in? Was that even legal? "Oh, my word!" After all, privacy laws were a big deal nowadays. She huffed a sigh and marched back down the hallway to see her mother hanging up the phone.

"So, what did he say?"

"Nothing."

"Nothing! Mother I know he wanted to talk with you." A surge of pure anger clamped her jaw. She closed her eyes and mentally counted to ten, then fifteen. Mouth open, she inhaled, filling her lungs so she could push it all out, and hopefully the anger with it. It didn't work, the anger boiled. Without a word she left the room so that she wouldn't unload what she was thinking onto her mother. She who was noted for calm and collected bargaining skills came so close to losing her temper, it frightened her. Where were all those carefully honed skills when she needed them? Why could she deal with high-powered executives but be brought to her knees by a stubborn old lady who only wanted to die?

You could just let her go her own way, a mocking voice insisted.

"This is my mother we are talking about here!" She realized she spoke aloud to a voice that was inside her head.

The ringing phone caught her attention again. "Hello." Where had her soothing phone voice departed to?

"Ah, Ms. Ormsby?"

"Yes." Recognizing the nurse's voice, relief poured through her like a cooling stream. "I'm glad you called back."

"You sound a bit—ah, put out?"

"That's putting it mildly at the moment."

"I think I can understand why. I have a note here that I can talk with either of Mrs. Ormsby's daughters."

"Good. When I asked her what you'd said, she replied, 'nothing.'"

A chuckle in her ear helped lower her shoulder blades. She wasn't in this alone after all.

"Well, that's not exactly true. I reminded her of her appointment, like I said I would. And I asked if she would like to discuss having a home health aide come by when you leave, along with mentioning that if she couldn't make it into the office, we'd have a home health nurse come by and take her vitals, assess the situation."

"And she said?"

"'No,' 'no,' and hung up."

Gillian rolled her eyes, a cobweb up by the ceiling catching her attention. "Well, I can see some improvement. She is eating; usually I have to feed her but not always and not much. I can't get many fluids into her, but she makes it back and forth to the bathroom on her own. She's not running a fever, but she sleeps most of the time."

"Really sleeping or dozing? Laying with her eyes closed and…"

"I have to put a hand on her shoulder and shake her to wake her up."

"How long has this been going on?"

"I'm not really sure. Allie called me early this past week. That was the first I knew about Mother." If it sounded like they didn't communicate well, that was only because it was so. How long since she had called and talked with her mother? "Allie said something along the line of three weeks since Mother took to her bed."

"I see. Were you able to make contact with your sister?"

"Not yet." Why did a simple question like that make her feel like a failure?

"I've been writing notes for Dr. Isaacs to read in the morning. I'm sure he will call and talk with you tomorrow. For now I suggest you keep on with what you are doing."

They said their good-byes and hung up, leaving Gillian more frustrated on one hand and grateful for an unseen nurse, who took the time to listen and encourage, on the other.

Picking up her to-do list, she scanned down to see what she could accomplish today. SPEAK WITH ALLIE in capital letters headed the list. This time she dialed the home number first.

When someone picked up the phone, she swallowed a sharp retort. At the hello, Gillian smiled. "Well, hello, Sherrilyn, how are you? This is your Auntie Gillian."

"I know, I'd recognize your voice anywhere. Are you coming out here to see us?"

Get right to the point there. "I'm not sure how we are going to work that out. How'd you do yesterday?"

"We won and I scored the final point."

They talked soccer for a minute before Gillian said, "Can I talk with your mother?"

"She's not here right now. I think she's on her way to see you and Grandma."

"Oh, good. Any idea when she left?"

"Sorry, not really. You could try her cell, but you know she forgets to turn it on half the time."

"Yeah, I know. Thanks, sweety. Talk with you soon." Gillian hung up the phone. Seemed like most of what she was doing today was talking on the telephone, to everyone but the person she needed to speak to most.

Now to think through all she needed to say to Allie, not just what she wanted to say. As usual, she took out paper and pen and started a list. The sound of a key in the front door told her the scrimmage was about to begin.

Chapter Ten

Gillian?"

"In the kitchen. I'm pouring iced tea or would you rather have coffee?" *Keep it smooth and easy for a while at least.*

"Iced tea is fine." Allie set her bag on the chair beside the buffet on the north wall. A large ficus tree in the corner wore many yellow leaves since it had not been watered for a while. "Something smells good."

"I dug out a candle from the gift closet and have it burning."

"But Mother doesn't like candles. Says they are too dangerous."

"Mother isn't out here, and even though I aired the house out yesterday, it still smells musty." Gillian handed a full glass to her sister.

"Is she awake?"

"She was because I woke her and fed her breakfast."

"You got her to eat?"

"No, I fed her. Although late yesterday, she did eat some on her own when I brought it to her. She wasn't happy about getting bathed and the bedding changed, but we got it done."

Allie stared at her like she was a magician or something. She shook her head. "I am amazed."

"Yes, well..." Gillian sipped her drink.

"I was going to call you this morning but we were running late for church."

What about all the calls yesterday? Keep it calm, cool. "We have some decisions that have to be made and implemented before I leave tomorrow night, you know."

Allie cupped her hands around the glass sitting in front of her. "I've done the best I can."

"Allie, this isn't about you. This is about our mother, who can no longer stay alone or she really will die."

"Well, I can't stay here full time. I have responsibilities, too, you know."

Tell her about your job or lack thereof. Why? She never asks about me. That thought was a new one. It was true. She asked the questions regarding Allie's life when she called, but the questions weren't reciprocal. Had it been the same with her conversations with Mother? She'd have to think on that, but she had a feeling it was pretty much the same.

"I think right now we need to put aside any confrontations and see what we can do here." *Because if I start in on you, you truly will feel like you're a failure.*

"Yeah, but..." Allie glanced up.

Gillian fortified herself with more iced tea. Yeah, but...she'd forgotten how much she disliked yeah-but people. *We will not step back into our past ways of talking, we will not. I will not.*

"A nurse called from the clinic this morning to talk to Mother. He spoke with me first and called back when she was awake."

"How did that go?"

"Succinct. 'No, no,' bang."

"But how did you get her to talk?"

"Woke her and handed her the phone. Did you know the ringer is turned off on the phone in the bedroom and she is keeping it under the bed?"

Allie nodded.

"So how can you talk with her every day?" Gillian watched her sister go into a defensive mode, shoulders curved in, head down. Bad Gillian, bad to attack. She leaned forward. "Sorry, Allie. That just slipped out." She patted her sister's hand. Change of topic.

"He called me back and told me what he'd said. He took notes and will give them to Dr. Isaacs in the morning. I think two things need to be first on the list. Who's going to stay here and how will Mother get to her doctor's appointment? Oh, the nurse said he could send a home health aide by to help and a home health nurse, if we absolutely can't get her to the doctor's on Wednesday."

"They better be tough. Mother's not going to like this."

"Maybe not. You know how charming she can be when she wants." *With others, that is, not necessarily with her daughters.* "We can also rent a wheelchair if need be, to get her into the office."

"True." Allie drew lines in the condensation on the glass. She looked up. "But how will I make her go?"

"Tell her if she doesn't cooperate, she'll end up in a nursing home." Gillian glanced at her watch. "You want some lunch? We have plenty of leftovers. Mexican."

Allie shook her head. "I need to get back."

"Get back? You just got here." *Well, Gillian, how you manage employees is sure different from managing your sister.* Allie had straightened her spine, and a glint of defiance sparked from her eyes.

"Jefferson and I would like you to come for dinner. He's doing barbecue. This way you can see the kids, too."

"Just drive off and leave Mother for a couple of hours?"

"Do you have any other suggestions?"

"Yes, we sit here and make some decisions, a plan so I know what I need to do tomorrow to implement it."

"Well, if you know so much, you just go ahead and do what needs to be done."

"Allie, please. Let's put the animosity on hold. We have to work together on this."

"Work together? You'll be busy tomorrow, and then you're leaving and I'm left to..." Her inflection changed, mimicked Gillian. "To do what needs to be done."

Gillian massaged her forehead with her fingertips. Maybe a change of subject would help. "How well do you know Enzio?"

"He's a sweetheart and has been trying to get Mother out, too. Did he call?"

"Yes, and came by for tea. Brought napoleons."

"Did Mother see him?"

Gillian shook her head. "She was sleeping."

Allie waved toward the door. "I see you got the window fixed."

"I tried to, bought the supplies but..." Again she shook her head. "Adam fixed it Saturday morning." *Before I tried to call you all day. Let it go. Let it go.*

"That was nice of him."

"It was. Why don't you go in and wake Mother? I'll heat up something for her lunch."

"All right." Allie rose and headed down the hall with a speed that suggested she wanted out of the kitchen.

Gillian took the white boxes out of the refrigerator and lined them up on the counter. Near as she could tell, they hadn't accomplished one blasted thing. *Think, Gillian, think.* If she went ahead without consulting Allie, then she would be accused of thinking she was better than her sister and could run the whole show. If she left it all up to Allie, then she would be accused of ignoring her. So what was the bottom line here? She knew the answer to that one. Make sure Mother was cared for and forced back into real life again—if that was possible.

But what if their mother really wanted to die? Didn't she have the right to make that kind of decision? Not eating and not moving around could certainly precipitate dying. So, what was it Mother really wanted?

Gillian could hear Allie talking with their mother as she entered the bedroom with the lunch tray.

"If you help her sit up, I'll put the tray on her lap."

Mother shook her head. Allie glared at Gillian. Gillian clamped her jaw and smiled, set the tray on the dresser, and crossed to lean over her mother. "You can scoot up by yourself, or I will help you. Which is it to be?"

Mother huffed and glared at her elder daughter but pulled herself up enough for Gillian to stuff the pillows behind her. "I'm not hungry."

"I know, but it's lunchtime and I heated up some of the leftovers from last night. Adam brought over dinner and had hoped you would join us." She earned another glare for her efforts. Ignoring that, she set the tray in place. "You can feed yourself or I will help you or, or..." Glancing toward her sister, "Allie will help you." She waited for an answer from either of them, but when neither responded, she sat down on the edge of the bed.

"So, how did the soccer games go yesterday?" she asked Allie, picking up the fork. Even though she already knew the answer, she couldn't think of anything else to say.

"Wish you had been there, Mother. Sherrilyn made a spectacular save in the last few seconds, and her team won."

"Do you go to the games?" Gillian asked, handing the fork to her mother when she reached for it.

"She used to."

You can't answer for her if you want her to take part in the conversation. But Gillian kept her mouth shut again, sure by now she had the indentations of her teeth permanently embossed on her tongue. "Mother?"

"I don't like tennis much." She picked up her cup for a sip to wash down the enchilada. "Too hot."

Thankful for every bit of progress, Gillian glanced at her sister to see if she realized what was happening. Allie was busy studying her cuticles. Shaking her sounded like a helpful idea. But it probably would not be popular.

"But what about soccer?"

"Too noisy." Dorothy sampled the refried beans with melted cheese on top.

"I hear Enzio came by yesterday," Allie said.

"He did?"

"I told you he was coming, Mother, but you refused to see him." Gillian willed her mother to take a few more bites.

"Oh." She laid her fork back down on the tray and picked up her cup again.

"Sherrilyn said she hoped you would come to her next game."

Gillian watched as her mother pulled back into herself, slumping again and staring at her plate. "How about a couple more bites, then I'll leave you alone?"

Her mother glared up at her, picked up her fork, and stabbed a piece of enchilada. She ate two bites, let the fork rattle on the plate, and pushed the tray away.

Gillian grabbed it before the liquids could spill. Now that

was indeed a reaction. And any reaction was better than no reaction. "Why don't you help Mother to the bathroom, Allie, while I take this back to the kitchen?" As she left the room, she heard her mother grumble.

"I'm not a child, you know. I can go to the bathroom when I need to."

"But, Mother..."

Did Allie always switch into little-girl mode when dealing with their mother? Gillian promised herself she'd think more deeply on these things. She'd never paid much attention to the way the three of them interacted with each other before, although Mother was the one with the strongest and most dominant personality. She'd read an article about how members of families often stepped right back into the roles they'd lived when they were younger when they came home again to visit. Allie most assuredly was doing just that. But with Mother trying to die, Gillian was forced to act differently. Or chose to. She was able to deal with Mother differently, but what about with Allie?

She glanced outside to see a hummingbird zip by the window and door. What if she were to hang a hummingbird feeder outside her mother's bedroom window? How could she resist? But the thought died before going any further. Who would fill it when she wasn't there? If Allie couldn't take time to turn on the water for the yard, why would she bother with a bird feeder? Both thoughts made her grit her teeth again.

Could she ask Mrs. Gonzales next door to check on things like watering and a hummingbird feeder? Offer to pay her? Give her a key and ask her to come inside to visit with Mother? Would Mother allow that? Gillian sat down with pen and paper and added on to her lists, the major one titled "How to help Mother get going again." She glanced up when Allie entered the room.

"She refused to go to the bathroom and insisted that I pull the drapes again."

"And you went along with that?"

"What was I supposed to do? Drag her out of bed?"

Gillian heaved a sigh. "No, but you can encourage her to get up and at least sit in the chair for a while. We have to get her out of that bed. And why in the world would you close the drapes again? Let the light in there."

"Because she told me to."

"Well, little sister, at this point we have to make some decisions, and if you won't help me make them, then you have no right to get mad at me for doing what I think is best."

"I don't get mad."

"Oh, really? You don't return calls, you snap, get sarcastic, and refuse to use a little pressure to get Mother to do what is best for her."

"I was busy."

Always back to *I*. Instead of throwing something through the window, Gillian stabbed her pen into the pad of paper. "Look. I have to leave tomorrow night. Who is going to stay with her, and who is going to take her to the doctor on Wednesday?"

"Hire someone. I cannot stay here all the time, and you know she is not going to get up, get dressed, and let me use a wheelchair to get her around."

"So, what are our options?"

Allie sank into a chair, all the while shaking her head. "I just don't know." She heaved a weary sigh. "Cancel her appointment?"

"That's one idea. What about her friends?"

"Well, Alice died. She refuses to see Enzio. And I guess the others sort of fell away."

"Have you looked into Social Services to see what they might offer?"

Allie shook her head. "I suppose I can contact the director at the senior center and ask her what to do."

"Good."

Gillian leaned back in her chair. "What do you think Mother really wants?"

"To die. That's what she said."

"Come on, Allie, you know she's always been a master manipulator. What does she want from us?"

"To be left alone so she can die."

"You really think so?"

"That's what she said." The defensive tone returned.

"Did something happen to bring this on?"

"Well, as I told you, she had a bit of a stroke, a TIA, and then after that she told me she was dying."

"You think that's it?" Gillian narrowed her eyes, trying to think this through. "What else about the stroke? Was she incapacitated? She's an intelligent woman. What could she be afraid of?"

"Mother's never been afraid of anything."

"She's always wanted a lot of attention."

Allie shook her head again. "Where do you get this stuff? Mother has always been strong. She never played games, I mean head games. She used to play bridge."

"Strong, yes. And you never caused her a moment's concern."

"That is a bad thing?" Allie's glare sharpened to daggers. She rose to her feet and grabbed her purse. "Are you coming for dinner or not?"

"I think not. I really don't want to leave Mother alone for that many hours." She paused for a moment. "What if you all come here? I'll order pizza or something."

Allie stared at her. "But—but Jefferson said..."

"You want me to call and invite him?"

"No, I'll talk to him and call you back."

"You could call him, stay here so we can visit longer, and he can bring the kids. Any time is fine."

"I—I can't do that. He's not home right now. I'll call you."

Gillian watched Allie do her version of stomping out the door. *She never once asked when I would be coming back. Or if. Interesting.*

Chapter Eleven

Adam glanced down at Thor sitting beside him at the sliding glass door to the backyard. A whine and a tail thumping indicated Thor's one-track mind. Outside. He wanted outside.

Adam opened the door and the dog shot out, barking at a squirrel Adam had not noticed. The squirrel took refuge on the top of the fence, chattering his displeasure, punctuating the diatribe with a flicking tail. Adam chuckled to himself at the body language of the two opposing forces and shifted his attention to his father's nursery area. His dad was just stripping off his gardening gloves and putting away his tools. Since it was Sunday morning, neither of them cooked breakfast because they stopped to eat after church.

Half an hour later they climbed into Adam's truck and headed down the street.

"She's still here."

Adam nodded. "Gillian leaves tomorrow night. I wish you could meet her before she goes."

"Jen made me promise to come there for dinner today. You going?" Jennifer Bentley had been married to Adam's brother, Charles, who had died several years earlier. She and her two children lived in Oakland and kept in close contact. She, too, had expressed concern about Bill's lack of vitality.

"Nope, I wasn't invited."

"Oh."

Adam glanced over to see a puzzled look on his father's face. "Don't worry about it. I had told her I was taking the *Sea Dream* out."

"Are you?"

"I don't know. I thought we could stop and pick up the potting soil you wanted and I'd help you for a while. If you want me to, that is."

His dad nodded. "I could use your strong back for a bit."

"Great, valued for my strong back instead of my brains." There, he'd brought a smile to his father's face.

The parking lot was nearly full already. They parked along the outer perimeter and followed the people in through the carved wood front doors to be greeted by smiling people handing out bulletins along with their "good mornings." Adam followed his father as they took their usual place fifth row from the front, right side, as if they owned that particular portion of the padded pews.

"How you doing, Bill?" asked the man who always sat directly behind them.

"Good, James, good. How about you?"

"Can't complain, after all what good would it do anyway?" James laughed and glanced at his wife beside him. "Huh, honey?"

The Sunday ritual never changed, but while his dad didn't seem to mind, Adam really wanted to sit somewhere else and meet new people. The one time he'd tried that, his father had gone along with it, but led the way from then on. After all, the tradition had started many years earlier, and one of his father's favorite axioms remained. "If it ain't broke, don't fix it."

As they settled in for the sermon, Adam's mind wandered to thoughts of Gillian. Did she attend church? Her mother had certainly raised her that way, but had she stayed with her childhood training? Life in New York City would most likely not be conducive to that. At least all the big cities he'd spent any time in through the years had been that way. A chaplain aboard the aircraft carrier he'd been assigned to had made it his mission to reawaken the faith of his "boys" as he called them. Adam knew he'd never forget the man, thankful for his hard work and persistence. When his brother died in a freak accident on the ski slopes, Adam's faith was a solid bridge to his heavenly Father's comforting arms.

They were sitting in a booth at their favorite restaurant waiting for their order when Adam cleared his throat, determined to ask a few personal questions.

"Dad, how long has it been since you've seen a doctor?"

Bill squinted, thinking. "Nearly a year, I guess. Why?"

"Just wondering. You don't seem quite yourself lately. Jen commented on it, too, so it's not just me."

"So, is she going to give me the old quizzing when I get there?"

"I have no idea. Have you noticed anything different?"

His dad thought again. "I guess I get tired more easily. Figured I was pushing kinda hard at the shop." He smiled at the waitress who slid plates of food in front of them. "Thanks, Maggie."

"You are welcome. Can I get you anything else?"

Bill held up his coffee cup.

"I'll bring the pot. Anything else?" She smiled at Adam, who shook his head.

Adam waited for his father to spread butter on his pancakes and pour the syrup, before prompting him again. "Anything else? Pain anywhere?"

"Well, come to think of it, I got pain in my right foot some."

"Really?"

"Yep, dropped a skid on it Friday."

Adam shook his head. Leave it to his dad. "You'd tell me if you suspected something was wrong, right?"

"Most likely. Eat your breakfast before it gets cold."

Adam shook his head and did as he was told.

Later at the nursery he shouldered his father away from the bags of potting soil and loaded the dolly himself, paid for the items, and let one of the young men load the truck. Father and son wandered through the nursery to see what to mark for a display like the one Bill now planned to set up at his shop.

"I'll come back later and put this together," he told the clerk. "Have someone clear out that section over there."

Back home they changed clothes and headed out to the nursery in their backyard. While Adam mixed the potting soil with their homegrown compost, some dried steer manure and dirt from a pile, his father cut the soil in the cyclamen flats so he could transplant them into individual pots.

With his mixing done, Adam watched his father for a bit. "Back to our discussion, how about getting an appointment for a checkup?"

Bill glanced up from his plants. "I will if that will ease your mind."

"It would. Thanks." He saluted his father and whistled for Thor. Both males needed a good run. At least his father wasn't cantankerous like Gillian's mother. Sometimes one needed to thank God for favors large and small.

Chapter Twelve

Enzio called. He'd like to come over."

Dorothy shook her head, her eyes clamped shut.

"He's bringing something for you, but I can't figure out what it is. Says it is something you really like. Any idea what it might be?"

Another head shake, but this time the woman in the bed opened her eyes and stared at the ceiling. "What time is it?"

"Three o'clock."

"Is Allie still here?"

"Nope." *And I'm not mentioning she left in a huff.*

"She is always so busy with the children and Jefferson."

Gillian wondered if she should tell her she invited them all for dinner, then decided to wait until she knew they were coming. "How long since you've seen either of the kids?"

Dorothy shrugged. "They were here this summer."

Not since then and this is October? Strange.

"I saw the hummingbird again. Do you still have any feeders in the garage?"

"Don't think so. They broke after a while."

Gillian almost smiled. Her mother was actually volunteering information. "Do you want me to comb your hair for you?"

"Why?" Her mother glared at her. "You tell Enzio he cannot come."

"How? He said he doesn't have a cell phone and he'd be out and about."

Dorothy closed her eyes. "Leave me alone."

"Sorry, can't do that." Gillian crossed to the bathroom and retrieved a brush and comb. "You have a choice, visit with him like you are, or let me comb your hair and you can put on a blouse or one of those church sweaters."

"Gillian Ormsby, this is my house and I will say who can come and who can't."

"Guess you'll have to get back on your feet then, so you can do as you want. Right now"—she held up the brush and comb—"you have a choice, yes or no. Unless of course, you want to hide under the covers or in the bathroom."

"Comb my hair."

"Thank you, I will. Do you have any hairspray or styling gel?"

Another glare was her answer.

"Guess I'll use some of mine then." She returned a minute later with a small plastic bottle of hairspray and sat down on the edge of the bed. "You know this would be easier if you sat on the chair." *Sorry, Mother, I'm all grown up now and you can no longer intimidate me with that glare. The world I live in, I've been subjected to far worse glares than yours.* "How long since you've had a haircut?" Gillian brushed her mother's hair, then combed and sprayed it into some kind of style, difficult since it wasn't long enough to comb back and up and yet too long to let it hang. "I don't suppose you have a curling iron?" Another glare. "This will have to do. Do you want a mirror?" Gillian put back the brush and comb and fetched one of the church sweaters from the closet. Holding it for Dorothy to push her arms into, Gillian almost shook her head in frustration. There was no way she was going to forcefully dress her mother. So, if she didn't care, what difference did a sweater make? About the time she was ready to concede defeat, Dorothy growled and shoved her arms into the sleeves.

"I know Enzio likes iced tea, but would you rather have coffee?"

"He only drinks decaf."

"Do you have any?"

"No. He can drink iced tea."

"And you?"

"Coffee." Her eyes narrowed, daring Gillian to argue.

"Fine then, I'll make you coffee. If I were going to be here longer, I'd have taken out the coffeemaker I sent you. Far easier than your old percolator." For that she received another stony look.

"There he is," Gillian said on hearing the doorbell. "You sure you don't want to come out to the living room?" Sure that was a rhetorical question, she hurried down the hall to the front door. "Come on in."

Enzio smiled at her, his dark eyes dancing. "Am I welcome?"

"By me you are." She stepped back and motioned him in.

"And Dorothy?"

Gillian rolled her eyes and shut the door. "She's been talking a bit more, ate both breakfast and lunch, not much but better than nothing. So I see that as progress."

Enzio patted her arm. "You are good for her, my dear, whether she thinks so or not."

"I hope so. Please, don't expect too much."

"Don't you go worrying about my feelings. I've lived a long time and dealt with all kinds of people. I've learned that love conquers all. Sometimes it just takes longer than others." He held a silver-wrapped package under his arm.

"I don't have any decaf coffee, so is iced tea all right?"

"It most certainly is."

Showing a gentleman to her mother's bedroom made Gillian flip-flop between laughing and feeling embarrassed. She thought of asking if he knew the way, but that left her open to blushing. On the other hand, if he was a longtime friend, surely he'd been to the house often enough to know the master bedroom was a little beyond the bathroom. She stopped at the door and motioned him in before heading back to the kitchen. What she wouldn't do to eavesdrop on the conversation, the old mouse-in-the-pocket kind of thing. If her mother would even deign to speak at all.

At least her mother wasn't shrieking, "Get out" or some such nonsense. Or throwing things. Not that she could picture her mother doing that, but then she would never have believed her mother would go to bed wanting to die. When the coffee finished perking, Gillian fixed a tray with three drinks and headed for the bedroom. Pausing outside the door, she listened. Nothing. No one said anything. Surely they had been talking. Or at least Enzio had been talking.

"Here we go," she chirped and then entered the room. Enzio smiled at her. Her mother ignored her. Setting the tray on the end of the bed, she handed one glass to Enzio, passed the mug to her mother—who set it on the nightstand—and parked herself on the end of the bed with the other glass. "Can I get you anything else?"

Neither Enzio nor her mother responded, so she took a sip of her drink. Now what should she do? She looked over at Enzio, then to her mother, and back to him. He shrugged and drank from his glass. Her mother stared at her hands.

"So, Enzio, how has your day gone?"

"Good. I played bocce ball after church; went to the early service."

"Did you win?"

"I didn't do half bad."

"He won."

Gillian snapped her attention back to her mother. She was paying attention.

Enzio chuckled. "That I did."

"Do you play bocce ball, Mother?"

"Sometimes. I used to."

"And she won the women's division."

"Really? Is that a big sport around here?"

"Guess you could call it that. Mostly older folks play it. The game came from Italy." He set his glass down on the nightstand and leaned forward. "Easier on the shoulders than horseshoes."

Gillian saw that the gift had been unwrapped but was either still or back in the box. Should she ask? Her mother picked up her mug and took a sip of the coffee.

"I told her I can take her to the doctor on Wednesday. I'll get the wheelchair from the church if I need to."

"Thank you, that's very kind of you."

"No. I am not going," the voice from the bed proclaimed.

"Then you have to make arrangements with Allie." *Mother, that is so rude. Here your friend is trying to be nice to you, make your life easier, and you are being a brat.* But then perhaps there had been some brain damage with the TIA. At least personality-wise. Gillian thought back. Her mother had always been able to get things and people to do what she wanted. Once Dorothy focused on something, it might take some time, but it happened. How close was Mother to really dying? That thought piled even more guilt on the necessity for her to leave in little over twenty-four hours.

Enzio drained his glass and got up to set it on the tray. "I will be back tomorrow afternoon, Dorothy." He leaned over and patted her hand. "Thank you for the visit."

Gillian walked him to the front door. "Thank you for coming. I'm sorry she was so rude."

"You are welcome. You do not need to apologize for her behavior. You are doing your best, but you are up against a strong will."

Gillian nodded. "That I know for sure. I will lay out her clothes before I leave. I know she can dress herself, but will she? I'm just not sure."

"Maybe I should ask Adam to help. Between the two of us we could force her to come along." His chuckle told her he was kidding.

"I wish I didn't have to leave." The statement surprised her. But saying it to herself again, she realized that it was the truth. Did she really have to be in New York by Tuesday morning? Yes, she and Scot had a meeting scheduled, but could it be postponed?

"Rest assured that we will take care of things here, and hopefully you will be able to return before long." Enzio pulled a folded piece of paper from his chest pocket. "Here are some contact numbers to get someone to help if you decide to do that. I don't know anything about Dorothy's finances, but getting help through the doctor and Social Services will take longer."

"I can manage to pay for help for a while for her. I just never expected we would be at this stage yet."

"And you shouldn't be. But God willing, we will see what we can do." He started to leave and turned back. "If you can get an extra key, I can come and go without bothering you or Allie."

"I will take care of that tomorrow. I plan on getting one for Mrs. Gonzales, too. I see her car is back, so I will go over and talk with her this evening or tomorrow."

"Good." He patted her hand. "You are a good daughter."

Her eyes misted over as she watched him stride down the walk. A *good daughter.* Was she really?

Time picked up speed and whirled her through her to-do list. She'd just hung up the phone again when she heard the doorbell. A familiar form filled the porch side of the screen door.

"Adam, how good to see you. Come in." The glint in his eyes made her smile wider.

"No thanks, Just thought I'd see if you need anything. Thor and I are on our way to the school for a run."

"Oh." Funny, why did she feel a tinge of disappointment?

"Dad and I will check on your mother after you leave. Just wanted you to know that."

"You don't happen to know of anyone I could hire to stay with her, even part time, do you?"

"Not off the top of my head." Thor whined behind him. "You tried the newspaper ads?"

She nodded. "I'll call the services in the phone book tomorrow."

"Good. We gotta go." He turned to leave, then threw over his shoulder, "Don't stay away too long, okay?"

Gillian watched Adam jog out to the sidewalk and turn down the hill. Though she wasn't a runner, a fast walk sounded like a good idea.

Mrs. Gonzales agreed to take care of watering the lawn and plants. There was no one available to stay over with Dorothy twenty-four hours a day, but Gillian would look for someone, or rather three someones, since her mother needed coverage for three eight-hour shifts. When Gillian checked online for the price for caregivers, she nearly choked. Companions were expensive, let alone nurses. Her mother would never agree to this.

When she called and talked with Allie about the information she'd learned, it was like talking to a stranger. In fact, a stranger would have been a lot more concerned.

"So you are saying you can only come every other day?" asked Gillian.

"That's for this week. I have to have time to work this out."

"I see." Even though she didn't. "I was hoping to interview someone tomorrow, but that just won't happen. I'm leaving the list of numbers here for you to follow up on. Enzio says he will get her to the doctor's appointment on Wednesday."

"Good, because my Wednesday is out."

"Why didn't you say that at the doctor's office?"

"I hadn't entered all of my calendar into my cell. When I got home and checked, I realized my morning was already full."

But you couldn't be bothered to let me know that. "What about dinner tonight?"

"Sorry, but Jefferson got tied up in a project at the neighbor's and sends his regrets."

"I see." She swallowed her inquiry about her and the kids coming and settled with, "Will I see you before I leave tomorrow?"

"I'm not sure. I'll let you know."

Gillian clamped her teeth to keep from ripping her baby sister up one side and down the other. With all the damage caused by the tongue biting and teeth clenching, her dentist would be able to afford a new Lexus. "You do that. Bye."

Pacing did no good. Stomping didn't, either. Instead Gillian grabbed the window cleaner from under the sink, retrieved the paper towels from the rack, and went outside in the backyard to attack her mother's bedroom window. Back to the pantry for the step stool. Her mother always despised slamming doors. But there was a certain release of frustration accomplished by a good door slam, except the door in this case was a slider, so it wasn't nearly as effective. Standing in the garden and screaming would most likely result in the neighbors calling 9-1-1, thinking someone had been injured.

Surely that window had never been scrubbed so hard. The paper towels were a shredded mess. And still Gillian wanted to scream.

Dorothy's bedroom window changed from water spotted and dusty to sparkling in a matter of minutes. On to the kitchen window and the sliding glass doors. Gillian's arm ached and now the birds would probably fly into the glass. How could her sister be so—so petty? Bratty? Shouldn't a forty-plus woman have some sense of responsibility? Of family? Gillian rubbed her shoulder. Now she had physical pain to go along with her rage. What happened to counting to ten? She'd be at ten thousand by now, and it still would not have done any good.

She used the glass cleaner to scrub the grime off the patio table. She'd washed it before, but now she scoured it, both the top of the glass and the underneath. A female Anna's hummer hovered two feet away from her face, zipped down to examine the clean table, and returned to eye level to hover a few seconds more.

Gillian could not help but smile, no matter how mad she was. "Aren't you beautiful?" she whispered. The hummer flew higher, hovered, and then headed for the roses. "That does it. I am putting out a feeder even if I have to go buy one. Surely if I hang one outside Mother's window it will get her attention." She ignored the in-her-head voice that asked "Who will fill it when you are gone?" and returned to the kitchen to put away her cleaning supplies. She found a box marked bird feeders in the garage and brought it into the kitchen. Inside were tubular seed feeders, two quart-size hummingbird feeders, and a tray type of seed feeder with a cover. She remembered her mother spreading sunflower seeds on a flat one like this when she was a little girl.

After washing the feeders and leaving them turned upside down on the kitchen counter to dry, she poured herself a glass of iced tea, one for her mother, and headed down the hallway.

"Mother?"

"I thought you left."

"No, this is still Sunday and I am here." She set the iced tea on the nightstand. "I brought you something to drink."

"What were you banging around out in the garage for?"

Gillian paused in mid-sip. Her mother had noticed all the noise. How about that? "I was looking for hummingbird feeders. I found the box."

"Oh." Dorothy pushed herself halfway to a sitting position.

"You want some help?"

"No."

Gillian set her glass down and stacked the pillows behind her mother's back. "I wish you would come out and watch her."

"Who?"

"The hummingbird."

Dorothy reached for her glass. "I don't feed them anymore."

"Why?"

A shrug, but at least it was a response.

"Are you hungry?"

"No."

"I'm thinking of leftovers for tonight; we hardly made a dent in them at lunchtime. Unless you'd like salmon again. There are those fillets in your freezer."

"Is Allie coming back?"

"No." Gillian drank a slug from her glass. "Do you know someone we could call to come and stay with you?"

Dorothy shook her head and tipped it back to stare at the ceiling. "I told you. I don't want anyone to stay here. I don't need anyone to stay here. You go back to your New York life and I will be just fine."

"Mother, I can't just leave you like this."

Dorothy glared at her again, rolled over, and pulled her covers up.

What would the glass being thrown against the wall sound like? More important, feel like?

Chapter Thirteen

Hanging up the hummingbird feeders felt like a declaration of war. Or maybe it was an act of war. The declaration had been made when she broke the windowpane to enter the house. Gillian watched out the kitchen window as her shimmering avian friend found the feeder. It hadn't taken her long. Hummingbirds used to be one of her mother's daily delights. She'd kept the feeders filled and planted her yard and garden to be a friendly place for both birds and butterflies. That thought brought Gillian to another. Where was the birdbath that was always kept full so the feathered guests would have the water they needed for drinking and bathing?

She'd not seen one in the garage. Surely her mother had not thrown it away. Gillian, now on a mission, headed for the area around the gate to the backyard where her mother used to keep gardening equipment under a shed roof attached to the house. Sure enough. The rakes and hoes hung on hooks, a tiller, lawn mower, and a couple of garbage cans with firmly clamped lids took up most of the graveled area, leaving just enough room for the concrete birdbath. Why had Mother put it away? But then the why of her mother's most recent actions would take far more understanding than Gillian was capable of at the moment. Since the birdbath came in two pieces, she carried the top part out first and set it on the concrete patio. When she alternately dragged and rolled the heavy stand out, her shoulder, the right one still unhappy with all the window washing, yelped at her. Though dusty, the birdbath had been scrubbed before its retirement. She retrieved the brush from under the kitchen sink, cleaned the concrete using water from the hose, and looked around for a place to put it. In the rose bed would be good; the sprinkler system would fill it while watering the plants.

Once the birdbath was in place and filled, she fetched herself another glass of iced tea, her pen and pencil, and sat down at the patio table. Interesting that her years in New York hadn't totally obliterated her training from childhood. Not that she'd thought of feeders and birdbaths and sprinkler systems while living in her high rise condo. Besides which she'd never been back to her mother's house for a length of time when she needed to spend hours in the backyard.

The hummingbird left the feeder and hovered over the patio table for a moment before going on to the roses.

"You're welcome." Gillian watched as her new friend perched on a rose cane and proceeded to groom her feathers. Back to her list of things that should be accomplished before she left. The countdown had begun; she had twenty-six hours before she needed to leave for the airport, giving herself an extra hour to return the rental car. When the phone rang, she returned to the house, not realizing she was chilly until she stepped inside to the warmer kitchen.

"Hi, Gillian, Enzio speaking."

Even the timbre of his voice made her smile. "I know."

"My accent gives me away."

"Not so much your accent as just your voice. You always sound happy."

"Now that, my dear, is a very good compliment. How is our patient doing?"

"As little as possible. She's trying to ignore me."

"I see. And how well is that working?"

"I've been busy outside. Good thing the grass is all dead because then I don't have to mow it."

"So, how are things with Allie?"

"You don't want to know."

"I see. Well then, on to the reason I called. Do you have errands to run tomorrow or will you be on the phone all day?"

"Both. Mother insists she does not need someone staying here."

"And Allie isn't volunteering?"

"No, and she has a full morning on Wednesday so she cannot take Mother in for her appointment."

"Then we will do as I suggested. I will come pick her up and if she is not dressed, she will go in her housecoat and slippers."

"Better you than me." Gillian blew out a sigh. "I just hate to leave her and let her sink right back into the way I found her."

"I understand that. But we have more of a plan in motion now. I know Adam will come help me."

"And Mrs. Gonzales says she will come every day to check on her. I gave her a key also. And no, I've not told Mother how many keys I have given out. Of course that might get her out of bed in pure fury."

"Have I mentioned, Gillian, how grateful I am that you came?"

That stopped her. "I—ah, thank you. I'm grateful, too. Right now my life isn't going the way I'd planned, but—well, we shall see."

"Do you have to return to New York?"

"Yes, I think I do."

"You don't sound too positive."

"I know, but I've never been in a position like this before."

"Are you coming back?"

"Most likely, but I'm not sure how soon I can manage it." She pulled out a chair and sat down. "One thing for sure, I will buy new phones for this house. Being shackled to the wall is torture." As she'd hoped, he chuckled.

"Call me tomorrow when you know your schedule and I will come stay with Dorothy while you are gone. If I talk long enough, she might get up just to get away from me."

It was her turn to chuckle. "Thank you, I will."

After she'd hung up the phone, she went to stand at the sliding door, looking out at the sorry yard. Well, at least it was in better shape than when she had arrived. And so was her mother. Be thankful in the small things. She'd read that somewhere. If only Allie would cooperate. If only Mother would cooperate.

At least she made the hummingbird happy.

The first call Monday morning was to Scot Hudson, her former boss in New York City. When she said she was coming in on the red-eye, he paused before answering.

"You needn't be there when the doors open, you know."

"I know, but I just want to get it over with. Do you know what you are going to do next?"

"I'm going to take a much needed vacation; my wife has been busy studying travel brochures."

"And then?"

"Sign up with a headhunter, call in whatever favors I can, and update my résumé."

She wanted to ask if he had any prospects but decided it didn't sound like it.

"When I land somewhere soon, I will let you know. I'd hire you in a heartbeat."

"Thank you." Just the knowledge that he considered her that valuable brightened her Monday morning. "Will you be in the office?"

"Nope. I'm cleaning out my office as I speak, and after our meeting tomorrow, let's make it at Kathleen's Café, Joyce and I will be on a plane to somewhere. I did say ten thirty, right?"

"Yes." So much for changing the meeting day. "Good for you." They hung up and she dialed Shannon's number only to get the answering machine. After leaving a message regarding her plans for Tuesday, she attached her cell phone holster to her waistband before going to the back door to look out at the yard.

The hummingbird perched on the feeder outside the kitchen window, alternately feeding at the yellow plastic port and staring around for possible invaders. A variety of small birds clutched the perches on the tubular seed feeder. If only Mother would come out here and identify them like she used to do. A blue jay sat on the flat feeder, enjoying the sunflower seeds. Funny how some things Gillian remembered even though she'd not thought about the birds since the last time she visited.

At eight a.m., she started the phone calls to the service agencies. No one had anyone available today. She would have to come in and fill out forms. Did her mother have long-term care insurance? And yes, her mother was seventy-three and on Social Security, which at this point seemed very unsocial and not too secure.

She made the coffee, oatmeal, and two slices of toast, placed the items on a tray, and carried the tray to the bedroom. Once her mother was awake, Gillian settled the tray across her mother's thighs and picked up her coffee mug along with one of the bowls of oatmeal with a spoon. She took hers to the chair and sat down to eat.

"The hummingbird is enjoying the feeders. What kind did you say she is?"

"Anna's. I don't know why you wasted your time putting them out. No one will be here to fill them."

"I talked it over with Enzio and Mrs. Gonzales. They have agreed to refill the feeders and come and check on you every day. It doesn't look like I can get someone in to take care of you for tonight."

Dorothy looked up, her eyes slitted, her brows flat out. "I told you, I do not want someone here. I don't want anyone here."

"Well, you have a choice. Either someone here or I'm sure Dr. Isaacs is going to insist on a nursing home or an assisted living facility." She didn't say she was going to visit several of the assisted living places in the afternoon. She'd hoped Allie would come with her, but once again her sister hadn't returned her phone call. "You cannot just stay here and let your life slip away."

"Allie will come."

"I hope so. But she said she cannot come every day or stay here nights." *And besides that, she was being a total snit.* Gillian ate her oatmeal and sipped from her coffee, leaning over to pick up the bedroom phone when she heard the kitchen ringer. She answered the greeting, and then held the handset out to her mother. "It's Dr. Isaacs."

She watched as her mother glared at first her, then the phone, and held it to her ear.

"No." Pause. "No." Pause. "I don't think so." Another glare and she handed the phone back to Gillian.

"She's not cooperating." Dr. Isaacs did not sound surprised.

"I guess you could say that." Gillian wished she'd opened the blinds all the way. "She ate a little last night and has her breakfast in front of her now, but she's still in bed."

"Did you try to locate a caregiver?"

"I called all the referrals, but no one can come today."

"No one is going to live here," her mother said.

"You heard that?" His chuckle said he did.

"Well, will she be here on Wednesday?"

"Yes, I've made arrangements for someone to bring her."

"Good. I'll talk with her then. Have you checked into any assisted living homes?"

"This afternoon, but I can't really see that happening." She hung up after he said good-bye and returned to her coffee, glancing over to see how much her mother had eaten. Never had she thought she would be here, literally forcing her mother to eat.

"I am not moving."

"Then you have to make the effort to get strong again."

"You just don't understand."

Gillian flinched at the whining tone. When had that started? If only Allie were here to answer these questions. Staring at her mother, she shook her head. "No, I guess I don't."

"I'm dying. I had a stroke and I'm dying."

"Have some more of that toast. You make the best peach jam. I found it in your freezer." *I will ignore the whining. I will ignore the dying. I will...* The doorbell ringing interrupted her affirmations.

"Who could that be?"

"Not Allie, she has a key." Gillian headed for the front door, recognizing the tall form through the taut lace curtains. She unlocked it and pulled it open. "Adam, how wonderful to see you. Come in." She stepped back for him to enter. *You have no idea how glad I am to see your friendly face.*

"Good Monday morning to you, too." He looked into her eyes and dropped his voice. "How bad is it?"

"You don't know me that well; I should be able to fool you."

His grin brought a warm feeling to her middle. "Your eyes give you away."

"You are too perceptive. I can hide a migraine from a boardroom full of clients when I have to."

"You aren't dealing with your mother then. Business is different."

She led him into the kitchen. "The coffee is fresh. We had peach freezer jam on toast. Would you like some?"

"Sounds good. How is our patient today?"

Our patient. She smiled back at him. "Which one, Mother or me?"

"There is a difference between patient and patience."

She poured his cup of coffee and plunked two slices into the toaster. While she'd never been a comfort food addict, that second piece of toast felt more like a necessity than a choice. "You on your way to work?"

"Yes, I thought of going in early, but I wanted to see you again before you left, so here I am."

"Thank you. You have no idea how grateful I was to hear that doorbell."

"Any news from New York?"

"My boss has cleaned out his office and will be heading

somewhere on a vacation with his wife by tomorrow afternoon, after he meets with me. I am hoping he has both more information for me and a possible job lead. When he returns, if he finds a position and can hire help, he will call me. In the meantime, I'll clean out my office tomorrow." *And then I start looking for another position.* The thought of no job made her stomach clench.

"Will that be a big job?"

"Four or five boxes I imagine." She buttered and spread jam on the toast and poured herself a fresh cup of coffee. "So, how does your day look?" Anything to change the subject. Taking a chair at the table, she sat down and they both took one of the halves of toast she'd cut.

"Normal. There will be a stack of stuff in my inbox, a pile of pink slips of calls to return, and hopefully all the staff will be there. I'm going to need a new clerk, one of my best and most dependable women is nearing her mandatory pregnancy leave. Finding good part-time help is difficult."

"Like finding someone to come in to take care of Mother for tonight. Pretty impossible."

"Does she need someone at night?"

Gillian shook her head. "I check on her before I go to bed and I sleep through the night. But I would hear her if she called for help."

"How about one of those alarm buttons I've seen many older people wearing around their necks? They seem like a wise choice for someone who wants to live alone."

"*Live* is the questionable word."

He huffed and shook his head. "This is so hard to understand, to accept. My mother fought like a tiger to live…"

"And my mother just wants to die." She pushed the plate of toast over to him. "I can't understand it, either. My mother has always been so strong. Demanding for sure, but she's the last person I would have expected to act like this."

"Is Allie coming over?"

Gillian shrugged. "Enzio will come and stay here while I check out retirement—or rather, assisted living facilities. He says he's going to keep on talking to Mother until she gets up to get away from him."

He glanced at his watch. "Sorry, but I'd better be heading out. What time do you leave for the airport?"

"Sevenish. Hopefully after the traffic."

"Can I have your cell number?"

"Sure." She picked up her purse and dug out a business card. "I should have given you this before. Not that I have a position there, but the cell number is accurate."

"Do you mind if I call you?"

She stared at him. "Not at all. I'd be delighted."

"Good." He put the card into his chest pocket and stood. "Dad and I'll be checking on Dorothy."

"I know. Thank you." She followed him to the door. He paused on the stoop.

"Come back soon."

From the look in his eyes, she realized he wasn't thinking about her taking care of her mother. This was personal. She watched him stride down the sidewalk and around the front of his SUV. *What would... Stop it, Gillian. You live in New York and he lives in Martinez, California, opposite ends of the country. And on top of that, he loves boating and monster dogs. And you love life in the big city. Don't you?*

Chapter Fourteen

She hadn't said when she'd be back. Or if she was coming back.

Adam closed the door on his thoughts and turned into the parking lot of the nursery in Pittsburg, upriver from Martinez. Never in his wildest dreams had he pictured himself running a nursery. But since it helped his dad, it was worth every minute. Besides, which, he enjoyed the business.

As he made his way to his office cramped between the cut flower and arrangement division and the designer pot displays, he greeted both employees and customers and kept a sharp watch to see if any plants needed watering or were looking wilted. Nothing cost them customer satisfaction more than neglecting the plants.

"Adam, when you have a minute, could we talk?" Suzanne, his soon-to-be-on-leave favored employee, asked as he went by.

"Sure, but after noon, okay?"

"No problem." She turned to the next customer, not happy about being confined to the cash register since she loved working outside helping customers choose the perfect plants.

He shut the office door behind him. He usually had an open door policy, but he needed a few minutes of quiet reflection. Now, if a certain New Yorker would just stay out of his mind, along with the sight of his father's weary eyes as he left in the truck for the other store. Adam and Gillian had a lot in common, dealing with an aging parent.

A miraculously short stack of pink slips disappeared in a few minutes with most being completed; only two messages left on answering machines. He flipped through the papers in his inbox, dealt with two, and left the remainder for later.

"Come along," he told John, one of his assistants, on the way out to the fall flowers. "You go get the forklift and I'll join you out by the deciduous trees."

"Another yard display?"

"That's right. I have the plan right here." Adam slapped the pocket of his short green apron, the first thing every employee donned as soon as they opened their locker. He'd planned out one display to show a fall garden, using the colorful foliage of both trees and shrubs against a background of solid evergreens in their large containers, along with various size pots of chrysanthemums, flowering cabbage, and other fall bloomers. Last June a man had come in and bought the entire summer-theme display. Although yard displays took up a lot of time, that extra effort did wonders for the bottom line.

The main delivery trucks arrived on Tuesdays and Fridays, so Adam could use the trees, shrubs, and flowers already in stock and fill in with the new plants when they arrived.

"I asked Ricky earlier to clear out some space near the front of the yard," he told John.

"I helped him; we're ready to go."

"I think we'll use a couple of those artificial rocks, too."

Within minutes he had the trees chosen and tagged with green tape, doing the same for the rocks. He decided the pond area needed sprucing up, too, so he jotted himself a note. Moving on to the shrubs and evergreens, he tagged them, too. What else did he have to put in the display that had been hanging around for a while? Nowadays garden art played a big part in yards, and they had a good selection of that, too.

As John brought in the trees, they set them in place and began filling in around them with the shrubs and smaller flowers. By the time lunch rolled around they'd finished, and already customers were commenting on their work. They surrounded other displays of plants with solid masses of chrysanthemums, including all colors and varieties. Where people usually might buy one or two gallon-size plants, now the shopping carts were leaving full to overflowing. Seeing a solid mass of color made buyers want the same. One plant wouldn't achieve good results.

"Did the pumpkins come in?" he asked.

"They did. Are you serious that we are going to carve them?" John tucked his leather gloves back over the ties of his apron.

"Carve and plant them. I saw a great idea in *Sunset* magazine. So if things slow down, set Carlos and JD to carving the tops out and cleaning out the seeds. When they have a few done, I'll show them what I want or I'll put on a demonstration for the customers."

"Okay." John took the forklift back behind the main building, and Adam went in search of Suzanne.

She joined him in his office as soon as a replacement could be found for checkout duty. "I have a problem," she said quickly.

"Okay, what's up?"

"The doctor says I need to get off my feet more, to ask for earlier leave. I hate to do this, Adam, but..."

"Consider it done." He glanced at his watch. "You're nearly finished for today, right?" At her nod, he continued. "Were you on the schedule for tomorrow?"

"I was supposed to open."

"I see." He pondered for a moment. "You just take care of that baby. We will deal with the rest."

"I hate to leave you in the lurch like this."

"I know. That's why I value you so highly. Prompt employees are getting fewer and harder to find. Keep us posted on how you are doing." He stood and came around the desk to shake her hand. "Don't look so sad. All will be well."

"That's what you always say."

"That's only because it is true. Payday is tomorrow. You want to come by for your check or shall I mail it?"

"My husband can pick it up after work, if that's all right."

"It will be at the front desk as usual." He watched her leave. Who could he depend on or train to take her position? John was already working full time. He went down his list of employees. Most had been there over a year and many for several years. His father believed in treating his employees well, like he did his plants. If only he took care of himself as well as he did his businesses.

By the end of the day Adam had called two other employees in and divided Suzanne's hours between them. "I know you wanted more flexibility, Sam, but right now I need extra help."

"We head south right after the New Year," the older man said. "We've been snowbirds for four years now and don't want to give that up."

"Just help me get through Christmas and you'll have my

blessing. You don't happen to know of any other seniors who might be interested in part time work?"

"I'll ask around."

"Thanks. Be here at seven thirty in the morning and John will walk you through the opening procedures. Openers and closers are on a higher pay scale, so you can expect a raise in your next check."

"Thanks, Adam." Aging brown eyes twinkled through Ben Franklin–style frames. "That new display looks real good. I think we already sold it."

"Great. Go ahead and fill the order with matching plants and we'll leave that display up. Might have to take out the rocks and garden art if they want those exact ones."

"They are talking delivery."

"Okay, get back to me with the particulars. Thanks for doing a great job. They buy it; you might want to take a couple of gallon-size chrysanthemums home to Hazel." Adam shook the man's hand and watched him return to the nursery. Now there was a man he'd like to have working full time. Staring at his desk calendar, he thought a few minutes. Maybe it was time to do a presentation or two. He jotted himself a note to call the senior center directors and set up speaking dates to present employment opportunities.

Dark had fallen by the time he left the nursery, but since he was going against the traffic, he turned onto Highway 4 in record time.

No lights were on in the living room at Dorothy's house and the rental car was gone. Should he go check on her? Most likely Gillian had just left, so he'd look in on her mother tomorrow evening. He slowed down, then eased on up to his own driveway.

His house was dark, and Thor met him at the door. Usually his father got home about five and would have let Thor out and started dinner. "Grandpa not here, fella?" He pulled the mail from the box beside the door and carried it into the kitchen to leave on the counter before opening the back door. Thor headed for his personal relieving space along the back fence like he'd been holding it all day. Where was his father?

Adam checked the answering machine; the light flashed but none of the messages were from his dad. Glancing at his watch, he knew the Martinez store was closed. He dialed his father's cell phone and heard it ring on the table in the entry where they routinely dropped keys and phones whenever they came home. Now what to do besides make sure his father had his cell with him every morning? Was it forgetfulness setting in or just being stubborn because Bill hated using the cell phone? He found his father's address book in the basket by the phone and flipped down to find Keith's, the assistant manager, cell phone number.

After the greeting, he said, "Say, you don't know where my dad is, do you?"

"He left a bit early. I don't think he was feeling very well."

"How early?"

"Oh, just after four, I think. I was busy with a customer and am not exactly sure."

"Did he mention any errands or anything?"

"No, not that I can remember. He didn't take his cell phone again?"

"Nope, and he's not here and not been here. Okay, thanks."

Adam punched the OFF key and went to the sliding door to stare out into the backyard. Would his dad have stopped at the grocery store? For three hours? Fear slithered up his spine. He let Thor back in, poured the kibble in the dog dish, and refilled the water bowl.

"There you go; glad someone in this family is happy." He grabbed a bottle of iced tea from the refrigerator, dashed off a note to leave on the counter, and headed back for his truck. He knew the route his father usually took home. Driving it would at least give him a feeling he was doing something useful.

He had been driving only a few minutes when he looked ahead to see the flashing lights of an emergency vehicle in the Safeway parking lot. Parked right behind a white truck. Could it be his father's? As soon as he could see the business emblem on the side door, his heart hit overdrive.

They were loading a stretcher into the back of the white emergency vehicle with red lettering.

Adam stopped behind them and bailed out of his truck. "That's my father."

"Oh, good. We tried to call his emergency number," the EMT said.

Adam nodded and stopped at his father's side. His eyes were closed and he wore an oxygen mask over his mouth and nose. "What happened?"

"We're not sure, but he was asleep in the truck and one of the shoppers stopped to check on him. When he didn't respond, she called 9-1-1. Does he have a history of heart problems?"

"Not that I know of."

"We're taking him from here to county, so you can follow us."

Adam took his father's hand, careful not to disturb the IV drip the EMTs already started. "Dad?"

His father blinked and slowly opened his eyes. "Sorry."

"They're taking you to county. Would you rather go to John Muir?"

"No." His eyes fluttered shut again.

"We're ready to roll, sir."

Adam stepped back and watched as the technicians slid the stretcher the rest of the way into the vehicle. He turned back to his SUV, grateful he'd not brought Thor along, although at the moment, comfort from his four-footed friend would have helped.

The admitting clerk insisted Adam fill out the paperwork before proceeding through the magic door to find his father. He gritted his teeth and filled in all the information he could readily recall. "I don't have his Medicare card but if you'd let me go see him, I could get it." He knew his voice sounded abrupt, but better that than leaping over the counter and scaring the woman half to death. She'd surely call some of those sheriff's deputies who guarded the penal patients to haul him out.

The woman took the clipboard back. "I understand. Just have a seat and I'll go see how things are going."

He'd learned during one of the emergency trips with his mother that time in the ER telescoped, each minute seeming like an hour. Back then he'd been supporting his dad. Now his dad was the patient. *Does he have a history of heart problems?* The question pounded through his mind. If he did, he'd never mentioned it to his son. His dad had been remarkably healthy all his life, even through the trauma of his wife's cancer and death two years earlier. But as they'd discussed on Sunday, he'd been more tired lately. Maybe it was more than just getting older as he'd said.

Why hadn't he forced his father to go to the doctor for a checkup sooner? Because force would have been what he'd had to use, and he couldn't see himself doing that. As if it would work. At least by waiting he'd had his father's cooperation. Too late but no fight. Big help.

He checked his watch. Three minutes had passed. *At the top of the hour I swear I'm busting down the door. Patience.* His years of military training kicked into gear. Stay calm. He was about to go seek information when the door opened and the clerk returned, coming over to stand by him.

"The doctor is working with your father right now and asks that you wait a few more minutes."

"Have they done an EKG?"

"They are doing that right now."

"Good. Thank you for telling me."

"When you get his medical card, will you be sure to bring it to me?"

"Of course." Why were hospitals so demanding regarding paperwork? Rhetorical question. He knew the answer. The insurance companies would not pay their bills if all the paperwork was not completed. Something like the government when he'd been in the navy. He ordered himself to relax, glanced at the television mounted high up in a corner, checked out the magazines, and pulled out his cell phone. He glanced up to see the woman behind the desk staring at him and shaking her head. Oops. Signs said NO CELL PHONES. He nodded and rose to take it outside. Grateful that his cell phone stored called numbers, he pulled up Keith's number and hit the green lit icon.

"I found my father," he said right after the hellos. "The EMTs were putting him into an ambulance in the Safeway parking lot. We're at county; they're checking his heart."

"What happened?"

"I'll tell you all the details later, but I'm going to need to get his truck home. Can you come and help me when I know more what's going on?"

"Yes, of course. But he's on the schedule for tomorrow."

"On the work schedule?"

"Yes, he said he'd take another employee's place since we are running short right now. So I wrote him in."

"Well, I hate to do this to you, but you'd better unwrite him. I'll call you as soon as I know anything." After hanging up, he tapped his chin with the cell phone. Should he call Jennifer or wait until he had more information? A thought caught him in the back of the knees and nearly dropped him to the ground. Who else was there? Only he and Jen were left of the immediate family. And the children, of course. His father was the last of the siblings on his side, and his mother's only sister lived in Florida. That left him to make all the decisions if his father became incapacitated. While he'd known this before, how could he not, there was more than one kind of knowing. This one was visceral and packed a punch he'd not been prepared for.

Who can I call? The pastor? Gillian? *Gillian, where had that come from?* He'd only known her since Friday.

Chapter Fifteen

She already had e-mail messages when she turned her phone back on after the airplane wheels touched the ground. The first one made her gasp.

Hi, Gillian. Miss you already. My dad is in the hospital, strange story, overnight at least, heart but not terrible. Just a shock. Didn't check on your mother last night due to all this. Light was not on in the living room is all I know. Sorry. Hope you had a good flight. Good meaning uneventful and on time. Adam.

She e-mailed him back as the plane taxied to the gate.

Dear Adam. Flight was just like you hoped. I even managed to doze off, which never happens to me on an airplane. Sorry to hear about your father. That must have been a terrible shock. Hope he is already feeling better. G.

She followed the herd to baggage and picked up her suitcases, a nice man loading them on a cart for her. She kept herself awake in the taxi from the airport to her building. Leaving her suitcases for the porter to bring up later, she unlocked her front door and, dropping things as she went, sat down on the edge of her bed and again checked her e-mail. With no reply from Adam, she typed in another message.

My flat seems so small and so empty. I watered my two house plants and thought of Mother's yard. Hoping there are boxes down in the basement here. I can't call the house yet, too early. Time zones are the pits. Any more news on your dad? G.O.

When the alarm went off at eight, she felt like she'd been dragged up from the bottom of the sea. Her eyes didn't want to focus as she stumbled into the bathroom and a shower. At nine she called Shannon's number and learned she was still working. Only the upper management had been let go so far. She didn't sound sure of anything, other than looking forward to seeing Gillian after her meeting with Scot. Once dressed in a corporate suit, black seemed appropriate for the day, Gillian changed purses, checked her briefcase to make sure her computer and all its accoutrements were there, and flipped open her cell phone again to find a message from Adam.

Update. Dad is looking much better, grumbling about being locked in or down. He's not, of course. Has more tests this a.m. I'm ready to leave for work. Short staffed. Hope your day goes well. Emptying an office is one of those things to just get done. Ran this morning. No lights and no cars at your mother's. Thor is worn out, or so he says. Adam.

Guilt wrapped slimy fingers around her throat. She should be there and not here. She tried reading the paper on the subway but found she couldn't concentrate. Rather than walking as she usually would, she caught a cab from the station to the restaurant where she was meeting Scot.

"Good morning," he said, rising to greet her with a hug. Caught by surprise, Gillian sat down where he indicated.

He didn't look good. Or was it just her imagination?

"So, how is your mother? How was your trip and how are you?"

"Mother still insists she is dying although I got her to eat and drink more than she had been. So I guess one could say the trip was a success, but I don't feel that way at all."

"You've had a rough weekend."

She nodded. "But it's not like it was a picnic here."

"No, it wasn't. This has been a shock to a great many people." After giving their food orders, Scot continued. "The new owners have let all the upper management go; the severance papers and packages are all arranged so this was well planned. The remainder of the staff will be either incorporated into their staff or let go. Production will continue as usual."

"I see. Did anyone have an inkling of this?"

"Not those I've spoken with. But the Fitches have been incommunicado."

Gillian poured cream in her coffee and stirred in sugar. Today she needed some body along with her caffeine. "So you're saying…?"

"I'm saying my office is cleaned out, Joyce booked our tickets, and we are on the way to the Mediterranean this evening. I will be gone a month. I suggest you do the same. Plan a month of R&R and meet me back here and we'll find someone who wants our expertise." He sat back for the waitress to place dishes of food on the table. "Thank you." He turned back to Gillian. "If that doesn't agree with you and you find something else, go with my blessing and the highest recommendation possible." He paused and stared into her eyes. "I do want to work with you again if at all possible."

"Thank you." Gillian swallowed. "I—ah..." She heaved a sigh and sniffed back tears that she adamantly refused to shed. "Thank you."

"So what will you do?"

She raised her chin a notch. "I'm going to eat my breakfast, clean out my office, and return to California for a month. Then we'll meet again. Just like you said." She surprised herself with the calm behind her words. As if she'd been planning her life just this way for the last year. He hugged her again once they were outside, then strode off down the avenue, slinging his jacket over his shoulder.

"God bless." She turned the other direction and entered the office building just as she had for twenty-plus years. At least she now had a plan.

* * *

Hi Adam, Took only four boxes. Brought it all back in a cab. Surely there should have been more after working there for twenty-five years. They even took my laptop because I had company information on it. Of course they had purchased it. Had to copy personal stuff to my flash drive. No answer at Mother's. Enzio must not be there yet. And they didn't find anyone else to help. Could throttle my sister. Going out to lunch with my former assistant. G.O.

She hit SEND and glanced at her watch. Talking on the phone would be more satisfying, but he would be at work and she hated to bother him. Besides, she had plenty to do to get ready to leave again for California. Paper and pen in hand, she sat down to make another of her lists. She started with the first one, call the airlines.

Halfway down her list, she checked her messages.

Picking Dad up around four. Says he's been poked and prodded enough. Will check on Dorothy. Have you called Allie? I'm surprised she's not there. If you were here, I'd take you out to dinner to celebrate your new life. The adventure is beginning. When you're done grieving the end of an era, you'll see that. Adam

She answered immediately.

I hope you are right. Why do I feel so out of place in NYC? This has been my home for over two decades. I love this city. Has grief addled my brain? I signed papers to say that I agree with their retirement package. Didn't even try to negotiate. Not like me. G.

She'd just hit SEND when another message showed up on her e-mail.

Enzio's car there when I went by so all is well on that front. No results yet on Dad's tests which made him testy. But that's normal. They are talking several different procedures based on the test results. He can't go back to work until later in the week. I think I'll live at the job. Home is not where the heart is at the moment. Oh, oh. Poor pun. Going to take Thor for a walk. Want to come? Adam

How delightful a walk sounded right now. If only he were in NYC they could walk in Central Park. Or wander the park down at the Battery. Or go window shopping on Fifth Avenue. She ignored the walking idea and added three more things to the bottom of her list, so she could feel like she was accomplishing something instead of playing on the e-mail.

> *That's good news. Thank you. I know if someone isn't there Mother will slip right back into former behavior. Talked with Enzio. He said she is grumpy. Now isn't that a surprise? I have an idea. More later. G.*

Gillian finished typing and tucked her cell phone into her purse. She glanced at her watch. Seven fifteen. What all did she need to pack? Or could she just close the door and walk away. Her list started with: empty the fridge. She'd take the food next door to Mrs. Hepplewhite and the house plants, too.

Her phone rang. She flipped it open and put it to her ear.

"You can't do that."

"And hello to you, too." Adam. Her heart kicked up a gear. Closing the front door, she set her purse on the floor and sank into her recliner. "Can't do what?"

"Say you have an idea and more later."

"But I did."

"I know you did." His voice softened. "So, now that I can talk rather than type, what's your idea?"

"I'm leaving New York."

"When?"

"Probably Thursday. I need to shut off some things and cancel others."

His chuckle made her heart skip a beat. Why was she feeling warmer all over? Could be that she was wearing a turtleneck sweater and jeans, warm clothes, but the day was blustery.

"You really are coming back?"

"I didn't say that."

"I know, I'm reading between the lines."

"I haven't made my reservations yet."

"Could you do the red-eye tomorrow? I'd pick you up."

"I'm going to need a car."

"Rent one out here; it's cheaper. How long are you staying?"

"I don't know for sure. At least until Mother gets back on her feet." *Now why did I not tell him I have one month to get that to happen?*

"Then what will you do?"

Should she tell him about the agreement with Scot? That was the crux of her mishmashed thinking right now. The most important thing was to return to Martinez and get her mother back in the real world. Then she would see.

"No dreams of what you would do when you retire?"

"I am too young to retire."

"Look on the bright side; you can have an entirely new career. That's what I did."

Gillian shook her head. "But I loved what I was doing and my company and living here and..."

"Did you never want a family?"

"Nope, not really. At least not enough to give up what I had to make it happen." She ignored an age old dream that popped up its head.

"No man in your life?"

"Off and on, but again, nothing that made me want to change my life."

"I see."

"My goal was to shatter that glass ceiling and be the first woman to make the top echelon of executives at Fitch, Fitch, and Folsom, and I did it."

"Really. How long ago?"

"Three years and nine months." *But obviously I couldn't*

hold on to it. The thought pressed her back into the recliner. She propped one elbow up on the arm of the chair and rubbed her forehead with her fingertips. What was she going to do now? "Look, I need to run. If you don't mind, I'll take you up on the offer of a ride. I'll e-mail you my itinerary as soon as it's set."

"Good. I'll see you then."

"Thanks. Bye." She clicked off the phone and rested her forehead against the slim metal case. All was working out well. So, why did she feel like crying? Actually more like bawling. Next step. Get something to eat. Go out or order in. She hit the button for the local deli, gave them her usual order, and hung up. One thing accomplished. Next? So many things depended upon if she was really moving away or just taking an extended leave.

No sense trying to call her mother and perversely, she didn't feel like calling Allie. Let her stew over Mother for a couple more days. *Come on, Gillian, she's had the responsibility for years. No, she hasn't. Mother has been on her own and doing just fine until a short time ago. Allie hasn't done more than take her mother to doctor appointments and lately do some shopping for her. Perhaps fixing food but I've not seen any indications of that.* Internal arguments were impossible to win.

The ringing of the outer door forced Gillian out of her chair to the panel by the entry hall, so she could punch the button to let the food delivery person enter the building. She stood by the open door, and when he arrived, she took the plastic bag of white boxes, paid and tipped him handsomely, and set the food on the table. This would be the last time she'd order from the Corner Deli. One more last time. The day had been full of last times. She glared at the packing boxes still sitting in her living room, blinking back the heat in her eyes and sniffing back the drainage in her nose. She rolled her eyes up to stare at the ceiling; someone had once told her that was a way to keep from crying.

Her cell phone chimed. Checking the screen, she saw a number she didn't recognize, but the area code matched her mother's.

"Good evening, my dear." The warm rich voice answered her hello.

"Enzio." She pulled a tissue out of the box by her chair and dabbed at her nose. "Thank you for calling. How are things there?"

"First of all, are you all right?"

"Of course, why?"

"You sound like you might be catching a cold."

She knew even her chuckle sounded weepy. "No, it's called fighting off the tears." Might as well be honest with him, he'd probably figure it out himself.

"Ah, I was afraid of that. Crying isn't a bad thing you know."

"Easy for you to say." *Now, Gillian, that wasn't very nice.* Her mother might be in bed in her room in California, but she still managed to sit on her daughter's right shoulder and monitor her manners.

"Hard day?"

"Yes. But I've made it through and I've made some decisions."

"Good for you." His voice alone could make one feel better. How could her mother ignore him like she did? "So, how did things go with Mother today?"

"I don't think she is very happy with me."

Gillian couldn't stop the chuckle. "That makes two of us. What did you do?"

"Spent most of the day with her, like I said I would. She

said it is hard to sleep knowing there is someone sitting staring at her." His chuckle brought forth one of Gillian's.

"Could you get her to eat and drink?"

"Somewhat. Not a lot at a time, but three meals. Allie was not able to find someone to spend the night, so Dorothy is on her own again until morning when I will be picking her up for her doctor's appointment. She still says she is not going. I am bringing a mutual friend of ours from the senior center to help your mother dress. I don't think she would really want to go in her robe and slippers. Although I threatened as much."

"Thank you, Enzio, I don't know how we'll ever be able to repay you."

"Repay? I don't think so. This is what friends are for."

Gillian set her phone to speaker and took it over to the table. All of a sudden she was ravenous so this way she could eat and talk at the same time. She retrieved a fork from the kitchen drawer and sat down. "Have you seen or heard from Allie?"

"Not directly, but she got a call through to your mother to say there were no helpers available. Dorothy said she'd told her to not worry, she didn't need any help."

"And Allie took that as a good excuse to not even come by?"

"I guess so."

She could hear some doubt in his voice. What was Allie's problem? Did she not care? No, that wasn't it. "Guess Allie and I need to have some heart-to-heart discussions."

"So, when are you coming back?"

"Tomorrow night on the red-eye if I can get a flight. Usually there's room on those planes."

"Do you want me to come pick you up?"

"You are such a sweetheart. But no thank you. I would have rented a car, but Adam offered to come get me."

"Oh, he did, did he?"

She ignored the knowing quality of Enzio's voice. "If you have e-mail, I'll send you my itinerary as soon as I know it."

He gave her his e-mail address and continued. "How long are you staying?"

"I'm not sure, but I'll close up here and then decide what to do some other time. Getting Mother back on her feet is my first priority."

"Mine, too. I'll let you get back to what you need to do. I'm glad to hear this, Gillian. I'll see you on Thursday."

"Call me after you've been to see Dr. Isaacs, would you please?"

"I will. Good night."

She snapped her cell shut and heaved a sigh, this one of relief. Mother was provided for. Gillian finished her dinner and put the leftovers in the refrigerator for lunch the next day. Amazing how things were falling into place. For a woman known as a detailed planner, she sure was making rapid-fire decisions. Maybe this really was the way she was supposed to be going.

"Ladies and gentlemen, we should be at the gate in twenty minutes. Thank you for choosing..."

She removed the ear buds and shut off the player, stuffing it all back in the case she kept on her lap, dozing until she felt the familiar thump of wheels on the tarmac.

On the ground and even on time. Adam would be waiting. It had been a long time since anyone had offered to meet her at an airport. Her back ached a bit, but then she'd flown business class since she was flying on her dime now and didn't want to use so many miles credits for first class. Especially since she might not be traveling for business as much anymore. If at all. If she ever had a job again, or even a business of her own. That thought had entered her mind somewhere over the Midwest. What kind of business might she be interested in starting?

The seat belt sign flashed off and the lights on. People stood immediately to retrieve luggage from the overhead. For a change she didn't have a briefcase along, just her travel purse and an overnighter in the overhead. The two big suitcases in the luggage compartment trashed her rule about always traveling light.

She followed the lines and signs to the baggage area and waited for the luggage to arrive.

"May I help you, ma'am?"

She knew the voice immediately and turned with a smile. "Adam." What was there about even his voice that made her heart flip?

He grinned at her. "At your service. How many bags?"

"Two, very big ones. The cases are black and I have a bright green strap around each one."

"How was your trip?"

"The entire thing or just the flight?" Gillian shook her head, not coming up with a good comment. "I'm glad it is over." Watching the bags coming off the line, she pointed. "That one is mine."

Adam excused himself and wedged between two other people to lift the bag off the conveyor. He pulled out the handle and handed it to Gillian. "Your other one is coming right up."

Setting the second one down, he smiled. "You must be living right to get both bags near the beginning." Taking the two handles, he nodded. "This way."

When they reached the SUV in the short-term parking lot, Gillian figured they'd walked a mile already. For a change, she'd packed the stilettos and worn walking shoes with her jeans and camel silk and wool–tailored jacket. As she'd expected, the air outside the terminal was chilly.

"I saw your mother today. Enzio was just leaving. Mrs. Gonzales had been over earlier, so I'd say she was well watched over."

"How did she seem?"

"I don't know. She was sleeping. Enzio said the trip to the doctor's really took a lot out of her."

"I'm not surprised when the only walking she's done is to the bathroom and back to bed. Even with a wheelchair the trip would be wearing. What do you know about your father's tests?"

"Not much. Tomorrow we get the results." He stopped at the black SUV and clicked the key. The rear door rose and he swung the three bags inside. "Are you hungry, thirsty?"

She shook her head. "Just tired. Does Mother know I'm coming? I called and left a message for Allie."

He slammed the door down and led the way to the passenger seat, opening the door for her. "She really has the ringer off on the phone in her room?"

"Yes, crazy isn't it?" She climbed inside and turned to catch a smile. What a nice man. Nice wasn't the best word, but right now she was too tired to come up with a better one. Dawn would already be pinking the sky in New York, but in California it was still dark.

"One good thing about this time of the morning is the lack of traffic," Adam said as he paid the parking fees and pulled onto the entrance ramp for 101 heading north to the Bay Bridge.

"There's no fog."

"I know, October is one of the best months in San Francisco, but then you must remember that."

"We didn't go to San Francisco a lot when I lived here. When we did, it was a real treat." She caught a yawn with her hand and stretched her shoulders and upper back. "Sorry."

"You're welcome to kick that seat back and take a nap, if you want."

"No, thanks, then I might be wide awake when I get there."

"At least you won't have to break in this time."

"True." *But what I have waiting for me is nothing short of daunting.* The thought she'd managed to subdue in the last couple of days assaulted her again. What if she couldn't get her mother back on her feet after all?

Chapter Sixteen

Even a suitcase banging against the door frame didn't wake Dorothy.

After checking on her mother, Gillian walked Adam back to the front door, trapping another yawn on the way. These yawns were coming so fast she could barely talk between. "Thank you. I am so glad I didn't have to drive." Yawn. "I probably would have been forced to go to a hotel and come out here this morning."

"Don't be in a hurry to get up. You earned sleeping in."

"But what about you?"

"Don't worry. I'll be asleep before my head hits the pillow. I can get by on a couple of hours. Night."

"Night." She watched him walk out to the truck; then she shut off the front light. She broke two of her life rules by not bothering to remove her makeup or brush her teeth before going to bed. It didn't stop her from falling asleep right away.

A ringing phone finally returned her to consciousness. Sort of. She reached for her phone on the bedside stand, realized she wasn't in her condo, and leaped out of bed. They'd hung up by the time she reached the kitchen. Was that a click she heard on the line?

"Who's there?"

Amazing, the phone had awakened her mother. "Mother, it's me, Gillian." She walked back to her mother's room, only to find her sitting up, eyes staring in fright.

"Gillian. When did you come?"

"Sometime in the wee hours of the morning. Thought sure my banging the suitcases would wake you." She stretched and yawned again.

"I—I didn't know you were coming."

"If you'd let the phone ring in here, you would have known. I tried calling three times. Today I am either buying an answering machine or adding it to your phone service."

"I don't need those things."

"Maybe you don't, but I do."

"How come you came back?"

"Well, it's a long story. How about I make us some coffee and I'll tell you?"

"You scared me half to death."

Gillian could see from the round eyes that she really had frightened her mother. "Sorry," was cut off by another yawn. Gillian ambled into the kitchen and set the coffee to perking. Some time today she was dragging out the coffeemaker, too. If she was going to live here, she would make things work for herself. The hummingbird sat on the feeder, and right before Gillian's eyes, a male hummer with a brilliant purple/pink bib on his throat hovered above her.

"Ah, so there's been something going on here, eh? He sure is handsome. Were I a hummingbird, I'd go for him." *So, are hummingbirds monogamous? Surely there is a book on Mother's shelves that will tell me more about hummingbirds—well, birds in general.* She stepped out the door to see a flock of small birds splashing in the birdbath, drinking from the edge, or sitting on the canes of the roses, preening their feathers. Bath time in the backyard. Let's see, she'd made her mother take a shower last Saturday and this was now Thursday. Time to go through that hassle again. Was that tiny spears of green grass she saw poking through the dead cover?

Wide awake now, Gillian felt lighter than she'd felt a week ago before they turned down her proposal at the good old Triple F's corporation that no longer existed. At least she was doing more than just existing. She stretched her arms straight in the air and then dropped forward to wrap her hands around her ankles and stretch her hamstrings and all the muscles way up to her neck. The hummer feeder was still more than half full. Someone must have filled it while she was gone, or there just weren't a lot of the little birds around. The seed feeder, however, was nearly empty.

She drew in a deep and cleansing breath, let it out, and returned to the kitchen. Lots to do today, and the first item was to find out what had happened at the doctor's office. Or perhaps it would be wiser to unpack first so she wouldn't have to iron all her clothes. After brushing her teeth and slipping into a pair of light sweats, she carried two mugs of coffee into Dorothy's bedroom.

Low and behold, the bed was empty. Gillian quickly drew back the drapes, pulled the blinds so the slats were flat open, and raised them. No coverings over the windows. Ah, joy. The sun poured in, as much as possible with the overhang of the roof. But still light, blessed light. And the two hummingbirds had moved to this feeder.

She heard the toilet flush and the water run, and then her mother opened the bathroom door. "Oh, close those; it is too bright in here." Her mother shielded her eyes with her forearm. "Gillian, I can't see."

"Just stand there a moment and let your eyes adjust. You'll be fine. Has Allie been here since I left?"

"No, but I talked to her on the phone." She shook her head. "That Enzio, he wouldn't go home."

"Oh, really. Good thing someone was here for you."

"Oh, I am so tired. Yesterday was just awful." She sat back down on the side of her bed. "Just terrible."

"If you want to drink your coffee in the kitchen..."

"No! I don't want coffee. I don't want anything. I just want to be left alone." She swung her feet up on the bed with no difficulty as far as Gillian could see, and started to lie down.

"No, let's fix your pillows. We need to talk."

"Later."

"Nope, now. It's nearly ten and I have things I have to do today."

"Like what? You just got here." Dorothy muttered as Gillian fluffed the pillows and waited for her to scoot back. Gillian took her arm and helped her when she started to slump too soon.

"There now. Here's your coffee."

"Drink coffee, I just have to get up to pee." But she took a sip, holding the mug with both hands.

"Okay, what did Dr. Isaacs say?"

Dorothy shook her head, almost more like a shudder. "That man."

Obviously her mother didn't like what he'd had to say. The thought almost made her smile. "Well?"

"He said I'm healthy as a horse and to get out of bed and back to living." The words came out in a grumbled, angry rush. "He just doesn't understand."

"Understand what?" Gillian leaned forward, elbows on her knees, coffee mug between both hands, and stared at her mother over the rim of the cup.

"I'm dying, that's what."

"Far as that goes, Mother, we are all dying. And none of us knows the day nor the hour." Where had that come from? Sounded an awful lot like a Bible verse she'd memorized oh so many years ago. What was going on? Coming back to this house, she found herself praying more than she had for years. Sure, she prayed in church, when she attended, but this was uncanny. Knowing she needed to ponder on this strange behavior, she turned her focus back to her mother.

"You didn't have a stroke." The whine was back.

"No, I didn't. Tell me what it was like."

"No. I'm exhausted." Dorothy held out her half full cup. "And if Enzio comes, tell him I am—I am...oh, I don't know. All of you, just leave me be." She slid down and pulled the covers over her head.

"I'll be back with breakfast, or rather brunch, after I shower and get ready for the day. What would you like?"

"Nothing."

"Sorry, that's not on the menu."

"Go away."

"Then you'll just have to eat whatever I bring you. There's a male hummingbird outside your window. He sure is beautiful." Gillian waited a moment in hopes of a reply, but when it didn't come, she left and went to her room to unpack. Sliding open the closet doors, she groaned. There was maybe two feet of space to hang her things. Though it had been fine before, it wouldn't work now. She checked the drawers. The top one was the only empty one. She checked the closet in the other, smaller room. Full. Dresser, full. Her mother's sewing machine sat against one wall, protected by a quilted cover. The chest of drawers next to that held sewing supplies.

Okay, she'd have to clear out enough space in her room

to hang her things, but where would she find clothes hangers? Back to her mother's room to check the closet. There were a few empty hangers, but not enough. That would be at the top of her list to find. Opening the closet door in her room, she hauled the coffeemaker box out to the kitchen, three other boxes into the sewing room to set in the middle of the floor, and a tall plastic container of wrapping paper beside the boxes. She'd sort later. Although crammed in, the hangers she had held the clothes from one suitcase. Her underwear went in the drawer and her shoes on the floor. One suitcase could go out to the garage. When she came back in, she peeked into her mother's room. Dorothy was sound asleep; gentle snores attested to that.

What sounded good for breakfast? She glanced at the clock. The day was flying by and she couldn't figure out how to catch it, or at least slow it down. Out of the shower, dressed, makeup applied, and ready for the day, Gillian returned to the kitchen. She set a pad of paper and a pen on the counter to start a shopping list. Hangers, a plastic crate, answering machine. She erased the last item and added a note to check with the phone company. Both hummingbirds sat on the feeder in front of the window. Other than the roses, there was nothing else for them to feed on.

Setting the oatmeal to boil, she brought out the tray and set two places, one for her mother and the other for herself. Outside again, she checked the roses. No buds left, so she cut a full-blown creamy blossom with brilliant pink edges to put in the bud vase. With an unfolded napkin as a miniature tablecloth, the tray looked very nice, if she did say so herself.

The ringing of the phone made her stop stirring the raisins into the oatmeal. "Hello."

"Oh, pardon me, I must have the wrong number."

"No, you don't have the wrong number, Allie."

"Gillian?"

"Was the last time I checked."

"You don't have to be sarcastic. When did you get back? Why didn't you tell me you were coming? How long are you staying?"

"Have you checked your messages?" At that moment, Gillian wished she had told her sister about the company takeover. But she hadn't so now she'd have to deal with more questions than she wanted to. "Look, I have breakfast about ready for Mother. Where are you?"

"Just turning on to Morello."

"All right, I'll tell you the whole story when you get here. Are you drinking coffee?"

"No."

"Okay, then I won't make more. See you in a few." She hung up the phone, dished up the oatmeal, and carried the tray into the bedroom. Top priority had just become to get her mother out in the kitchen to eat. Clicking into cheery, she set the tray on the dresser. "Breakfast is served, madam." While the French accent sounded cheesy, she would give anything to make her mother smile, let alone laugh. How long since Dorothy had laughed?

"Go away."

"Nope. Come on, our food is getting cold." She pulled back the covers and reached for the opposite pillow. "I am here to help you." Stroking her mother's bare arm, she cringed inside at how thin it had become. "Come on, Mother. Let's get you sitting up."

Dorothy huffed, but she sat up and pushed herself back against the pillows. "Anything to get you…"

Gillian's mind finished the old saw. "…off my back." *Mother, you've not seen anything yet.* She set the tray on her mother's lap and picked up her own bowl and utensils before sitting on the chair. "There wasn't any bread or I would have made toast."

Dorothy picked up her spoon. "Is there brown sugar on this?"

"Yes, it melted in." Gillian ate a few spoonfuls. "What kind of rose is that?"

"A very poor specimen of Double Delight."

"It smells wonderful. Let's leave it in here so your room smells good." She heard a key in the front door. "Allie is here."

Dorothy closed her eyes and shook her head. But at least she kept eating, slow as she was.

"I'll tell you, hearing your voice on the phone gave me a shock." Allie neglected to even say hello.

"Sorry, it's a long story."

"Hello, Mother." Allie came around the bed to halfway hug her mother. "I see you are eating. How wonderful." She kissed the top of her mother's head and turned to Gillian. "Okay, what gives?"

"First of all, I lost my job."

"Why didn't you say anything?"

"I never had much of a chance, and I was reeling from it myself." She glanced at her mother, who was staring at her.

"So why did you go back to New York?"

"I had to empty my office and sign some papers, plus a meeting with Scot, my former boss. I finished that on Wednesday morning, but all I could think of was Mother here by herself."

"You did not need to come back for me," Dorothy grumbled.

"You're right, Mother, I did not need to, I wanted to."

"So." Allie stretched the word into three syllables.

"So, I did what I had to do, closed up my condo and caught the last flight last night." Gillian finished her oatmeal and wiped her mouth with her napkin, outwardly trying to look as calm as if it had been a normal day.

"How did you get here?"

"Adam met me at the baggage claim area and brought me here. We thought sure our banging around with the luggage would wake Mother, but it didn't."

"I didn't know until the phone rang and rang." Dorothy took a sip of coffee and made a face.

"That was me. I figured you would call me back like we usually do if you heard the phone ring," Allie added.

"I heard a voice say hello. Scared me half to death. Someone was in my house."

Gillian rolled her lips together to keep from smiling. Those were the most words she'd heard her mother utter at the same time since she'd come back to Martinez last Friday.

"So now what?" Allie sat down near the foot of the bed.

"So now I'm not sure." Gillian caught her mother's glance and picked up the tray, setting it in its usual place by the door. *Do I tell them about the month I have or not?* "I just knew that I had a job to do here and the sooner I could get back, the sooner we'd get Mother back on her feet."

Dorothy shook her head slowly from side to side. "But what if I don't want to get back on my feet?"

Gillian shrugged. *Please, God, let me be the winner in this battle.*

Chapter Seventeen

But why didn't you tell me you were coming?"

"I left you a message on your phone. Have you checked lately?"

Allie sputtered, then had the grace to look sorry. The two sisters had moved to the kitchen after their mother had ordered them out of her bedroom. Gillian dumped the coffee grounds in the trash under the sink.

"Mother saves those for the compost pile or to spread under her roses."

"Really." Gillian looked in the bag to see coffee grounds scattered all over the trash. "Then I will next time. Thanks." She refilled the basket and set the percolator on the burner. "This isn't bad coffee, you know."

"Actually I prefer flavored coffees, but I drink this when I am here. Or tea. There's herbal and black teas above the stove."

Gillian sat down at the other end of the table so she could watch her sister more easily. "Back to your question. I tried to tell you about my job when I was here, but, Allie, you were so rarely here there was no time." Might as well lay it out on the line. "And then you never returned my calls. So I just had to go ahead and do what I could."

Allie stared down at her hands. "You could at least have told Mother."

"I could have, but when I left here, I wasn't sure when or if I was coming back. Had the new owners offered me a job, I would probably have taken it." She snorted gently, more like a huff. Shaking her head, she nibbled on the inside of her cheek. "I'm neither old enough nor ready to retire."

"So what are you going to do?"

"Like I said before, I really don't know. And I haven't had a lot of time to give it much thought." *And if I start thinking on it, I want to either sob or run screaming.* "I had my life all planned out."

"Well, at least you've had a life."

Gillian stared at her baby sister. "What do you mean? I thought you loved your life."

"Nothing." Allie pasted a smile on her face that didn't quite reach her eyes. "Just a smart remark. I do love my life, my husband, my children." She glanced at her watch. "I can't stay too long, I..."

"Allie, what are you running from?"

"What do you mean? I'm here for ten minutes and you are already criticizing me?"

Had Gillian been standing she would have taken a step back, or two. Where had that come from? She raised her hands, palm out in the surrender salute. "I give. Let's talk about Mother and what has to be done here." She watched Allie's shoulders slump and her eyes lower to return to staring at her hands. Think on this later, Gillian told herself. That is the same thing Mother does. "Did anyone tell you what went on at the doctor's?"

"Mother just muttered when I talked to her yesterday. Said she was too tired to talk."

"Well, when I asked her this morning, she said he said she

was healthy as a horse and then ordered her to get out of that bed and get back to living or something along those lines. I'm expecting Enzio to call any time, but he wouldn't have gone into the examining room to see the doctor with her. He was just the transportation. Have you talked with him?"

"No. I think the coffee is ready." Allie got up to pour. "Sugar or cream?"

"No thanks, black is fine." Gillian watched her sister as she added sweetener to her own and brought both mugs to the table. Something was bothering Allie, but at this point she had no intentions of talking about it. The signs were the same as when they were younger. But Miss Perfect Allie shouldn't be bothered by anything really important. She had everything she wanted. "Thanks." Gillian stared at her mug. "Any suggestions on how to get Mother out of bed?"

"You really believe she is not sick, not really dying?"

"That's what I think, but until I talk with Dr. Isaacs, how would I really know? I know she can eat and feed herself. She can walk to the bathroom and back to bed. Once she has more nourishment, she should get stronger. Enzio spent the last two days with her just to make sure she was all right physically." Gillian heaved a sigh. "But she still thinks she wants to die. All because she had a small stroke. There must be something else going on here; we just have to figure out what it is."

"What if I look up TIAs on the med-line and print out what they say? Perhaps reading about it would help. Or if we read it to her."

"Good idea, anything is better than watching her get weaker and weaker. Mother has always been such a strong woman that this just does not make sense."

"I'll do that this evening. Do you have your computer here?"

"Nope, the buyout company wanted it back and I've not purchased a new one yet. That's another thing on my to-do list. In the meantime, I get e-mails and such on my cell."

"Then I'll bring the information by tomorrow. What else?"

"I'll put in a call to Dr. Isaacs. He'll probably return it after seeing patients. I would have assumed he would order more tests, but mother didn't mention that. If he wrote a prescription it would be in her purse, right?" The thought of going through her mother's purse or any of her private things made Gillian cringe. Nobody looked in her mother's purse.

"I'll check." Allie got up and went to the bedroom, returning with a black leather handbag that had seen better days. She sat down and began rummaging, then looked up, shaking her head. "Nothing."

"Well, is that good or bad?"

"Good. He must have checked heart, lungs, blood pressure, eyes, ears, and so on. Did you ask if he ordered blood drawn for a blood panel?"

"No. Didn't think of it." Since when did her little sister talk as if she knew a lot about medical things? She'd always shuddered at the sight of blood and always said she knew nothing about medical procedures. Come to think of it, she'd acted dumb about medical things when Gillian had been there last week. Something strange was going on. "But I will."

"I'll ask her. I'm going to wake her before I leave so she knows I was here. Sometimes when I've come to visit, she doesn't remember."

"Often?"

"No, just recently. That's why I called you. Sometimes I couldn't wake her up all the way."

Gillian started to ask why she didn't call the paramedics but knew that would sound like an accusation. Besides she remembered Allie saying Mother would refuse to go, and the EMTs wouldn't force her.

Allie returned the purse to the bedroom and tried to wake her mother. "Mother, I'm here and we need to talk. Mother." The tone changed slightly from sweet to demanding. "Mother."

"You have to shake her shoulder." Gillian raised her voice to be heard down the hall.

"Mother, you need to wake up now." The enunciation was sharper and Allie had slipped into her scolding-the-children voice. "I'm sorry, but I can't stay long." The sweet tone returned, so obviously she'd managed to wake their mother.

Gillian debated going back to the bedroom or outside where the sun shone warm and the birds sang. How could her mother stand to stay in that dark room? What would happen if she took down the drapes and the blinds? Said they had to be cleaned and just didn't get around to putting them back up. She added to her list: *Buy basket of flowers to hang outside Mother's window.* Perhaps the hummingbirds would appreciate that, too. After all, now she was going to be here to water things.

"Gillian?"

She headed for the bedroom on command, stopping in the doorway. "What?"

While Dorothy was still lying down, she at least looked alert. "When did you come?"

"About three a.m. You didn't stir."

"Why did you not let me know you were coming?"

"I told you. I called three times but you never answered. That's why we're getting an answering machine or service. Who do you have for your server?"

"She means who do you pay your telephone bill to?" Allie spoke gently.

Thinking she needed interpretation zinged Gillian, but she ignored it. Anything to communicate.

"AT&T. I've always been with them."

Gillian came around and sat on the foot of the bed. "Where do you keep a copy of the bill?"

"What are you going to do?" Dorothy's voice quavered.

"Look, if I am going to be here a while, an answering service is important. If you don't want to pay for it, I will. It can't be more than five dollars a month. If you don't like it, we'll take it off when I leave."

"You're not leaving now, are you?"

"No, Mother, I can be here as long as you need me." *And by then I have to have figured out what will happen next. Unless Scot comes through like he said.*

"What about your job?"

At last, interest in something besides sleeping. "My company was bought out and they let all the management personnel go. The takeover was last Friday. I went back, did all the things required, closed up my condo, and here I am." *You're stuck with me.*

"But you have worked there all your working life."

"I know." *And I planned to retire from there at age fifty-two with a sound pension, sufficient investments, and a plan for the rest of my life. Not rich but indeed comfortable. Now here we are, six years early with a buyout but no job.*

"Why didn't you tell me?"

"I was in a state of shock. I saw the news on the ticker tape that runs along the bottom of the screen on news shows. First I'd heard of it."

"Oh, Gillian, that's terrible." Allie leaned forward. "I am so sorry."

"Thanks, there is no turning back for sure." She looked at her mother. "So if you want me to stay here, I will. If you want me to move, I can do that, too. But not until you are up and running."

"Of course you can stay here." Mother looked one shade south of indignant.

But do you want me to stay here? Can and want are two different things. I'm not a deadbeat crawling home because I have nowhere else to go. She felt like pounding the walls, perhaps going out to weed in the yard would be a good thing. "Thanks." Gillian glanced at Allie, who was rolling her eyes. How about that, Allie did understand.

"Besides, once I am gone the house will belong to the two of you anyway."

Definitely, it was time to weed or go shopping or…

Interesting how her mother ignored her comment about being there as long as she was needed. When the doorbell rang, Gillian headed to the front door. "I'll get it." Who would be here now?

"Hello, Enzio, how good to see you." She pushed open the screen door. "Come on in."

"I see Allie is here, too. I can come back later if you like."

"No, you know now is the best time. I was just telling my gruesome employment story."

He set a white cardboard box on the table. "I just brought us all a little treat."

"If you say napoleons…"

"No, I brought cannoli this time. I wasn't sure if you've had that before."

"Pardon me while I wipe away my drool."

"They are delicious. Is your mother awake?"

"Yes, come on in. I just told her my news. The coffee is hot to have with our treats."

Gillian kept one ear tuned to the bedroom. The greetings seemed to go fine. Mother was not screaming "Out! Out!" After a bit she ambled back there. Mother was now sitting upright and Enzio sitting on the edge of the bed. She left to bring in a couple of folding chairs. They still hadn't talked about the appointment with the doctor, and Gillian still hadn't called his office. After dialing his number and leaving a message with the receptionist, she brought the extra chairs into the bedroom.

"I could have done that." Enzio jumped up and finished carrying one around to sit beside Allie.

Although Dorothy didn't take part in the conversation, at least she stayed awake and seemed more alert. A bit later Gillian and Allie brought in two trays with coffee mugs, plates and forks, and the delectable cannoli. When everyone had theirs, Gillian took her first bite and closed her eyes in bliss. Talk about melting on the tongue.

"As good as the napoleons?" Enzio asked.

"Do I have to make a decision?"

"When did you have napoleons?" Allie asked.

"Friday or Saturday."

"We need an Italian bakery in San Ramon."

Gillian glanced at their mother, who had eaten at least one bite and now had powdered sugar on her face. That was good. She watched as Dorothy reached for the coffee mug on the nightstand. Another good harbinger.

"So, are you ready to go get the rental car?" Enzio asked.

"Any time." Gillian ate the last bite and mopped her mouth. "That was so good, thank you."

"Why are you renting a car?" Mother asked.

"Because I need transportation."

"What is wrong with my car?"

"I don't know. Nothing, I imagine." Gillian had seen the

car in the garage. Her mother had always kept everything up to perfection. "You want me to drive your car?" She stared from her mother to her sister. Mother never let anyone drive her car. Allie shrugged. Dorothy nodded. Enzio winked. "But what if I dent it or something?"

"I have insurance."

"Ah, well, thank you. I need to do some shopping this afternoon."

"The keys are hanging on the board in the kitchen."

They were actually having a conversation. Some real give-and-take.

"I need to go," Allie said as she stood. "I'll be back in a day or so." She leaned over and kissed her mother's cheek. "Thanks for the treat, Enzio. Good to see you."

"Then I am not needed as a chauffeur this afternoon. Dorothy, I guess you are stuck with me for a while." He waved Allie off and moved over to take her chair and sit closer to the bed.

Gillian followed Allie to the door. "We still haven't made any decisions."

"Well, it appears to me that Mother is doing much better and you don't need me here. I'll call you later." With that she headed out to her car, leaving Gillian to stare after her.

There it was again, that underhanded bit of sarcasm. What was going on with her sister that was causing her to act like this? Gillian shut the front door to keep the breeze from cooling the house too much. Just think, October and the doors could be open. Yes, there were cheery fall days in New York, but certainly not like this.

She stopped by the bathroom to check on her makeup and hair, changed her shoes, and grabbed her purse before poking her head in the bedroom door. "I'll get as much done as fast as possible. How long can you stay, Enzio?"

"Oh, three hours or so?"

"He does not have to stay to watch me sleep," Dorothy grumbled.

Gillian tucked her grin back inside. "Is there a garage door opener in the car?"

"Yes, of course." A glare accompanied the comment.

Gillian started to say she could get her own car, but decided against it. She would eventually have to buy a car, if she stayed in California, but using her mother's avoided that necessity for a time. Come to think of it, she'd never bought a car in her life. One did not need an automobile in New York City. She kept a driver's license only to rent a car when she traveled. "Bye."

She put the car in reverse, backed out of the garage and down the short driveway. The Buick was definitely not a sports car. So many changes in her life in such a short period of time. When was she going to spend time thinking out her own future? A plan was necessary. But planning in the unknown was far different from planning with a secure job with a future. Or waiting for Scot to find something. So many *ifs*. Maybe that was why she was feeling like she was walking down a rocky path blindfolded.

Chapter Eighteen

Adam gave his father strict instructions to do nothing.

"Do you mind if I sit in my recliner and watch television?"

"Dad, you know what I mean. The doctor said to take it easy for a couple of days."

"He didn't say my life was supposed to screech to a halt." Bill tossed his son a half grin.

"You can let Thor out, fix yourself some lunch, or read a book, but not go out to your babies. They can get along without you for another day. I checked on them. Oh, and you can talk on the phone. Please call Jennifer, or she will strangle me."

"I hardly think so." Bill made shooing motions with his hands. "I'll be fine."

Adam hoped Gillian was still asleep as he drove by her house. If only she had met his father so she could go up and check on him. Strange, that they needed each other to check on the other's parent. Three hours' sleep had not been enough. He should have gotten up a bit earlier to run, to force the blood to get moving in his veins and arteries.

Instead he felt like a slug—the slimy crawl-on-the-ground variety, not the bullet kind.

"Lord, I know You are taking care of my dad, forgive me for trying to do Your job, but You're going to have to talk mighty loud to get him to listen right now." Adam took the shoreline road to stay off clogged Highway 4. Sometimes going east on the freeway was easy, other times it bottled up. That was why he usually left for work earlier. With the SUV windows down, he could smell the marshes along the river, tasting the tangy bite of fall. White pelicans floated on one inlet, egrets and herons patrolled the shallows while ducks grazed the bottom, tail feathers in the air. The drive to the Pittsburg nursery was always a chance to see more of the water-bird kingdom; the way home a time to unwind and observe nature again. Coots paddled the ponds along with a goodly variety of ducks and some geese, mostly Canada geese. With blue sky and a good breeze this would be an ideal day to be out on the water. Especially with Gillian. If he could talk her into sailing with him.

The nursery gates and doors were already open when he arrived, the way they should be. John was still working with his new opening man. Adam waved at them both and went directly to his office. He immediately called his father. When the phone rang four times, he almost headed back to his truck, but his dad finally picked up.

"I told you not to fuss about me."

"I know and I'm not, but in all the rush, I forgot to feed Thor."

"He already told me, rattled his dish until I got the point."

"Thank you. Looks like I'm the one needing reminders."

"We'll get through this, don't you worry."

"Right. I have the nursery newsletter here in front of me; how about we cancel that birding trip in November?"

"Now why would we do that?"

"Well, to take some pressure off you."

"No pressure, the birders meet in our parking lot and Henry leads the walk. I don't have to go unless I want to."

"All right, you promise?"

"Adam."

"Okay, are there any other changes you want?" They went through this every month. Adam wished he had someone to delegate this job to. At least the printer came up with the graphics. When there was no answer, his throat tightened. "Dad?"

"I'm thinking. I usually have a copy right in front of me, you know." He paused a bit more. "Did we put a blurb in there about special sales coming in December?"

"Yes."

"Good, then that's about it. You're taking it to the printer today?"

"Yes. And we'll send it out to our e-subscribers when the printed one is delivered." They had pretty much cut out sending monthly mailers through the postal service due to cost but handed out a printed calendar version to all who came in to shop. The latter was due to Adam's insistence. The e-mail letter always contained an extra coupon to encourage more people to sign up for it. "All right then, I'll talk with you later. Take it easy."

His father hung up grumbling.

Adam sat for a minute, trying to corral his thoughts. Should he have stayed home with his father? What if the test results came back and Bill couldn't work any longer? What then? But another thought calmed him. His father would have his babies to tend. He much preferred time in his backyard than time spent at the nursery. So his dad would be fine. They would hire a manager for one or both of the stores, and Adam would oversee the entire operation.

He glanced at his watch, the urge to call Gillian paramount, but it was too early. He'd stop on his way home, if he could hold off that long. Thinking about her made him smile. Amazing how he had come to care for her in such a short time. Had someone told him this could happen, he'd have laughed. "Get back to work, Bozo, you can't spend the morning daydreaming." Gathering up his computer disc and the mock-up of the newsletter, he picked up the outgoing mail and headed for his car. On the way, he swung into a Starbucks. Today he needed a triple-shot venti latte. He should have stopped before work, but the drive-in coffee shop had been out of his way then.

Latte in the SUV's cup holder, he dropped the mail off at the post office, checked the post office box, and headed for the printer. He took his latte in with him, when he saw a line waiting for service.

"Hi, Adam," said the man in front of him. "How's life?"

The two of them had gotten acquainted at the local chamber of commerce meetings Adam usually attended.

"Good." *Liar, crazy would be a better word.*

"Missed you at the meeting Monday night."

"I know, I was planning on going but my dad wasn't home when I got there. Found him being loaded into an ambulance in the Safeway parking lot."

"Is he okay?"

They moved closer to the counter. "Today he's unhappy because the doctor told him to take it easy for a couple of days until the test results come back."

"Maybe I should send him some flowers?" Both the man's eyebrows and the corners of his mouth lifted.

Adam snorted. "Thanks for the thought, but for some odd reason we always have plenty of flowers." It did give him an idea, however.

"Hope he gets well quickly." The man stepped up to the counter, and one of the clerks waved Adam over to the farthest cash register.

"Hello, Adam, must be newsletter time again."

He laid the manila envelope on the counter. "Sure is, and I'm even early this month."

"We appreciate that. Same quantity as usual?"

"Yes. All the instructions are in the envelope."

"Okay, we're good to go." The clerk handed him a copy of the order form. "You know, I got more compliments on those pots you helped me plant. I keep telling people to come by the nursery and ask for you." She grinned at him. "I know, anyone there can help. Just teasing. Hope you have a good day."

"You should come see our newest idea. Planting in cleaned out pumpkins. Chrysanthemums are especially gorgeous."

"Really? What a clever idea. Do you have some ready for purchase? I have a dinner to go to this evening. That would be fun to bring as a hostess gift."

"I'll put your name on one." He went out the door with a wave. Shame he hadn't had one in the car. Oh, well, one sold. He'd show a couple of his employees how to make them so they'd have a good supply in stock. When he returned to the nursery, he handed an instruction sheet to one of the women to copy for him and had the guys set up a table with the cleaned-out pumpkins on it and chairs in front. When they were ready, he picked up the mic to the loudspeaker and invited the customers to join the employees for the demo in five minutes. With a cleaned-out pumpkin on the table, he removed a chrysanthemum from a four-inch pot and, after filling the pumpkin about a third full of potting soil, set the plant in and filled in with dirt around it. "If the pumpkin is not full enough you can add more plants. Water it and add a bow on a stick." He set it out for them all to admire. "One more good thing. When the pumpkin gets too soft, plant the entire thing in the garden. The pumpkin fertilizes the chrysanthemum." His audience clapped and swarmed the table to give requests. Adam turned to John. "We need to make them daily since the pumpkin might begin to rot in a few days. We'll tell people to put a plate or clear plastic saucer under it."

"And the price?" one of them asked.

"I think fourteen ninety-five sounds about right. Probably nineteen ninety-five if someone asks you to make a larger one. Use various sizes of pumpkins and the price depends on how many plants are used."

He left them to make up a few more and watched as two customers bought three of them, including his, while they were being finished. Looked like it was going to be a successful idea.

By the end of the day, they'd sold ten and had orders for more. He needed to get them on sale at the other store, too. "I'm leaving now," he told John.

"Early? You never leave early."

"I know, but I'm going to deliver some flowers on my way home. And I'm going to stop by the Martinez store and have them start making pumpkin planters, too. Had no idea this could be such a hot item. Oh, pick out a bunch more from the stack of pumpkins in front. We need to prepare some for the carving demo on Saturday. I'll bring in the instructions, and we'll set one of the high school kids to carving for practice."

"What's wrong with faces?"

"This article shows carving just the outer shell. Works of art. Next year we should have a pumpkin carving contest." He nodded as he spoke. The idea had just whizzed through his mind.

"Divided into age groups. What do you want to use for prizes?"

"Gift certificates from here and stores around town."

John nodded. "Great idea. Should bring in lots of buying customers. And the pumpkins could be used in the November display, too."

"We might just try wreath making in December. Blast, and I took that newsletter to the printers already." He dug out his cell phone and clicked on the number in his directory. "Thanks, John." He left with a wave, flowers tucked into the angle of his arm and cell phone to his ear. Grateful that he was able to add another announcement box to the newsletter, he drove to his father's store and instructed two employees to clean out pumpkins. After he planted one, the crew got excited, and after he talked about the success at the Pittsburg store, they were even more enthusiastic.

"We can sell more than they can," someone said. And thus the challenge was issued.

"We'll tell you tomorrow what the prize is for the winning store." Adam couldn't believe he was saying such a thing. They'd never done a sales competition between the two stores before. He drew Keith aside. "You call John and challenge him. Tell him this is with my blessing. The contest will run until the end of the month."

Keith shook his head. "This is wild. Does your dad know yet?"

"Nope, it all came about because of an article I read in *Sunset* magazine. How have things gone today?"

"Good; the traffic has been good and sales are steady. We need to order more chrysanthemums."

"Great. Make me a list of what you need. We'll let Dad place the orders. Not sure when he will be back to work."

"He only called twice. I'd say that's pretty good."

Adam clapped the man on the arm. "You're a good man, Keith. I'm glad you work for us. Thanks again for helping me get the truck home. Oh, and have someone clean out the pumpkins in the afternoons and then they can be planted the following mornings. Take special orders if you need to."

"We'll do it."

Adam said good-bye and returned to his SUV. Now he could stop to see Gillian. Or perhaps he should go home first and get Thor? Nope, Gillian first. But when he parked on the street, there was no rental car in the driveway. He picked up the flowers and rang the doorbell. He rang it again. No answer. Five o'clock. Was she still shopping? Had someone taken her to get a rental car? Why, oh, why, didn't he call ahead? Feeling like a balloon with a slow leak, he turned back to the car. Talk about going from high to low in less than an hour.

When he parked at the house two doors up, he could hear Thor barking. The dog always recognized the sound of Adam's vehicle and welcomed him home. Adam gathered up his things, including the mixed bouquet of flowers, and strode into the house. He realized the air must be nearly out of his balloon because all of a sudden he felt drained, ready to sit down with a glass of iced tea and do absolutely nothing.

Other than to talk with Gillian when she returned. That idea put a smile on his face. "Sit, Thor." He placed the flowers in the sink and looked around for the dog. Oh, he was still sitting. "Good dog, Thor, come here. I'm sorry." He bent over to get his ear sniffed and snuffled, then rubbed his dog's ears and head. "Such a good dog you are. Where's Grandpa?"

Thor immediately went to the open screen door. Adam followed him, and sure enough there was his father out there with his babies, all the plants he started either with seeds or by cuttings. Years earlier, Alice had named them Bill's babies. Adam slid the door open and stepped out, Thor right on his heels. "I thought you were taking it easy today."

"I am. Just walking around out here, looking at things. Haven't dug anything up or moved anything or even watered anything. Just looking isn't doing anything."

"Are you walking?"

"Yes."

"I rest my case." Adam ambled out to join his father. "Did the doctor call?"

"Nope. He said tomorrow." Bill settled into a chair he kept out there between his planting beds. "Sit down, you make me nervous."

"Did you call Jennifer?" Adam sat down on a brick step that divided the two levels on the slope. Thor came over and sat beside him, his head right where Adam's hands were.

"I did. She's bringing dinner tonight."

"Wonderful."

"She gave me a lecture on taking it easy, too. Did you put her up to that?"

"Nope. I stopped down at Dorothy's with some flowers, but no one was home."

"Oh, I'm sure she was home, just sleeping. I do hope that daughter of hers can get her up and living again. Can't believe she figures she's dying. Last person I would have expected that from."

"Gillian is nothing if not determined."

"Something going on there?"

"What do you mean?"

"Oh, I got me a feeling you have a powerful interest in the woman."

"She's not 'the woman.' Her name is Gillian."

"Well, do you?"

"Do I what?" *How did he figure this out already?*

"Have an interest in her?"

Adam pushed out a heavy breath. "Yeah, Dad, I guess I do."

His dad leaned forward and thumped him on the shoulder. "Well, it's about time."

Thor leaped to his feet and yipped, heading for the closed screen door. "Thor, halt." The dog skidded to a stop before flailing through the screen door and turning it into shreds. "I'm coming. Jen must be here with the dinner. Was she bringing the kids?"

"No idea. Maybe we could eat out here at the patio table."

"I'll see." Adam went through the kitchen and living room to the front door, getting there just as the bell rang again. "I'm here. Thor, sit." He opened the door to find his sister-in-law standing on the step with a wooden basket in each hand. He held the door open. "Sorry, we were out in the back."

"He couldn't stay inside any longer, eh?" She reached up and kissed his cheek. "Been too long since we've seen you."

"I agree. Here, let me take those."

She handed him her baskets and slung her purse off her shoulder to set by the entry to the kitchen. "How is he?"

"Seems fine to me. Perhaps that was a singular episode." He pulled back the folded dish towel. "Mmm, looks good."

"Enchiladas, refried beans with cheese, and an apple

crisp for dessert. I hope you have sour cream. I brought salsa I made from tomatoes, homegrown at that, and guacamole. Oh, and tortilla chips."

"Smells as good as it looks. Where are the kids?"

"Soccer and homework. Lissa Marie is picking Lawrence up. I left the same thing at home for them." She went outside to greet Bill.

Adam watched her go. Tall, slim with shoulder-length sun-bleached blond hair, she carried herself like the model she'd dabbled as for a time. White capri pants and a red and white striped T-shirt. She always looked like she'd just stepped off the page, no matter what she wore.

He pulled plates and silverware out of the cupboards, digging out cloth napkins for a change. "Had I known what you were bringing, I would have made sangria." He raised his voice so she could hear.

"That's okay, I'm driving. Put the enchiladas in the oven at three hundred while we eat our chips and dips."

He did as she told him, finding a basket for the chips and bowls for the dips, whipping up the sour cream before filling the bowl. He took the lids off the salsa and guacamole and dug into the latter with a triangular tortilla. "Umm." Jen made the best guacamole anywhere. He put the beans and the enchiladas on two racks in the oven and carried the hors d'oeuvres outside. "Come on over to the table. Jen, you're getting stains all over the back of your pants."

"Oh, well." She brushed her rear off. "I have a good prewash spray."

The three of them sat in the dusk green–padded chairs at the table, each digging a chip into the bowls.

"What can I get you to drink?" Adam asked.

"You have any of that green tea I had here before?"

Adam nodded. "At your service. Dad?"

"Nothing right now."

Was he looking a bit gray around the eyes again? Adam studied his father. Was he breathing harder?

Bill glared at his son. "Go get the drinks and quit looking at me like I'm some sort of strange specimen. I'm fine. If I weren't I would tell you."

Jennifer's laugh tinkled like wind chimes. "Get real, Papa. You've not been feeling good for a long time, and you never said a word. You just think we were too stupid to notice."

"No, never stupid." He laid his hand over hers. "Just don't want to worry anyone." Thor nudged his arm with a black nose. "All right, one chip and that's all."

"Dad, he's not supposed to beg at the table."

"He's not begging, I offered."

Adam set the bottles down along with glasses of ice. "Well, should we say grace now that we've all tried the food?" They joined hands and Bill said the simple grace he'd taught his boys almost before they could talk. "God is great, God is good..."

Grace said, they started eating.

"So, Adam, what's new in your life?" Jen asked.

Adam started. "Ah..."

"Adam is interested in a woman," Bill said.

"Dad, what a way to put it." Adam stared at the twinkle in his sister-in-law's eyes. "Her name is Gillian Ormsby. She's here to take care of her mother, two doors down."

"You mean Dorothy? What's wrong with her?" She looked toward Bill. "Why didn't you tell me?"

Of course Jen knew Dorothy. All the years the families had shared meals and celebrations. After all, Dorothy and Alice had been such good friends.

"She thinks she's dying." Bill took another chip and crunched it.

"That's no joke."

"No, not usually, but she's not. She just thinks she is."

Adam leaned back and watched Jen's face. Introducing her to Gillian would be a good thing. Shame he'd not been able to bring Gillian home with him. If she wasn't back by now, surely…, possibly…, something had happened to her.

Chapter Nineteen

Oh, no!" Gillian stomped on her brakes, strangling the steering wheel.

The impact slammed her back and then jerked her forward.

A second impact came from behind, the cars screaming like wounded animals. The sounds of crashing seemed to last forever. *Mother's car. I've wrecked Mother's car.* Gillian sat without moving, waiting for her heart to slow down. She moved arms, legs, neck, and shoulders. Everything worked. No blood anywhere. But then she'd been almost stopped before the impact.

Someone tapped on the window. She looked out to see a man standing there and rolled down the window. "Are you all right, ma'am?"

She nodded. "I think so. Just yanked around a bit."

"Good. Sit tight. The police will be here any minute."

"What about the other people?"

"I don't know. I'm right behind you and someone else is behind me. You're safer if you stay in your car."

Gillian nodded. *But it's not my car. It's my mother's car, and she's never in all these years put a ding in it. What am I going to do?* She heard the sirens and saw flashing lights in her rearview mirror. Even if she called her mother, no one would answer. What to do? She rolled her head around, stretching neck and shoulders. All she needed at this point was whiplash.

Another police cruiser pulled up, followed by an ambulance that passed her and stopped several cars ahead of her. So was someone really injured or was this a precaution? Okay, what did she need to do? She checked behind the visor for an insurance card. None there. So she unsnapped her seat belt and leaned across the seat to flip open the glove box. Sure enough, the insurance card sat right on top of the car's instruction manual.

She saw an officer talking to the people in the car ahead of her, then he nodded and walked back to her car, stopping to check the license plate and jotting down the number. Gillian rolled the window down again. Good it was electric because now her hands were shaking so severely she couldn't have grasped a turning handle.

"Are you all right, ma'am?" The concern in his voice brought immediate tears.

"I was until just a minute ago, when I started to shake."

"Good, that is perfectly normal. No blood or pain anywhere?"

"No, sir." Funny saying sir to a man far younger than she.

"Can I see your license, registration, and insurance card?"

She handed them to him. "How many cars are involved?"

"Five. Good thing everyone was going so slowly." He looked up from the cards. "This vehicle belongs to Dorothy Ormsby?"

"Yes, she's my mother and she's never gotten a dent in it. Prides herself on her driving, and here I have it one time and look what happened."

"Sorry." He walked back to the front of her car and then to the rear, then back to the window. "I think you'll still be able to drive your car. The bumpers did their jobs and this is a heavy vehicle. We'll let you know when you can try." He handed her back her cards. "You'll need to contact your insurance company and file a claim."

Things I've never done in my life. Who do I ask? Enzio would know, but so would Adam. She glanced at the clock and dialed his cell phone. He should be home from work by now.

"Gillian?"

At the sound of his voice she burst into tears.

"Gillian, are you all right? What's wrong?"

"A-an ac-ci-dent." She stuttered through the tears. "I—I'm not—hurt." She sniffed and cried some more. "H-high-way six eighty near P-pleasant Hi-ll."

"What are you driving?"

"M-mother's c-car." The sobs intensified.

"Oh, no. But you're not hurt?"

"No. Wait." She laid the phone down so she could blow her nose. Now that she'd cried, she heaved a deep breath, mopped her eyes, and picked up her phone. "Five cars. Slow traffic so the damage is not extensive. An ambulance is here, but I don't know if anyone needs it. There is another car behind me."

"So you not only got rear-ended but damaged the front, too?"

"Yes."

"Well, at least you won't be deemed responsible. I'll come and get you and order a tow truck."

"No, the officer looked at it and said he thinks it's drivable. I have to wait until he comes back to tell me when. Sorry I turned into a blubbering mess." Glancing in the mirror on her visor she shook her head. Now she looked like a raccoon.

"No problem. Shock does that to you. So, how can I help?"

"You already did. If it can't be driven, I will call you back, okay?"

"Do you want me to call your mother?"

"No, her bedroom phone is turned off. Enzio was there for a while but I'm sure he's gone home by now."

"His car was gone when I came home. I knocked on the door, but no answer."

"How am I going to tell her I wrecked her car? She never lets anyone drive her car and she did me, and now this."

"Let's find out how bad the damage is first. We can take it down to the auto repair in the morning."

He had no idea how good the "we" sounded right now. She was not alone in this; she had a friend who would help. She dug out a clean tissue from her purse and scrubbed at the mascara line down her cheek and the smears under both eyes.

The police officer was back. "Go ahead and start it up, see if any warning lights come on."

When she glanced in the rearview mirror, she saw that the car behind her was already gone. She turned the key and the engine purred like usual.

He handed her his business card. "Good. I want you to back up and test the brakes. Then you can swing out and across the lanes to where there is no glass and continue on. I suggest you head on home since you could be a bit shocky still."

She did as he told her.

"That front bumper seems secure enough. Be grateful you weren't in a little car like the one two ahead of you."

"Thank you."

"You're welcome. Somewhat different here than in New York City, right?"

She nodded and pulled out around the car in front of her. The ambulance was gone and a wrecker was getting ready to tow the first car. *How am I going to tell Mother?* The thought made her stomach churn worse than the accident had. Had there been some way she could have avoided it? Was this due to her lack of driving experience? The questions bombarded her as she turned onto Pleasant Hill Road and followed it up the hill to a right on Morello Avenue. Morello led to home and what she would do. Her cell rang and she fumbled to get it. "Hello?"

"Where are you?" Adam's voice filled the car.

"On Morello heading north."

"How is the car doing?"

"Like the officer said, it drives fine but I can hear some rattles."

"Most likely the damaged bumpers. You'll have to go fill out accident forms and call your insurance agent in the morning. Why don't I meet you at your house and look at it and we'll go from there."

"Thank you. I hate to impose like this."

"Impose? This is the kind of thing that friends are for."

"But if you have plans for tonight..."

"We've finished dinner; Jen is here and she said to tell you hi. She'll probably come with me to look at it. She used to work as an insurance adjuster."

"Thank you. I'm coming under the freeway."

"Okay, see you in a few."

She saw him waiting on the sidewalk when she was halfway up the hill. A streetlight spotlighted both him and the attractive woman standing beside him. She'd heard of Jennifer from her mother, who had attended family events with Alice and the rest of the Bentleys. No one had ever mentioned how striking Jennifer was. The couple looked like two of the hoi polloi out for a stroll. They should have been in Hollywood rather than small-town Martinez.

Adam opened her car door and Gillian swung her legs out to stand, but she decided to wait a moment for the quivering to stop.

"You need a hand?" Adam asked.

Jennifer joined him. "Still shaking?"

"Some." Gillian rolled her head around on her shoulders and stretched first one side, then the other.

"Whiplash?" Jennifer asked.

"I don't think so. I was nearly stopped before the collision. And the bump from behind wasn't bad." She glanced up. "You are Jennifer, right?"

"Oh, I'm sorry." Adam apologized and officially introduced them. "Are you ready to stand?" He held out a hand.

Gillian took his hand and let him pull her up, ducking to miss banging her head on the doorjamb. "Thanks." She stood still a moment more and then took one step, followed by another. She wasn't dizzy and the quivering had pretty much disappeared.

Adam stayed by her side, but Jennifer took the heavy flashlight and checked out both bumpers. "They'll have to be replaced, but I don't see any other damage. Oh, wait, there's a dent here." She pointed to the driver's side, front.

Gillian stared at the damage, reminding herself that it could have been so much worse.

"Those bumpers did exactly as they are supposed to, protect the car and driver. Replacing them is no big deal. A couple hours' work. They can smooth out that dent so you'll never know it was there." Jennifer smiled at Gillian, reassurance in every look and word.

"Really?" Gillian sniffed back the tears that threatened, tears of relief this time. "I don't know how I'm going to tell Mother."

"Do you have to, right now I mean?" Adam asked.

"Well I..."

"You can take it in for the estimate tomorrow. They'll give you the information. I'll give you the name of a repair shop and tell them you're coming. They're honorable and work fast. You can rent a car for overnight or so and go pick it up when it's finished."

"Don't I have to wait for all the claims and such?"

"No, for this limited damage, you can go ahead, but be sure to notify the insurance company. You'll have to pay the deductible. Your insurance company will go after those deemed responsible. If you can show Dorothy that all is well, that will make it easier, I think."

A feeling of relief caused her to lean against the front fender.

"Did you get insurance information from those in front and behind you?"

"Ah no."

"Did you take pictures?"

"Nope." How to feel stupid in two simple statements. "I didn't get out of the car. The officer said to sit tight, and that's exactly what I did. I do have the officer's business card."

Jennifer patted her arm. "Don't worry about it. There will be plenty of information available."

"I just didn't think. All my years in New York, I've only driven on vacations. I've never had an accident before."

"Why don't you pull it into the garage and not worry about it for now? Have you had dinner?"

"No."

"I'll go get the leftovers, if that's all right?" Jennifer offered.

"Jennifer brought enchiladas, chips, the whole meal."

"Thank you. I—I don't seem to be computing real well right now." Gillian watched Jennifer walk down to the sidewalk.

"You want me to drive it in?"

She nodded to Adam and stepped back while he did so. After he parked the car and pushed the remote to lower the garage door, he followed Gillian into the quiet house.

Gillian checked on her mother, who was sound asleep. Had Dorothy heard anything she would have been sitting up, or at least paying attention. Gillian shrugged and continued on to the kitchen, turning on lights as she went. One glance at the kitchen clock and she heaved a sigh. The accident happened at four thirty and now it was eight o'clock.

"Coffee?"

"No, thanks." Adam took a chair at the kitchen table. "You go ahead."

"I have iced tea, but I think I need something hot." She stared at the pot. Making fresh seemed a futile effort for this time of night. Instead she poured leftover coffee into a cup and set it in the microwave. Reheated coffee was never the best tasting, but right now… "It could have been so much worse." She needed to remind herself of that over and over, otherwise guilt would eat at her.

"When those things happen, often you can't avoid it."

She heaved another sigh. "I know, I guess."

A discreet knock at the front door announced Jennifer's arrival. The microwave dinged at the same time. Adam rose and headed for the front door while Gillian took her cup from the microwave, cupping the heat between her hands.

Jennifer took over, setting out the chips and guacamole, fixing up a plate of enchiladas and refried beans and heating it in the microwave. "Do you want me to make a plate for Dorothy?"

"I'll go ask her but I doubt it. She never has liked to eat late and she was sleeping." Gillian returned to the bedroom. "Mother?" She crossed the carpet and shook her mother's shoulder. When she blinked, Gillian asked if she wanted dinner.

"No. Enzio forced me to eat earlier. I want to sleep."

The word *forced* made Gillian smile. "All right. I'll see you in the morning."

"Yes."

Well that went better than it would have a few days ago. Gillian comforted herself with that thought and the other; Mother didn't ask about her car.

She returned to the kitchen, the fragrance of enchiladas drawing her back. The thought of friends lightened her load. She needed to get her purchases out of the trunk but probably not until morning.

Adam and Jennifer didn't stay long after nibbling on the chips as Gillian ate her dinner. She walked them to the door, drooping under the onslaught of exhaustion. Though her mind knew this was a normal reaction, her whole self grumbled in disgust.

"I'll be here at nine then to follow you down to the adjuster's office. We'll get this taken care of," Adam assured her.

"Thank you."

"Call me if you have any questions," Jennifer added. "I left my phone number on a pad on the table. And if you wake up with a lot of pain, you'll need to get to a doctor."

"All right." Gillian covered a yawn. "Thank you both."

"You sure you'll be all right?" Adam asked, his gaze drilling past her manners.

She nodded. "See you in the morning. I'll make sure Mother eats early." *Or perhaps I'll just let her sleep. That might be easier in the long run.* The more she talked with her mother, the more tempted she would be to tell her about the accident. "Night. And thanks for the delicious dinner."

So this was how having friendly neighbors made one feel. Protected and comforted. Especially when one of them was so willing to help, so often. And so charmingly.

Chapter Twenty

You think she'll be all right?"

"Adam, you're worrying like an old hen." Jennifer glanced at him as they strolled up the hill. "She just needs a good night's rest and some perspective. Right now every time she blinks, she hears the crash again. It will probably wake her up during the night, too."

"Something like posttraumatic stress?"

"Sort of. Especially someone who has driven as seldom as she has. Once the paperwork is all finished and the car repaired, she'll be fine."

"Not to change the subject or anything, but what do you think about Dad?"

"He looks good to me. I still can't believe you didn't call me."

"You know how he is. Doesn't want to bother anyone. With me he just didn't have a choice. When I saw them loading him into the ambulance, I about had a heart attack. Thank God for people who see a possible problem and check it out."

"Do we know her name?"

"And phone number. I can get her address by the reverse

directory, just haven't taken time to do that yet. I'm going to send her some flowers, probably a flowering plant."

"Would you like me to do that for you?"

"I'd appreciate that a lot. Also, could you call Dad tomorrow? He still can't go back to work; all the test results aren't back yet."

"So, he'll go out and play with the babies."

"True. And he is most happy there. I don't think he'd mind a bit if he never went back to the shop."

"Why can't he retire?"

"Said he isn't ready yet. I asked. But I'm afraid if I suggest it, he will think I am trying to take over and send him over the hill."

"Oh, for Pete's sake."

Thor waited inside the screen door, whimpering for them to hurry in.

"I've not taken him for a walk or run yet, so I better go do that. Will you be here when I get back or do you want to come with me?"

"Think I'll stay and talk with Dad. I have an idea I've wanted to discuss with him." She leaned over to ruffle Thor's ears. "You get a bit impatient, don't you?"

Adam took the leash off the hook by the door and snapped it on Thor's collar, setting him to quivering with anticipation. "Dad, I'm taking Thor for a walk. Be back in half an hour or so."

"Where's Jen?"

"I'm here and I'll be right there." She reached up and planted a kiss on Adam's cheek. "She's nice."

"Who? Oh, you mean Gillian?"

"Go after her."

"Jennifer Bentley!"

"I mean it. You already have that look in your eyes when

you think no one sees you watching her. I've not seen you with that expression before, and it's about time."

Adam left, shaking his head. Women. What was it she thought she saw? Surely he wasn't wearing his heart on his sleeve. Gillian was a lovely woman, but she didn't like sailing. Said she got seasick whenever she was on the water. Besides that, he hardly knew her at all. How could a New York City executive be interested in a man with no definite goals who worked at his father's business? She'd said she had her life all planned out. Right, but look what happened.

He picked up the pace to a jog to keep Thor happy. He should have brought the Frisbee; he'd be able to see it in the lights at the school yard. They trotted down the hill and turned right on the path that bordered the street. Up and over a little rise and across the road to the long driveway. At this time of night he could let the dog run free.

Once on the grass he stopped and removed the leash. "Okay, fella." He waved his arm in their signal for go and Thor took off. He raced around Adam, ever widening his circle until Adam waved him back in. "Don't go out so far, I can hardly see you." He started running alongside the drive and then curved over into the field and back toward the road, putting on enough speed to raise his heart rate. Thor returned to run beside him, so Adam angled around and ran back to the school again. Good thing he was wearing shorts or he'd have been drenched. When he needed to stop for breath, Thor flopped down beside him, sides heaving. "I wonder if she likes to run or jog or even walk?" Thor thumped his tail, ready to go again. "Nope, we'll take it easy going home." Adam snapped the leash back on, and the two jogged back to the bottom of the hill that was their street.

Jen's car was gone. She usually tried to be home before the kids went to bed. Not that Lawrence needed to be tucked in any longer. Boys who were juniors in high school were a bit touchy about things like that. And Lissa Marie, at nineteen, half the time ended up as a closer at the Starbucks where she worked while going to college in The City, as San Francisco was often referred to by the residents across the bay.

He really should plan a day to take them all out sailing. While they'd adjusted to their father's death as well as could be expected, Adam had promised his brother he would be there for his family. During the past summer, Lawrence had worked for him at the nursery and probably would again next summer.

Adam locked the door behind him, and Thor made a fast trip to the water bowl. Bill was in the family room watching the news. "So what happened in the world today?" Adam asked.

"Mayhem, murder, and mistrust."

"That sounds delightful and inspiring. I'm going for a shower." When he returned to the family room, his dad was sitting in his chair, the television off. "You want anything to drink?"

"No, thanks."

Adam retrieved a bottle of green tea from the refrigerator, unscrewed the top, and chugged half of it before ambling back to join his dad. "So, how are the babies?"

"Doing well. If I weren't working I'd be able to spend a lot more time out there, perhaps hybridize more of the irises."

"True. Do you want to do that?"

"I think I do. Jennifer and I were talking, and she asked me point-blank why I keep going into the store." He shook his head. "I couldn't even tell her why because I think the only reason is that I don't want you to have to work seven days a week."

"So, what do you see as choices?"

"Well, I keep on managing my store and you the Pittsburg one. Or I cut back to half time and let Keith manage it with you overseeing him. Or . . . " The silence stretched.

"Or . . . ?" Adam stretched the word out.

"Your mother and I always said we would retire and travel all over this country. That won't happen now. But I have the babies. I'm thinking that if I bought some land so I had more room . . . " He nodded slowly, his gaze far away.

Adam watched his dad pondering his options. Which brought him back to his own question: what did he want to do with the rest of his own life? "There's another option. Sell out altogether and do what you want without worrying about the stores."

"Do you want to do that?"

Adam shook his head. "I have no idea. I've done the things I've wanted to, and now I don't know. I'm happy doing what I'm doing, but I'd be happy not doing it, too. This has to be your decision." A picture of Gillian getting out of the car, still shaking, skidded through Adam's thoughts. How long would she be tied up taking care of her mother? Would she look for a job in this area or return to New York? What difference did it make to him what she did? He thought of that for a moment. While he wasn't sure of the where and when, he knew for certain that he did care what she did, and he hoped she wasn't leaving again.

His dad folded the newspaper that had been laying on his lap and stuffed it into the magazine rack. "Well, we don't have to make a decision tonight, that's for sure. Did you lock the door?"

"I did."

"Sure was nice to see Jen. Think I'll go watch Lawrence's soccer match on Saturday."

"Good idea. You want to go sailing on Sunday?"

"I'll think on it. Night."

Adam glanced at the clock, wondering if it was too late to call Gillian. After ten. She'd probably taken a hot bath like she'd said and crashed. Bad choice of words even for a thought. He checked the lock on the back door and turned out the lights on the way to his bedroom, Thor padding beside him. He could text her, and if she heard the bleep, good. If not, that was all right, too.

He unhooked his cell phone and typed,

How are you feeling? A.

Laying the cell along with his keys, change, and billfold on the tray on the high chest, he got ready for bed, then retrieved his cell to check.

Drowsy and no longer shaky. G.

He flipped back the light comforter and sheet on his bed and sat on the edge.

Good. I know that was a bad shock.

With my mother's car, no less.

She won't beat you.

But she will be disappointed.

Adam continued.

True, but she'll get over it. Besides it will be all repaired by Monday.

You don't know my mother.

I've always heard good things about her.

Yeah, well, appearances can be deceiving.

The two of you don't get along?

He propped himself against the headboard on a stack of pillows, and crossed his legs at the ankles.

Didn't use to. We'll see now.

Allie could do no wrong?

How did you pick up on that?

My male intuition.

He rolled his eyes, sure that would get a rise out of her.

Didn't know there was such a thing.

I learned it in the navy.

LOL.

I'll see you in the morning.

That thought made him smile.

Thanks for your help.

You're welcome. Sweet dreams.

Night.

He clicked his cell shut and reached for the top book

on his stack. He usually had two or three going—one devotional, a novel, and a business book—and tried to read bits of each of them every night. But when he opened the pages, he saw Gillian's face. He turned out the light and rolled over.

"I'm taking Gillian to get her estimate and down to Roger's to have him fix it before I go to the shop."

Bill looked up from reading his paper. "Good. Tell her I feel for her."

"I was thinking of inviting her and Dorothy up here for dinner."

"Dorothy out of bed yet?"

"Not that I know of."

"Well, let's not wait for that to happen." Bill laid his paper down. "She is one stubborn woman when she gets set on something. This is Friday, right?" Adam nodded. "Roger most likely won't be able to finish the repairs today."

"Probably not. There might be more than I saw last night with the flashlight. But if we get it there, he'll get at it."

"All depends on how busy he is."

"Take your phone outside with you."

"I have it right here." Bill slapped the holster on his belt. "And, yes, I will call you as soon as I hear from the doctor."

Adam grinned and headed for the garage. He must have been a bit overprotective the way his father talked. *Oh, well, we all have to learn how to deal with new things*. He parked on the street in front of the house two doors down and whistled his way to the front door to ring the bell.

Gillian answered and stepped back for him to enter. "Good morning. I'm about ready. Just want to pick up Mother's tray. I couldn't leave her without making sure she had eaten."

"Have you talked with Allie?" He studied Gillian, noting

slight circles under her eyes, but otherwise no worse for the experience. Khaki slacks, a scooped-neck yellow T-shirt, and a yellow cardigan made her look like a bit of sunshine flitting around the kitchen. She shook her head, setting her hair to swinging but returning into perfect order.

"I'll be right back."

When she returned to the kitchen, she cleared off the tray, put the dishes in the dishwasher and the tray in the pantry. "There. I left her a note with my cell number on it. I have no idea if Enzio is coming; I left a message on his answering machine. And"—she glanced around the kitchen and then up to him—"thank you for helping me with this."

"You are welcome. I'll be on the downside of the drive. Just follow me, I'll take it slow so you don't get left behind."

Once they were on the road, he took her back to Pleasant Hill via Morello and into the parking lot for the estimator. Gillian parked at the line where a sign directed customers who needed estimates and exited her car to go into the office. Adam joined her and held the door open.

An hour later Adam and Gillian were finished and back in their cars. She'd handled the process with perfect ease, in spite of not having all the paperwork, charming the older clerk behind the counter and the younger estimator outside. Adam had enjoyed watching her in action. She was obviously well honed in negotiations, laughing at herself and her lack of experience, causing the two men to take care of her problems with eagerness. He wondered if her people skills were natural or the product of intense training.

Next he led the way to the auto body shop his friend Roger owned. They'd met at a chamber of commerce meeting soon after Adam moved to the area.

As expected, Roger had looked over the paperwork, studied the bumpers, and agreed to begin the repairs promptly. He had apologized that he couldn't finish the work today, however, and the shop was closed for the weekend because he was to serve as best man at a wedding.

"Otherwise I'd work on it tomorrow, too."

"That's fine," Gillian said. "I'm just grateful it won't be tied up longer."

Roger handed Gillian a copy of the work order and another piece of paper. "We have a deal with a local car rental company, so take this certificate with you. That will save you some money there. Does the insurance include rentals in a situation like this?"

"I have no idea. I'll just pay it and see about that later. Thank you."

Adam guided her to his SUV and held the door open for her. He might be at the shop before noon at the rate they were going.

"You can just drop me at the car rental if you want to. I know you need to get to work."

"That's okay. I thought perhaps we could swing by a coffee shop I know and I'd treat you to a cup of coffee."

"Add a doughnut and you're on."

"Okay. This place has good scones, too."

Her phone rang and she dug it out of the holster on her purse. "Allie, where are you?" She glanced at Adam and rolled her eyes.

He got the impression this was not a call she wanted to take.

"Gee, I'm sorry to hear that. No, Mother ate a bit for breakfast and grumbled at me when I said we'd do a shower this afternoon. I'm going to buy two baskets of flowers and hang them outside her window. Hopefully watching the hummingbirds will encourage her. Good. Well, keep me posted. I was hoping we could have a family get-together on Sunday." She slid the phone back into the holster and heaved a sigh. "Well, I don't have to worry about her coming and demanding that I inform Mother about the car."

"They're going somewhere?"

"Out to Half Moon Bay as soon as the games are done. They'll be back Sunday night." She raised her hands in the air. "One more thing to be really grateful for."

"You want to go sailing with my family then? I'm hoping to take the boat out Sunday afternoon."

"I would like to, but I'm no fun on a boat. I'll just get seasick and make everyone miserable."

Adam shrugged. "When you see a doctor, just ask for a prescription to overcome motion sickness. They have some good ones now." He pulled into a parking lot and parked in front of Mamie's Coffee Shop. "I'll get you out there yet." He wasn't sure if that was a threat or a promise.

Chapter Twenty-one

Gillian opted for a car with a trunk instead of the sports car she'd first considered, purely because she needed space to haul the hanging baskets. Stopping at the nursery on Alhambra Avenue that she knew belonged to Adam's father, she purchased one basket of pink petunias and another of red. She thanked the young man who had helped her, especially for the reminder that if a frost was predicted she would need to cover them. After tucking the trailing branches in carefully, she closed the trunk.

Next stop, the Knob Hill Market for some microwave-ready food for lunch and dinner, and salad mixes and fixings. Leaving there she noticed the list of movies playing at the theater across the street. Would there be any chance she could talk her mother into going to a movie?

What had Dorothy's social life been like? Or did she have a social life, other than the senior center, church, and her garden? She used to belong to some other organization, if Gillian could just remember its name.

"So why didn't I buy some other bedding plants?" she asked herself as she followed the streets back to her mother's house. Her mother had many pots that needed filling, and since so many plants survive the winter here, they could be a real brightener for both front and backyards. Fresh plants would bring beauty back until the shrubs and flowers already established grew back or were replaced. She shook her head, amazed that she was thinking along these lines, acting as if she were really going to stay here instead of returning to New York and seeking another job.

Since she'd bought some prepared clam chowder, she decided to serve that for lunch. Did her mother like clam chowder? Maybe the two of them should make a list of Mother's likes and dislikes.

She drove the car into the garage but didn't lower the door until she could take the baskets out. "Mother, I'm back," she called as she entered the house.

No answer. She checked on her mother. How could anyone possibly sleep this much? "Mother." At least Dorothy's eyes blinked open without Gillian having to touch her shoulder.

"You came back. I dreamed you left."

"I did leave to do some errands. But I am back now and thinking we'll have clam chowder for lunch. How does that sound?"

Dorothy shrugged.

"I brought a surprise. I stopped at Bentley's and got two hanging baskets so the hummingbirds will feed right outside your window where you can enjoy them."

"You never give up, do you?"

"Nope. You're stuck with me so let's make the best of it. Would you like a shower before or after lunch?"

"Neither."

"Well, then. I'm hungry so we'll eat first. Then I'll hang the baskets and then your shower." *You sound like Miss Merry Sunshine,* Gillian thought as she brought the groceries into the kitchen. *At least Mother isn't asking about her car.*

After she'd served their lunch and they were eating in the bedroom, Gillian asked, "Mother, how long since you've been out of your bedroom, other than to the bathroom? Not counting the doctor's visit, of course."

Dorothy blinked and shrugged. "I don't know. What day is this?"

"Friday. I came home the first time a week ago." Last Friday, who would have dreamed such cataclysmic changes would occur in her own life in one week?

While Dorothy appeared to be thinking, moving her head back and forth with such small movements, Gillian wondered if there was something wrong. Had Mother had another TIA? "I don't know."

"You don't remember the date you took to your bed?"

"It wasn't all of a sudden, you know. I just couldn't see any sense of getting up and I knew that was because of the stroke."

Gillian let that one pass. Dr. Isaacs had said most people didn't even recognize they'd had one. "Mother, you still haven't told me exactly what the doctor said."

"He checked me over, all the normal things, ordered an EKG and blood work, and said if nothing showed up I was healthy as a horse and to get out of bed and back to life."

"You told him how you felt?"

"I told him I was dying—and he laughed. He said that he and I were too ornery to die so young." She locked her arms across her chest, making the dishes on the tray rattle.

"I see."

"Enzio read to me yesterday. I think he ran out of things to say."

"Did you enjoy being read to? I know I do. That's why I

either buy or rent audio books. I have several if you would like to hear one."

"I fell asleep. I think he did, too, sitting in that chair."

Goodness! We're actually carrying on a conversation. "Allie called, they are going to Half Moon Bay after Sherrilyn's soccer game and will be back Sunday night."

"Oh." Dorothy pushed the tray away, so Gillian picked it up. Most of the chowder was gone and half of the coffee. She'd done well.

"I'm going to hang the baskets now. I'll use the step stool in the pantry."

"You be careful out there."

"Yes, Mother, I will. Can I get you some juice to drink?"

With a shake of the head, Dorothy turned on her side and pulled the covers up. "You could close the blinds."

Not likely. Gillian took the tray back to the kitchen and retrieved the key to the side gate from the board where the house keys were carefully labeled. Now that was like the mother she remembered, not this pitiful remnant in the bedroom. She was just heading outside to open the gate, when her cell phone rang. *Ignore it and keep going.* She could always call back or...she snatched the phone out of the holder on the fourth ring, not bothering to check the caller ID.

"Hi."

The sound of his voice made her smile. "Hi, yourself. I'm on my way out to hang up the pots I bought at your dad's nursery."

"Those big ones?"

"I guess they are the big ones. Two took up most of the trunk."

"Why don't you wait and I'll stop on my way home? They're heavy."

This made her smile wider. She who was Miss Independent in New York found herself being assisted by a very nice man. "If I have trouble, I'll wait." *But I am pretty strong.* Hand weights helped with that. Which reminded her. She'd need to buy some here since she hadn't brought her own.

"The reason I called, would you like to come to church with us on Sunday? Dad and I attend the early service at eight thirty, then we go out for breakfast."

"What church do you go to?"

"A new nondenominational one on Morello."

"I'd like to but..."

"But your mother?"

"Yes." She thought a moment. She'd been running errands, so leaving Dorothy alone for a short while wasn't a problem. She knew her mother wouldn't mind at all. Allie would be out of town. "Yes, I'd like to go." The answer surprised her. She thought she was going to say no.

"Good, this way you'll get to know my dad. He's looking forward to meeting you."

She heard him respond to a question from someone in the background.

"Call you later; I have to go."

She hung up and tapped the phone against her chin. Strange, or rather surprising, how she was settling into life here. Cleaning house, buying plants, working in the yard, making friends, and now going to church. This wasn't the way she'd thought it would be at all. Not that she'd given her future a great deal of thought since arriving back at her mother's house. She should be making plans and decisions, listing her name with headhunters and working on her résumé, especially since she'd never needed one in all these years.

Yes, she'd made decisions all right like which plants to

buy, what groceries were needed, what car to rent, and now to go to church or not. But none of those choices would have any effect on her long-term plans. She needed to decide what she wanted to do with the rest of her life. Of course Scot might get a really good thing going again and call her to help him. They worked well together. But could she count on that? Was she wise to depend on a nebulous hope, or should she begin her job search in San Francisco? Soon.

One month. Surely she could take one month here with her mother to help her back on her feet, to return the yard and garden to their former condition so her mother could enjoy them again. Could she believe that all this was part of God's plan for her? After all, she used to believe that about her life in New York. Was there any good reason not to believe that way again? Just because the company was bought out, it wasn't her fault. Staring out at the weeds, sticks, and dead plants, surely getting the yard back in shape was a worthy goal, for a month at least.

She shoved her phone back in the holster and headed outside to deal with the baskets. One thing at a time and this was the most important right now. She'd heard someone say, "Just do the next right thing." The only question was, was this right thing, the best thing? Maybe she should call Adam back and put church off for another week. Was decision remorse the same as buyer's remorse?

Gillian positioned the folding step stool under the hook, removed the hummingbird feeder, and went to the car for the baskets. The man carrying them both had made it look easy. So much for her weight training; these were heavy. She set the baskets on the concrete apron in front of the garage and fetched the wheelbarrow from the gardening shed by the garage wall. Putting them in carefully to break off as few branches as possible, she wheeled the baskets around to the back. Good thing she had purchased chains for hanging them. Standing on the top step, she attached the end of the chain over the hook and let it dangle. Now to get the wire hook for the basket into one of the links.

Standing on the first step of the three, she held the basket by the sides and aimed for the chain link. By the third try and miss, she set the whole thing back in the wheelbarrow. Surely this should not be so difficult.

Her phone rang and she wandered over to the lawn chairs by the table to sit and talk with Enzio. "Thanks for calling."

"Isn't caller ID a handy thing? What are you working on, you sound like you're puffing."

"Trying to hang these two baskets of petunias I brought home for the hummingbirds. I want Mother to see them out her window. Maybe it will be an encouragement for her."

"Do you need a hand?"

"I hate to admit it, but I'm not managing very well on my own."

"Good, I wanted to come over anyway."

"You know you don't need an invitation."

"A man likes to know he is needed."

"I think that's a universal need, not confined to the male of the species."

"Are you in need of a sinful treat?"

"My dear Enzio, any time is the right time for something sweet. I'll make some iced tea. It'll be ready by the time you get here. Bring some for Mother, too. I'll make sure she is awake."

"See you in a bit."

She left the baskets and stopped in the kitchen to turn on the teakettle. Shame she hadn't started sun tea that morning. It tasted much better than brewed. Now there would be no time for her mother's shower. Unless they waited till evening after Enzio left. Content with that, she entered the bedroom, then changed her mind before waking her mother. She and Enzio needed to talk.

She poured the brewed tea over the ice cubes about the time he rang the doorbell. Inviting him in, she handed him a glass and led the way to the outside table. "I have something I need to tell you."

"Does it have anything to do with the rental car sitting in the garage?" He set a white paper bag on the table.

She nodded. "I was involved in a multicar accident on the six eighty late yesterday afternoon. Only the bumpers were damaged on Mother's car, so today it went in for repairs. I should get it back Monday." She nodded at his question before he asked it. "I am fine, was nearly stopped when I hit the guy in front and someone hit me from behind." She sipped her tea. "I've not told Mother yet. You know how she is about her car. I couldn't believe she offered it for me to drive and then this happened."

"You've had some adventures already." He opened the bag and held it out to her.

"Macaroons." She reached inside for one. "I love macaroons. In fact I love all Italian bakery things, if you haven't guessed."

He took one, too, and leaned back in the chair. "Those are the baskets?"

"Yes. I just need someone to lift them from the bottom so I can slide the hook into the chain link."

"Won't take but a minute. The grass is starting to come back."

Gillian turned to look at the slender spears. "Amazing what a little water can do. Do I need to fertilize it?"

"Not usually at this time of year. It'll go dormant once it

gets cold. In fact there's a cold front moving down from the north. You might want to plan a cover for the baskets or just not put them up yet."

"No, I want Mother to see them. The hummingbirds are so feisty." She nibbled on her cookie. "I was thinking of buying plants for pots and some to put around the front door. Do you think the jasmine will come back?"

"Possibly. Pansies always make it through the winter. Cyclamen is just coming into the stores. Snapdragons are good winter flowers, too, along with primrose."

"You are a wealth of information. No wonder you and Mother became good friends. Did your wife garden, too?"

"Betina took care of the flowers, I did the vegetables. Now I do it all and it's not nearly as much a pleasure." He set his glass down on the table. "Let's get those baskets up. You needn't worry, I'll keep your secret."

"I plan to tell her, but not until the car is back in the garage, all restored to pristine condition." Together they had the baskets hung in a minute, and Enzio trundled the wheelbarrow back to where it belonged. "Amazing how handy four hands are instead of just two."

"Have you met Angelina Gonzales, next door, yet?"

"Yes, last time I was here and asked her to water the plants and check on Mother." She studied his face as he stared at the glass in his hands. Something seemed to be bothering him, if the wrinkling forehead was an indication. "What is it, Enzio?"

"I was thinking I would tell you my idea, but I think I must run it by Dorothy first."

"Good idea or bad?"

His eyes twinkled as he grinned at her. "Oh, I think it is a very good idea, but for now I, too, have to keep a secret."

"I told you mine."

"Ah, but this one—I can't spoil it."

"Enzio, dear man, have I ever mentioned that I abhor secrets?" At his raised eyebrows, she added, "Mostly ones that I don't know."

"Soon, my dear. Soon." He patted her hand. "Let's go see if we can irritate your mother."

Chapter Twenty-two

I can't come with you to church this morning. She's dead."

"What?" Adam found it hard to even recognize her voice between the sobs. "Gillian?"

"Yes. It froze last night and our hummingbird is dead."

"I-I'm sorry." *Please don't cry.* He tried to subdue the idea that she was really overreacting to the death of a little bird. There were lots of hummingbirds around the area. Listening to her cry made him want to go see her, hold her. No one should have to cry alone, and he was sure her mother was sleeping right through this. "Have you told your mother?"

"No, I'm the one who's been feeding her, and I brought the baskets for her to enjoy and..."

Does she mean her mother or the hummingbird? Adam stared out the sliding glass door to where his father was uncovering the babies. He'd covered them as a precaution, like he always did. "Did you cover the plants like I suggested?"

"Yes, the plants are fine but the hummingbird is dead." She hiccupped and he heard her blow her nose. "I know it is a little thing and this is so silly and it doesn't make sense and I don't make sense and I'm a mess."

Lord, I really need some help here. "Why don't you put the hummingbird in a shoebox or something with some soft tissues? Put it in a dark place. There is a thing called torpor that hummingbirds go into. When they warm up, they come out of it and are extremely hungry."

"All right." She sniffed again. "Thanks."

"I'll stop by on my way back from church."

"Okay."

Gillian did as he said, stroking the little body, enchanted in spite of her tears by the perfection of such a tiny creature. She closed the lid after punching air holes in it and put it in the pantry. Stopping into the bathroom to wipe the mascara off her face, she studied the figure in the mirror. All dressed for church in a slubbed silk jacket, tailored silk cream shirt, and matching slacks, gold chains and earrings, and her face a mess.

Whatever had come over her? She washed her face, reapplied her makeup, and stopped in her room to change clothes. And make plans for the day. Walking into her mother's bedroom, she glanced out at the still covered hanging baskets. "You want another cup of coffee, Mother?"

"I thought you were going to church."

"I was, but I found the hummingbird lying on the sidewalk and I couldn't quit crying. Silly I know, but I have enjoyed her so much."

"Sometimes the birds fly into the windows and that kills them, but sometimes they are just stunned and after a while will wake up and fly away."

"Adam said this might be torpor at work. I have never heard of such a thing before." She leaned against the doorjamb. "I put her in a box in the pantry."

"I've seen them come alive again. Go out and bring the

feeder in and set it in a sink of warm water. If she lives, warm sugar water will help her more." Dorothy pushed herself upright against her pillows. "The hummingbirds are my favorites, too."

Then why did you... don't go there, Gillian told herself. *Just appreciate that your mother is actually talking with you and not telling you to go away.* "I'm warming up a cup of coffee. If you want some, I'll make fresh. Or there's orange juice. I bought a half gallon yesterday."

"Orange juice, I think."

Gillian made sure her face didn't show the shock she felt. *What is happening here?* She warmed up her coffee, poured the juice, and returned to the bedroom. Handing her mother the glass, she sat down on the chair. "When do you think I should take the covers off the baskets?"

"Any time. Once the air has warmed past freezing." Dorothy sipped her orange juice.

"How about a shower?"

"I will but after a bit." Dorothy leaned back against her pillows. "Is Enzio coming today?"

"I don't know. Do you want him to?" A shrug was her answer.

"You look like you're feeling better." Gillian glanced out the window and saw the male hummingbird hovering around the baskets. "I'll be right back." Outside, she removed the covers from the baskets and took one of the feeders down to take inside to warm up. "I hope she comes back to you." Setting the feeder in the sink, she ran warm water to cover it and weighted it down with the wet dishcloth. Did she dare look yet? She returned to the bedroom. "Do you think I should check on her?"

"How long has it been?"

"Half an hour? I'm heating up the feeder in the sink."

"Give her a bit more time."

"I went online and found some books on hummingbirds. One is written by a woman who had a hummingbird winter over in her sun room. I thought I'd like to order it."

"You might try down at Wild Bird's Unlimited. They carry books about birds, besides seeds and feeders." Dorothy drained her orange juice and set the glass on the nightstand. "In answer to your question, I am feeling better. Weak, though."

Thank You, God. "You have some color in your face again." *You're still so thin that I wouldn't recognize you as my mother, but we can deal with that.* "How about I change your bed while you take a shower? Do you want me to wash your hair?"

"The chair is still in there?"

"Yes."

"I can call you if I need you?"

"I'll be right here."

Her mother heaved a sigh. "Then we'd best get to it." She flipped back the covers and turned to sit on the edge of the bed.

"I'll go start the shower." Gillian did so and stared for a moment into the mirror. Was this a miracle? What had brought about the change? She turned to see her mother holding on to the door frame, so she opened the shower door enough to unlatch it and stepped back.

"Can you help me take off my nightgown?"

Dorothy sat down on the chair in the shower with a sigh, the water beating down on her chest and lap.

Gillian took the shampoo off the rack. "If you tip your head forward to get wet, I'll wash your hair. I know how good that feels." After massaging her mother's scalp with her fingertips, Gillian left Dorothy to rinse and wash. Gillian stripped off the linens and remade the bed, finishing just as the shower water turned off. With the sheet and blanket folded back on an angle, the bed looked inviting.

Once Dorothy was in a fresh gown with her hair fluffed with the hair dryer, she walked back to the bed with Gillian beside her. She was breathing like she'd just run around the block or lifted weights, and when she sat down, it was more like collapsing than sitting.

"How about if I rub some lotion into your arms and legs?"

"If you like." Dorothy lay back in her bed, huffing out a breath and rolling her head from side to side.

Gillian found the bottle of lotion on the shelf under the nightstand and poured some into her hands. She began with her mother's arms, working in long soothing strokes like the massage therapist did with her, massaging each finger. By the time she finished the legs and feet, her mother was sound asleep. She pulled the blanket over Dorothy's shoulders and patted them. "You earned this rest, Mother. 'Heavenly Father, thank You for bringing my mother back.'"

After starting the sheets in the washer, she tidied up the bathroom and hung the towels on the rods, then returned to the kitchen just in time to answer the telephone. As always, Enzio's voice made her smile.

"She's doing better. Sleeping now because she just had a shower and shampoo. Hard to believe how weak she is."

"It will take time to rebuild her strength. What do you think made the difference?"

"I don't know, but I'm sure grateful." She told him about the hummingbird.

"Have you checked on her?"

"Just about to."

"Good. I'll be over in a while. I thought I'd bring lunch."

"You don't have to do that."

"I know, but I want to. See you in an hour or so."

Gillian hung up the phone and glanced at the clock. Nearing ten thirty. She opened the pantry door and paused in delight. She could hear a scrabbling sound from the box. She took the warm feeder back outside and hung it, then returned for the box. Lifting one corner, she peeked in to see the hummingbird sitting and looking at her with one beady little eye.

"You're alive." She felt like laughing but kept it to a smile, one that stretched her whole face. Stepping out the back door, she went to the feeder and gently lifted off the box lid. The hummingbird looked at her, shook her body to ruffle her feathers, tipped her head back, then fluttered her wings and flew out of the box, straight to the feeder where she sat drinking for the longest time. Gillian watched her without moving. She'd held the hummingbird so close to her that she could see every minute feather, the long thin beak, and the slight sheen of green on her back. So very precious and alive. *I wish I had shown her to Mother. Earlier this little bird looked so dead and now she is alive. Like you, Mother, you are coming alive again.* Gillian raised her face to let the sun shine its benediction down on her skin and her closed eyes. She heard the male zoom by her shoulder. With her eyes closed, she could hear so much more. The hummingbirds clicking, the birds at the feeder, children playing up the street. A wealth of sounds, songs of life. A bumblebee droned by, his buzz different from the honey bees, heavier and more erratic.

Gillian inhaled the perfume of a newly blossoming rose. She stroked the petals with the tip of her finger, soft but firm, not wet but not dry, either. All these things, gifts she never had in New York. But they were all here, in her mother's backyard, in spite of the lack of water and care, they survived.

Like Mother is surviving. Like I am a survivor. All these gifts on this Sunday morning. Lord, I am rich beyond measure. She sat down at the table to watch the hummingbirds now feasting at the hanging baskets, to let the sun warm her, the slight breeze kissing her face. She pulled another chair out so she could put her feet up and let all the tension drain from her body.

So much to do, but she had time to do it tomorrow. Or the next day. Right now she could just enjoy. No lists. No rush. Time to just appreciate.

"Well, talk about a beautiful picture."

She looked over her shoulder to smile at Adam. "Come on out."

"The door was unlocked and I didn't want to disturb you by ringing the bell."

"Have a chair. Can I get you something to drink?" She started to get up, but he laid a hand on her shoulder.

"You just sit there. I have a feeling you don't do that very often."

"You're right, I don't." Her shoulder felt cool as soon as he lifted his hand, but the warmth that went into her bones remained.

"How's the hummingbird?" He sat down across the table from her.

She nodded toward the baskets. "Him and her over there. When I peeked in the box, she was staring right at me, so I brought the box out here. I had warmed the sugar syrup in the feeder, and she waited a few seconds, just watched me, and then flew out. She was not afraid at all."

"They aren't. Dad and I've had them fly into the house several times. If the door is open we guide them out again with the broom. Half the time, they hitch a ride on the broom. I'm glad she's all right."

"Me, too."

"How's your mother?"

"Doing so much better. Even talking, not just yes or no, but in complete sentences. She's sleeping now; the shower exhausted her."

"You want to go for a walk?"

She pondered for a moment. "No, I don't think so. Enzio is bringing lunch any time and I said I would be here. But thanks." She cocked her head to the side. "But another time, perhaps?"

He nodded. "I'm taking the boat out this afternoon, I was hoping I could talk you into trying it." He smiled and stood. "Another time."

She shaded her eyes with one hand since he was backlit by the sun over his shoulder. "You don't give up, do you?"

"Nope."

"You could stay for lunch."

"Dad's waiting and Jennifer and Lawrence are coming, too. Enjoy your day."

She watched him as he slid open the screen door and walked through the house. Could she go out on the boat and not be barfing over the side? She'd ridden on a boat once off Long Island. It had not been pleasant. But like Adam had said, perhaps there was a medication that could prevent seasickness. The real question was why did he insist she should want to go out on his boat?

He and Jennifer were a striking couple. Had he ever thought of his sister-in-law romantically? Sometimes that happened. "I hope not," she muttered as she stood up and pushed the chairs back in. She cranked up the umbrella and went into the kitchen for a wet cloth to wipe down the table.

Why had that idea bothered her so? After all, she and Adam weren't even really friends yet, but somewhat more than acquaintances. She laid her hand on her shoulder where his hand had been. Was it still warm or was she imagining things?

Something was going on. Enzio had brought lunch as promised, and her mother has actually gotten up! Not only that, she had joined them for lunch in the backyard. Now Gillian stood at the kitchen window watching Enzio and her mother at the patio table, their heads together, his smile broad enough to split his face. Her mother was actually smiling and nodding. Dorothy leaned back in her chair, shaking her head, but Enzio was being his most charming. How could she resist whatever he was selling her? Gillian brought the iced tea pitcher outside to refill the glasses. "You two look like two kids plotting mischief."

"Oh, not mischief," Enzio replied.

"Is this part of the secret?"

Her mother frowned slightly, started to say something, then caught Enzio's slight shake of his head.

"Well, when you get around to telling me..." Gillian swallowed a chuckle. Two kids, they really were acting like two kids. What a change. How could she say thank you enough?

Chapter Twenty-three

Gillian watched the hummingbirds while drinking her first cup of coffee on Monday morning. Hearing them click at each other made her smile. Since it was still chilly out, she wore rust-colored sweats with a down vest and kept her hands warm by holding the coffee mug. The lady hummer had already buzzed by to check out the red in Gillian's clothes, flying back to the feeder when she discovered Gillian wasn't a flower.

Something strange had been going on yesterday, but Gillian had no idea what.

The thoughts still made her restless. Here she should be rejoicing that her mother was improving and instead she was feeling confused. No, maybe concerned was a better description. Of course, she'd been concerned ever since she'd arrived here the first time. Now she felt more like apprehensive—there that was the right word. Like that old saying, "waiting for the next shoe to fall."

Her mother was sitting up in bed, her hair combed, and staring at the clothes she had laid out. "Good morning," she answered Gillian's greeting. "I cannot believe how weak I am."

Gillian rolled her lips together. Wait until she called Allie and told her all that had gone on. She wouldn't believe it, either. "I guess sleeping so much does that to one. I can help you after you eat if you want." She set the tray with two plates on the bed, smoothed out the blankets, and put the tray on her mother's lap. "Enzio brought an extra loaf of bread yesterday, so we have good sourdough for toast."

"That Enzio." Dorothy shook her head.

"He's quite a character." Gillian sat in the chair and held her plate on her lap. Maybe this was the last time they'd eat in here. She took a bite of her toast. "You know, we can't get as good a sourdough in New York as here. Must have something to do with the climate."

Her mother glanced up at the window where the hummingbirds were visiting the pink and red blossoms. "Determined, aren't they?"

Gillian nodded. That one comment made her investments of time and money worth every penny and minute. "I was so thrilled when she flew to the feeder yesterday morning, I nearly cried. I was sure she was dead."

"Good that you are finding interests here. Do you miss New York?"

Gillian pondered the question. "Possibly, when I allow myself to think about it. But I don't think I've felt so relaxed for years." *The corporate world is a pressure cooker for sure.*

"Good. You're not in a hurry to leave then?"

"I'm here as long as you need me."

"Then what?"

Gillian stared out at the hummers. "I don't really know."

"I always found that gardening is a good way to clear the mind, help one to think more clearly."

"I can remember you saying that years ago. But there aren't a lot of places to garden in the Big Apple."

"No, I suppose not." Dorothy removed the tray from her lap.

Gillian picked it up. "If you want help dressing, I'll be right back."

"Thank you, but I think I'll rest a bit first."

"I've made a list of things I want from the nursery. Thought I'd plant the pots by the back door."

"Get plants that don't freeze. Pansies are really hardy."

"Okay." Gillian felt like dancing her way back to the kitchen. Her mother was getting better, no longer talking about dying. When could she ask her what brought about the change? She answered the ringing phone as she set the tray down.

"Hi, this is Roger. Your car is ready."

"Wonderful. Thank you, I'll be right down." She hung up and the thought hit her. How would she get the rental car back to the lot? Too late to call Adam, he'd have left for the store. Enzio? She dialed his number, but it went to the answering machine so she hung up. There was no way she wanted to listen to Allie get all excited about it. *What am I going to do?*

She put the dishes in the dishwasher and went to change clothes. She no longer needed to wear sweats. That was for sure. A short time later, Gillian backed the rental car out of the garage and headed for Roger's Auto Body Repair. While she had the address from the work order, she still made a couple of wrong turns before she found it. Another thing to add to her list. Either put the GPS service on her phone or buy a separate portable unit. Since she never drove in New York, she'd never needed one before.

After she inspected the new bumpers, which looked perfect as far as she could see, she paid the bill. "I have a favor to ask," she said as she put her credit card back in her wallet. "Is it possible someone could drive one of these cars over to the rental place so I can turn mine in?"

Roger, his A's baseball cap pushed back on his head, grinned. "Sure we can do that. In fact I will. I'll drive the Buick and, if you like, lead the way?"

"Thanks. Once this one is back in Mother's garage, I will feel great relief." She drove Roger back to his shop after turning in the rental, and he made suggestions on the easiest and fastest way to get to Pittsburg and Adam's nursery.

"You won't have any trouble," he said as he exited the car. "Although you do know, his dad's nursery is closer to your house?" He winked at her and touched the brim of his cap.

"Thanks for your help."

"Any time."

She followed his directions to Highway 4 and headed east. The big old Buick seemed to float along the freeway. Now she could tell her mother the story without feeling badly. The car looked every bit as good as before. She took the exit Roger had suggested and turned into Bentley's Garden Store just minutes later. When she didn't see Adam's SUV, she scolded herself for not calling him before she left. A surprise didn't do much good if the surprisee wasn't there.

An older man, wearing the official green, collared T-shirt, smiled at her. "Can I help you with something?"

She nodded and returned the smile. "Yes, I intend to plant some large pots for fall color." She pulled an article she'd torn from one of her mother's magazines from the outside pocket of her leather purse and handed it to him. "Sort of like these, but I need plants that can live through frosts like the one we had last Saturday night."

He glanced down at her article. "Do you have the sizes of your pots?"

She shook her head. "I didn't think of that, but I can show you. By the way, is Adam here?"

"Nope, but he'll be back soon. He went to pick up the printing."

"Thanks, I'll watch for him then."

"Let's get a cart and we'll pick out what you like." She showed him the sizes of the two tall pots and the two low ones she'd put by the front door. If she bought extra plants, she'd form groupings in the patch of dirt by the front door and along the rose bed. That's what the article suggested. "I'm going to need some potting soil, too."

"Are the pots full or empty?"

He showed her the different plants including some spiky grasses, round purple-colored decorative cabbages, several trailing-type plants, and some chrysanthemums. Although she nixed the ivy, her shopping cart filled up quickly. She added a couple of six-packs of pansies to please her mother.

"Now, do you need anything else?"

"Not that I can think of. Any suggestions?"

"We have gourds like that article shows in a basket if that might interest you."

She studied the pictures and then shook her head. "I'll try these to start with."

"Well, look who's here."

The sound of Adam's voice brought her around to face him.

"I wanted to surprise you."

"You did that. I see John has found the things you needed?"

"Yes, he did." She turned to the man. "Thank you. You've been most helpful."

The clerk at the cash register waited patiently, but when Adam nodded, she took out her pricing wand and started ringing up the purchases.

"You have time for lunch before you head home?"

"I think I can manage that." She smiled up at him, almost taking a step backward. She'd not had a man affect her like this for years. Not since Pierre, and she'd managed to forget him for most of the time. While she'd dated in college, none had been the man she was waiting for.

"Good. Let me get a couple of things done and we'll go in my car. You can leave yours parked here."

"Will my plants wilt in the trunk?"

"I don't think so, we won't be gone that long."

By the time one of the clerks had loaded all of her plants into the car, Adam drove up in his SUV and jumped out to come around and open the passenger door for her. Climbing up into the truck made her glad she wasn't wearing a straight skirt.

He got in and slammed his door. "Okay, Mexican, seafood, Thai, or Chinese?"

"Ah, what's easiest?"

"Seafood is the farthest away."

"Thai?" She'd not eaten a lot of Thai food, and besides it might be interesting to sample the variations between the East Coast and the West Coast.

"Good, that's the best around here." They drove a couple of blocks before he pulled into a strip mall and parked in front of a narrow restaurant. "I know it doesn't look like much, but the food is superb."

Once seated, they studied the menu on the wall that had pictures of all the entrées and brief descriptions of each.

"You can order any dish and tell them how spicy you want it."

"What is good?"

"Everything."

She glanced over to see him studying her and not the menu. She swallowed; suddenly her throat was dry and heat seemed to be creeping up her neck. "I—I can't make up my mind."

"Fish, beef, pork, or chicken?"

"Chicken."

"Okay, look at three, seven, and fifteen. They're all excellent."

"Fifteen."

He left her sitting at a table and went up to the counter to order. From the way the short man greeted him, it was obvious Adam came here often. He placed their orders and returned to the table. "I forgot to ask what you wanted to drink so I just ordered Tai tea for both of us. Is that all right?"

"Fine."

"So how were things at your house this morning?"

Gillian leaned forward. "I cannot believe the difference in my mother. She got out clothes to dress today but then decided on a nap first after breakfast. I said I'd help her, but I bet I find her dressed when I get back."

"That's wonderful. And I see you have her car back."

"Yes, and in perfect condition. Roger drove the Buick over to the rental agency for me. He's sure a nice guy."

"That he is. Did you hear from the insurance company?"

"Not yet. How was the sailing?"

"We had a great time. Jen had Dad laughing so hard, I thought he would collapse. We stopped for dinner near the marina."

"You look a bit sunburned."

"I know."

The man at the counter brought their orders, his smile rounding his cheeks. "Your first time here, eh?" He nudged Adam. "You introduce us, no? Bring pretty lady here, very good."

Adam grinned at him and introduced Gillian. "This is Mr. Ray Yang. He makes sure everyone gets the best food, the best service, and he never forgets a name."

"Gillian? New name I not heard before." He set an extra plate of interesting looking food on the table. "You try this, tell me what you think." He moved the plates around to make room for an extra plate. "You need anything else?"

Adam shook his head. "As usual, excellent."

"You tell me that after you taste." He smiled, nodding at the same time, and returned to his post.

Gillian picked up her fork, but laid it down again when Adam bowed his head. "Thank You, Lord, for food, friends and this day, amen."

"Is he always friendly like that?"

"Always, there are no strangers when he's around." Adam used chopsticks and lifted a prawn to his mouth. "Do you use chopsticks? I didn't think to ask."

"No, I do better with a fork." She took a bite of her chicken. "Um, you were right." She watched him eat. "How did you get so dexterous with chopsticks?"

"One of my tours of duty was to Japan. Over there you eat with chopsticks or go hungry, so I learned."

"How long were you in the military?"

"I put in my full twenty years, mostly based on aircraft carriers. I hadn't liked the idea of submarines so opted for the big ships. Moved my way up to commander, head of IT, which meant a lot of computer work. When I'd put in my twenty years, Charlie and I decided to start a business producing programs for the navy."

"What did you like about the navy?"

"Seeing the world. And I've always loved boats and airplanes. I thought I'd go for thirty years, but Charlie had a really great idea so I opted out."

"Do you regret changing course?"

"Not at all. I'd have missed those years working with my brother, and then when he died, I couldn't sustain any interest in the business. So I sold it."

"Losing him must have been terrible for all of you." She watched his face, his quick blinking making her want to take his hand. Obviously the loss was still hard to bear.

"It was. Life was going so well and then he was gone." He laid his chopsticks down on the edge of his plate. "He wasn't just my brother, he was my best friend. We did everything together. Boating, skiing, the business. He married Jen and then it was the three of us."

No woman in your life? But she decided not to ask that question. He'd not mentioned anyone.

He checked his watch. "I better get back." His smile made her heart trip. "Thanks for the surprise."

"You are welcome." She'd only eaten half of her lunch and asked for a take-out box. As they left, Mr. Yang came around to escort them to the door.

"You come back now, bring Gillian with you. I make her something special."

"Thank you, Mr. Yang. I will be back," Gillian promised before they returned to the SUV. "I ate too much." She leaned against the seat. "Those servings were huge."

"And cheap. The best food for your money anywhere around here. We should have bought an order for your mother."

"I'll give this to her. There's more than enough there." She held up the little white take-out container.

"If you want, I'll lift those bags of potting soil out of the trunk for you when I get home this evening."

"Thanks, I can manage. Me and the wheelbarrow. Maybe I can get Mother outside to supervise my planting."

He parked beside the newly repaired Buick. "I'll see you when I get home."

"All right." She caught herself on the intensity of his gaze. "Th-thank you for lunch."

His voice deepened, just slightly, but her suddenly sensitive hearing picked up on it. "You're welcome."

He got around and opened the SUV's door for her before she had her seat belt unsnapped and had picked up her purse.

She unlocked the Buick door, her hand shaking slightly. "See you." He was still standing there watching when she glanced into the rearview mirror as she drove away. She heaved a sigh, of what she wasn't sure. "My word but he packs a punch," she muttered to herself. *How did I not notice that before?*

The clock on the dash showed nearly one thirty when she turned into the driveway. Enzio's car sat at the curb. She unlocked her mother's car trunk, lifted it to give the plants fresh air, and without opening the garage door, walked to the front door.

Two suitcases waited just inside the door. Was Enzio moving in? The thought shocked her. "Mother?"

"Back here."

Was that a dog bark she heard? Gillian headed to the backyard where the voices had come from. Enzio and her mother were seated at the patio table. A dog, fluffy and white with a couple of black spots, ran around the yard, sniffing everywhere.

"Why the suitcases?" she asked, stopping beside her mother.

"Because we are going on a cruise." Enzio answered her question.

"You are what?" Surely her hearing had taken a vacation.

"Your mother and I are going on a cruise. We have to be at the pier at four thirty. The car will be here for us in about half an hour. Oh, and I have a special favor to ask you. My dog sitter had an emergency and obviously I can't take Winnie with me. Would you please dog-sit while we're gone?"

Chapter Twenty-four

Gillian? You here?"

A dog started barking. A dog here? It sounded like a little yapper.

"I'm in the kitchen, Adam. Come on in."

Adam strolled into the kitchen to find Gillian sitting at the table, staring at the wall. "What's the matter?"

"They're gone."

"Who's gone?"

"Enzio and my mother." She shifted her stare from the wall to him.

Adam pulled out the chair next to her and sat down, ignoring the fluffy dog who sniffed his pant leg and darted back to hide behind Gillian's leg. "Gone where?"

"On a cruise."

"What?" Adam's eyebrows drew together. "As in cruise on a ship?"

"Uh-huh. A big black car picked them up and away they went." She stroked the head of the dog who had jumped onto her lap and now kept a careful watch on the visitor. "I still can't believe it."

"Maybe you better start at the beginning. After all, it wasn't that long ago that you and I had lunch."

"I walked in through the front door and saw two suitcases sitting there." Gillian pointed toward the front door. "Enzio's car was parked exactly where it is right now. I asked who owned the suitcases, and they dropped the bomb on me."

"Was this planned?"

She shook her head. "Enzio saw an ad for a remarkably inexpensive cruise, leaving today. He called, bought two tickets, came here, convinced Mother to go along, packed her suitcases, told her whatever else she needed they would buy on the trip, asked if I would please watch the dog, and said a car would pick them up. It did and away they went."

Adam tried not to, but the snort made it past his resolve. He rolled his lips to keep from laughing. The look on her face didn't even hint at humor. But all he could think was this was the funniest thing he'd heard or seen in a long, long time. "I..." *Choke, cough.* "I..." He couldn't hold it any longer. A deep belly laugh broke out that brought the dog to her feet.

"Well, I fail to see the humor in this. After all..." The dimple in her right cheek deepened. "Adam Bentley, this is a serious matter."

"Why? Two people took off on a cruise. It's wonderful. I hope they have the time of their lives."

"But Mother is so weak..."

"He can get her a wheelchair. This is the best thing to get her off her dying kick. If I'd thought of it, I'd have bought them the tickets." His grin pleaded for her to laugh, too.

She chewed on her lower lip. "But what if..."

"What if what? If she needs a doctor they have a good doctor on board. I take it they are heading south?"

"Yes, it's the last cruise from here heading south. They are going through the Panama Canal and into the Caribbean." Her lips twitched.

"Good for old Enzio. He's got more life in him than..."

"Mother couldn't get hold of Allie, so she left a message on both the answering machine and Allie's cell phone. Allie's going to be fit to..." A giggle escaped.

"I love it!" Adam threw back his head and laughed again, slapping his hand on his knee. "Wait until Dad hears this."

"You don't have to tell the world, you know." Gillian heaved a sigh along with another chuckle. "I still can't believe it. My dying mother is already aboard a cruise ship bound for Florida or Texas or I don't know where. They left the itinerary here somewhere." She shook her head again. "They were going to leave me a note. Can you believe that? A note!"

The little dog jumped down and went to stand by the door, looking over her shoulder at the two laughing lunatics.

"Your dog wants out."

"She's not my dog." She wiped the laughter leaking mascara away with her fingertips. "So I am a dog-sitter until they get back." She let the dog out. "Good thing we have a solid fence in the backyard. My mother has never owned a dog."

He swallowed and drew in a deep breath. "Did you have any clue?"

"Nope. I figured he cares about her a great deal." She narrowed her eyes. "He told me once that he had a secret. No, but that couldn't be this because he said he only knew of the cruise this morning. But perhaps..." She nodded, tongue digging at her inner cheek, "maybe he was trying to tell me that he loves, or is in love with, my mother."

"Sure could fit. They've been friends for a long time, and he certainly has been here to help her and you every moment you needed him."

"Maybe that's what got her turned around? I keep thinking on that. What made the difference that she finally responded?"

"You say finally, but when you think of it, it wasn't really that long."

The phone rang. Gillian glanced at it then back to Adam. "You want to bet?"

"Allie?"

Nodding, Gillian answered the phone and then held it away from her ear.

Adam could hear Allie literally screaming. "...on a cruise? Why didn't you stop her? What is the matter with her? With him? I can't believe this. Gillian! Are you there?"

"I am, but you about broke my eardrum." She flinched and held the phone out again.

"...can't believe you let them go!"

"Allie, calm down. Now!" Had she been in the same room, Gillian might have resorted to slapping her little sister to stop the hysteria. After all, that's what they did in the movies. Worked every time. She glanced over at Adam who was fighting not to laugh again.

"How could she do this to me?" Shouts faded to a plaintive whimper.

"Allie, she didn't do anything to you. If we're going to play that game, you can take the dog, too."

"The dog?"

"Enzio's dog is here. I am the designated sitter since his usual one bugged out."

"And you let him impose on you like that?"

Gillian rolled her eyes. Adam sputtered.

"Who's there?"

"Adam."

A silence hummed over the wires. "How long will they

be gone?" Her voice finally sounded normal although a bit weepy.

Gillian wanted to say until they got back, but she opted for, "Two weeks, I think."

"What will you do?"

"Take care of the dog, plant the pots, clean up the garden. There's plenty here for me to do."

"Go out to dinner with me." Adam spoke loud enough for Allie to hear him.

"How will you do that? I mean the dog?"

"I will put the dog, whose name is Winnie, in her crate with a couple of toys and lock the door on my way out."

"You don't have to get sarcastic."

"Well, in case you haven't figured it out, this was as big or a bigger shock to me. I almost came back to an empty house and a note."

"True." Another silence. "I cannot believe this. A week ago she was trying to die and now she's on a cruise. What happened?"

"I would like to say it was all my doing, but I think Enzio had more effect on her than I did. I just irritated her by making her eat and drink. And talk at times. Oh, and shower and go to the doctor and… I was doing my best."

Adam nodded and gave her a thumbs-up sign.

"So, what will you do now?"

"I've already told you."

"No, I mean, you know about a job or…"

Gillian heaved a sigh deep enough to curl one's toes. "My dear sister, I have absolutely no idea. All I was focused on was getting Mother back up and living again. I have two weeks here to take care of Winnie. Perhaps I'll come up with some ideas in the meantime."

"You could come to Sherrilyn's soccer game on Saturday.

Spend the day with us. Jefferson will show off his barbecue skills." Her voice was tentative, not screeching like a crow like when the conversation had first begun.

Gillian recognized an olive branch when she heard one. "That would be fun. Let's plan on it." She said good-bye and set the phone on the stand.

Hearing Winnie at the door, she opened it and let the dog back in. She'd never had a dog in all her life. "What am I going to do with you?" she asked, staring down into the dark button eyes.

"Feeding her before we leave would be a good idea," Adam's deep voice suggested.

"Sounds good." She picked up the sheet of instructions from the table. "Let's figure this out." Winnie sat watching her and trotted along beside her as Gillian pulled a container of dry dog kibble out of the pantry. Enzio had lined up two metal dishes on a rug in front of the stationary panel of the sliding glass door. One bowl held water, so she poured the kibble into the other one. "Okay. And you get a tablespoon of canned food on top of that."

Winnie danced with her to the refrigerator, watched while Gillian scooped the canned food onto the dry, and then began eating daintily.

"Nothing like Thor, that's for sure."

"No, she doesn't scare me half to bits."

"He's the most gentle and well-mannered dog around."

"He's big enough to frighten an elephant." Gillian placed the covered can back in the refrigerator and returned the kibble to the pantry. "I don't know how to take care of a dog."

Adam tapped the information paper. "Everything you will need is right here, even to the commands she knows. Winnie, what a name for a dog. You let her out after she eats and then put her in the crate and we leave. Simple as that."

"But what if she cries?"

"She'll quit. It's not like we're going to be gone for three or four hours. Dad is taking care of Thor, you will have taken care of Winnie, and we will go get something to eat before I faint."

Gillian rolled her eyes. "Faint from hunger, right." When Winnie went to stand at the door, she let her out and gave Adam an amazed look.

"Dogs like routine, some more than others. She really is settling in with you quite nicely."

"Enzio says she sleeps right along his thigh when he is sitting in his recliner watching television, and beside him all night. But don't think I'm ready to share my bed with a dog, no matter how cute and fluffy."

She gave Winnie a chew bone in the crate along with a few toys and let Adam lead her out of the house. She paused at the door. No whining, no whimpering, no barking. Maybe this wouldn't be so bad after all.

"Can we eat close by? All of a sudden, I am really tired."

"Sure. There's a great burrito place down by the Lucky store, plus an excellent place next door that serves Chinese. One over by Nob Hill has both Chinese and sushi. The Burrito House would be fastest."

"That sounds good. How about I treat you this time?"

"How about that is not a good plan?"

"Well, it's not like we're dating or anything."

"Says who?"

She stared at him. Did he really consider they were dating? The tone of his voice sure indicated as much. "I . . ." She shrugged. "I just thought you were being helpful to the new girl on the block." *That you treat everyone the way you've been treating me.* A warm glow started in her middle and spread outward.

They ordered their dinner and sat at a nondescript table.

"Ambiance is not on the menu here." He used his paper napkin to brush crumbs off the sand-colored table. "But if you like burritos, these are a full dinner."

When the cook called Adam's order number, he went up to the tall counter to pick up the food. Gillian noticed a woman watching Adam. He did turn heads. It wasn't that he was so handsome, not that he was ugly, but he had a presence about him. The sharp posture of his military background added to the sense, but it was his ready smile that cinched the attraction. He radiated concern and goodwill.

He set the basket in front of her, the burrito as big around as an average mouth and probably seven inches long, all wrapped in thin foil. "Enjoy."

"I'll never eat all of this."

"So, you add them to the leftovers in your refrigerator. You won't have to make lunch all week." He unwrapped his burrito, splashed some red sauce on it, and took a bite, his eyes closing in delight. "Mmm."

Gillian omitted the sauce. She was not one to burn her mouth in order to think the food was good. But the combination of rice, beans, grilled chicken, and who knew what else reminded her that it had been hours since lunch. She wiped her mouth with a napkin. "You sure know how to pick 'em."

"Restaurants, you mean?"

She nodded.

"I know. I like good food. My mother was a marvelous cook, and she taught her sons how since she had no daughters, so we all like good food. I'm not partial to fancy places, but if the food's not really good, I don't go back."

"What do you like to cook?"

"Comfort foods, I make a mean pie, and now that we

have a bread machine, I like playing with that, too. I'm afraid we are gadget freaks. My father says it is time to clean out the cupboards again. Did you cook much in New York?"

Gillian shook her head. "I usually got home too late to fix much. Often stopped by the deli on the corner and bought whatever was the special for the day. Mr. and Mrs. Levy pretty much made sure I ate. She was always trying to fatten me up. I kept yogurt, eggs, cheese, that kind of thing, along with fruit in the fridge. Bagels were my chief breakfast food. No one makes bagels as good as the delis in New York."

"You'll find some good ones in The City. I've not researched bagels in our area, but not the grocery stores, that's for sure."

Gillian ate half of her burrito and folded the foil over the open end.

"I'll get you a bag." Adam crumpled up the little piece he had left and took their baskets to the trash containers by the door. When he returned, he guided her to the door, his fingers just touching the middle of her back. She could still feel the spot later when he walked her to the front door of Dorothy's house.

"Thank you."

"You are most welcome." He grinned at her. "Do you have a key or do we need to break the window?"

She held her key up and inserted it into the lock. Immediately she heard Winnie bark.

"Ah, the big watch dog." Adam touched her shoulder and stepped back. "Sleep well."

"Night." She'd thought for a moment he was going to kiss her, but now she wasn't sure if she was disappointed or glad. She shut the door behind her and turned to watch him as he cornered the garage. The barking intensified.

"I'm coming, I'm coming. You don't have to announce it

to the world." She let the dog out. After a wagging greeting that earned her a pat, Winnie made for the door, looking over her shoulder to make sure Gillian understood what she wanted.

"So," Gillian said, as she opened the door, "who's in charge here after all?" She thought about her mother and hoped she was having a good time. The question still nagged at her. What had been the key that got her mother on her feet?

Chapter Twenty-five

She woke in the morning to the sensation of being watched. Who could be in her room? She'd locked the doors. Easing her eyes open a slit, she saw the source. Winnie sat on the pillow staring down at her. When the dog saw Gillian's eyes opening, she yipped and ran to the foot of the bed. When Gillian didn't move any farther, the dog ran back, bounded onto her chest, and whined again.

"Oh, I get it, you have to go out."

At the word *out,* Winnie leaped from the bed and ran out of the bedroom to be heard at the back door.

"I'm coming." Gillian rammed her feet into her slippers and shuffled down the hall. At least she only had to open the door, not go outside. Winnie darted outside, did her business, and scratched at the door. The dog whipped over to her metal dishes, drank from the water, and stared down into the empty dish, then up at Gillian. "You sure do make your wishes clear, your highness." She followed the routine from the evening before and when the dog was eating happily, staggered back to her bedroom. Seven a.m. There would be no sleeping in from now on, that was for sure. If only she had taken the time last night to set up the coffeemaker. But then she'd not planned on having a dog sleep with her, either. She'd given up the night before, quickly learning who had the upper hand, or paw in this case.

Donning a light robe over her pajamas, Gillian located the still-in-its-box coffeemaker and carried it back to the kitchen. She'd bought her mother one just like the one she had at her condo, so there was no learning curve. It would be ready by the time she'd finished her shower. From this day forward, she would have coffee from the moment she entered the kitchen, dog or no dog.

The question that was now her nemesis attacked while she was in the shower. *What will I do for the rest of my life?* A picture of a certain charming man up the street floated through her mind while she dried off. The picture returned while she brushed her teeth. The dog whined from outside the closed bathroom door. "Can I not even have the bathroom to myself?" But trying to ignore Winnie was like trying to turn off the rain. Gillian opened the door and the dog danced in, a squeaker toy in her mouth. By the time Gillian had her makeup on and was fully dressed, she'd decided that verbal toys had to go. Or at least be confined to the crate for when she was gone and Winnie needed to entertain herself.

After breakfast, she adjourned the house to work in the yard. The shades of brown in her mother's glazed pots promised to set off the colors of the newly purchased plants. With the magazine article weighted down by a rock on the table, she got to work. By the time she had the pansies planted in one pot and the decorative cabbage with white alyssum in the other, she found Winnie covered in dirt. The little dog had made an impressive hole for one of her size. What a mess.

"Okay, little dog, you are going to get tied up so you don't run out the gate when I take these to the front porch." She got out the long leash, hooked it on the dog's collar, and slipped the looped end under the table leg. The dog came with three kinds of leashes; was there a hint there?

Winnie let her know of her displeasure as Gillian rounded the house on her way to the front door. Setting the two pots on either side of the step, she stood back to view her work. Though the arrangements looked good and did indeed add color, the two taller pots behind them would set them off. Returning to the backyard, she let the dog loose again and tried digging into the tall pots. It might be tomorrow or next week before she could plant them they were so dried out.

Her phone blipped, letting her know a text message had arrived. She removed her garden gloves and flipped open the phone.

Having a great time. All is well. Love E. and D.

"Well, I'll be." Gillian glanced down at the dog who was staring up at her. "You have the dirtiest face. You need a bath." But first, she had two more pots to plant. She found a pronged hand digger on the wall in the shed and stabbed that into the wetter of the two tall pots. Stab, soak, stab, soak. She repeated the process over and over again and it was working.

This time the phone rang, not just blipped. "You want to bet that is Allie, all excited?" She looked down at Winnie, who just stared up at her.

"Hello."

"You got the text message?"

"I did. I'm grateful he sent it."

Allie sputtered. "I just can't get over it. Them leaving like that. Did they have separate staterooms?"

"How should I know?" *What difference does it make? I'm not the bedroom police.*

"Well, you at least got to say good-bye."

"True and I also got to keep the dog."

"What are you doing?"

"Softening the dirt in the two tall pots by the back door so I can plant them, then I am going to get cleaned up and go shopping. After I bathe the dog, who's been digging in the yard."

"Oh, I'll let you get back to work then. Bye."

Gillian glared and snapped the phone back into its holster. *What? Was she afraid I was going to insist she come help me?* As if insisting anything with her little sister had ever worked.

Gillian stared out over the dead garden as she watered the plants and set them in the shade. What would it take to bring this yard and garden back to some degree of beauty? Leaving the hose barely dripping into the pots, she decided she'd finish tomorrow. After brushing most of the dirt off Winnie, she let the dog back in the house and set about getting ready to leave with Winnie right at her feet the entire time. "Can't you find something to do beside try to trip me?"

Winnie wagged her tail, never taking her eyes off Gillian.

Once ready for shopping, she took her lunch out to the patio table and let her thoughts take over. So, apart from the yard, what should she do with this month at her disposal? Emulate her boss and take a vacation? The answer sat at her feet staring up at her in a most pathetic way. Of course she could put Winnie in a boarding kennel. But her mother and Enzio had left the house and the dog in trust to her. Besides which, there was no place she really wanted to go. At least not by herself.

"I don't know, Winnie, but it seems to me that the best bet for the moment and these next two weeks is to stay right here. What do you think?" The little dog about wriggled herself inside out. Gillian leaned over and picked her up, and for her effort got a clean chin. "I hope my makeup isn't bad for you, the way you keep ingesting it." She cuddled the fur ball under her chin and stroked her head and ears. "You sure are an affectionate little thing." And there was something comforting about having this bundle of fluff around her feet and now on her lap. Maybe there was something to be said for a dog in one's life after all.

Purse on shoulder, dog in crate, Gillian headed for the garage. "You be good, Winnie. I'll be back soon."

Sometime later, list in hand, Gillian entered the electronics store and pulled out a shopping cart. She needed more than just one or two things. At least she knew what she wanted in a laptop. Up and down the aisles she chose computer, printer, GPS, and a phone network with three receivers. In addition, she picked up a combination CD and DVD player with decent speakers and a handful of her favorite CDs. Some of the CDs were duplicates of those she owned in New York, but who knew when she'd be going back there. That was another one of those decisions she would need to make after her mother returned. She added some office supplies and headed for the checkout counter. Now she could listen to music and play movies if she wanted to.

Back in the car, she drove to the bank she'd noticed on her way in and withdrew cash from the ATM. If she stayed here she'd have to find a local branch of her bank or transfer her accounts. The big *if.* Such a little word to convey so much.

So many decisions. But how soon did she need to make them? After all, the thought of living with her mother when she returned, while an option, was not what she'd want for her life. She reminded herself again that she had only one month and she'd be heading back to New York. Possibly. Probably. But she didn't like to procrastinate. "Get in and get things done" had always been her motto. But what good had it done? Here she was at forty-five years old with her entire life in chaos. Obviously not of her own doing. As if that were any consolation.

She swung into a Starbucks with a drive-through and ordered a sugar-free vanilla latte venti but with only two shots of espresso. And a chocolate-dipped biscotti. Next she stopped in at a real estate office and asked for a map of Martinez.

"Are you new to this area?" the woman asked.

"I'm here visiting my mother." That was at least part of the truth.

"If I can help you in any way, let me know." She handed a business card across the counter. "After all, you might decide you like living here."

"Thanks." Gillian waved the map. "Who knows?"

Later that afternoon she installed and organized her new computer as Winnie lay beside her on the sofa, dreaming doggy dreams. Gillian smiled at the antics. Waiting on the computer programs to load took far more time than she had realized; she had had IT people doing it for her at Fitch, Fitch, and Folsom. She heard a car door slam, and Winnie leaped to her feet, barking before she even had her eyes open.

"Come on in," she called as the big shadow opened the screen door to knock.

Adam looked down at the white fluff barking at him from

right in front of his feet. "Well, she sure decided this was her house quick."

"She already rules things here, but I did not take her in the car with me." Gillian patted the sofa. "Enough, Winnie, come." The dog growled one more fierce bark, and, glancing over her shoulder, returned to sit by Gillian's feet, glaring at the newcomer.

"And she slept in her crate?"

"Well, not exactly. But she sure settled down when I got under the covers on my side so she could stretch out along my back."

"I see. So much for no dog sleeps in your bed, right?" He stared at the various boxes, plastic bags, and Styrofoam packing. "I guess you did go shopping."

"Have a seat. I'm waiting on this to finish loading."

"Did you get all the pots planted? The ones by the front door sure look nice."

"Nope, still trying to get rock-hard dirt in the tall pots to soften enough so I can dig it out. Discovered that Winnie likes to dig. A lot. That little white face was more black than white when I finally realized what she was doing."

"What was she digging for?"

"How should I know? I haven't learned to speak dog yet."

"You and feisty there want to walk with Thor and me?"

"Are you sure Thor won't eat her in one gulp?" Her fingers flew over the keyboard. "Ah, that's done for now. I still have to install the printer, but I can do that later. I thought you two usually ran."

"We do, but we can walk."

"All right. We heard from Enzio today. By text, no less. Having a good time. All is well."

"That's it?"

She nodded. "Allie was a trifle upset."

"I bet. I'll be back in about fifteen or twenty minutes. Does that work for you? Oh, and Dad and I are ordering pizza for tonight. You want to join us?"

"I haven't had pizza in a long time. Sure." *So casual, just like we've been neighbors for years. Is this what life in the 'burbs is like?* "Can I bring anything?"

"Nope. You like everything on it?"

"Everything but anchovies."

Adam rose, which sent Winnie into a growl. "Are you a runner?"

"Nope. Tried jogging but my feet hurt." *And my knees and hips. Ugh.*

"Were you on concrete?"

"Pretty much."

"That's why." And out the door he went.

"You be nice to him, you silly dog. He's the best friend we have." She got up to answer the phone; she hadn't set the new ones up yet.

"Hi, Gillian, this is Jennifer, Adam's sister-in-law."

"Well, hi. How nice of you to call."

"How are things going there? Adam told me about the exodus. And that you get to dog-sit."

"Winnie and I are learning to get along. Or she's training me, I guess you could say."

"I was wondering if you would have time for lunch one day this week. I could come out there."

Gillian quickly reviewed her calendar in her head. "Wednesday or Thursday?"

"Good, how about Thursday. I'll pick you up, say, twelve thirty so we miss the lunch crush?"

"Great. Thanks." Gillian hung up, smiling at the prospect. Maybe she'd have a friend there, too. Heading for the bedroom to change into walking shoes, she shuffled her toes toward Winnie, who pounced on her foot. "I think I need to learn how dogs play. And I'm getting a chance to maybe make a new friend. What do you think?" Winnie jumped onto the bed beside her, head cocked, black eyes dancing. "You know, you look like a wind-up toy. You want to go for a walk?" Off the bed and down the hall to the kitchen Winnie went, her yipping sounded a lot like a giggle. Was it the word *walk* or *go* that set her off?

Maybe having a dog would get her out walking every day. Especially if she could walk with Adam. Thor, however, was another matter. She took the leash off the hook by the back door. Another adventure about to begin. She'd been doing a lot of that lately. New adventures, that is. *Maybe I'm just going to have adventures for the rest of my life.*

"You're sure he's not going to eat her?" Gillian asked when Adam and Thor arrived.

"He won't eat her. We'll just let them get acquainted. Thor, sit." The huge dog did just that. "Okay, bring her out and let them sniff."

Her heart pounding, Gillian did as he said. The two dogs sniffed each other before Winnie returned to sit behind Gillian's feet, a slight growl voicing her displeasure.

"Okay, let's go."

"That's it?"

"They'll adjust." Adam and Thor took the street side and the foursome headed down the hill, Thor heeling and Winnie trotting in front.

"I bought a GPS."

"Good. Do you know how to install it?"

"Bought a portable one; I'm sure I'll figure it out."

"Call me if you have trouble."

"Are you this helpful to everyone?" She caught a frown on his forehead.

"Hmm, have to think on that. Most people I meet aren't beautiful, charming, and caught in crazy circumstances."

"Adam." In spite of her, a warm glow suffused her middle. *Did he really think that or was he being polite?*

"You have to admit you've been in an unusual situation."

"More than one."

"I rest my case. We follow the path along the road." He indicated a turn to the right.

"Do you always go the same way?"

"Pretty much. We get a run at the school except Saturday mornings when they play soccer or baseball there. Otherwise we take the truck down to one of the parks."

"Jennifer called me."

"Good. I think the two of you will really hit it off."

She wanted to ask, "So, are you and she a pair?" or something along that line but refrained. "Tell me about her family."

"She's been a widow for better than three years now, daughter, Lissa Marie is nineteen, going to college, and working in The City. Son, Lawrence, is seventeen and a junior in high school. Good kids. She's done well with them."

"Does she work? Outside the home, I mean."

"A lot of volunteer stuff, manages my brother's estate, tries to keep tabs on Dad, and I..." He paused. "I've tried to get her dating again, but she says she's not ready."

Guess that answered one question, she thought, at least from his point of view. They crossed the road and into the school driveway.

"I let Thor off leash here, but I'd not recommend that for Winnie until we know she'll come when called and not run off."

"Okay. You go run, too, if you want. We'll just walk around."

"You sure you don't mind?"

"Not at all." She watched as Thor ran in ever broadening circles around them. When Adam took off, Thor ran beside him. Although the two males looked to be having a good time, Gillian had no desire to run or even jog. But she and Winnie could walk fast. By the time they headed up the hill, her heart rate was indeed up and Winnie's tongue was hanging out. All Gillian really wanted was a chair and a tall glass of iced something.

Chapter Twenty-six

"He's not in the habit of eating guests for dinner."

Gillian glanced up at Adam. "You sure?"

"You're chewing your lip."

"No, I'm not."

"And when you're nervous, you chew your lip."

"Whatever makes you think that?" She clamped her teeth together. Caught for sure. "Smart aleck."

"You ready?" He waited before reaching for the door handle.

"Oh, for..." Gillian inhaled a deep breath and let it out. "Yes."

Adam grinned at her. "He's going to love you." *I know because he and I have similar tastes, and while I'm not sure I'm in love yet, I think it is on its way*. He opened the door and let Thor go first.

"Maybe I should have left Winnie off at Mother's."

"Gillian, you are dithering."

She rolled her eyes and went through the open doorway, since he was holding the door.

Adam hung up Thor's leash, and, taking her arm, led her back to the family room. "Dad?"

"Out here."

"He's out with his babies." He grinned when her eyebrows rose. "Mom called all his plant starts his babies because he is so protective of them. Really it's a mini-nursery out there." He ushered her out the sliding screen door to the slate patio.

"I think it is too chilly to eat outside tonight. The pizza is in the oven." Bill raised a trowel in greeting.

"Dad, meet Gillian and the fluffy thing down there is Winnie. Gillian, my father, Bill."

"Ah, I now have a face to go with such a lovely name." Bill held out his hand after wiping it on his pant leg. "All these years I have heard about you and now we finally meet. Welcome."

"Thank you. I can tell where Adam got all his charm."

"No, no, that came from his mother. I'm the curmudgeon nurseryman who would rather play with his plants than converse with humans."

"I don't think I'm going to believe that. Not for a minute. What are you working with out here?" She looked over his tables and planting masses.

"I start some plants with cuttings and then I hybridize irises; that's my real hobby. Someday I hope to introduce a new bearded iris."

"Really? But don't you divide iris rhizomes to propagate them?"

"Yes, and we do that after I have one that I want field trials on, but you need to pollinate for seeds to come up with new varieties." He led her over to the seed beds. "Now these are my newest ones, pollinated this year, the real babies. Those are from other years." He indicated carefully marked rows of irises.

"And do you have some with real promise?"

"I do. I'll show you them in the spring when they bloom."

"He has pictures of his best. He won a prize in an iris show one year."

"Really, how exciting."

"About like watching grass grow, I imagine," Bill said with a droll nod. "Enough of this, let's go eat dinner before the pizza dries out."

Adam touched the middle of her back to guide her and beamed when she threw him a smile over her shoulder. She'd just made a lifelong hit with his father by showing interest in his babies. What a woman.

"Hope you like supreme with all the trimmings." Bill pulled a pizza box from the oven and set it on the table. "There's salad if anyone wants."

"I'm fine. Pizza is a treat." Gillian handed her plate to Adam, who'd picked up the pie server. "One is fine."

Adam shrugged and served them all before taking a bite of his own. "So, how is this different from New York pizza?"

Gillian looped a string of cheese over her finger. "I have no idea. I don't do pizza in New York very often. I mostly eat at the corner deli. Mrs. Levy makes sure I get the specials of the day so there is variety."

"You don't cook?" Bill stared at her.

"Not often. Easier this way." She closed her eyes, the better to savor the flavors.

Adam watched the exchange; the shock on his father's face, the bliss on Gillian's. He glanced over to see the two dogs lying on the rug in front of the sliding glass door, as if they'd been friends for years and not hours. Hard to believe this was indeed Gillian's first time in the Bentley home.

"So, tell me about life in New York." Bill reached for another piece of pizza.

"Well, I have a condo in Greenwich Village, which isn't

a village at all but a part of Manhattan. I worked for a company that was taken over with all the management personnel let go. My former boss is taking a month's vacation, and he said that when he comes back and finds something else, he will call me. So I came back here to take care of Mother, and you know what has happened there."

Adam made sure he wasn't staring at her. The monthlong hiatus was news to him. Why had she not mentioned that? Would she really go back, or was this a pie-in-the-sky kind of thing? He had a feeling there were a lot of things he had yet to learn about Ms. Gillian Ormsby.

Bill shook his head. "Dorothy retreating to her bed wasn't like the woman I've known all these years. But then going off with Enzio was a shock, too."

"Good to hear you say that. I wondered if I was the confused one, gone too long to not have seen this coming."

"I was trying to figure what caused this for her, and I got to wondering if it had to do with her good friend dying and the stroke happening so close together. Those two women did a lot together, you know. Alice always said Dorothy was one you could count on no matter what the emergency. Rock solid."

"Good thinking, Dad. You know that might be a part of it, at least."

Gillian nodded. "I've sure been questioning what the catalyst might have been. I know Mother has always been terrified of strokes, so maybe all she heard the doctor say was stroke, not the degree of it."

"Depression can bring on all kinds of strange things."

Adam focused on another slice of pizza. Was his father speaking of himself in a rather oblique way?

Bill nodded and slapped his hands on the table. "Guess you just got to find new things to live for when you get dealt a bad hand. I'll clean up here; Adam why don't you show her your mom's scrapbooks? No better way to learn about the family than that."

Adam took Gillian's hand. "Come, the master has spoken."

They spent the next hour poring over scrapbooks. The albums filled one of the bookshelves of a built-in entertainment center that took up an entire wall of the family room. Bill joined the couple after he cleaned up the kitchen, and then he told some of the stories that went along with the pages.

"Thanks for such a delightful evening," Gillian said when she caught herself yawning. "We better get on home."

"I'll walk you down." Adam stood and stretched. "Come on, Thor. Let's walk." He took her hand when they reached the sidewalk. "Thanks for coming. I haven't seen Dad that animated for months."

"He's had a hard time, losing first a son, then his wife. I can't begin to understand how bad that is."

"Mom said that losing Charlie was the worst thing that could have happened. She said it left a hole in her heart, and I don't think that had time to heal before the cancer struck. For Dad, I think losing her was the harder of the two, if one can quantify such tragedy."

Gillian squeezed his hand. "And you tried to pick up the pieces?"

"I guess." They turned into her yard. "You have the key?"

She nudged him with her elbow. "Of course." She let go of his hand to dig in her pocket and pull out the key on a ring of its own.

But when she started to turn to open the door, he stopped her, tracing her jaw line with one finger, raising her chin. He bent his head and touched her lips, as if tasting first, before he kissed her again. When he raised his head, he smiled. "Night."

"Thank you for the evening."

"You're welcome." He watched as her hand shook slightly when she tried to insert the key. When the door opened, she turned to stare up at him, then followed Winnie inside.

"Come on, Thor. Let's go before I'm tempted to do that again."

Chapter Twenty-seven

Dear Gillian and Allie,

Your mother and I were married by the captain of the ship last night. Be happy for us. We are delighted. Love Enzio and his bride. P.S. I'm going to make sure she learns to use the computer. E.

Gillian stared at the e-mail message, the first one to arrive on her new computer. Probably the most shocking she'd ever received. She saw that both hers and Allie's names were on the contact line. Surely the phone would begin ringing any moment. So they got married. She leaned her head against the cushion on the recliner, Winnie snoozing by her side. What did this mean for her? Far as she could figure, just a new member in the family and she already adored him, so what was the catch?

Allie. Allie would be all upset, most likely hysterical. But why? She didn't want to take care of Mother. She'd proven that by calling in Gillian when things got rough. Not that she'd made a mistake, all things considered. This temporary move to the West Coast had been a good thing. She closed her eyes and ran the last couple of weeks through her mind like a newscast, starting with the failed proposal at work and now reading this latest announcement. A giggle escaped where on a movie screen would be printed THE END. Instead of a phone call, Mother and Enzio had e-mailed. Besides which, she knew her mother had chosen to not learn the computer. Who'd have thought they'd do such a thing? Meaning both e-mail and the obviously not planned marriage. She thought back to Enzio and his secret. Maybe asking her mother to marry him had been his secret. Or at least that he loved her.

She thought of forwarding the message to Adam, hoping he would see the humor in it, too. Hitting the FORWARD key, she knew Allie wouldn't. What had happened to her sister's sense of humor? Had life mashed it at some point, or could it be resuscitated?

Gillian hit REPLY and set to typing.

> *Congratulations. I couldn't be happier for you both. Welcome to the family, Enzio. Love and myriad blessings, Gillian*

After flipping through her e-mails to make sure there was nothing else important, she turned off the computer and sat stroking Winnie. The walk with Adam and Thor had been a pleasure, and she knew she was already in love with his father. Bill Bentley was a delightful man. The pizza was good, but the conversation made her feel like she was already a friend. She figured she was more than just a friend when Adam kissed her good night on the doorstep. *Tender* was the best word she could think of. Kind of like a hello kiss with hints of forthcoming desire.

She touched her fingertips to her lips. How long had it

been since she'd been kissed by a man, other than a friendly bussing that usually missed her skin?

Winnie whined and leaped to the floor, glancing over her shoulder so that Gillian would get the point.

"I'm coming." Letting the dog in and out was becoming ingrained. In fact, having the cuddly little canine was becoming a habit. A nice one, but she reminded herself that Winnie belonged to Enzio and would return to Enzio when he and her mother got back from their cruise.

She'd just finished dressing when the phone rang. "You want to bet that is my sister, my highly irate sister?" Winnie cocked her head and then scampered to the kitchen to wait by the phone. "After today we will not have this dinosaur running our life." She picked up the receiver.

"Did you know about this?"

"Allie, how would I know about it? I got the e-mail the same time you did." She pulled a chair over by the phone and sat down. This promised to be some conversation. "Why are you crying?"

"Our mother got married and we weren't even invited, and you wonder why I am crying?" She sniffed again and blew her nose. "Such a terrible thing to be left out like this."

"Allie, get a grip. It's not a terrible thing. We can always have a reception when they return. They are happy; that's all that counts. Think about it. Two weeks ago Mother insisted she was dying, and now she is partying on the high seas and is married." She almost threw in a comment along the lines of *at least she didn't have to get married*, but knew that would not go over well.

"If she loved us, she would have waited until they got home again so we could be with them." Sobs led to a hiccup. "This just isn't like Mother at all; she could have called."

Gillian heaved a sigh. Allie was sounding like her mother

of years ago. If you loved me—what an old tune that hadn't worked then and wouldn't fly now. "Of course she loves you. And I adore Enzio. If he were a few years younger..."

"Gillian Ormsby, what a thing to say."

"Well, he's a sweetheart, and if you'd been here and seen how lovingly he cared for her...Allie, he brought her presents and sat with her while she slept, and all the time she was nasty to him." *Like she was to me.*

"I—I feel so left out."

"Allie, this isn't about you. It's about them and their happiness. You'd better not try to call them in the state you are in."

"I wouldn't do that."

"Good thing."

"I don't know how to get ahold of them. Cell phones don't work out at sea."

"Don't tell me you tried." Gillian closed her eyes. *Please, God, no.*

"I did but I didn't leave a message."

"Thank goodness for small favors. When they get on land again, they will most likely call. You didn't e-mail them, did you?"

"No."

Her sister still sounded like a whiny little girl, pouting because she didn't get her own way. *Is that the way she treats her husband, too?* The thought came out of nowhere. Gillian felt like she had run into a glass wall. When had all this started? She didn't remember Allie acting like this when they were growing up. "Sorry, what's that you said?"

"I said you don't have to act like you're smarter than I am."

Whoa. "Sorry if I sounded—ah, condescending. This was a shock to me, too. After all, I was the one taking care of her. I certainly didn't plan this."

"Seems to me no one did. He saw an online special and just went out and bought the tickets?"

"And then convinced our mother to go with him. I don't know how he talked her into it. I really don't."

"But she is so weak."

"I said that, and he said he'd get her a wheelchair. Allie, they were already having fun. Mother was smiling. You know she has always dreamed of going on a cruise."

"I promised I'd take her."

"Well, I'm sure she'll want to go again." At least Allie seemed to be calming down. The two of them had to have some time together to work things out. "Did you have a fun weekend?"

"Well, Sherrilyn's team lost their game, but we had a good time out at the beach. For the first time I went someplace and didn't have to be worried about Mother."

And has all the worrying done any good, changed anything? Gillian knew this wasn't fair. After all, she seemed to have missed the family worry gene. "I'm glad you all had fun."

"With all that has gone on, I forgot to mention Halloween. Would you like to come out and see all the trick-or-treaters? The little ones are so cute."

"Halloween? Good grief, I never thought of that. There might be kids coming here?"

"Probably, parents usually drop their kids off at safe neighborhoods. Your street would qualify, I'm sure."

"Then I better stay here." *All I need is some vandalism because the house is dark.* She glanced at a calendar on the wall. "I'll be there on Saturday for sure. You need to e-mail me the directions. Do you mind if I bring Winnie?"

"Winnie? Oh, Enzio's dog. I guess. Sherrilyn will be delighted."

"You don't have a dog anymore?"

"Nope, we decided not to get another one after Butch died. I better get going. My list for today is long. We'll talk soon, and I'll send you directions for Saturday. Same e-mail addy?"

"Yes. Thanks for calling. Bye." Gillian hung up and headed for the coffeemaker. She needed a restorative cup like she needed air. First thing after the coffee, plant the tall pots. She'd already checked the soil, which was now moist enough. At least the plants wouldn't shift personalities as fast as her sister did. From baby to breezy in how many seconds?

She took her coffee to the patio table and resumed yesterday's task. The hummingbirds buzzed by her a couple of times, no doubt checking to see if her pink shirt was an especially sweet flower. The clouds playing tag with the sun meant shifts from hot to cool. After removing the plants from the plastic nursery containers, she set them in the pottery pots, then moved them around to get the desired arrangement. After filling potting soil in around the stems, she watered them in, added more soil, and wove the branches together like the man at the nursery told her to do. It did indeed make them look like they'd been growing in the pots for some time. She stepped back to view her handiwork.

"Nice." Nodding while she reached for her coffee cup, she took a swallow and made a face. Cold. Iced coffee was fine, but this was neither hot nor iced. She tossed the remains into the pots. Fertilizer, that's what she'd forgotten to add. The article said to sprinkle fertilizer pellets on the dirt before planting. Back to the shed. Fertilizer also came in liquid form. She mixed that as directed and watered all the newly planted pots. Something had been chewing on the pansies.

A trail of shiny goo over the edge of the pot identified the culprit. A snail or slug. Sure enough there under the rim of the pot she found a granddaddy snail. It crunched satisfactorily when she gave it the bottom of her heel. "Yucky things. What did Mother use to do to kill snails?" She could remember being assigned the job of locating and disposing of snails. Other than bagging them, tying the bag tight, and tossing it in the garbage cans, what did she put out? Good, a reason to call Adam. She heated another cup of coffee and sat down at the patio table with her cell phone.

She hit the TEXT button.

Lovely morning. How do you kill snails?

Sipping her coffee, she stared at the upper side of the property beyond the low rock wall. The upper garden that used to be all vegetables now hosted dead plants and poles with dried-out clinging vines. The weeds were growing just fine without water. If she cleaned it all out, the yard would at least look better. Besides, she might find a few plants still alive.

Her cell beeped.

Put out snail bait, around pots or in them. Will attract and kill snails. A.

Thank you. I'll look for some.

I'll bring a box when I come home.

Thanks. Good. Adam to the rescue again.

You want to walk tonight?

A smile lit her face.

Good idea.

She glanced down at the dog snoozing in the sun. At least she wasn't digging today.

See you six-ish.

I could make dinner. She hit SEND before her brain realized what her thumbs had typed.

Good. Ask Dad?

I will.

See you. A.

So now she had company coming for dinner and no idea what to fix. "What have I done?"

Winnie looked up as if to ask, "Are you talking to me?"

"No, go back to sleep. This is my problem." But when Gillian went back inside, Winnie followed her. A grocery list. She checked the pantry. Staples but no dinner food. The refrigerator. Plenty of leftovers, but no food for company. She grabbed her paper and started the list. She'd seen fresh pasta and sauces at the grocery store.

After shopping, she allowed herself two hours out in the garden, digging and pulling out dead plants. The refuse pile grew as foot by foot she reclaimed the soil. A fast shower and she morphed into hostess for her guests.

That evening the table looked lovely with her mother's good dishes on a seldom-used tablecloth. Gillian had even found candles in the save-for-some-fancy-day box in the bedroom and cut all the remaining roses to make a centerpiece. She'd put one of her favorite CDs on the player. This was so different from New York, where she'd pick up all the fixings, including flowers and candles, at the market, set it up, and then pretend she entertained often.

"Mmmm, something smells good," Adam said as he and his father entered the kitchen.

Bill handed her a pink cyclamen plant with foil and a bow. "Thought you might like this."

"Thank you. So you're back to work?"

"As of last Monday."

"Good for you. How are you doing?"

"Can't see any difference. Other than the medication the doctor put me on takes some getting used to."

She nodded and glanced down at Winnie, who was dancing about their feet but not pawing at their pant legs. Enzio had trained her well.

Bill leaned over and petted the dog, then picked her up. After cleaning his ear and chin, she snuggled into his chest and quieted as he stroked her.

"You have a friend for sure. She's so shy." Gillian motioned to the table. "Dinner is ready, so how about if we eat right away?"

"Fine with me." Bill set the dog down and took the back chair. "This sure looks pretty."

"Can I help you?" Adam asked.

"Yes, the salads are in the fridge. If you could put those on the table, I'll get the bread from the oven." When they sat down, Bill bowed his head so Gillian did, too. "Would you like to say grace, Bill?"

One of these days she would have to get comfortable saying grace, she thought. At the amen, she passed the bread. "Who ever would have dreamed that I'd be serving dinner at my mother's house?"

"Well, I for one am glad you're here." Adam's smile sent

her heart into overdrive. Would he kiss her again tonight? Not that she'd given the first kiss more than a thousand or so thoughts.

"Thank you."

After the salads she served the linguine with prawns in marinara sauce, sprinkling parmesan cheese on top. As they raved about how good everything was, she did not mention she'd been shopping, just accepting their praise with nods and smiles. If that was being deceptive, too bad.

After dinner, they moved into the living room for coffee and dessert. She curled in the recliner. "Make yourselves comfortable."

"If I get any more comfortable, I'll fall asleep." Bill stretched his arms over his head. "This getting old is the pits."

"So, you don't have to go back to work. We can manage; you have a good man in Keith. We can make it work." Adam leaned forward. "And you have plenty to do with propagating your plants."

"That's so true."

"At least you have a job to go to that you like to do." Gillian sipped from her china cup.

"I know, and I'm grateful for that. The nurseries have been good to us."

"How many years have you had them?"

"Opened the one here in Martinez in the seventies; it was just a small place that we later expanded. Let's see, we opened the Pittsburg store in 2001. Alice insisted we include fresh flowers and the garden art. She always had a good sense for what would be a profitable next addition. We put in the water feature sections just a couple of years ago." He caught a yawn.

"Gillian's trying to decide what she wants to do with the

rest of her life. I think I have an idea, at least for an interim job." Adam smiled at her. "I need another person on staff. How about coming to work for me?"

Gillian stared at him. Working in a nursery? "But I don't have any experience. I mean I don't even know all the names of the plants."

"You can learn. And you have a keen sense for what looks good together. Have you ever run a cash register?"

"Back in high school, but they are slightly different today."

"You could learn that quickly."

"I have an idea." Bill looked from his son to Gillian. "How about you buy Bentley's Garden Stores?"

Chapter Twenty-eight

Deal with one thing at a time, Gillian reminded herself.

Winnie whimpered and extricated herself from the blankets when Gillian half rolled on her. She scrambled to her feet and shook her head.

"Sorry, Winnie. I'm not used to being concerned about a bed partner." Gillian stroked the dog's head, but the action failed to derail her mind.

Adam says come to work for him and Bill says buy the whole company. Her stomach felt like she'd been struck a body blow. Both ideas imploded in her mind, and yet the conversations went on as if nothing had happened. She glanced at the lighted clock on the nightstand. Twelve thirty. She who never had trouble falling asleep had been stewing for an hour. Going to work out in the Pittsburg store was an easy thing to solve. Either do it or don't or ask for an extension. If Adam thought she could handle the job, she figured she could. After all, she learned new things quickly and she did have some gardening background. Surely much of what she'd learned as a child would come back as needed.

But it was just a job, a fill-in job until she could figure out what she wanted to do with the rest of her life. Surely she who could put together plans for multimillion-dollar proposals could learn to run a cash register. And she did need income eventually or she'd be forced to pull from her retirement funds. Or sell her condo in New York. Okay, she put those ideas away.

But buy the company? Was Bill out of his mind? Whatever had made him bring up an idea like that? She tried looking at it from all sides, but she didn't know enough about the business to look at it objectively. Number one: She had no idea what Bentley's Garden Stores were worth. Number two: She had no idea if she wanted to run the business. Number three: What would Adam think? She'd not been looking at his face when his father dropped the bombshell. From the sounds of things, they had discussed selling it before. And number four: Did she want to invest her retirement money in a business?

She rolled over again, this time the other way so as not to bother the dog. *This is not something you have to solve tonight, so put it away and go to sleep*. Easier said than done. For even if she weren't thinking on Bentleys, she did have to come up with some kind of plan for the rest of her life.

Interesting that she'd always worked toward the same goals, achieved them, and worked harder to make the successes solid. There had never been a Plan B. She flipped to flat on her back and practiced the deep-breathing exercises that made her relax. By the fourth inhale, hold to ten, and exhale, her body began responding, warmth stealing from her toes upward. When she reached the floating feeling, she knew sleep would creep in. Until Adam walked across her mind screen. Yes, there was definitely an attraction there. As they said, chemistry. Yes, he met her long-ago-dreamed-of criteria: honest, dependable, sense of humor, good-looking, intelligent, successful. But relationships took time, and she'd only known him a couple of weeks, been on a couple of dates. Enjoyed herself immensely.

But did she want to forget all about New York and instead live on the West Coast? Did she want to live so close to her mother and her sister, both of whom managed to frustrate her beyond measure? If she went back to New York, she could pretend that Allie was the woman she thought she was, not the whiner she'd found her to be lately.

If she stayed, she could be a real auntie to Sherrilyn and Benson, something she'd regretted at times that she hadn't been an exemplary aunt. She could get to know her mother again and enjoy Enzio. Working with dirt and plants and the out of doors would be about as opposite from what she did in New York as possible.

Winnie snored on.

Her mother had always said that God had a plan for her life. For everyone's life. How had she gotten so far away from the teachings of her childhood? Could she find her way back?

She awoke to the sun in her face. What time could it be? Winnie whimpered. Gillian threw back the covers and charged down the hall to let her fluffy friend out. Good thing she'd let her out late the night before or surely there would have been a puddle somewhere. Eight thirty. She never slept this late, was always up by seven no matter what time she went to bed.

She stared at the coffeemaker. No fresh coffee aroma. She'd forgotten to set it last night. She'd been too distracted by her reactions to the Bentley men and their ideas. Obviously she'd not be working today, at least not at the nursery. With Winnie back in and fed, the coffee started, she left the door to the bathroom open enough for Winnie and let the shower beat her fully awake. Gillian wondered if she went to work, how would she manage to accomplish all the things she wanted to do around here?

First on the list, besides sprucing up the backyard, was to tear apart her mother's bedroom and deep-clean it. She doubted it had been painted in all the years she'd been gone. A nice cream color would be a change from the dingy blue. But even before she considered painting it, it still had to be thoroughly cleaned. It smelled musty. Her mother used to be such a finicky housekeeper. When had that begun to decline? Surely more than a couple of months. If only she could ask Allie without her getting all defensive.

What would it cost to hire a painter? If she stripped the room, it shouldn't take more than a couple of hours. Sitting in the kitchen to eat her breakfast, she got out the phone book and looked up painters. The list went on for pages. Short of closing her eyes and stabbing at one, how could she find someone who was reputable? No one had been available to fix the broken window. But this was a bigger job. *Start with A.* Able Painters had a license number, was bonded, and promised both quick and reasonable work. After only one phone call, she knew someone would come that afternoon to give her an estimate. Yes, they worked on Saturdays and no, there wouldn't be an extra charge for weekend work.

This seemed too good to be true. She could go to lunch with Jennifer and be back in time to meet with the estimator.

Gillian continued her list. The phone's ringing interrupted her.

"So, how is your morning going?" Adam's deep voice sent an electric charge up her arm.

"I just found a painter. I'm going to redo Mother's bedroom as a wedding present."

"Good idea. Who?"

"Able Painting?"

"They have a good reputation. I met the owner, Madison Able, at a chamber meeting. She's a dynamo."

"I wonder if that is who I spoke with."

"Could be." He broke a brief silence. "I was serious last night about needing help out here."

"I thought you were. Did you mean full time or part time?"

"Part time. About twenty hours a week. One of my best employees had to go out on maternity leave early."

"That sounds even better. Yes, I'd like to do that." There, she'd committed herself, at least for a while.

"Good. How about you start training on Monday?"

"I could get the bedroom finished by then. Thank you." And maybe a good section of the garden.

"Thank you. Plan on working full days Monday through Wednesday and then we'll put you on the schedule."

"You—you really think I can do this?"

"I think you'll be a natural."

Now the warmth of his voice curled in her stomach. "Thank you."

"Want to walk this evening?"

"Sure." She clicked off the phone and heaved a sigh. Life was moving forward, that was for sure.

Lunch with Jennifer was as pleasant as she thought it would be. Jen told her more of the family history including about the death of her husband, Charles.

"How did you get through that?"

"God got me through is all I can say. I had to keep going for the children's sake, and Mom, Charlie's mother, in spite of her own grief, held on to me and loved me with all she had. Her faith built my faith, and while God seemed far away at times, I always knew He was there for me. You just never think these things can happen to your family, you know?"

"I've never gone through anything like that really. I was so young when my father died that I hardly remember him. I guess losing my job like this has been about the worst thing that has happened."

"I never wish such grief on anyone, I tell you that. While the kids have seemed to respond well, I am sure there will still be repercussions."

"What is Lissa Marie majoring in?"

"She's not sure yet. Might be communications. She reminds me so much of Charles, the same sense of humor, sparkling eyes, and dedication to work." Jen dug a tissue out of her purse and dabbed at her eyes. "Even now, I cry sometimes just at the memories. You never know what will bring it on."

"And then Alice died?"

Jen nodded. "She fought that cancer so hard, but it took her anyway. The family has had hard times."

"I was afraid my mother was really going to die."

"I'm glad you came in time. Bill said you pulled her through. He really admires you, the way you pitched right in and didn't let her buffalo you."

Gillian shifted her silverware around. How to bring up the subject?

"Would you ladies care for dessert today?" the black-garbed waiter asked.

Gillian shook her head as did Jen. "No, thanks. But the meal was delicious." She waited while the young man cleared their plates. "I would like some more iced tea, though."

"I'll be right back with it."

"Thanks." She turned back to Jennifer. "Did Adam tell you he asked me to work at the Pittsburg store?"

"No, we've not talked. That's marvelous. I know they are shorthanded at both stores. Finding competent help is difficult at times." She leaned forward. "Are you going to do it?"

"I am. I start on Monday." Gillian glanced at her watch. "I need to be home by three. I have a painter coming to give me an estimate on painting Mother's bedroom. I'm redoing her room for a wedding present."

"What a great idea. I can't get over that she and Enzio went on a cruise and got married. I wish Bill could find someone again. Did he seem all right when he was at your house the other night?"

"I guess." *Until he dropped the bomb on me.* "Do you know much about the nursery business?"

"Not a lot. But Bentley's has a great reputation. Bill has built a solid business and run it wisely."

Tell her. Don't tell her.

"I know he has mentioned selling it. I think he's just tired. And this heart thing hasn't helped."

"He said I should buy it." There it was out. Relief slipped out like a sigh.

Jennifer cocked her head slightly to the side. "Did he now? I'm surprised."

"I was shocked. Right after Adam asked if I'd like to come to work for him."

"Do you want a business of your own?"

"I don't know. I was at the top of the ladder until they jerked it out from under me. Do I want to climb it again with another company?" She nodded her thanks to the refilled iced tea. "I just wish I knew what I want to do with the rest of my life."

"Well, I know one special man who is glad you came to Martinez. Don't count him out."

"Adam?" Even saying his name made her smile.

"Adam. I've never seen him interested in a woman before, not in all the years I've known him. Ever since Charles died, Adam has done all he could to help us out. I cried on his shoulder many a time. He is the big brother I never had."

That statement put the thought of them as a couple to rest. "Sailing seems pretty important to him."

"Oh, it is. He has always loved to sail, says that is where he does his best thinking. He's a good sailor, too. He was disappointed you didn't come with us on Sunday."

"Jennifer, I get so seasick, boats are not a pleasure for me."

"Next time I come out, I'll bring the patches the doctor prescribed for Lissa Marie. She has always been the same way, but now she can sail and loves it. You can try it out and see if it works for you, then get them from your doctor."

Which means I will need to get a doctor here. Guess I could go to Dr. Isaacs. She glanced at her watch. "We better be going."

"Please say you'll try the sailing with the patch to help you. It means so much to Adam."

Gillian could not turn down the look of entreaty on Jen's face. "I will try." Once she had the patches in hand she had no further excuses. Not particularly liking boats was not acceptable. Another commitment made.

Jen signed the credit slip and they both stood.

"Thanks for lunch. My treat next time."

"I'm looking forward to lots of next times." Jennifer's smile made Gillian feel like they'd already been friends for years.

She got home just before the paneled truck marked ABLE PAINTING parked behind Enzio's car.

By the time she and Madison had finished, she felt like she had another new friend. They examined several paint chips, decided on the color, and set an appointment for eight a.m. on Saturday morning to begin painting.

She'd just seen Madison Able out the door when another idea clobbered her. She was supposed to spend Saturday with Allie and her family. Surely Allie would understand that she wanted to have the bedroom all finished before the newlyweds returned. And getting it done this quickly was as much a shock to her as to Allie.

A huff puffed out her cheeks. Might as well get the dirty deed over with. Allie's answering machine clicked on so she left a message. "Hi, Allie, I just hired a painter to paint Mother's bedroom. I want to redo the bedroom as a wedding present and time is limited. She can do it on Saturday, so I will have to take a pass on the games. I should still be able to come for dinner. The painting will be done by three or four. Let me know if this change works or if we should just get together another time." She hung up and stared at the phone. Allie did not like changes being made in her schedule. But considering that the lovebirds had already been gone for almost a week, she didn't have a lot of extra time. Gillian slapped her hand on the table. She hadn't mentioned her new job. But she'd not had to listen to Allie either whine or be angry at her, either. That was a relief.

What a shame, to dread talking to her baby sister.

Chapter Twenty-nine

W*hat time would I have to call her to not get the answering machine?* Gillian glared at her cell phone the next morning. Was Allie taking the kids to school already? Why couldn't she return calls?

Winnie left her watch-the-birds spot in front of the glass door and came over to stand in front of Gillian. Head cocked to the side, the dog appeared to be interested in whatever her new friend had to say. Gillian slapped her knees and Winnie jumped into her lap. Cuddling the dog had already become a relaxing habit. "So, what do you think I should do?" She imagined her New York coworkers' surprise if they saw her. Winnie stretched up to give her a quick chin lick, then turned around and made herself comfortable.

"You know, dogs have a mighty easy life." One ear cocked, and then Winnie leaped to the floor toward the front door, a sure signal someone must be there. Winnie had quickly become Gillian's early warning system.

Gillian got up to follow her, immediately recognizing the outline of the visitor. She unlocked the door and tried to swallow the upbeat of her heart. "Good morning, Adam. Come on in."

"I was on my way to work, but I wanted to see you before I drove out there."

"What's up?"

"Dad and I got to talking and I just want to make sure that you want to come to work at the nursery, that you're not doing it just to be nice or some such."

Gillian rolled her eyes. "Yes, I want to work at the nursery. I had no idea that I wanted to, but I do and I appreciate the offer."

"You didn't even ask what the pay would be. I know it is nothing like you were getting, but..."

"But it will help pay the bills." *And give me good experience. Not that I plan to run a cash register for the rest of my life, but this will be a welcome change.*

"Okay. How about dinner tomorrow night? Just us."

"I don't know. I was supposed to spend the day and evening with Allie and her family, but now that the painter is coming I've had to change that. I'm not sure if she still wants me to come for dinner or not."

"And she hasn't returned your phone call?" His eyes said what he thought of that.

"Nope. Neither one."

"Well, let me know. Walking tonight?"

"Of course." She really had enjoyed their walks. Winnie chasing Thor around the school yard was always good for an uplift. The two dogs brought more laughter than a professional comedy act. While Thor could eat the little fluff ball with one bite, he played with her gently, as if knowing he could hurt her.

"See you then." Adam leaned forward and touched his lips to hers. "See you." His eyes said more than his mouth conveyed.

Gillian put her fingertips to her lips as he walked out the

door. That was one way to become wide awake. She'd just finished making her bed when Winnie went tearing to the front door again.

"Gillian?"

"Back here." Allie. Now this was some surprise. Gillian tossed the throw pillows in place and headed for the kitchen. "Coffee?"

"Yes, please. Is it fresh perked?" Her grin said she was teasing.

Gillian rolled her eyes. "No more perking here. I got the new coffeemaker up and running." Gillian pushed the ON button and inhaled as the machine ground the beans before making the coffee.

"Nothing but the latest?" Allie leaned over to pet Winnie, who had decided she knew this person and more barking was not necessary.

"I sent her this two years ago. Wonder what else is stuffed in that closet?"

"Everything that couldn't be used immediately or saved easily." Allie straightened.

"I'm going to work for Adam. On Monday."

"On Monday? Well, good for you."

Gillian's mouth opened but no sound emerged.

"And tomorrow the painter is coming?"

"Do you think she'll be pleased?" Gillian got two mugs out of the cupboard.

"I don't know. Mother really doesn't like change, especially these last couple of years. She's almost paranoid about it. What color did you choose?"

"A nice cream. You want to go shopping with me for new bedding and lamps? Is your morning all booked up?"

"No, that's why I came up here. I don't have to be back until I pick up the kids after school."

"You have the entire day off?"

"Well, not quite. I was hoping you could do lunch."

Gillian filled their cups. "I most certainly can. The garden can wait and I can strip the bedroom tonight." Together they moved to the table.

"So, you think you'll stay here?"

"At least for now. But I can't live with Mother forever. She and Enzio will need the place to themselves."

"They'll probably decide to live at Enzio's. His house is really nice."

"He said he has a big garden." Gillian sat down and propped her elbows on the table. "So what will she do with this one, put it on the market?"

"I doubt it. I'll bet she's planning on you living here."

Gillian stared at her sister. Where was all the contention they'd had every time they talked? "Are you serious?"

"What? It's not good enough?"

Now, that sounds more like my sister. "No, that's not it at all. Mother'll need the money. What if they need to go into a retirement center?"

Allie shrugged. "The house is to go to us when she dies, that's what her will says. She made me read it a couple of months ago."

Gillian sipped her coffee, wishing she had a doughnut to go along with it.

"Those flowers look good by the front door."

"Thanks." *Ask her,* an inner voice prompted. "Allie, are you happy?"

Allie straightened, her eyes hooded. "What do you mean?" The sharp edge had returned to her voice.

Gillian sighed. Might as well keep on going. "Well, the other times we've talked, you've been so touchy. As if you might go off like a rocket any moment."

"I don't think so!"

"Well, that's just my observation. I know Mother's attitude frightened you."

"Easy for you to say. You hadn't been watching her decline for the last months. Doing less and less and then not getting out of bed. I was sure she was going to die before you got here."

"I can understand that. But I wondered if it was more than that." She rimmed the mug with the tip of her finger, wishing she'd not started this. When she looked up again, Allie was wiping a tear away with a tissue, then blew her nose.

"Good old Gillian, problem solver, mighty brain come home to help her poor dumb sister." A mean glint flashed in Allie's eyes.

"Allison Miller, whatever has come over you?"

Winnie jumped up on Gillian's lap, shivering.

"You always did everything perfectly. Honor roll, a job, college, a career, a big, fat huge success. And you did it all on your own. No help from your mother."

Gillian stared at her sister, at the same time trying to swallow the words boiling in her mind. *Keep it soft. Use your conflict resolution training*. "Allie."

"Don't patronize me." Slapping her hand on the table, Allie leaned back in her chair, arms locked over her chest. "All I've heard for years is 'why can't you be like your sister?'"

"Wait a minute!" Gillian's voice ratcheted up a notch. "Just wait a minute. You have always been Mother's darling. Allie, who could never do anything wrong, the sweet girl, so pretty and cute and obedient, my yes, sweet little Allie. You did everything Mother wanted you to do, including getting married to a good man who was going places and having the perfect family. Two children, right on schedule."

Allie shook her head, her jaw clenched. "You have it all. A condo in New York City, an executive…"

"Did you want that?"

"Taking care of Mother was the straw that broke this camel's back. I have to take care of everybody!" She nearly shouted the last word.

She didn't answer my question. Gillian moved her head around to release the tension and bit back a sarcastic reply. "So, answer me. What do you want?"

Allie tipped her head back and stared at the ceiling. "Sometimes I want to run away."

"I think everyone feels that way at some time or another."

"Did you?"

Gillian tried to think how to answer that. If she said no, Allie would feel worse, if she said yes, it would be a lie. "I made sure I took vacations."

"I have never had a vacation alone."

"So, take one. Jefferson could handle the kids for a weekend. Or he could take vacation time to stay home with the kids while you left."

"What kind of mother and wife wants to run away from her family?" She shook her head. "Besides, I might not want to come back."

"Allie, wait a minute." Gillian held up her hands, traffic cop–style. "Think back. You heard how wonderful I was doing. I thought you were Mother's darling. What is going on here?"

"Two sisters, who aren't the best of friends?"

"No. Two sisters who were being manipulated by a mother trying to make them do better, be perfect. Be everything she was not, have everything she never had."

"Gillian, you are out of your mind." Allie rose to pour herself more coffee.

"No, I think I'm onto something."

"Well, I don't want to talk about it anymore. If you want me to go shopping with you, we better get going. Then we can have lunch and I'll bring you back here."

"I have one other question."

"What?" Allie's voice returned to short and sharp.

"I don't expect an answer right now, but I want you to think about it." Gillian spoke slowly, trying to get her mouth around her idea. "If you could do anything, anything at all, what would you like to do the most?"

"In the next two hours or..."

"No, in general. With your life?"

"I thought that was your question, what will you do with the rest of your life?"

"I'm working on it. I need to make some choices, but I'm waiting until Mother and Enzio return before I make a final decision." The feeling of Adam's kiss flashed across her mind. Perhaps he was another consideration to take into account.

"You have to admit, you had it all." Allie dumped the remainder of her coffee in the sink, tossing the words over her shoulder as she put the cup into the dishwasher.

"Stop there, I had it all perhaps. I had what I set out to accomplish. But now that is gone and I..." She moved her coffee cup in a circle. "Actually, now I have nothing."

"Nothing in New York, you mean?"

"I guess." Her mind continued with the thought. *What have I lost? My position, where I had power and respect and work that I enjoyed because I had power and respect, working with people I respected—well most of the time. The money was a big part of it. I could pretty much do whatever I wanted if I could find time to do it. One thing I never had was time to spend in ways not connected with my job.* So she no longer had seventy-hour workweeks, either. Nor the pressures of her job. She could go out and work in the garden if she wanted to. She put her cup in the dishwasher and shut it with a snap.

"At one time, I wanted a husband and children, but that never happened and now it is too late. Let's go shopping. Winnie, outside." She opened the back door for the dog to go out. "I'll be ready in a minute. Let her in will you please?"

Once they were in the car and heading down the hill, she turned to Allie. "Why do you never return phone calls?"

"Sometimes I do."

"But not usually, why?"

"I forget to turn my cell on and I don't think about the answering machine until I'm running out the door. There, are you satisfied?"

Gillian shook her head. "Nope. How am I to get in touch with you then?"

Allie shrugged. "Guess I'll have to make more of an effort." Something in her voice made Gillian think she didn't really want to make more of an effort.

"Doesn't Jefferson get tired of not getting a response when he calls?"

A half shrug and a slight pout and she answered, "I guess."

"That doesn't bother you?"

"Sometimes."

"You mean not a lot?" Deciphering the meaning behind the words was getting tiring.

"Look, I said I'll try harder. What more do you want?" Allie stopped for a red light. "Besides, everyone is always demanding something from me."

Gillian stared out the window, wishing she had more answers. *Let it go,* a voice inside her head commanded. *But Allie is my baby sister, and I really want her to be happy.* But she knew from all her years of studying people and attending training sessions on being an effective manager that only Allie could make Allie happy. Letting go of old issues took a lot of work. That she knew from intense personal experience.

Saving Allie was not her job.

But learning to get along was part of being a family, something she'd not had to pay a lot of attention to when separated by a broad continent. More to think about later, especially the part about Allie feeling that everyone continually demanded things of her. Had she been doing that, too?

"Where do you want to go to look for the bedroom things?" asked Allie.

"Where do you suggest?"

"Depends on how much you want to spend." Allie listed the stores in the immediate vicinity.

"Well, not high end and not cheap, either. Somewhere in the middle, but where we have a good selection. I figured with cream walls, we could go about any direction."

"Just remember, Mother does not like frou-frou and fluffy."

"Neither do I."

Before they got out of the car, Allie stopped and stared at her sister. "Why are you doing this if Mother might not even live there again?"

Gillian thought a moment. "I want her to have something nice and new to go along with her new life. Besides, I can't think of anything else to give her."

"That she won't put away to keep it nice?"

"That, too."

Sometime later they dropped the large-size bags in the back of Allie's SUV and got back in.

"That was fast." Allie started the vehicle. "Where do you want to go to lunch?"

"No idea." Gillian glanced at her watch. "You only have an hour. How about the burrito place by Lucky's? That's the only fast-food place I know about."

"Sounds good to me."

With their orders in front of them, they looked at each other across the table. "Do you realize how many years it has been since you and I had lunch together in a restaurant without anyone else?" Gillian sat shaking her head. "I remember one time I wanted you to come to New York in the worst way so I could show you some of my favorite places. I called to ask, but you were so pregnant the doctor wouldn't let you fly."

"I would have loved to come." Allie unwrapped the end of her burrito. "I thought about bringing Sherrilyn and surprising you, but I figured you would not have time, so I never followed through." She took a bite, continuing to shake her head. "And those times you came home, there was never even time for a real visit."

Not that the three of us knew how to really talk to each other anyway. Gillian just nodded. At least she and Allie were talking now. *And Mother was even talking with me before she left.* Was that what this whole thing was about?

When they drove up to the house, she turned to her sister. "So, do you want me to come for dinner tomorrow night, even though I'll miss the games?"

Allie looked at her, question marks all over her face. "Why would that make any difference? Of course we want you to come. As soon as you can."

"I'll call you before I leave."

Allie rolled her lips together. “I’ll make sure the phones are turned on. You need help carrying all that in?”

“No, you get going.” Gillian pulled the bags from the car and set them on the concrete, then waved to her sister. Now that was about as big a turnaround as Mother made. What was going on here?

Chapter Thirty

So, are you ready for the great onslaught?" Adam asked Gillian as they headed home after their walk.

"You mean Halloween?" At his nod, she shook her head. "I've not prepared at all."

"Come up to our house, we can share the duty," Adam suggested.

"But I haven't bought any candy."

"We have plenty. Dad bought out the big bags of candy section at the Rite Aid. We better have lots of trick-or-treaters."

"I thought that was going out of style." Gillian checked both ways as they reached the road again after walking the school grounds. Both dogs and Adam were panting like they'd run miles. "Keeping kids off the streets and all that."

"We live in a designated safe neighborhood. Parents drop kids off by the carload. I think there should be an age limit."

"Guess I'll put Winnie in her crate then."

"Just leave your lights off. That's the sign that there are no treats at that house."

"My word but things have changed since I was a kid. We used to have fun on Halloween."

"We did, too, though some of our fun was never shared with the parents." These walks were becoming the highlight of his day. Just the two of them, well, four including their canine friends.

As they neared the house, Winnie picked up her pace, pulling at her leash.

"Come on up right away. I'll get a shower and we'll be ready by dusk, which isn't far off."

Gillian unlocked the door and unsnapped Winnie's leash so she could run ahead for a drink. Had Gillian known she was going to Adam's, she'd have fixed something to add to the dinner at least. This cooking on a regular basis was new for her. She fed the dog, locked her in the crate, and headed up the hill. Small bands of costumed children were already starting at the bottom of the hill.

"Come on in," Bill greeted her at the door. "Glad you decided to join us. We'll take turns answering the door." He gestured to a plastic bin of a mixture of wrapped candies. "You dump a few pieces into each bag. Don't let the kids pick because there isn't time. Last year we had over a hundred. Jen and Lawrence came out to help, so he kept track."

"I really enjoyed meeting Jennifer. You know..." She paused and smiled at him. "You have a wonderful family."

Bill blinked and nodded. "Thank you." The doorbell rang. Thor yipped and she picked up the goodie bin.

Adam took turns, too, and while one answered the other two demolished a bucket of fast-food chicken with all the trimmings.

"I know, I'll just open the door and you distribute the wealth. Tag-teaming 'em." Adam warned Thor about his vocals and took up his position behind the door, opening it as soon as the bell rang. Gillian tried to greet each of the children, but after a while just dumped in the candy.

"Here." Bill refilled the bin, making sure he got a chocolate bar for his efforts.

The horde let up just after eight, with only a few stragglers, mostly young teens with wild makeup and fewer costumes.

"Well, we went through fifteen pounds of candy. After the next group, let's turn off the light."

Gillian collapsed on the sofa, shaking her head. "I can't believe this. Did my mother do this every year?"

"She came up here a couple of times. Allie and the kids have joined her after they grew older." Bill tossed the last bars into the offered pillow cases. "That's it, kids. Happy Halloween." He waited until they reached the sidewalk and turned off the light.

"Welcome to the burbs." Adam sat down next to Gillian. "They don't trick-or-treat in NYC?"

"I have no idea. At least not in my part of the city." Gillian took the small packet of M&M's he handed her. "Thanks." After popping a couple into her mouth, she continued. "Well, tomorrow is a workday for me with the painter coming."

"You want some help?" Adam was leaning against the back of the sofa, eyes closed.

Gillian turned to look at him. "Are you volunteering?"

"I am."

"I plan to dig more in the garden, too."

"I'm game."

She turned to Bill. "Have I mentioned what a good son you have?"

"Better save the compliments until you see how he does. I heard he's a bit of a slacker on weeding."

"Come on, I'll walk you home before my reputation is permanently shredded." Adam stood and pulled her to her feet. "Tonight was baptism by fire. You are officially a member of the Bentley family now."

When they reached her door, Gillian could hear Winnie barking.

"Fierce watch dog." He wrapped both arms around her, pulling her close. "Gillian, where have you been all my life?" He rested his chin on the top of her head. "You smell sweet like honeysuckle or jasmine." He bent and kissed her. "And taste better. Night."

He could feel her gaze following him, so when he reached the sidewalk, he turned and waved. "See you in the morning." Now that was the way to end a day. Maybe they could make a habit of it.

"I say just rip it all out."

Adam shook his head. "You can't do that. If I remember right, there are perennials in here that would be dormant now. That would be criminal to destroy those."

Gillian blew out a breath. "Makes sense, but my idea would be easier."

"Since when is gardening ever easy?" Adam mounted the two railroad tie steps to the garden area. "Some things we can tell by their foliage."

"Even when it is dead?"

"Not dead. Dormant." The look on her face made him smile. "Just look at this as training for your new job."

"I think I understand cost estimates and production proposals better." She pulled on a pair of her mother's gardening gloves and stared across what looked more like a plant cemetery than a thriving garden. "Surely Mother started to retreat long before she took to her bed."

"Were there any stakes in the garden shed?"

"What kind of stakes?"

He measured two feet or so with his hands. "Wood, flat wood. Usually comes in bundles."

"I didn't see any." She bent over to pull out mustard plants. "Good grief, do these roots go clear to China?"

"Near there. Was there a digging fork?"

She shrugged and used both hands to pull, leaning against it with all her weight. Slowly the plant released its hold on the soil, and she staggered back when it gave up. She banged the root ball against the ground to dislodge the clumps of dirt.

Adam headed for the shed area. Surely Dorothy had what he needed. "I can bring down the tiller when we figure out where the perennials are." Not surprising, all the tools were cleaned and hanging on the rack on the wall. He loaded forks and spades into the wheelbarrow and took it all out to the garden. He'd take the chipper in the corner out later. He arrived back in the garden just in time to see Gillian win the war with another mustard but end up on her rear in the dirt for her efforts. Hiding a grin, he parked and picked her up from behind.

"You might wait and loosen the big ones with the fork."

Her mutter made his grin fight to get out. "Okay, we need a plan here."

"I plan to get this mess cleaned up and…" She picked up the wilting plants and tossed them in the wheelbarrow. "How could she let this go like this? The garden was always such a source of pride for her."

"Depression'll do that to you."

"But how could she have been so depressed and Allie didn't pick up on it?"

Adam let that comment lie and prowled the parameter looking for familiar foliage. "Here are the peonies."

"Oh, I loved the peonies. Big fat blossoms." Gillian came

to stand beside him. "There used to be several colors, pink, red, and white. I think I remember pink tinges on the white. Mother would pick the peonies and we would take them to the cemetery to put on my father's grave. I haven't thought of that in years." She pointed to fluffy branches with bright red berries. "What are those?"

"Asparagus. And these are daisies, I think. Not sure if they'll come back or not."

Winnie's barking caught Gillian's attention. "The painter must be here. I'll go get her started. You want something to drink?"

"Yes, please. You might want to brush the dirt off your rear before going in the house."

She glared him a look that said a whole paragraph, but did as he suggested.

Adam watched her walk away, smiling both inside and out. When she got something on her mind, she wore determination like a flak jacket. *Bet she is something in a boardroom. I'd rather have her on my side than across the table.*

Sometime later, with the pile of weeds on the second wheelbarrow full, they turned at a "halloo" from the fence.

"I brought lunch."

"Thanks, Dad." Adam wiped his dripping forehead with a bandanna from his rear pocket. "You should be wearing a sun hat. Your face is getting red," he told the woman beside him.

"Oh, great." Gillian headed for the gate to let Bill in. "Let's eat at the patio table."

"Looks like you're accomplishing a lot," Bill said as he set his baskets on the table. "I brought drinks, too."

"You are one sweet man." Gillian removed her gloves and brushed her hair back with the back of her wrist.

"All I did was go to the deli." He started setting out wrapped sandwiches and chips. "They wrote on them so we'd know what was what."

Gillian and Adam washed at the hose and, wiping their hands on their pants, took the chairs in the shade.

"Wonder what Dorothy did with the arbor?" Bill asked after starting on a roast beef sandwich.

"That's right, I'd forgotten about that, too." Gillian held the iced drink against her forehead.

"It's up behind the compost heap. Looking much the worse for wear."

"Wonder if it is worth repairing?" Bill looked to Gillian. "I remember right, it's an old one, probably antique status by now. Do you mind if I look at it?"

"Not in the least. Do you know if she worked out here during this summer?"

"No idea; I've not been much of a neighbor lately. You might ask Maria Gonzales. She kind of keeps an eye on the neighborhood."

"I will." Gillian wrapped half of her sandwich. "I'm going to see how Madison is doing."

"She's got the window taped." Adam nodded over his shoulder. "Taping takes about as long as the painting."

"Or longer. I always hated that part, but your mother didn't mind."

Adam caught himself in a quick look at his dad. He'd not mentioned his wife much this last year. Come to think of it, sitting down with the scrapbooks had been the first time. Maybe he had more to thank Gillian for than he'd realized.

After lunch they checked out the arbor, and Adam promised his dad he'd bring it home when he came.

"Let's take it now. I have some time…"

"Okay, now is fine." Jubilance felt good. The three of them picked up the arbor and hauled it up the hill.

"That thing is heavier than it looks." Gillian puffed as they set it down in the Bentleys' garage where Bill's workshop covered the back wall.

"That's what makes it worth repairing." Bill was already tapping with a hammer to look for dry rot.

Adam took her hand as they strolled back to "the project" as he was beginning to refer to it. "You want me to show you how to start the chipper?"

"Not today." She stretched her neck from side to side. "I'm not used to this kind of labor."

"You want to come sit in our hot tub?"

"Later, maybe. I have to go out to Allie's for dinner."

"Then we better get back at this." He studied what they had accomplished. "Why did you say you were doing this?"

"Crazy, isn't it? But I guess I just want to surprise my mother."

"What if she's not even going to live here?"

"Then a renovated yard will bring a better selling price. Like everything else in my life, this, too, is up in the air." She pulled her gloves back on, twisting her wrists around.

"Sore?"

"Uh-huh."

"I found a row of carrots." Gillian waved one in the air a bit later. "She did plant some things this year."

Her joy was contagious, so Adam smiled back at her. *And that's important to you.* He pushed the wheelbarrow up to where they were stacking the refuse that would become compost to rebuild the soil. He dug down into the bin that looked the oldest and brought up a handful of rich, black compost. Sniffing it, he smiled at the fragrance.

"What are you doing?" She had come to stand beside him.

"Checking to see if the compost is ready."

"Is it?"

He held out his hand. "Nature's gold. Your mother has the traditional three bins. We use this one, toss the middle one into here, and start over in the first one with all the ground clippings, some horse manure, green grass clippings, kitchen refuse, all the good stuff to make the soil rich. You dig down to the bottom and you'll find handfuls of earth worms, God's earth tillers."

Gillian stared up at him. "You love this, don't you?"

"I do; I think it is genetic."

"My mother loved it, too. As did I when we ate the produce and picked the flowers. And since I've been home, besides aching in every muscle, I think I'm relaxing for the first time in a long, long while."

Adam touched her cheek with a gentle finger. "I'm glad. You better get some aloe on your face or you'll be peeling in a few days."

She tipped her head, trapping his hand between cheek and shoulder. "Thank you."

"You're welcome. You want to come to church with us tomorrow? I was going to take the boat out after, but I can come and help if you like."

"I like."

Chapter Thirty-one

Gillian studied the directions Allie had sent her. Finding their Danville house shouldn't be that difficult. She took the turnoff indicated, and a few minutes later, after only two wrong turns, parked on the street in front a house that looked big enough for a family of ten. "Okay, Winnie, here we go."

As she'd driven down the 680, she'd been thinking on the work in the yard—and Adam. Considering how quickly her month was flying by, she had to remind herself that a job might be forthcoming in NYC. She was supposed to be on vacation.

The tall young woman who came flying down the steps to greet her surely couldn't be Sherrilyn.

"Auntie Gillian, you finally came."

"Sherrilyn, what happened to you?"

Long blond hair swung forward to shield her face, then Sherrilyn hooked the fall behind her ears. "I grew some, huh?"

"Some! Sweetie, you are gorgeous." Gillian smiled at the blush that suffused her niece's face. Wrapping both arms around the girl, the two rocked in a hug until Winnie whimpered at their feet.

Sherrilyn dropped to one knee and extended a hand to be sniffed and inspected before Winnie gave it a lick and glanced back to Gillian as if asking permission. "Can I pick her up?"

"Winnie loves everyone, so see how she reacts."

Sherrilyn petted the little dog and rubbed down her back, all the while murmuring lovey words. Winnie spun in a circle and planted both front feet on the girl's knee, staring up at her. "Oh, she is so cute. Come on, let's snuggle." With the dog tucked under her chin, she led the way into the house.

"You haven't been to this house, have you?" Sherrilyn turned to Gillian.

"Nope. As your mother reminded me, it's been five years or more since I was in California. Plenty of time for both you kids to get all grown up."

"We might be taller, but one of us is not so grown up."

"Where is Benson?"

"Out helping Dad. Mom's in the kitchen." She unclicked Winnie's leash and handed it to Gillian. "The yard is fenced so she'll be all right."

"So, did you win this morning?"

"We did. That puts us in first place for the league. You have to come to one of my games. Or all of them. I can't believe you are really here. And with a dog, even."

"Can't beat that, can you?" Allie met them at the archway into the kitchen, gave her sister a half hug, and turned back to her preparations. "So, how does the paint job look?"

"Wonderful. And Adam helped me out in the garden, so that is looking better, too. But having one room painted just makes the rest look shabby." Gillian looked around the enormous kitchen with the commercial-size stove set into a bricked-in archway, cherry cabinets, and brushed steel appliances. "Lovely. A room like this might make even me want to cook."

"Don't you have a kitchen in your condo?" Sherrilyn perched on a stool, still cuddling Winnie.

"Oh, I do, but four or five of them would fit in here. And the view." She crossed to look out to the backyard where a waterfall ran into the swimming pool. "You have a hot tub, too?"

"We do. I should have told you to bring a swimsuit." Allie pulled a tray of dough-wrapped sausages from the oven. "How about putting these into those baskets? The drinks are already outside. Tell Dad that he might want to start the heater. It's cooling down pretty fast."

"We're eating outside?"

"Jefferson has tri-tip on the barbecue, his specialty."

"Mom, we have to have a dog again. One like Winnie."

"We'll talk about that later." Allie handed Gillian a tray with cheeses and crackers. "Just put that on the counter out there." She paused. "Did you bring a warmer jacket?"

"Nope."

"Sherrilyn, go grab Auntie Gillian a jacket off the coat rack. We can't have her freezing on us this first visit."

Oh, we'll save that for later? Gillian was glad she thought before she spoke. She wasn't sure if Allie was in a rush because Jefferson said dinner was ready or if she was nervous. So she obediently donned the denim jacket and took her designated platter out the door. Benson, too, had surpassed her in height, and she had a feeling he was not done growing. When he stood up to greet her, she did find traces of the little boy she remembered in his grin.

"So, I hear you're a tennis star now." She accepted his halfhearted hug and patted his shoulder.

"Ah, don't believe everything Mom says." The red in his cheeks deepened.

"Gillian, I was beginning to think Allie had been making you up." Jefferson hugged her as if there had not been a lapse of years since the last time he saw her. "Stunning as ever, I see."

"Thank you. You all look wonderful. True California tans, blond hair, the works."

"Got to keep up the image. Sit down, make yourself at home." He waved the spatula in his hand across the matching outdoor furniture that looked like tan wicker. "I need to turn the veggies."

After dinner the family spent time getting reacquainted. They drew the chairs up near the open fire pit, and while Allie and Sherrilyn fixed the dessert, Jefferson leaned forward. "I was really sorry to hear about the buyout. I probably saw it the same time you did, but I figured you already knew."

"Nope, total shock. Never dreamed I'd be out here for more than three days."

"Do you know what you are going to do next?"

She told him of her boss's offer. "But that is all up in the air, too. If this, if that. So Monday I start working at the nursery with Adam. He needs some part time help and thinks I can manage that."

"Of course you can, but what a waste of all your experience. You thought of looking for something in San Francisco?"

"Not really. I promised myself I'd take a month's vacation and so that's pretty much what I am doing." *Along with contemplating buying a business.*

"Right, along with redecorating your mother's house, restoring the yard, and working in a nursery. Sounds like a real vacation to me."

"She said she'd come to our games." Sherrilyn set a tray

with plates of apple pie on the table. "Mom is bringing the ice cream."

"Do you know how to play tennis?" Benson asked.

"Sorry, no. Never had the time or the desire to play sports of any kind."

"Do you watch baseball?"

When she shook her head, he stared at his father. "We got to take care of her."

Gillian laughed along with the others at her nephew's concern. "You'll have to come watch the Yankees play when I'm back in New York."

"Don't say that. I'm praying you'll stay out here." Allie set the pie now crowned with a scoop of ice cream in front of her.

Gillian looked from the pie to her sister. "Thank you, for both."

"Both?" Allie glanced over from serving her husband.

"The pie and the prayer." *Does she really mean that, or is she being polite?*

"Well, if you, or rather when you..." Jefferson corrected himself after a glance from his wife. "When you decide to stay here and if you want an executive position again, I might have some leads for you."

Allie laid a hand on her shoulder as she handed Benson his dessert. "See, I told you, we all want you to stay."

You told me that? When? Gillian took a bite of her pie. "This is just as good as I remember Mother's pies being."

Jefferson winked at her and made the okay circle with thumb and index finger. *How could Allie not be happy with this family?*

"You want to go to church with us in the morning?" Adam asked her on the phone. He called after she arrived home from the dinner with Allie's family. "Sorry, I should have asked you earlier today."

"What time?" She smothered a yawn with a hand over her mouth. "Sorry."

"We'll pick you up at seven forty-five. Dad likes the early service best."

"Is this a dress-up church or more casual?"

"Both." His chuckle warmed her ear. "No matter what you wear, you always look gorgeous."

His compliment made her blink. "Thank you, kind sir."

They said good-bye and Gillian rolled over to pet the dog. "That man is getting to me, Winnie. Am I ready for this?"

Sitting shoulder to shoulder with Adam in church felt just right. His baritone singing of hymns and praise songs made her throat catch. As they left the church, she had no idea what the sermon had been about, but she knew she wanted to repeat the experience. Perhaps forever.

"So how did he measure up, as a weed puller, that is?" Bill asked after the waitress handed around the menus at the local pancake house.

"He identified a lot of the dormant plants for me, and we cleared a fair-size area. Hard to believe it has been let go so bad. I was here at Christmas a few years ago, and the garden was lovely even then. I seem to remember lights and pink flowers at the front door, but lights in the garden, too." She shook her head. "Maybe I am confusing memories."

"Dorothy used to string little white lights over the arbor, back in the days when she and Alice were still in the garden club. They dropped out several years ago when there was a tiff over something stupid. Neither of them liked politics."

Adam watched his father. More memories. He sure owed Gillian a vote of thanks for this.

"I think they just got tired of the bickering." He nodded his thanks for a full coffee cup. "So, are you taking the boat out this afternoon?"

Adam rolled his eyes. "No, I'm committed to liberating more of the garden."

"You do realize this is a monumental sacrifice on his part?" Bill smiled at Gillian.

"Well, I am grateful. I'm sure once I start work, time will speed up. By the way, which store won the pumpkin award?"

Bill rolled his eyes. "His did. They had a head start."

Adam burst out laughing. "Any excuse is a good excuse. We just tried harder. Did you post the sign-up list for the wreath-making class? We already have ten signatures."

"I'm sure Keith did. He's almost as competitive as you are."

"You have leftover pumpkins?"

"A few. Those pumpkin-potted plants, I dare you to say that one fast"—he grinned at Gillian—"really depleted our supply."

"We ran out. Why don't you put a sign on those left that they are free and include instructions on how to turn a pumpkin into pumpkin pie?"

"I'll just put up free and they'll be gone." He turned to Gillian. "That old arbor needs some repairs, but basically it is still sound. Do you want it painted white or green?"

"White. Think I'll plant pink climbing roses on it. That's the way it used to be."

"Wait until bare root roses come in, in January."

Adam watched consternation sweep across her face. What was she thinking? About her mother? Or perhaps not being here. He kept trying to ignore what she had said, about being here for a month on vacation. Surely taking the job at the nursery meant she was thinking of staying on.

Bill spent the afternoon repairing the arbor, and Gillian and Adam freed more of the garden, even spreading finished compost on the perennials and spring bulbs they discovered.

"Next Sunday we go out on the boat." Adam leaned back in the patio chair, stretching his arms above his head.

Gillian stared at what was left of her manicure. *How can I convince him that is not a good idea?* "We'll see. Mother and Enzio should be back by then, so I hate to make commitments."

"Heard any more from them?"

"Not after dropping the wedding bombshell. I do want to give them a reception, or rather, Allie and I do." She scrutinized the garden. "You said you'd show me how to start the shredder?"

"I will." He drained his iced tea. "I wonder when the oil was last changed." He smiled at her blank look. "It's a gas machine, not electric. Runs like a lawn mower. I better check both of them. After all, you might have to mow the way the lawn is coming back."

"Do you mow year-round here?"

"All depends on how cold it gets." He shoved back his chair. "I'll go check those while you spread more of that compost so we have a bin to shred into."

That evening on their way back from running the dogs, Gillian stopped in the front yard. "All those good things happening in the back and I've ignored the front but for right around the door." She snapped a dead-looking branch off the jasmine. "Brittle as can be. What a waste."

Adam dug down farther and did the same. "Looks like

this one is still alive. Don't give up on it yet. We'll spread some of that compost out here, too, and see what spring brings."

"It used to smell so sweet."

"It will again." He put his arm around her shoulders and drew her close to his side. "I hope you're not so stiff and sore from gardening that you can't work tomorrow."

"Fat chance." She elbowed him in the ribs gently. She held up her hands, fingers spread wide. "Looks like I'll have to give myself a manicure. What a mess. Gloves should have protected my hands more."

"That's okay. Manicures are not required to work in a nursery." He kissed her, a lingering kiss this time. "See you in the morning."

Chapter Thirty-two

Are you ready?"

Gillian nodded. "Mrs. Gonzales is coming to let Winnie out a couple of times. I can't think of anything else."

Adam identified points of interest for her on the drive to Pittsburg, but that did nothing to soothe the butterflies cavorting in her middle. Others had told her of the agonies of starting a new job, but she'd not had to suffer through them since she started at the Triple F. Surely they wouldn't put her on the cash register the first day.

"You're being unnaturally quiet."

"I'll be fine."

"John will be handling much of your training since that is part of his job. I'll introduce you to those working there and show you around the store. If you have any questions, please ask so we can help you."

"Right."

He parked his SUV and came around to help her out, but as soon as he opened the door, she stepped down.

He leaned closer and dropped his voice. "We've not eaten any new employees for some time. You're safe."

"Funny man."

After the initial walk around and introductions, Adam retired to his office to meet with a possible new supplier, and John took over.

"We'll start with the cash register, since that is the most intimidating part of the job, unless you've worked with one in the last few years?" When she shook her head, he continued. "Everything is computerized now, so our stock is monitored by sales. At the end of the day when we do a readout, we know everything that has transpired that day. And how to order for restocking."

She glanced up to see Adam watching them. She forced her attention back to John's instructions and the location of the cheat sheets.

"You use the wand to read the bar codes, but it helps if you know the general pricing structure in case bar codes are missing." He handed her several pages of lists. "We ask that you take the time to study these; it will help you in the days ahead."

"I see."

When they took a break for lunch, Adam appeared with takeout from the Taco Bell. "I forgot to tell you to bring a lunch."

She collapsed in a chair at the table. *Was she just slow or was the cash register out to get her?*

That afternoon she had a lesson on sales etiquette, one on phone procedures, and spent an hour observing an older woman, named Marge, who ran the monster machine with perfect finesse. She turned to Gillian when there was a lull. "I have a feeling that my first day and yours are much the same. I was terrified of this thing." She patted the cash register affectionately. "Jumbo here just likes to test you, but once you become friends, he's loyal to the max."

"You mean that machine, right?"

"I do. Here, you practice and I'll coach you." Marge set several pots on the checkout table. "Have at it. Remember, you have to push the button on the wand to make it read."

Gillian nodded and scanned in the prices, hit the subtotal, and smiled at Marge. "Will there be anything else?"

"No, thank you. But don't hit the total, we'll cancel this out." She came back around the counter and hit the CANCEL button. She patted the tan monster. "Good job."

"Thanks, that helped."

"Life got a lot easier here when they installed the new system with bar codes."

"You worked here long?"

"Ten years with Bentley's. I started out at the Martinez store." She smiled at Gillian. "They're a great company to work for, more like family." She turned to wait on another customer. "Here comes John."

"I have a bunch of paperwork ready for you to fill out in the office," John said.

"Okay." When she signed the last form, she looked up. "Anything else?"

"What size shirt do you wear?"

"Ah, a medium."

"Okay, I'll get three of those for you and an apron. You need to wear blue jeans or khakis, sturdy shoes, and a smile. You already have that last part down well." His grin let her know he was teasing. So far, this new job seemed to be working out.

"You want to go walking?"

Gillian stared at the man through bleary eyes. "I walked fifty miles today, why would I want to go again?" Monday eve. Day one on the job. Results: her feet hurt, her back hurt, her legs hurt, and she figured she could sleep for a week. And here she thought she was in good shape. In spite of all her walking in NYC, there was a big difference between padded chairs, carpeted floors, a fine desk, an assistant getting her coffee, phone conversations, and working on a computer versus concrete floors, hefting plants, trying to learn where things were, and a cash register named Jumbo. Gremlins inhabited the ugly machine and leaped at her throat every time she drew near.

Of course some of the stiffness was from two solid days of heavy-duty gardening, as Adam had warned her.

"You want me to bring dinner?"

No, I want you to forget I exist until at least Wednesday—or Friday. "No, thanks, I have plenty to eat in the fridge." She tried to open the SUV door, but her hand cramped. Stifling a yelp, she pushed again only to look up and see him opening her door.

"Do I need to carry you into the house?"

The glint in his eyes made her smile. A fake smile for sure but the most she could manage. "No thank you." *I will walk if I have blisters an inch deep.* While she knew she did not really have blisters, her feet could light a fire.

"You might consider a hot bath."

"Right after I feed the dog." Even though Mrs. Gonzales had come over and let Winnie outside, the little dog had to hold her bladder a long time. Good thing she'd thought in advance. She knew that riding with Adam would mean a long day, she just hadn't computed how long.

"Do you have sturdier shoes you could wear tomorrow?"

She looked down at her poor feet. Her Keds looked good, matched her khaki pants, and were usually comfortable. "I have walking shoes that will be better." With more support and a far thicker sole, along with more inner padding, she used them to walk to and from the subway and to the office building at home. Walking was always easier than standing.

He leaned over and caught her chin with one finger, looking into her eyes. "It will get easier, I promise." His gaze dropped to her lips, but instead of kissing her, he stroked her cheek. "I'm sorry. You don't have to do this, you know."

"You want to bet? I'm not a quitter." *Gillian, you talk a sound talk, but can you walk it? Nasty word—walk.* "Same time in the morning?"

He nodded.

Later Winnie sat on the rug by the tub and studied Gillian. Head cocked to one side, she did a little whimper and laid down.

"That's a good dog. I'm not used to having supervision in my bath, you know." Gillian adjusted the rolled-up towel she had behind her neck and turned on the hot water faucet with her toes. She'd have to let some of the cooling water out pretty soon if she added much more.

When her chin sank into the water, she jerked upright and pushed up the lever to let the water out. Drowning in the bathtub would not help. Of course then she wouldn't ache anymore, either. Rising to her feet, she wrapped one of the bath towels around her body and stepped from the tub. Once dried, lotioned, and in her pajamas, she let the dog out and in, drank a glass of water with two pain pills, and fell into bed.

"You might not be a quitter, but not starting this could have been the smarter part of the equation."

Winnie snuggled closer to her side, offering doggie comfort.

By Wednesday she could tell her body was adjusting, still only a faint glimmer but improvement. The cash register had become her friend, and she'd even managed to increase a sale or two by suggesting something in addition.

"Will there be anything else?" she asked the woman waiting for her total. Having Adam standing off to the side made her fingers fumble on the keys.

"No, I don't think so, not today. But will you have more of those planted pumpkins tomorrow?"

"No, I'm sorry. Those are all finished."

"Shame, they would make a nice arrangement for Thanksgiving, too." She dug in her bag for her money. "You're new here, aren't you?"

"Yes, I am. Your total is twenty-six seventy-nine. Would you like some help out with that?"

The woman counted out the exact change, making the folks behind her in line audibly sigh. "Thank you so much, yes, I would."

"I'll take care of that, ma'am." Adam came around the counter and took over the woman's shopping cart.

Gillian checked out two more customers, one taking an extra bag of fertilizer they had on sale, before Adam returned.

"Thank you for being so gracious with that old lady," he murmured from behind her. "She's a faithful customer. I think she comes in sometimes just to have someone talk with her."

"Do you have her address?"

"I'm sure we do, why?"

"I just thought I'd drop her a card." She turned to the man who'd just walked up carrying a potted azalea. "Did you find everything you wanted?" Adam headed for his office, talking with John on the way.

"I need a plant for my mother's birthday. How long will this bloom?"

"You know, I'm new here and I have no idea, but I will find out." She crossed the few steps to Adam's office and stuck her head in the door. "How long will an azalea bloom?"

"Inside or out?"

"Inside, I think. It's a birthday present."

"Several weeks if it's not too hot in the room. Not in direct sunlight. Easy on the watering."

"Got it." She returned and told the customer all she'd learned. "Would you like some foil around that pot, or, we have some really attractive pots over there on the shelf. We can put a ribbon with the foil."

"Oh, good." He handed her the plant. "Foil please."

"If you'd like to look around a bit while we take care of this, you are welcome to do so."

"Thanks."

Gillian took the pot over to the wrapping bench. No one had showed her this side of the business.

John joined her. "You need some help here?"

"I do. While I've gotten potted plants, I've not fancied them up." She glanced over at the cash register, where there was no line for a change.

"Here, let me show you." John pulled a square of foil from the slot in a drawer under the table, a ribbon with bow from the wire overhead, and within seconds had it wrapped, fully disguising the pot. He turned and handed it to her, then smiled. "I'll do it again slowly if you want later when we have a lull."

"Thanks." She took the pot back, studying how he did that as she went. Silver foil with a pink bow to match the buds. Would there be a charge for this? And John had removed the price before wrapping the pot in foil.

She turned and caught John's attention. When he got to the counter she asked her questions.

"No extra charge and we are still cheaper than a florist. The eight inch pots are seven ninety-five." He pulled out a sheet of paper with figures on it. "Here's a cheat sheet. Get to know the size of the pots and you'll find the info here."

"I sure have a lot to learn."

"You already do the most important thing well." He smiled at her questioning eyebrows. "You charm the customers."

"Thanks." Compliments seemed more important than usual to her. Could be because she felt so unsure at what she was doing. When the promised lull came after lunch break, she joined John at the gift-wrapping bench. He showed her where the supplies were kept, demonstrated several wrapping techniques, and identified pot sizes. He left her doing several on her own to make sure she was comfortable. *After all,* she told herself, *this isn't rocket scientist stuff.*

She had Thursday off and worked a half day on Friday and all of Saturday. After work, she cleaned up the master bedroom and put the new furnishings in place. When she finished on Saturday night, she stood in the doorway and studied the room, seeking anything more that needed doing. The painting of a garden her mother had hanging on the wall didn't really do much for the new décor, but buying artwork for someone else was tricky.

When the doorbell rang, she invited Adam and Thor inside. "I have to show you." She led the way down the hall and stopped just inside the doorway. "What do you think?"

Adam stared around, nodding and smiling. "Is that a new chair?"

"Nope, slip-covered the old. New nightstands though so they'd match, and lamps." She straightened a corner of the new comforter. "You think she'll like it?"

"She'd be crazy not to. You've done a good job."

"Thanks." As they left the room, she trailed her hand along the wall. "The fresh paint in there makes this hallway look even more needy. I thought of having Madison give me an estimate for more, but Mother might have a fit."

"If she notices. Remember they will still be newlyweds, and usually the newly married don't notice much but each other."

"You really don't think it will be like that, do you?"

He shrugged. "You up to a walk?"

"Yes, Winnie reminded me that she is missing her walks."

"How did she do that?"

"Tried to pull her leash off the hook."

Halfway down the hill, he took her hand and smiled down at her. "Feels better this way."

"Just don't take off running then. I can handle walking." Mostly. She still stiffened up every time she sat down.

Chapter Thirty-three

I have something I want to read to you." Gillian tried not to chuckle as she cradled the phone between her shoulder and ear.

"Read away." Adam replied.

Dear Gillian and Allie,

We are having a wonderful time on our cruise. The scenery has been beautiful and the people where we've stopped friendly and charming. We have learned of another cruise that leaves Miami the day after we dock, our same ship actually, going to the Caribbean for ten days. We decided to take it but will still be home before Thanksgiving. We'll call you from Miami. Hope you and Winnie are getting along.

Love, Dorothy and Enzio

"Well, I'll be..." His voice wore a matching chuckle. "Have you heard from Allie?"

"No, but she probably hasn't gone online yet. Good thing Winnie and I are hitting it off so well. Looks like we'll be housemates for a while." She heard a click on the phone. "That's probably Allie. I'll call you back later." Gillian pushed the button to transfer the calls.

"Did you read the e-mail yet?" Allie's voice rose with each word.

"Yes, I'm glad they're having such a good time, aren't you?"

"Yes, but…I really miss Mother. She's never been gone like this." Now she sounded more like the little girl lost.

Not having lived nearby, Gillian tried to understand. Her years of distance made it much easier. "She has to be feeling good again; I think this cruise and the marriage are the best things that have happened to her in a long time." She didn't add the *forever,* but she thought it loud. "I know you want her to be happy."

"I do and I'm so grateful she isn't dying after all." She heaved a sigh. "Guess I just don't like change a whole lot."

"Most people don't. How about we plan a really great Thanksgiving? I was thinking we could invite all the Bentleys, too."

"That's a lot of people for that house. We usually invite Jefferson's folks, too. Why don't we just have it here?"

"Fine by me. I'll help cook, and everyone can bring something." Gillian thought of the times her flat had been full of people, a big Thanksgiving potluck with people sitting on the floor when necessary. "The more people the merrier." She could tell that Allie wasn't overly excited about all the people coming but decided not to mention it. "We'll have a wonderful time, you wait and see."

After they hung up, Gillian got ready for bed and called Adam back after she and Winnie were all snuggled in.

"So, how did it go?"

"All the Bentleys are invited to join us for Thanksgiving

at Allie's house. We're making it potluck sort of, everyone bringing something."

"Good, I'll bring the turkey, we have a deep fryer. Best turkey you'll ever taste. Perhaps I can bring the stuff and come early to cook it there."

"You want me to ask Jen?"

"That would be good. Dad always makes Mom's relish recipe, so we'll bring that, too." He paused. "I'm really glad things are going better between the two of you."

"Me, too. I wasn't counting on much there at first."

"You know, fear does strange things to people sometimes."

"True."

The next morning, Gillian joined the Bentleys for church again. After breakfast at a western-themed café on Contra Costra Boulevard, Adam asked, "You two want to go for a drive into The City and out to the beach?"

"Thanks, but I'd rather putter with my plants." Bill's eyes twinkled, remarkably like his son's.

"Sounds wonderful. So many years since I've been there. But I'll need to change clothes first if we're walking on the beach. Are we taking the dogs?"

"Nope, I hate leaving Thor in the car if we stop for dinner." Adam signed the receipt. "I won't mention the beach, or he'll be crushed."

Sailboats dotted San Francisco Bay as they drove over the Bay Bridge and down along the waterfront. Adam pointed out the changes along the way—so many new buildings, the ferry terminal. He explained about the collapse of the Cyprus expressway in the '89 earthquake as they passed Pier 39 and climbed up the hill past Fort Mason. They walked along the beach side of Crissey Field, watching the myriad kites, many of them two-handed or even two-person ones. The Golden Gate Bridge guarded the entrance to the bay. They drove through parts of the Presidio, which was no longer a military base, and down onto Highway 1 along the beach. They even found a parking place facing the ocean.

"Ah, what a treat," Gillian said as they walked down the concrete stairs to the sand. "This is so different from the Atlantic, all the breakers. Have you seen the Atlantic?"

"Yes, I kept looking for the ocean, thinking those smooth waters must be all bay. Long Island was not what I had imagined." He tucked their clasped hands in the pocket of his Windbreaker, pointing toward the north with his other. "See that tanker coming out from the bay? We saw it before near Alcatraz Island."

"Have you ever sailed under the Golden Gate?"

"A couple of times, but my little twenty-two footer seems mighty small when you get out on the ocean swells."

"I even got sick on a cruise ship, when the seas kicked up. Miserable."

"Sorry to hear that." They turned and headed south, enjoying the sun on their faces, the children playing in the edges of the waves, seagulls floating and screaming overhead. Two dogs ran past them barking and nipping at the foam. The hard-packed beach held no driftwood, no rocks—all flat sand sending the rollers back out to sea.

The wind picked up as the sun slanted toward the west.

"I'm getting hungry, what about you?"

"Salt air always makes me hungry." Gillian smiled up at him.

"I thought about eating over there." Adam pointed to a rock building across the highway. "They say the seafood is good."

"Fine with me."

They waited in the lounge until a table was ready, and then they were seated at a western-facing window. The fog bank that had hovered on the horizon had crept closer, so the anticipated sunset was more sun disappearing. The wispy clouds above turned vermilion and shades of rose and pink in spite of the low fog.

Gillian sighed. "So beautiful. What a treat to really see a sunset."

"Too many tall buildings in New York?"

"Sunrise is light showing up on the building across the way."

"Do you miss it?"

"The sunrise?"

"No, New York." He picked up her hand and slid his fingers through hers so they were palm to palm, watching her face all the while.

Telling herself to ignore his hand, she shook her head. "I thought I would, but I haven't been here very long, you know."

"Long enough for me to want—"

"What can I get for you folks to drink?" The black-garbed waiter stood with pad poised.

Gillian almost asked for a fan. Adam's intent gaze had caused a rush of heat to bloom on her neck and face. "Iced tea for me."

"I'll take coffee." His voice sent shivers up her spine. How could even those simple words sound sexy?

When their dinners were served, Adam reached for her hands and bowed his head. "Heavenly Father, I thank You for this day, for this food, and for bringing Gillian into my life. Amen."

Gillian focused on her prawns. *He thanked God for me.* The thought made her feel like she was suspended in air, floating on a cloud of happiness. He must be feeling the same way she was, as if given a precious gift with all the time needed to open it with great care and savor every moment.

He told her about growing up in Seattle, he and his brother on swim teams and learning to sail. "Mother called us her water babies. Have you been to Seattle?"

"On business trips. I thought Mount Rainier was a myth until I saw it on one trip. Too many gray days there for me."

"Have you ever been in love before?" he asked, totally catching her by surprise.

"I thought I was once. His name was Pierre, but when I realized he was not really the man I thought he was, I broke it off. What about you?"

"I was married when I was young, but after I was deployed, I received that ominous *Dear John* letter. She couldn't handle being alone and I was in the navy. I never saw her again; everything was done through lawyers and when I retired, I chose to live in a warmer climate."

"No children?"

"No, which made me sad and glad. So now I enjoy Jen's two kids and take care of plants and customers all day." He propped his elbows on the table and stared over the coffee cup into her eyes. "I'm glad you came back to Martinez."

"Me, too."

Leaving the restaurant, he kept his arm around her shoulders. Back home, he walked her to the door, and this time when he kissed her, he meant for her to know he cared. When he lifted his head, he gazed into her dark eyes. "Thank you."

"I'm supposed to be the one to thank you for such a lovely day."

He kissed her lightly again. "We'll do lots more lovely days, okay?"

She put her key in the lock and floated into the house. Winnie whimpered from her crate. *Back to the real world,* she told herself. But she understood there had been a major shift in their relationship and knew he believed the same.

She worked Monday, had Tuesday off when she cleaned out the garden area, and worked at the nursery Wednesday morning. In between they walked the dogs every evening and shared their life stories. When she got home on Wednesday it was after three and the gray clouds suggested rain might be coming. She turned the heat up and took care of Winnie before bringing her laptop out to the living room. With the television on, she flipped through her messages, stopping at one with an unknown name. Was it spam? Her filter managed to dispense with most of that, so she opened it.

Dear Ms. Ormsby,

My name is Mark Hassleton and I am Senior VP of R&D for Cranston, Inc., the company that purchased Fitch, Fitch, and Folsom. I was looking through back files and came across a proposal you submitted just before the acquisition. It is marked declined but I found it very interesting. I am looking for sharp people to fill out the remainder of my team. Might you be interested in meeting with me? I'll be available for the rest of the afternoon if you'd like to call. I'm looking forward to talking with you.

His contact information was under his signature.

Gillian read it again. Surely this wasn't a joke. She leaned back in her chair. *He thinks I am still in New York. Too late to call now with the time difference.* She stared at the television screen but had no idea what the heads were talking about. A possible job again in New York. A job that would do more than pay the daily expenses. A job that might be the perfect transition for her canceled career, that might answer that question, what am I going to do with the rest of my life?

She Googled the company name and read all she could find about them online, then went to the *New York Times* and brought up the business section to read more. The firm definitely had good credentials. Since she'd not been able to contact him today, the earliest she could meet with him would be Friday. A frisson of excitement traveled her spine.

But how would she tell Adam?

She was on the work schedule for Friday and Saturday.

All of a sudden, she had obstacles. Big obstacles. Obstacles she did not want to face.

Adam would be here any minute to walk the dogs and she hadn't changed yet. The doorbell rang while she was tying her shoes. Winnie ran barking to the door but stopped as soon as she realized who it was. Hobbling out, one shoe on and one off, she opened the door. "Come on in, I'll be ready in a sec." She sat down on the recliner to put her shoe on and watched the dogs sniff each other, the canine equivalent of a human hand shake. As she retrieved her light jacket, she made the decision. She'd not tell Adam until she'd talked with this Mark person.

Thor heeled with thinly disguised obedience, his whole body quivering in anticipation of a run. Winnie walked slightly ahead of Gillian but not pulling on her leash like she had at first. As soon as they reached the fenced school yard, Adam unsnapped the leash and Thor tore off in ever-widening circles. Winnie waited for Gillian to release her and made a straight line to intersect the circling.

"Do you mind if I run?" Adam asked.

"Not at all. I'll just walk the driveway to the creek bed and around the perimeter." Actually having the time to ponder was a good thing. When she got home she would start her lists, for and against.

"Are you all right?" Adam asked as they strode back up the hill to home.

"Just tired, I guess."

"Dad will have dinner ready. Do you want to join us?"

"Thanks but I think not. My chicken soup really sounds good." *What a pathetic excuse,* she thought. *Why not be up front and just tell him? Because—because he might get mad, be disappointed, not say anything, say too much, check one of the above.* How would he feel about a long-distance courtship? If that was what was going on between them. A rather old-fashioned word, but it sounded more important than dating.

She made sure she smiled as she and Winnie peeled off for their house. "See you in the morning."

"You want to ride with me?"

"No, thanks, I'm only there half a day again."

When she turned off the light, she was no closer to a decision of whether to go or not to go. But how could she decide when she didn't have any of the particulars yet? As she lay in bed, her mind wandered back to church on Sunday. One thing she did remember the pastor saying. "When in doubt, ask God." *You used to pray, to ask Him things. You also know He answered. That job you had at Three F was a case in point.*

Gillian heaved a sigh that stirred Winnie. "God, You know I've been remiss in all things pertaining to You. But it looks like I am being pulled back, or at least surrounded by people who really do live Your way. Adam and I haven't talked about a lot of spiritual things yet, but I'm sure we will.

He talks to You as if You are sitting right next to him. I want that." Saying that stopped her. Did she really mean it because she knew God could read her heart and mind and see what she really believed? "I do mean it. I do. Right now I need wisdom to know how to handle this new situation. Am I to go back to New York to work?" She stared out the window, recognizing a sadness that clung to that idea. "Perhaps there are ways to work that out. I trust that You are going to show me what to do. Thanks in advance. Amen." She rolled on her side to stroke Winnie's silky fur. As Shakespeare had said, "The die is cast."

She called Mark at seven a.m. and introduced herself. After they talked for a couple of minutes, he said, "Can you come in this afternoon?"

"Not really. I am in California."

"California? I thought you lived here in the city."

"I did, I do. But we had some family problems and I came out to help."

"When can you be here?"

"If I can catch the red-eye, I'll be there tomorrow."

"Ten?"

"All right." She forced herself to remain calm, to sound professional.

"I even have your old office so you know the way. See you then."

Gillian clicked off her phone and sat staring out the kitchen door. The hummingbirds flashed past. She got up and poured herself another cup of coffee, then started her list to get everything done in time. As soon as the kennel opened, she'd call to see if they had room for Winnie. She jotted the number down so she could call from the car.

Getting ready for work, she chewed on how to talk to Adam. He'd ask her all kinds of questions that she had no answers for.

She called Allie as she backed the car out of the garage. She decided it must be a miracle day when her sister answered. Gillian explained what had happened.

"But I don't want you to leave again. I like having you here. We all do."

"I know, I like being here, but I at least need to check this out."

"I guess. What are you going to do with Winnie?"

"Put her in the kennel. I'm calling them next."

"I'll pick her up after I get the kids at school. Will you be home by then?"

"Yes, thanks. This is a big help." She hung up; that saved one phone call.

Once at the nursery, she tied her apron on and looked around to see where Adam was. If she weren't on the schedule for Friday and Saturday, this wouldn't be such a big deal. She would be back by Monday. Since putting it off was making her stomach queasy, she found him and asked if he had time to talk for a minute.

"Of course." He stared into her eyes. "What's wrong? Let's go in the office."

Gillian forced herself to take several deep breaths on the way.

He shut the door behind her and motioned to a chair. She shook her head. "I'll stand."

"That bad?" The joke didn't quite make it to his eyes.

"Bad or good, all depends." She took another deep breath and dropped her shoulders. "I had an e-mail last night from a man in New York City. He is senior VP at Cranston, Inc. That's the company that bought us out."

Adam leaned his haunches against his desk, ankles crossed to match his arms. "And?"

"And he read that proposal of mine that was turned down and wants to talk to me about a position there."

"I see. That's quite a compliment."

"I talked with him this morning. He was surprised to learn I was in California, so I said I could meet with him tomorrow morning instead of today. I'll take the red-eye tonight." She wished she could see into his eyes, but he was staring at his arms. "But I am on the schedule for the next two days and I don't want to cause you any more trouble either." *Adam, talk to me.*

He heaved a sigh and looked up at her. "Of course you must go. This could be a big break. I'll take you to the airport tonight. Did you get a flight?"

She nodded. "Right after I talked with him."

"What about Winnie?"

"When I called Allie, she volunteered to dog-sit."

"I see you've made all the arrangements. But I shouldn't be surprised. You are most efficient."

She knew he was paying her a compliment, but it didn't feel like one, more like a dagger slash. "I—I better get to work."

"I'll have John change the schedule."

"Okay." She waited another moment, hoping he would say more, but what more, she had no idea. When she turned and left, she would not have been surprised to see that a giant chasm had opened across the room.

Chapter Thirty-four

He'd been more friendly the day he thought she was breaking into the house. The ride to the airport seemed like forever. Gone was the warm laughter, the glances that made her heart thump. It was like he'd gone behind an opaque screen that allowed only necessary conversation.

"I'll call you," she said as she stood on the sidewalk in front of the terminal.

"Right."

"Move along," the traffic officer ordered.

Adam raised a finger to touch her cheek. "Take care." He walked around his SUV and drove off without a backward glance.

Fighting tears, Gillian pulled her over-nighter along to the ticket counter. How would she sleep after this? She almost dialed his cell to ask him to come back for her.

Staring out the window into the ebony night, with only the light flashing on the wing, she let her mind wander. Not that she could have controlled it at this point, but she did need to sleep. Morning would come far before she was prepared. From the sounds of it, she could step right back into her former life as if her new life in California was really just a vacation. *But I loved New York.* She closed her eyes. Loved. Past tense. What did she love about it? Memories scrolled through her mind. She had loved her job, moving up through the ranks, usually seen as a bright, rising star. But a vision that cost her a life apart from the job and the company. How many real friends did she have? People around her at work. All right. How many of them had called her or even e-mailed her after the buyout? Two: Scot and Shannon. How many had she called or e-mailed? Two: Scot and Shannon. She did love the thrill of the challenges, making money for the company and thusly for herself. She liked her lifestyle. *Had* liked. Was it because she didn't know any better? She leaned her forehead against the cold window. Now compare that life to her new one in California. Adam. Her heart ached that he'd not even looked back when he drove off at the terminal. Her sister and her family. She'd just begun to get close again, did she want to lose that? Could it grow long distance? Her mother and Enzio. Would they come to visit her? Even Winnie. Having a dog in a high-rise apartment building with a seventy-hour-a-week job didn't compute. The garden, her new job at Bentley's. New friends in Bill and Jennifer. A life. A real life. She'd just fallen asleep when they announced the descent into La Guardia International Airport.

When she walked into her New York condo after what seemed an eternity of travel, she stared around as if wondering if she was in a new land. That houses, condos, flats, all needed to be lived in, or they started to decay was most assuredly a true statement. She'd only been gone, was it a month now? No, less. After hanging up her coat, she dragged herself into the bedroom, set her alarm to ring at eight, and collapsed in the bed. It was far too early to call Adam.

* * *

Walking into the building where she used to spend most of her waking hours, she punched the elevator button for the twenty-second floor. She stepped off to see that the new company had not changed a thing other than the signage. Same gray-blue carpets, same light gray walls, although the arrangement in the reception area now showcased fresh flowers rather than silk.

The same receptionist.

After their greetings, Gillian leaned forward and dropped her voice. "So they kept everyone but management?"

Cicely nodded, her smile as bright as ever. "They're a great company to work for. We even all got raises when we decided to stay."

Shannon had told her the same thing on one of their phone calls. "Glad to hear that. I'm here to speak with Mark Hassleton."

"I'll see if he is ready." She pushed the requisite buttons and nodded. "Good to see you."

"Thanks."

He was standing at the door to her old office and reached out to shake her hand. "Welcome. Hope you had a good flight. Come in." He looked every inch the rising young executive, even to the horn-rimmed glasses.

Gillian shook his hand and entered the office. She'd wondered if this would bother her, but she never felt a twinge. As if she'd gone through a door and closed it on her former life.

"Please, have a seat. Can we get you anything? Coffee, water?"

"No, thank you." Was her assistant now working for Mark, too?

"Thank you for coming. I was surprised, to say the least, when you said you were in California. What part?"

Gillian responded to the chitchat and kept her hands from smoothing her skirt or showing any other sign of nervousness. She'd not done this since that first interview those many years ago. Usually she was the one on the other side of the desk, interviewing possible employees.

"Like I said, I was impressed with your proposal." He leaned back in his chair and studied her over templed fingers. "From everything I've read about you, I knew I needed to call. You had a long history with Fitch et cetera, working your way up the ladder. I'm sure the buyout was a shock."

She nodded.

"The way I see it, I would like you to step back into the same position you had before, with the same responsibilities only probably a few different management styles. I can offer you a rather generous signing bonus, an increase in salary of fifteen percent, and profit sharing. You'll find our performance-based bonus program one of the best in the city for a company of our size."

"How many other women are in the upper echelon of management?"

"None."

"So, I'll be your token female in the boardroom?"

"I wouldn't put it quite that way."

"But yes?"

He nodded and leaned forward. "You have always been a team player from what I have ascertained, and while I cannot tell you the specifics, Cranston, Inc. is on the verge of a huge explosion. Being part of this period of growth will be exciting and a real challenge for us all." He leaned forward again, looking right into her eyes. "Are you interested?"

Gillian waited before answering. "When would I need to start?"

"What about Monday?" His smile made her think of a big cat locked in on its prey.

"I have another job, and I would have to make arrangements there."

He didn't like being deflated. "Oh. I see. How much time would you need?"

"Probably two weeks. That would only be fair."

He stared at the pen on his blotter, then picked it up. "While I wish you'd start Monday, two weeks it is." He looked back at her. "Anything else?"

"So, am I to understand that the position is mine, should I decide to take it?"

He nodded.

Gillian stood. "Thank you; then I will let you know my decision on Monday."

He stood to walk her to the door. "If you have any questions, please don't hesitate to call." He handed her a business card. "That's my private cell number."

"Thank you."

Cicely wasn't at her desk as Gillian left the reception area. When she walked out on the street, she was surprised to find that she'd been in the meeting for nearly an hour. Since the sun was still shining in spite of gray clouds looming, she decided to walk back to her condo. The breeze had a bite to it as it kicked up bits of trash and the last of the leaves, so she belted her coat and headed out. As always, she loved New York City. The people rushing, taxis honking, store windows to enjoy, the sense of energy, going places. She stopped at the Corner Deli for a sandwich and chatted with the owner, who wanted a full history of all she'd done since she left.

Back in her condo, she sat down at the table to eat. How could any place feel so empty and cold? No Winnie, no flowers, no hummingbirds. But worst of all, no Adam. Here it was noon and in California he was just getting to work. No, he'd been at the nursery for better than an hour. She reached for her cell and started to dial, then snapped it closed.

Bringing her laptop out of her briefcase, she turned it on, and while it booted up, she went into the kitchen to make a cup of tea. What would it take to pack up this condo? What would she do with her things? The microwave pinged and she dipped her tea bag in the hot water. Using boiling water was always better, but she ignored that and took her cup back to the living room.

Not a lot of messages on her e-mail. She opened the one from Allie.

> *Winnie is not happy. You need to come home soon. I hope your interview went well. Call me when you have time. I love you, Allie*

Such a change.

Gillian hesitated before opening the one from Adam. A simple one-liner.

> *Just remember, there is a heart waiting for you here.*

She burst into tears. So much for being a competent executive who controlled her emotions as she led her staff. She was a woman in love. She blew her nose and took that thought out to look at again, to savor, and seek out the facets. *I love Adam. I do. I like Adam. I do indeed.* She went to stand at the window. *Do I love New York and this new job to the exclusion of my life in California?* Two pigeons flew by and then returned to light on the outside ledge. They certainly weren't hummingbirds. And there was no place for rosebushes and a birdbath.

Get real, Gillian. Look at the money you'd be making. You were very comfortable before, but with the increase and the bonuses? Your nest egg could grow exponentially. So, would Adam come to New York if she asked him? The gray clouds that had been forming opened up and dumped a deluge. Gray outside, gray buildings, no sunsets to speak of. A woman with a red umbrella hurried along, out of place with the rivers of black ones.

Can I afford to live in California without a real job? But then I haven't looked for one, either. I like what I'm doing, working at the nursery. Back and forth her mind swung, a pendulum in motion. She clasped her elbows with her hands and headed to the bedroom for a sweater. She'd not felt this bone deep chill in months; was this a portent of the coming winter?

Gillian sat back down at the computer and read Adam's message again. To her, the e-mail looked like an apology for his attitude when he took her to the airport. "Just remember there is a heart waiting for you here." *Call him. Don't call him.*

The call she made instead made her smile all over.

Chapter Thirty-five

Adam turned on Munson Street, the final blocks to home. What an intolerable day. He'd kept hoping that Gillian would call or at least answer his e-mail, but nada. How could a woman he'd known only a few weeks have captured his heart so completely? He stared at Dorothy's house, which he now thought of as Gillian's. Empty. Just like he felt.

He drove two houses farther and into the driveway. His father's truck was parked in the regular place. How could the whole world go on as regular as the sun when he failed? He climbed out and slammed the door. A long run would do both him and Thor a lot of good.

Something smelled mighty good. "Dad, I'm home."

When there was no answer, his heart lurched. Dad must be out with his babies. But where was Thor, who always met him at the door? He dropped his keys on the tray like always and meandered into the kitchen.

Gillian turned from the pot she was stirring. "How's your heart?"

He crossed the kitchen in two steps and swept her into his arms. "It's in overdrive." The kiss they shared could have heated the frying pan. He sat down at the table and glanced out the back door to see the two dogs romping in the backyard, then pulled her onto his lap. "All right, put me out of my misery."

"I turned the job down."

"I've figured out how we can manage with you back there and me here . . . you turned it down?"

She nodded. "I don't want to live in Manhattan again. I e-mailed Mark and told him I declined. It was a mighty good offer."

"Do you want to take the job?"

"No."

"Even if I moved to New York, too?"

She started to shake her head and stared at him. "Would you do that?"

"I thought about it—a lot. If I had to, we could make it work."

She still shook her head. "The money was appealing, I can't deny that. I'd be doing the same job as I had before—I liked it then. But now I've had a taste of a different life. And I like it."

"Have I mentioned that I love you?"

"I think that's what your e-mail said, but I love to hear the words." She leaned closer and kissed him, then laid her head on his shoulder. "I wanted to surprise you."

"You did."

She held up her arm, showing him her wrist. "See this?"

"Yeah, so what?"

"This is not an ugly watch. They say this is better than the patch because there are no side effects. I thought we'd try it out on the boat tomorrow after church."

"You better stir your cooking over there; I think it is starting to burn."

Gillian leaped to her feet and whipped the pan off the burner. She stirred it with the wooden spoon. "We're okay."

"We most certainly are. How did you get Dad involved in this?"

"A simple phone call. He was delighted."

"I'm sure he was. Do you have to go back?"

"I thought maybe we could take a trip there together."

"As in a honeymoon?"

"That could be a very good idea."

Epilogue

Sunshine drove away the fog on Thanksgiving Day. With the entire family gathered, the seams of Allie's house stretched to fit. While some of the males stayed glued to the football games on television, the hubbub in the kitchen reached epic proportions. Dorothy and Enzio teamed up to get the hors d'oeuvres together, at the same time telling the girls about their adventures.

Adam came in from the patio to say half an hour until the turkey was done. Jefferson had the ham heating on the covered barbecue.

Adam dropped a kiss on the back of Gillian's neck as he passed by.

"So what do you think of our idea?" Enzio asked.

"Which one, the worldwide tour or living at your house?" Gillian smacked Adam's hand as he snitched a radish rose in passing.

"Both." Dorothy turned to her daughters. "I cannot believe I really wanted to die. Think of all I'd have missed out on." She smiled at Enzio. "He spoils me rotten."

"'Bout time someone spoiled you." He winked at Gillian. "But she fights spoiling tooth and nail."

Allie raised her eyebrows at Gillian. "You really think he's right?"

"Not a bit surprised."

At the table, they all clasped hands for grace. Enzio cleared his throat. "I'd like to offer the grace if I may, and then I thought we could go around the table and everyone say what they are most thankful for." He looked around to find everyone nodding. "Dear Heavenly Father, I thank You for all the blessings I see around this table, for creating us all a new family as we come together as Your children. I thank You for my new life with Dorothy and all the adventures we are having, for the love we share. For health and the true happiness we find in You. I thank You for the food so lovingly prepared and for our great country. Most of all, I thank You for loving us."

Dorothy smiled at her new husband and then her daughters. "I am thankful that you three confronted my fear after the TIA. I was terrified I'd be helpless, like your father before he died, so I tried to die before that happened." She raised a hand to stop their responses before they started. "Fear doesn't make sense at times. Just thank God with me."

Gillian nodded, sniffed, and used her napkin to dry her eyes.

As the rest of them each said something they were thankful for, Gillian tried to sort through her overflowing heart of joy. When Adam said he was most thankful for loving her, she sniffed. "I thank You, Lord, for Adam, for love, and new life." She squeezed his hand, feeling the new ring on her left hand. The marquis-cut diamond insisted on sliding to the side.

And everyone said, "Amen."

Reading Group Guide

1. An old adage says that as you age you will become more of whoever you were when younger. If you don't like things about you now, what are you doing to change those dislikes before you get locked into bad habits?

2. As you watched Gillian struggle with her mother, what do you think she might have done differently?

3. Have you been through a similar situation, and if so, how did you handle it? Are you pleased with the outcome?

4. Typically when siblings come home, they step right back into the roles they played as children. How do you see that happening in your life?

5. Many people are being forced into starting their careers over, like Gillian was. What advice would you give someone in that situation?

6. Working in a garden, no matter how small, can bring healing on so many levels. What have you experienced in this area?

7. Heroes come in unlikely packages at times. How would you recognize one?

8. Gillian has found herself falling away from her childhood faith and upbringing. What experiences have you had in your life where life chips away at faith, rather than helping it grow?

9. What do you have to be thankful for? Make a list and share it with those you love.

About the Author

Award-winning and bestselling author LAURAINE SNELLING began living her dream to be a writer with her first published book for young adult readers, *Tragedy on the Toutle*, in 1982. She has since continued writing more horse books for young girls, adding historical and contemporary fiction and nonfiction for adults and young readers to her repertoire. All told, she has more than sixty-five books published.

Shown in her contemporary romances and women's fiction, a hallmark of Lauraine's style is writing about real issues of forgiveness, loss, domestic violence, and cancer within a compelling story. Her work has been translated into Norwegian, Danish, and German, and she has won the Silver Angel Award for *An Untamed Land* and a Romance Writers of America Golden Heart for *Song of Laughter*.

Lauraine helps others reach their writing dreams by teaching at writers' conferences across the country. Her readers clamor for more books more often, and Lauraine would like to comply, if only her ever-growing flower gardens didn't call quite so loudly.

Lauraine and her husband, Wayne, have two grown sons, and live in the Tehachapi Mountains with a watchdog Basset named Chewy. They love to travel, most especially in their forty-two-foot motor coach, which a friend has dubbed "The Taj," their home away from home.